Nicola Thorne was born in Cape Town, South Africa. Her
father was English and her mother a New Zealander, and she
was brought up and educated in England.  in
Sociology at the London School of Economics, but she always
wanted to pursue a literary career, and worked as a publisher's
reader and editor while writing her own books. She has written
a number of successful novels under the pseudonym of Nicola
Thorne, including *The Daughters of the House*, *Where the
Rivers Meet*, *Affairs of Love*, *Never Such Innocence* and
Yesterday's Promises. She lives in St John's Wood, London.

By the same author

NICOLA THORNE

Bright Morning

GRAFTON BOOKS

A Division of the Collins Publishing Group

LONDON GLASGOW
TORONTO SYDNEY AUCKLAND

Grafton Books
A Division of the Collins Publishing Group
8 Grafton Street, London W1X 3LA

Published by Grafton Books 1987
Reprinted 1988, 1989

First published in Great Britain by
Grafton Books 1986

ISBN 0-586-06875-9

Printed and bound in Great Britain by
Collins, Glasgow

Set in Times

The morning will come.
Brightly will it shine on the brave and the true;
kindly on all those who suffer for the cause;
glorious upon the tombs of heroes.

Winston Churchill in a broadcast
to the French Nation, 21 October 1940

CONTENTS

Family Tree of the Earls of Askham

From *Never Such Innocence* (ends 1915) to the beginning of *Bright Morning* (1939)

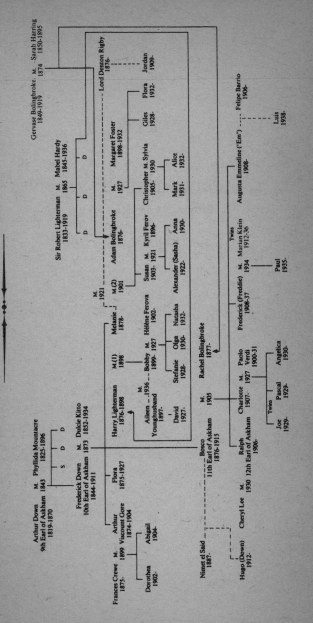

PART 1

... wars and rumours of wars
St Matthew's Gospel ch 24 v 6

Summer 1939–Spring 1941

CHAPTER 1

That year Chanel showed flamboyant gypsy-style dresses in red, white and blue, the French tricolor in organdie embroidered with poppies. In the summer of 1939, it seemed as if she were carried along by a burst of patriotic fervour, although, despite the signs of storm, no one could then guess how symbolic that brave display of the national colours would prove to be.

According to *Vogue* Paris was enjoying '*une saison de grande élégance*'. It danced, went to the races, and attended parties and fashion shows as if those habitual socialites – the arbiters of fashion, good taste and high living – could control the destinies of nations, curb the territorial ambitions of Hitler, Stalin or Mussolini.

There were echoes of war, certainly, but they seemed very far away as Charlotte Verdi gave the skirt of her gown a final swirl and looked at herself appraisingly in the tall mirror. Mademoiselle Chanel, still almost as chic as her most beautiful mannequin, stepped back, scissors in hand, putting a last minute tuck in here or there, deftly snipping at a loose thread.

'*Excellent, ma chérie,*' she murmured and went to resume her place on the staircase. Charlotte swept into the famous mirrored salon, surrounded by the *beau monde* of Paris and the world's fashion press, nodding at them with a disdainful tilt of her head, for the climax of the show.

Afterwards she hurried down the main staircase mixing anonymously with the crowds struggling towards the exit. There were smiles, waves, raised hands, and then there was Arthur pressing forward waiting to kiss her on the cheek and escort her to his small Citroën parked outside in the Rue Cambon.

Charlotte had changed into one of Chanel's neat little navy blue dresses with white revers which flattered her tall, graceful figure. A large navy straw hat shaded the upper part of her face and, as Arthur pulled away from the kerb, she sat back with a deep sigh.

'Tired?' Arthur glanced at her sympathetically but only briefly, his eyes on the traffic.

'Tired's not the word.' Charlotte groped in her bag for a cigarette, lit it and blew a long thin stream of smoke out of the open window. 'Thank heaven that's the end. And tomorrow,' she stretched out her arms and gave Arthur a brilliant smile, 'home!'

'You still think of England as home.' Arthur said this as a comment, rather than a question.

'Of course. Don't you?'

'For me it *is* home.' Arthur paused for a moment. 'I wish it really *were* for you.'

Charlotte didn't reply but continued to gaze out of the window of the small noisy car Arthur kept at his base for use when he was in Paris. Home, for her and her children, really was Paris; home for the four of them was France. What Arthur meant was that he wished that she and her family would move permanently to England to live with him.

'We really have been engaged for too long you know, Charlotte,' Arthur said nervously, realizing it was a tricky subject.

'Oh dearest Arthur, not just now,' Charlotte pleaded.

'When?'

'When we're at home with Mother,' Charlotte promised; but Arthur knew that there was always a next time, and a time after the next time. Charlotte, successful and independent, was happy as she was.

The house where Charlotte had her ground-floor apartment had once belonged to a famous French courtesan who had shared her favours with, among many others, the last Emperor of the French, Louis Philippe. In the early years of the present

12

century Hôtel du Maurois had been turned into five rather grand apartments, but the one on the ground floor was easily the best because it incorporated many of the former *grandes salles* of the original eighteenth-century house: the high ornate gilded ceilings still remained, and it enjoyed the exclusive use of a beautiful, extensive and well laid out garden.

The Hôtel, constructed round a quadrangular courtyard, was approached through an arch. To the left of this was the flat occupied by the concierge, a small, bent, apparently ageless woman called Marie. As the car stopped Marie came forward to open the door for Charlotte, leaning forward urgently to speak to her before she had time to alight.

'What is it, what is it, Marie?' Charlotte began to laugh as she gently pushed the old woman away from the open door. 'I can't tell what you're saying. What princess?' They spoke in French.

She stared at Marie who gesticulated towards the apartment, her gnarled old face puckered with excitement.

Arthur came round to the kerb side of the car, straightening the jacket of his RAF uniform.

'What is it?'

'Someone is here. Marie calls her "The Princess" but I don't know which princess she means.'

'Oh, we know *so* many princesses ...' Arthur airily waved his hands before bending to help Charlotte out of the car.

'Well, we know a few.' Charlotte stuck up her nose at him and preceded her old servant to the door of the apartment which opened onto the paved courtyard.

It was dark inside the large hallway but light streamed in from the half-open door of the main salon.

'Hello?' Charlotte called feeling slightly apprehensive because of the silence. She pushed the door wide open and stood on the threshold peering in.

Slowly the figure sitting in a chair near the French windows rose to greet her.

'Hélène.' Charlotte rushed forward, her arms extended.

13

'Oh, *Hélène*!' She placed her arms round the bowed shoulders of the woman, who put her head between her hands as though she were crying.

'Hélène ... I didn't think it was so *soon*.'

'Is anyone with you?' At the sound of footsteps Hélène looked up nervously towards the door.

'Only Arthur ...'

'I don't want *anyone* to see me.'

'Right.'

Swiftly Charlotte released her cousin and went to the door, leaning out with her hand to her lips.

'Please go into the small sitting room,' she said to a bewildered Arthur, 'and get Marie to bring you and us coffee. I shan't be long.'

'Who is it?' Arthur stammered,

'Hélène ...'

'So *soon*?' Arthur's voice was hoarse with surprise.

Charlotte nodded. Then quietly she withdrew into the room and shut the door.

'You haven't run away have you?' she said slowly walking towards her visitor.

This made Hélène smile. She looked up.

'*I'd* quite like to have stayed there. It was so peaceful. What was there to come out for?' She gave a gesture of hopelessness. 'Apparently, something to do with the international situation. Everyone seems to think there'll be a war. They feel the fewer people they have in prison the better. My release was ordered yesterday. I spent the night in a hotel.'

'All alone? You should have telephoned.' Charlotte crouched by her side. 'Your mother? You didn't phone her?'

Hélène opened her bag, withdrew a crushed packet of cigarettes and nervously lit one. Her thin, fine hand was shaking.

'How could I tell her *I* was free? They have to be prepared for it ... they, and the children. The fact that I had young children was given as one of the reasons for my release, on the

14

grounds of compassion.' Hélène gave a bitter smile. 'Little do the authorities know what my children think of me...'

'That's not true.' Charlotte drew up a chair and took hold of Hélène's free hand. 'I saw Stefanie only last week and she said ... they do think a lot of you. They missed you a lot.' Charlotte's voice trailed off because she knew Hélène was too intelligent, too perceptive to be deceived.

'Olga might miss me, or even Natasha. But Stefanie ...' Hélène vigorously shook her head. 'Stefanie hates me. She felt the scandal more.'

'That's not true at all. Oh dear ...' Charlotte rose and walked to the window. 'It's time to start afresh Hélène, with your daughters and your parents. The State, by releasing you early, has shown compassion, given you a chance to know the daughters who, as you say, you don't really know. Who don't know you. You've been away three years. It's a long time in childhood. It is time to begin again.'

'Just now I can't face them.' Hélène looked up as Marie crept in with two cups of coffee.

'This is Princess Hélène,' Charlotte said taking the tray from the concierge. 'You were perfectly right to let her in. She is my cousin by marriage.'

Marie sighed with relief. She loved Charlotte so much. She was terrified of offending her, of doing the wrong thing – because Charlotte was stern, she was strict: with a busy career, three children, and a home to run she felt she had to be.

As Marie closed the door Hélène put the hot coffee to her lips and sighed with satisfaction. 'Much better than in prison. For coffee at least, I'm glad to be here.' For the first time she gave Charlotte a warm, relaxed smile.

'How are all the family. Your mother? Ralph? And Cheryl?'

As Hélène bent her head again to sip her coffee Charlotte saw that the colour was returning to her face, though, blonde and fair complexioned, she had always been pale. In the old days it had the air of aristocratic hauteur; now it was clearly the pallor of the gaol.

'They're all very well, Mother especially, as busy as ever. Ralph and Cheryl are pretty nearly always apart. Arthur and I are flying over for the weekend. Why, if you don't want to go home, don't you come with us? It will help you unwind before you meet your family – or do you terribly want to see them?'

'I only terribly wanted to see you,' Hélène said without emotion. 'Only you and Susan have stood by me, Charlotte. My mother came to visit me three times in prison – she said she found it too distressing – my father not at all. Hardly any of the family came, but in the three years I was in prison you and Susan came often.'

Charlotte sat down again, nervously rubbing her hands.

'Don't hate your family, darling. It *was* a terrible shock for them.'

'A terrible disgrace you mean, for a Ferov to be jailed for killing her lover! *That* is what my family cannot get over, and never will.'

'They *will* get over it, now that you're free, now that they don't have to go and visit the prison. They *will* soon forget as you establish your life again, as you...'

She stopped speaking abruptly, and Hélène said softly: 'Exactly. As soon as I what? What can I do? What am I fit for? The divorced, penniless wife of a millionaire; the daughter of a Russian prince who has brought disgrace on the family; the mother of three girls who hate me for the shame I brought and because of what they think I did to their father. How can *I* establish my life again? What *is* there left for me to do?'

For a long time Charlotte gazed at her. Just then she couldn't quite think of an answer.

A few days later Charlotte and her mother Rachel sat together on the terrace at Askham Hall overlooking the lake. It was a dear, familiar spot where they had spent many happy hours – alone or with the family. The two women were reminiscing and Charlotte sighed once again, as she so often had in the past, at all times and all ages since she was a little girl.

'How I *wish* I had known Papa. How I *wish* I remembered him more.'

'You were only seven when Bosco was killed. It's not surprising you don't.'

'If only he knew how much I missed him.'

'I'm sure he does, somewhere.' Rachel looked vaguely at the sky as one does on these occasions – the perpetual search for eternity, for consolation.

'You've never forgotten Papa have you, Mummy?'

'Never.' Rachel shook her head though now, twenty-four years after his death, her eyes no longer filled with tears at the memory. One could speak almost with detachment about a loved one so long dead – killed in 1915. Yet Bosco was and remained a part of her, not a ghost but a dear familiar; someone she often consulted in her heart when she was worried about the children or, now, the grandchildren; someone to whom she had turned for comfort when Freddie their second son was killed during the Spanish Civil War.

So the two women, Bosco's widow and daughter, sat in thoughtful, companionable silence for a moment, glad of the peace on that summer afternoon, aware of the calls from the tennis court where most of the others – Arthur, Ralph, Cheryl and Hugo – were more energetically spending their time.

'I thought that Hélène looked frightfully pale.' Rachel spoke at last, turning her head to look up at the house.

'She looks sickly,' Charlotte followed her mother's gaze, 'as though she were not well. I think Doctor Fraser should see her.'

'I suppose it's quite natural after three years. Those French prisons are awful I hear. What a blessing she was released.'

Charlotte sank back more comfortably into the old wicker chair. It was nice to have family about her – though the children were still at school.

'Privately I hear the French are far less sanguine about the international situation than they like others to believe. It appears they would quite like most of the gaols to be clear in case there is a war.'

'Oh please God there will be no war.' Rachel put her hands to her head. 'I cannot *possibly* live through another major war in my lifetime. Besides, it makes me feel terribly old.'

'Mother, you look wonderful.' Charlotte gazed at her fondly. 'Not a day over fifty.'

'In fact I'm sixty-two,' Rachel said, suddenly feeling, indeed, much younger. She knew she did look good for her age. She had not put on weight, or not very much, and her hair, though becomingly streaked with grey, was still primarily the same ash blonde it had been when she was a girl, though, perhaps, a little dulled by time. Of course she had the lines of age on her face; but they were soft, gentle furrows rather than deep creases, and the brilliant colour of those youthful blue eyes that had so captivated Bosco had not dimmed a bit with time. She was a handsome woman, always had been. She had never been an acknowledged beauty like her daughter Charlotte, whose haunting features were familiar to so many patrons of Chanel's salon or readers of magazines devoted to high fashion.

Charlotte, who had been lounging in her chair, sat up, alerted by something she'd seen, and got to her feet. She went to the edge of the terrace, looked down and pointed to the path that ran from the Grange across the lake to the Hall.

'Em!' she cried pointing. 'I can see Em with Luis.'

'And Felipe?' There was a note of caution in Rachel's voice as she got up, rather reluctantly, because she had been enjoying the rest in the company of a daughter she saw little of.

'No. No sign of Felipe.'

'Thank heaven for that,' Rachel breathed *sotto voce*, but not soft enough for Charlotte who glanced at her, her frown slightly disapproving.

'Oh Mum, you don't dislike him as much as that!'

'I detest him, as a matter of fact.' Rachel perched on the parapet that ringed the terrace. 'Isn't that an awful thing to say? I don't find he improves with acquaintanceship. I have tried very hard to like him, but I have failed.'

Em was puffing hard as she got to the top of the hill with her sturdy infant son in her arms. Charlotte ran down to meet her sister, taking the baby and, as she did, exclaiming:

'My, he *is* heavy. I can't think how you carried him all this way.'

'You know me,' Em grunted, 'sturdy. It's a good thing Mademoiselle Chanel never wanted *me* to model for her. I should regretfully have had to refuse.'

Em, considered plain by some, had many good features – none of the Askhams were really plain – but she cared little about impressing people and was content, or so she said, with herself as she was.

Rachel, smiling, helped her over the parapet to a cosy chair on the terrace. Her two precious daughters, seldom together, were with her and her newest grandson. Yes, Charlotte and Em together were infinitely precious. Tenderly she took Luis and balanced him on her own knee, kissing him. 'I don't see nearly enough of you,' she whispered.

'Mother, that's your fault.' Em's tone was terse. 'You never come and see us.'

'That's because I'm so busy darling.' Rachel's voice faltered uncertainly and she glanced rather guiltily at Charlotte.

'It's because you don't like Felipe.' Em looked hard at her mother. 'Be honest. You usually are.'

'Em, I don't want a row. Charlotte is only here for a few days. I thought it would be a happy time with Arthur and poor Hélène...'

'No one told me Hélène was here!' Em jumped up. 'Is she out of prison?'

'She's got indefinite parole, thanks, it seems, to the international situation.'

'Then where is she?'

'Asleep,' Charlotte said briefly. 'She has slept almost

continuously ever since we arrived, has her meals in bed. She's quite exhausted. It's the emotional upheaval of it all.'

'Did she go and see the girls?'

'She came straight to me. She didn't feel she had enough strength to confront them until she'd rested. The Ferovs virtually cast her off when she was sent to prison...'

'*They're* nice people to cast anyone off,' Em said grimly. 'Fascists.'

'Don't be political, Em,' her mother said reprovingly. 'For Hélène to go to prison was, in their eyes, a profound disgrace. I can't think your dear grandmother would have been very forgiving either if Aunt Flora or Aunt Melanie had been sent inside for murdering their lovers.'

'I can't ever see Aunt Flora having a lover,' Charlotte giggled then stopped, her hand to her mouth. 'Sorry. I shouldn't have said that.'

Rachel decided to ignore it. The whole family knew that for many years of her life Bosco's sister, Flora, had been in love with Rachel's brother Adam. When he married another woman she apparently committed suicide, though no one could ever have been certain. It certainly wasn't a physical love, but it was a great love, and Adam's behaviour had destroyed Flora who had been found drowned in the Nile on a visit to Egypt.

'Poor Hélène.' Em seemed suddenly restless. 'I would *love* to see her again. I'm so glad she's here; but I do feel so terribly for her. She has nothing but problems to face.'

'It *is* lovely being with you girls,' Rachel said quietly thinking of other problems. 'You can't really know what it means to me. I wish Charlotte would marry Arthur and live here permanently.'

'Here, Mummy? I certainly wouldn't live at the Hall.' Charlotte pretended to shudder. 'Since Cheryl's renovations I can hardly even bear to come here. Were it not for seeing you and Ralph, Hugo and Em, I wouldn't.'

The mention of Ralph's unpopular wife seemed to have a

dispiriting effect and the three women pointedly studied the lake while Luis played happily on a rug Em had spread for him with the toys she had brought for him. Luis was like Em, a sturdy little boy with her fair colouring and blond hair. With his fine bone structure and dark blue eyes Luis had the makings of being handsome when he got older.

'Where *is* Cheryl by the way?' Em glanced casually round.

'They're all playing tennis; Cheryl, Ralph, Hugo.'

'You didn't say you *wouldn't* marry Arthur,' Em glanced curiously at her sister. 'Usually when Mum brings it up you go all defensive. You *are* engaged to him after all. Don't you have a date for the wedding?'

'There are too many uncertainties,' Charlotte murmured uncomfortably. 'I don't actually want to return to England and Arthur wants to make the Air Force his career. We can hardly live in different countries, which we should be doing.'

'Anyway you don't love him,' Em said. 'That's the truth.'

'Oh Em ... why are you so cross today?' Charlotte looked at her sharply. 'You've done nothing but pick since you came over.'

'What do you mean "pick"?' Em looked at her indignantly.

'Well, that remark about the Ferovs being Fascists.'

'They are. I'm just being brutally frank. You have never loved Arthur and I don't know why you got engaged to him except to lead him on.'

'I'm going in to order tea,' Rachel said abruptly. 'Please sort your differences out while I'm gone.'

Charlotte looked immediately contrite and put out a hand to stop her mother but Rachel shook her away, gently but firmly, and disappeared through the French windows into the house.

'She's calling us to order.' Em settled back in her chair. 'Dearest Mum, she doesn't change does she?'

'Not a bit. I do miss her, and if anything would bring me back it would be Mum rather than Arthur. But I love Paris. I love my life there and my work.'

21

'Work *is* frightfully important, I do agree.' Em reached over to waggle a toy bear for Luis who had started to cry. 'I miss it terribly. Yet Felipe won't hear of me going back.'

'He's very much the dominating male, isn't he?' Charlotte squinted at her sister.

'Well, it's his point of view,' Em said defensively. 'He shares a lot with me about his ideas and his views. We discuss politics endlessly...'

'But he likes you to wash the dishes.'

'I don't actually wash the dishes,' Em protested. 'We do still have a maid. Why are you so nasty about Felipe, Charlotte? *I'm* not nasty about Arthur.'

'I'm *not* nasty about Felipe, dearest.' Charlotte groped impulsively for her hand. 'If I sound nasty I apologize. But I feel that you and your talents are wasted a bit, you know what I mean. You were very happy as a journalist.'

Em shook her head, her hand lying woodenly in Charlotte's lap.

'It *is* Felipe,' she said. 'Don't make excuses. I'm not blind and I know none of my family likes him. That causes me pain. The Askhams have plenty of money. The Grange is owned outright and not rented or mortgaged or anything. We both live on the allowance of one person, and the little money I have. If *I* want to keep my lover I can't see why that should concern anybody but us. Plenty of women, and I don't need to look hard to find them,' Em glanced at the house, 'are very happy to be kept by men. Felipe is a thinker. He has been terribly wounded, and also upset by the defeat of the Republic in Spain. He has to have time to recover.'

'I don't think it's that ...' Charlotte looked as though she was about to go on and then changed her mind. 'Anyway it's none of my business.'

'But I *want* to know,' Em said sharply, clasping her hand. 'It *is* your business and you're my sister. I want to know why the family doesn't like Felipe. Is it because he does nothing to ingratiate himself with them?'

'He certainly doesn't go out of his way to be pleasant but, after what you say, maybe he is merely sensitive. Do make him come over for dinner tonight and we'll all try again.'

Charlotte squeezed Em's hand hard, giving her an encouraging smile.

Felipe Barrio detested the Askham family and all it stood for. He was a Republican, the son of a miner from the Asturias, one of that band of brave men who had been put down by Franco before the Revolution began; and to him the aristocratic Askhams represented the Fascists that he'd fought against so hard. That is, Felipe had fought hard enough until he saw the way the tide was turning in Spain and then he'd got out. He'd seen the carnage ahead that Franco would inflict and he didn't want to die. He was a brave man but not a foolish one, and he felt he could best serve his cause from outside.

Now they were all in evening dress, except him. He had at least worn a tie and jacket to please Em, otherwise it would be trousers and an open shirt on a warm spring evening whatever the occasion.

Throughout dinner Felipe sat glowering at the Askhams, not attempting to disguise his contempt and consequent unease. As usual he ate and drank an enormous amount and said little. The family, who had done its best to welcome Em's man, the father of her child, were quite accustomed to his antisocial ways. Impeccably English and polite they attempted to ignore them.

As well as Felipe, Rachel sitting at the centre of the oval table, quietly observing, thought that there was an unusual amount of tension in what should have been a happy family gathering. Hélène had been persuaded to come to dinner with the greatest reluctance and sat there, apparently wrapped in her own thoughts, in a dress borrowed from Charlotte. It had been difficult to draw Hélène out all weekend; in many ways Rachel felt it was a mistake of Charlotte to have brought her. She was clearly apprehensive about facing her family, putting off the evil day which would appear much worse for being too long postponed.

Em was unusually argumentative, uneasy in the unaccustomed presence of Felipe with her family. Charlotte appeared brittle and thoughtful as though Arthur were a problem, and where would she and Arthur sleep tonight – alone or with each other?

Hugo, dear robust Hugo, could always be relied upon to fill the gap, the awkward pause, even though he was habitually ignored by his hostess Cheryl who had always nursed a grudge against him; she lost no opportunity of belittling or demeaning him. Hugo accordingly ignored Cheryl too though in a very courteous way, speaking only if spoken to in the course of passing or offering some dish or the other.

Looking around the table Rachel thought back on so many similar dinner parties at Askham Hall in the many, many years since she'd been associated with it and, although not all of them had been successful, few had seemed as fraught as this. Usually, whatever the external circumstances, the family could relax together. But tonight it was as though the international situation they were discussing imperceptibly affected them all; that family tensions were a microcosm of what was happening in the world at large.

Ralph, titular head of the family, sat at the top of the table, more thoughtful than usual, twisting the stem of his wine glass between his forefinger and thumb, trying to compose in his mind the best way to announce to his family what he had to say. Opposite him his wife, beautifully dressed in a gown by Schiaparelli, was making animated conversation with Ivo Hazard, an old friend of the family who had farming business to discuss with Ralph. He was the sort of man she liked – handsome, charming, clever and accomplished, a budding politician, a local councillor. On her other side was Arthur whom she also liked because he was Establishment. She didn't like people who protested, or failed to conform, or were lacking in that drive that had made her what she was, where

24

she was – Countess of Askham, Chatelaine of Askham Hall and, in London, a large town house. The fact that the family now left her largely in isolation didn't trouble her at all.

But tonight, despite the correctly dressed men sitting on either side of her, white starched fronts gleaming, bow ties correctly tied by their experienced valets, she wasn't totally happy. She loved formal dinner parties, but she preferred to be completely in charge of the guest list and tonight it was one of those occasions that she dreaded: an Askham dinner, planned by Askhams for Askhams to bring the family together. It was a reunion, and at such a reunion were the members of the family she detested most: her mother-in-law Rachel, her husband's half-brother Hugo, her anarchic sister-in-law Em with her boorish, oafish lover with his unkempt matted beard and his plebeian dress.

Most of all, however, Cheryl detested that un-establishment figure, that cuckoo in the nest, Ralph's cousin by marriage, Hélène Lighterman, formerly Princess Hélène Ferova, who had spent three years in gaol after sensationally killing her lover. The story, a sordid one of deceit and betrayal, had rocked France and England at the time – another unwelcome case of publicity for the family.

Cheryl found herself glowering at Hélène throughout the course of the dinner party. She had once been very friendly with the princess in the days when, as the wife of one of the richest men in England, Ralph's cousin Bobby, Hélène had had little to do but spend his money in the shops and boutiques of Bond Street and the Rue de Rivoli. Then, as a beautiful rich young woman of impeccable family connections – her family older than the Romanovs – she had not only been good company but had taught the naïve, rather gauche Colonial from Kenya how a woman, unexpectedly elevated to a title and a position in the world of high society, should behave.

How very different it was now, Cheryl thought, looking at the bowed head at the end of the table next to Ralph. Truly, Hélène *did* have a prison pallor and her appetite was apathetic.

Everything that was put before her she gingerly tasted, as though it had been offered to one of her ancestors in the days of Ivan the Terrible, and then pushed to one side. While the trauma of her time in prison drew various reactions, mostly of a compassionate nature, from the rest of the family, from Cheryl it only drew contempt, disgust and the kind of fear that people who break the rules occasion in those who, given different circumstances, are afraid they might. Conformity was too precious to Cheryl, too essential to her peace of mind, the possibility of its being shattered was too threatening and disturbing for her to relish the idea of entertaining a gaolbird under her roof. Her reception of Hélène had been icy; thereafter she had ignored her.

No, except for the presence of Ivo Hazard and Squadron Leader the Honourable Arthur Crewe it was a highly unsatisfactory evening. But the food was impeccable, the service perfect, silver and candles glittering on her exquisitely proportioned macassar ebony table by the French designer Emile Jacques Ruhlmann.

Cheryl saw Charlotte looking at her and flashed her a smile. Charlotte was possibly the one member of the family for whom she had made an exception. Here admiration was combined with envy: envy of Charlotte's looks, her grace, her elegance and popularity, the sense that, in some indefinable way, she was a completely rounded human being. One moreover to whom the fates had not always been kind; who had suffered.

Charlotte, glittering in a Chanel gown sewn with thousands of tiny pearls and sequins that emphasized her figure, was saying something to Ivo which was making him almost choke with laughter, but further down the table the talk was more serious. It was about the recently passed Compulsory Military Training Bill for all men between the ages of twenty and twenty-one.

'It is much too early for anything like that,' Rachel said

26

forcefully. 'It seems to me sometimes that our leaders are, willy nilly, hurtling us towards war.'

'You can hardly say that about Chamberlain, Mother.' Em's voice was contemptuous. 'I don't think he knows the meaning of the word "hurtle".'

'I know you despise Chamberlain,' Rachel leaned towards her daughter, 'but for those of us who were caught up in the last war it is almost impossible to envisage another. Some people, and I must say *I* am one of them, would do anything to avoid war.'

'Mother, I didn't think you were *that* much of an appeaser.' Ralph's voice was reproachful.

'I am *not* an appeaser, Ralph, in the sense that I would *totally* give in to Hitler and Mussolini over everything, but I would do almost *anything* to avoid a war.'

'The more we give them the more they want.' Felipe, whose English was poor, spoke slowly. 'Don't forget, Lady Askham, they took our country too. It is thanks to the timorousness of *your* country and America in not supplying us with arms that Hitler and Mussolini feel as brave as they do. That one can walk into Czechoslovakia and the other into Albania. Where next? How long will it take you to realize what these men are like?'

'You forget, Felipe,' Rachel said coldly, 'that I have personally had an encounter with Hitler and, believe me, I didn't like what I met. I have no doubt that he is an evil man; but I would like to think that, in the end, diplomacy and persuasion can succeed in place of violence. Hitler says that his territorial ambitions are satisfied...'

'And you believe that?' Felipe interrupted, thumping the table and drawing back his chair as though he were going to strike Rachel.

'I...' Rachel paused, which gave the urbane Ivo Hazard the chance to come to her rescue.

'Lady Askham is quite right in my opinion. No one wants war, of course they don't. But we have to watch the Germans very carefully, and the Italians. In my opinion the danger of war comes from these countries feeling they are threatened while England tries to secure alliances with the countries which surround them...'

'It is only for *their* protection,' Em said indignantly. 'How can you say...'

'But England has pledged to support not only Poland in case of attack but Greece, Rumania and Turkey. No wonder Hitler talks of a policy of encirclement.'

There were many people who did passively support Hitler, as the alternative to Stalin, and the right-wing country-loving, cricket-playing Ivo was, it seemed, one of them.

'Only *if* he invades ...' Rachel began to feel that she wasn't even convincing herself. Yes, she was a closet appeaser, a supporter of Chamberlain in his efforts to prevent war. She had lost her husband and a son in wars and she didn't ever wish to see another. Almost any price, it seemed to her, was worth paying to avoid war. Yet those supporting appeasement were becoming increasingly unpopular as the country did, indeed, seem to be preparing itself for war. Chips Channon the Tory MP had said, almost with relish, that he believed war was inevitable. Could it be that some people actually enjoyed war? Wished for it?

'Anyway I'm going to enlist,' Ralph announced abruptly in the small, awkward pause that followed. Steeling himself all evening for the announcement it now wasn't as hard as he'd thought it would be. He had imagined himself telling his mother first of all in private, but when it came to it he'd found he lacked the courage. He knew how she felt – first his father, then his brother Freddie.

'What do you mean you're going to enlist?' Cheryl's voice, raised in indignation, was the first to break the silence. 'You're hardly within enlisting age I would have thought. Twenty and twenty-one, I heard it was.'

'I'm thirty-three,' Ralph said with a smile. 'But hale in wind and limb. If war comes I want to be there and ready. If it doesn't then I shall only be in the Army for three years. That's the length of my commission.'

'It sounds as though you've made all the arrangements.' Rachel spoke strongly to avoid showing her fear. 'It sounds *very* definite, darling.'

'It is, Mother. Hugo and I have talked about this for a long time.'

'I can manage the farm on my own.' Hugo, who had quietly been talking to Hélène, sitting next to him, for most of the evening now intervened. 'Ralph began his career as a soldier, and it's where he feels he should be.'

'But he gave it up. He preferred to *farm*.' Clearly Cheryl was seething.

'Ralph sees this as a time of crisis.' Hugo smiled at the woman next to him. 'We might all be called to arms.'

Rachel, who could quite clearly remember 1914, felt as though her blood had run cold.

In addressing her again Ralph's tone was gentle, but earnest.

'I am *very* anti-appeasement, Mother. I think if we'd have shown Hitler we meant business there would have been no rape of Czechoslovakia. Next it will be Danzig and the Polish corridor, you know that. Personally I think if we *had* supported the Republic in Spain, with arms and a strong force, like Germany and Italy quite openly supported the Nats, Hitler would have thought twice about Czechoslovakia, and Mussolini would never have laid hands on Albania. They think we are weak and vacillating and that no one wants war. Well I don't want war, but I have a debt to settle – the deaths of Father and Freddie.'

Rachel tossed her napkin on the table and shook her head impatiently.

'Oh don't talk to me about revenge, Ralph! It's a foolish emotion. If one went round conducting vendettas one would end up like the Mafia, killing people all the time.'

'I can assure you, Mother, I would only want to avenge Father and Freddie if the opportunity presented itself. I would not seek a war because of it. But I am ready to fight. I have enlisted in the Guards from the first of next month.'

Once Ralph had shut the bedroom door he found himself faced, not for the first time, by a very angry wife. He knew that some members of the family referred to her as a viper and, again not for the first time, he agreed with them. Though she was a beautiful woman well endowed with charm and intelligence, Cheryl had a very ugly side to her which she showed quite often, especially to those closest to her. And yet Ralph had found himself eyeing his wife over the candlelit table, still admiring and still desiring her. For most of the time they lived apart, led separate lives – Ralph at his farm ten miles away and Cheryl flitting between London and the European capitals. Despite the extensive refurbishment she had made to Askham Hall after his grandmother had died, ruining it in the eyes of the family, she was scarcely ever there. Some people now thought of it as a tomb to Askham aspirations.

'I'm sorry,' Ralph said, seeing the expression on her face, her tongue visible between her lips. 'Do you mind so much if I spend the night?'

Remembering how beautiful she had looked in the dining room, and afterwards in the drawing room where a few hands of bridge were played in order to soothe the passions that had been aroused at dinner, he had wanted to stay the night; to hold her in his arms just once again, to try and recapture, however briefly, the good times they'd shared long ago – how many years? Nine? Ten? How long was it since he'd begun to see her as others saw her – greedy, calculating, remorseless in her quest for self-satisfaction. But he banished all this from his mind and moved towards her, his arms extended.

'Oh *that's* what you want, is it?' Cheryl's lips curled derisively. 'I should have known you'd want a little hanky-panky after all you had to drink.'

'Is wanting to make love to my wife "hanky-panky"?' Ralph

kept his tone mild and polite because he did want her; very badly.

'You know we don't have a married life.' Cheryl turned towards the mirror and began to unfasten her pearls, anxiously scrutinizing her face as she did as though for signs of ageing. Yet though older than Ralph she wore well. She could still have a child.

Ralph, approaching her gently, put his hands on her shoulders, his cheek next to hers. He was quite shocked by the violence with which she broke from him, saying:

'Get away! Keep away please. Is it not enough to make a fool of me this evening, and now you try and seduce me? Get away. If you insist on staying here go and sleep in the dressing room.' She rapidly crossed the room and drawing the counterpane off the bed threw it at him. 'There, wrap yourself up in this.'

'If I want to sleep alone there are plenty of rooms in which to do it.' Ralph carefully spread the counterpane on the bed turning it back as if for sleep. He felt a kind of desperation that came from thwarted desire. He knew that his desire for her was purely carnal and he despised himself. He didn't love her as a husband should love a wife, she had long ago destroyed that emotion; but he admired her as a lovely, desirable woman and, yes, now that he was enlisting in the Army it would be nice to leave behind him an heir as his father and brother had done, just in case ... The matter seemed to become more urgent now.

Breathing angrily Cheryl, a lit cigarette between her fingers, stood against the far wall, as far away from him as she could get, arms akimbo, watching him smooth down the bed.

'It's no good, Ralph,' she said. 'I'm not having you in my bed. I thought we'd got that straight? Oh, don't think I didn't *see* you looking at me tonight, know what was in your filthy mind. You treat me like some kind of whore. Well, I'm not. *I* am the Countess of Askham, and don't you forget it.'

Ralph sank dejectedly onto the end of the bed. He looked,

31

and suddenly felt, very tired and his desire was slowly ebbing away, heir or no heir, as it so often had in the past.

'I'm not likely to forget it, Cheryl. You have reminded me of it frequently in the past. If I did look at you, as a man does who longs for a woman, is it so bad? Is it so unnatural that I should wish to sleep with my wife who is a lovely and desirable woman, particularly so tonight, if I might say so.' Even the compliment failed to ingratiate him with Cheryl who twisted her mouth into an even uglier expression, but said nothing.

'Now that I am going to enlist and possibly go away, if war is declared, I would like nothing better than for us to resume our married life again, to try and be the lovers and friends that we once were…'

'Oh, the heartstrings.' Cheryl raised her eyes to heaven in an exaggerated expression of piety. 'The warrior going to the war is it now? What next I wonder? The wounded warrior perhaps…'

'Maybe the dead warrior,' Ralph said solemnly. 'My family has a poor history in wars. I just thought, Cheryl, that if I mentioned it…'

'*Mentioned* it, did you say?' Cheryl gazed at him stonily. 'Broadcast it to the world, more like. If you really want to know why I am angry tonight, Ralph Askham, it is because yet again you have made a fool of me in front of your family, sought yet *again* to debase me in their eyes.'

'Just how have I done that?' Ralph lay across the bed knowing that, tonight, this was as close as he would get to the wife he had been married to for ten years with so little pleasure or satisfaction.

'Wouldn't it have been at least *polite* to inform me that you intended to enlist? Don't you think *I* should have been the first to know, or is that too much to expect? It's just an indication of the way you really feel about me, Ralph; that is that I am an object rather than a wife, that you show me up in front of your entire family by making an announcement, a very important one, if I may say it, at dinner. The very least one would have expected was that you would have had the courtesy to tell me *first*.'

'If I was rude, I apologize,' Ralph said woodenly. 'It was not my intention to insult you; but I was worried about my mother.'

'Oh her!' Cheryl almost spat the words. 'Naturally you were more worried about *her* than me.'

'I know how she felt about my father and Freddie. I know that she only supported Chamberlain, for whom she has little personal regard, because she thought he presented the best chance of avoiding war. My mother *hates* Fascism, Hitler and what they stand for. Em has been in Germany, and they know just what conditions there are like, what they're doing to the Jews. But my mother thinks of me and the young men in our family – Hugo, Sasha, various cousins and those not old enough yet but who soon might be to fight in a war. I think most women think like this, Cheryl. All you think of is that your pride has been hurt because I should have told you first. I apologize. I should.'

He slowly rose and looked at her diffidently like the young man he had once been wooing a beautiful, experienced woman. He came over to her, but when he had reached the centre of the room he stayed where he was so as not to frighten her.

'I do apologize, Cheryl. I should have thought about that. I know I have disappointed you as a husband and as a man. Our marriage has not been happy and for that, surely, I am as much to blame as you.'

'I didn't think *I* was to blame at all,' Cheryl said stubbing out her cigarette in a large onyx ashtray by the side of the bed and immediately lighting a fresh one. 'Why should *I* be to blame for the failure of our marriage? I had so much more to gain from making it a success. Why should I want it to fail? Tell me please. Why?'

It was difficult, now, to summarize a situation that had worsened over ten years; to encapsulate into a few words the reason for the deterioration of their happiness and hopes. He thought he had married a greedy, selfish woman whose greed had only increased with the more she had. He knew that in her eyes he was weak. He tried to understand her too well and, like Chamberlain, had probably made the mistake of appeasement rather than a show of strength. Maybe a strong man, a brutal man was what she really wanted. But it was far too late for that now. Besides, he was not the type to take what he wanted by force.

'I think the fault for the failure of our marriage lies with us both,' he said at last. 'We should both have tried harder. Maybe if you feel as strongly as you do we should have a divorce rather than try again.'

Cheryl looked up at him in alarm, extinguished the fresh cigarette and moved quickly away from the wall to hurl herself into a long, low chair by the side of the bed.

'*Divorce* did you say? On what grounds?'

Ralph shrugged. He leaned against the wall, folding his arms, his hand stroking his chin. 'Incompatibility?'

'I believe there is no such plea, Ralph Askham, and you know it. Non-consummation is one plea, and *that* is certainly not the case with us – I hope we don't have to prove it. Adultery is the other and I most certainly have not been unfaithful to you and, if *you* have, believe me I shouldn't care. I would never ever sue you for divorce.' She pointed a finger imperiously towards the door. 'Sleep where you like tonight, Ralph Askham, and when you go to the war, if you do, don't expect me to wave you off. Whatever you do and whatever happens to you, believe me: I intend to remain Countess of Askham, with all the rights and privileges of that status, until the day I die. I will never grant you a divorce, never!'

CHAPTER 2

Stefanie Lighterman was approaching her eleventh birthday as, despite the gaiety of the Paris season, her adopted country prepared for a war that neither it nor anyone else, if the statesmen were to be believed, wanted. With her sisters, Olga and Natasha, Stefanie had been born in England; they were members of the Askham family through their father Bobby. Through her mother Hélène, Stefanie and her sisters were related to the noble Ferov family who had lived in great splendour in Russia until their assets were seized by the Bolsheviks, from whom they narrowly escaped with their lives.

It might have been thought that, by now, such children born in luxury and related to the nobility of two great countries would be living carefree lives of comfort and ease; but such was not the case with the three young Lighterman sisters. When their father had found out about their mother's adultery in 1935 he had banished not only her but his daughters, who reminded him too much of her, were too tainted, and he had never seen them again. His allowance to them had been minimal, and they had been brought up in what many would consider straitened circumstances in a large old-fashioned flat in a dingy apartment house behind the Gare du Nord.

Nor had the girls seen much of their mother either before the divorce or after: for the last three years she had been in prison for the murder of her lover. But none of them knew this – perhaps it would have been kinder if they had. There were so many mysteries. Nothing was explained to them. They grew up in ignorance, being taught that it was impolite to ask questions. Thinking that they had been abandoned by both mother and father, they developed into rather lonely little girls given to day-dreaming and make-believe. Their natural high spirits were constantly suppressed by the gloom of the large noisy apartment, draughty in winter, hot in summer, and by the depression of their grandmother, Princess Irina, with whom they lived.

The three girls with the same mother and father were yet very different to look at. Stefanie, tall and dark, resembled her father in his younger days, with his beautiful deep-set eyes and thick black hair. Nine-year-old Olga and seven-year-old Natasha were Ferovs; ash blonde like their mother with the same aquiline cast of features and deceptive air of serenity that had characterized that ambitious, passionate but unhappy woman.

One hot day in July, the sort of day when a girl of title and wealth would like to have been in the park or maybe the grounds of her country home with her nanny, Stefanie was standing in front of the window, her head pressed to the pane, humming a little song that was peculiarly tuneless. In the large badly furnished airless room behind her Natasha and Olga, heads bent over the table, were carefully colouring in a book that Cousin Charlotte had recently given them. They were close to Charlotte's daughter, Angelica, who was also nine and about to be sent to boarding school in England, much to their sorrow. Although Angelica led the kind of life the Lighterman girls might envy, spending a lot of time with various friends of her mother's who had large country estates or homes by the sea, Angelica and Olga, who had been born in the same month of the same year, were particularly close. Both had sweet, gentle natures, unlike the fiery Stefanie who, like her father, managed to be both possessive and aggressive, never completely contented with life. Only, in her case, there was more reason than her father, who had never known a moment's deprivation, never wanted for a single material thing since the moment he was born at Askham Hall in the year 1899.

Stefanie was gazing at the treeless street, its pavements baking in the hot sun. Her eye was caught by a solitary figure who had turned into it from a side street by the station and appeared to walk rather uncertainly, looking up at the houses as though searching for a number. Unexpectedly the person, a woman, stopped in front of the house from which Stefanie was peeping. She raised her head and Stefanie found herself looking into the eyes not of a stranger but of her mother: the mother who had abandoned them to go, where? They never knew and, being well brought up, were too polite to persevere when their questions remained unanswered until in the end all felt, with some justification, that some dark unpleasant secret were being concealed that it would be best not to know.

Stefanie took a step back from the window, not wanting her mother to see her. Maybe she would pass on and maybe it would be better if she did. Maybe not to know that dark secret would be better all round.

She looked at the bowed heads of her sisters, tongues poking out of their mouths with the effort of concentration, and then hurried towards the door; but even as she did the bell rang. It was an old bell with a stutter and it seemed to echo through the cavernous house. In better days, before the railway had been built, it had allegedly been a residence of some elegance. But all traces of that had long gone, and all that was left were peeling walls and patches of damp which in the hot weather caused the building to stink unmercifully.

Stefanie was already in the hall when her grandmother shuffled to the door of her room and stood on the threshold pulling her dressing gown around her although it was late in the afternoon. Poor Princess Irina was past caring – she of the perfect complexion, the well shaped eyebrows, rouged and perfumed cheeks, the stylish *coiffure*, had been finally defeated by fate, cruel fate which made her born to luxury, which she then lost, found again and lost once more. The final blow came when her disgraced and divorced daughter was sent to prison. Even in front of her granddaughters she forgot her dignity, lost that élan and sparkle which had seen her through so many vicissitudes. She spent most of the day in bed and when she was up she seldom dressed, but wore the same quilted, crumpled dressing gown that her friend Dulcie, Lady Askham, had given her for a birthday present ten years before. Oh, those days at Askham Hall, remembered so often as she shuffled about or solaced herself in furtive bouts of drinking.

'Who's that?' she asked Stefanie sharply, looking at the door.

'I think it's the wrong doorbell. Don't let's answer.'

'Of course we must answer! Open it, you silly girl! Maybe it's Cousin Charlotte back from England, or your Aunt Susan come to invite us to dinner.' The Ferovs had never had a telephone installed, so that people who wanted to invite them had either to write or call personally. It made for a certain amount of excitement, but for someone who had been an intimate of the last Empress of All the Russias it was a very bitter blow indeed to have been reduced to such straits. In Moscow the Ferov family had been among the first to have a telephone at the turn of the century.

Just then the bell rang again more insistently and, reluctantly, Stefanie opened it and stood looking unsmilingly at her mother.

'Hello.' Hélène took a step back as if she didn't recognize her eldest daughter. Three years in a young girl's life can bring about many changes. 'Why, it's Stefanie,' Hélène went on as if to reassure herself. She didn't lean forward to kiss her daughter's cheek or take her hand but said, rather timidly, her head on one side: 'May I come in?'

As Hélène stepped into the hall she was greeted by a loud wailing sound that for a moment sounded like a prolonged funeral dirge at the rites of some obscure religious sect. Irina had flung her arms in the air and then as Hélène came to a stop in front of her she fell upon her daughter who, for a moment, bore the entire weight of her mother's sagging body.

'Oh dotchinka, dotchinka,' Irina sobbed. 'Oh my dearest daughter, it has been so long, so long...'

'There, there,' Hélène said gently, trying to help Irina to an upright position. She looked over her mother's shoulder at

38

Stefanie who, reluctantly, took her bag and some flowers noting, as she did, that there were no other presents, nothing to make up for years of absence. 'Are you all right, Mother?'

'Sick to my soul,' Irina moaned, 'sick to death.'

The conversation was in Russian which the family spoke at home, ironically, as in Russia in the old days it had always been considered smart to speak in French.

'Come, Mother.' Hélène led her into the sitting room where Natasha and Olga stood with their hands behind their backs, gazing with astonishment at the scene, the unexpected visitation.

Then, after Irina had been settled in a chair, the two smaller girls were reintroduced to their own mother, greeting her awkwardly as though she had been a complete stranger.

It was a very odd sort of homecoming.

Later, when it was seen what little food there was in the apartment, Hélène went out to buy some, excitedly escorted by Natasha and Olga who, with the innocence of youth, had completely forgiven her. Stefanie, however, remained at home by the window, brooding as she had during the afternoon, waiting for them to return. Irina had recovered from her vapours, excited, after all, at the reappearance of the black sheep of the family. She had changed into a full-length dress of purple lace over gauze which she had worn on occasions when she was in waiting to the Czarina. She'd puffed up her hair, applied rouge to her cheeks and kohl round her eyes, though without the skill of former years, so that all her make-up was slightly blurred. Her lips, framed with magenta, looked quite garish as though she were in the final stages of terminal heart disease.

But she bustled about humming under her breath getting the table ready in the dining room with the best cloth, setting out the family silver and the tall crystal wine glasses, all of which had made the perilous journey from Odessa long ago.

Hélène came back with a shopping basket full of food and

more fresh flowers; the girls, each with shopping bags, their cheeks stuffed with sweets.

Still Stefanie watched – watched and said little. Even the smell of frying from the kitchen, the happy babble of family gossip, failed to excite her. When, eventually, they all sat down to the table she continued to stare at her mother, who suddenly leaned across the table as though to say 'boo!' and stared at her too.

'What is it? Has the cat caught your tongue? Have you seen a ghost?'

'Where have you been...'

'Stefanie, *that* you mustn't ask ...' Irina began but Hélène gave her mother a warning look.

'I've been travelling.'

'Why? Why did you leave us? Why didn't you write?'

'Ah Stefanie, that's not fair,' Irina began again, but Hélène once more interrupted her.

'No, she *has* a right to ask, Mother. She's a big girl.'

As Irina looking anxious bit her lip, smearing her teeth with colour, Hélène went on speaking, primarily to Stefanie who sat facing her across the table like judge and jury. 'When your father divorced me, so cruelly, sent us all away, I felt I too had to get away to have time to recover. I thought it was fairer to you that I should leave you with your grandparents, because I was in a very depressed state of mind. I went away to South America...'

'South America!' Natasha echoed, eyes shining, but Hélène hurried on: 'The West Indies, all over. Then when I felt better I came back, and here I am.'

'No card,' Stefanie accused. 'No letters.'

'Forgive me!' Hélène stretched out her arms, and it would have been difficult to ignore the appeal on that face, still lovely though bearing the marks, the indelible marks, of the penal years, still very very pale. But Stefanie ignored her mother's supplicant arms and bent her head, eyes fastened on her plate while Olga and Natasha began excitedly to ask questions about their mother's travels, to many of which Hélène, who had read extensively in prison, found she was able to reply. But Hélène's eyes remained restlessly on Stefanie as she fielded the questions. It was as though it was especially important for her that her critical eldest daughter should believe her.

'The thing I didn't want to tell you,' she said eventually, 'because it might hurt you is that your father married again. That is why he didn't want to see you. He has a new wife and a son, called David. He wanted to make a completely new life for himself and cut us all off. You can see how much it hurt me and, now, I know it hurts you.'

'Françoise Bethune has a new mother *and* baby brother,' Olga announced as though the blow were not such a major one after all. 'She says there are advantages in two sets of parents. Both her parents married again.'

'You see it is the modern age,' Irina lamented to no one in particular. 'It was quite unheard of in the days of the Czar.'

'*Now* we can meet them and see them?' Olga suggested. 'It would be very exciting. And you here with us ... oh Mummy!' Olga jumped from her chair and onto her mother's lap. Suddenly Hélène buried her face in her daughter's hair and only a visible effort of will prevented her from weeping.

'When will Papa be back?' she said, ruffling Olga's thick blonde hair so matched in colour and texture to her own.

'Who knows? God knows,' Irina said, raising her expressive eyes to the ceiling as though seeking confirmation directly from the Deity. 'You will see a change in your poor father too; but he sees friends, he reads the papers ...' Irina shrugged, 'he hopes.'

It was quite late when Prince Alexei Ferov arrived home and the children were in bed, Stefanie, reluctantly, the last to go. Even for her it had seemed the first normal evening, the first proper bedtime with a parent present that they'd had for years. Hélène laughed with them and cuddled them, doing things for the younger ones that she had never done before, because

41

when she was married to Bobby there had always been servants and nannies. For Stefanie she couldn't do anything but at least when she went to bed she kissed her mother and, suddenly, the touch of her flesh, the memory of a particular smell, a fragrance of flowers and a beautiful voile dress made the tears spring to her eyes. Then, at last, Hélène had pressed her so close that Stefanie thought she could feel her mother's heart beat. Or was it her own?

Hélène was deciding to go to bed when her father came in, but she came into the sitting room to greet him, fastening the cord of her dressing gown. Irina, who had wanted time to prepare him for the shock, looked on fearfully as her spouse screwed his monocle tightly into his left eye, peremptorily surveying his daughter up and down.

'It's Hélène,' Irina explained helpfully.

'I know that.'

'Do I have a kiss, Father?' Hélène remained by the door without approaching him.

'Why should I kiss you?' her father said. 'Haven't you...'

'Sshhh.' Irina frantically put her finger to her lips and pointed towards the long corridor to the room where the girls slept.

'Leave me alone, then, a little with Hélène,' Alexei pointed towards the door and, as Irina scuttled out, father and daughter faced each other.

If Irina had allowed herself to go to pieces Alexei Ferov certainly had not. He was a man of character and determination, a survivor, and he accepted what had happened to them, their many vicissitudes, not as the will of God, but as part of the lot of mankind. It was a quasi-religious, but mainly philosophical, belief; it had been a turbulent century and he and his family, like millions of others, had been its victims.

Throughout the years of exile Alexei had maintained, at whatever cost, the dignity and appearance of a Russian prince; one who had been born not only to great wealth but certain standards, an attitude of mind which had remained with him

42

when all else had gone. His clothes, made many years ago by the finest tailors in Moscow and St Petersburg, had stood the vital test of time, and, though maybe a trifle on the shabby side, a little frayed at the cuffs and round the lapels, were always kept clean, well brushed and eminently presentable. His carefully pomaded hair looked unnatural, being without a trace of grey, as was his perfectly waxed moustache which twirled up in correct military fashion at right angles at each end. Somehow everything was strictly but indefinably in keeping with the slightly decayed, but immaculate aristocratic image which he so carefully maintained. There were a number of men who resembled Alexei Ferov; who spent their mornings at the cheaper cafés on the quais of Paris drinking black coffee and reading the emigré press; but no one quite like him.

'We were better off without you,' Alexei said when he'd finished his appraisal of her. 'I don't know why you came back. The children had forgotten you. Why did you have to stir up trouble again? Don't you think you caused enough?'

Hélène swallowed hard. Her hair, normally pinned into a chignon at the nape of her neck, hung loosely down her back and her clear blue eyes and tragic pallor made her lovely.

'That's not the welcome I expected, Father,' she said in a low voice. 'I hoped, by now, that you'd have forgiven me.'

'But what you did was a terrible thing – an adulteress, and a murderess. Why didn't you lose yourself in some far off place instead of coming here?'

'Where could I go?' Hélène dejectedly flopped into one of the chairs, two of whose legs were propped up on uneven pieces of wood. 'You may not think it but I love my children. I love you and Mama. What I did was bad but ... I hope God has forgiven me. Maybe you could too? Is it too much to ask?'

'I no longer think of you as a daughter.' Alexei sat down after neatly creasing his trousers. 'You forfeited my love when you went to prison. A family that for so many centuries had served Russia with distinction, close to the Imperial Family – what, I asked myself, had it come to? You are not welcome here and I don't want you. You must go and live somewhere else, decide your own future. We have our lives, you have yours.'

'But what about the children?' Hélène's fingers played desperately with the knot of her gown.

'It is time your ex-husband made a home for them. They should have been sent to England. It is much too much of a burden for your mother and me, dearly though we love them.' He looked around the sitting room: it was sadly in need of a coat of paint, new furniture and carpet. 'We are too old for this place. It is cold. It leaks. With a little money we could find somewhere in the country...'

'Without the children you have *no* money,' Hélène said harshly. 'Bobby at least pays you for looking after them.'

'Yes but we're old. We want to live alone, have a bit of peace before we reach our graves. What you do I don't much care, but you must see your ex-husband again. He must give the children a home in England and leave us free. Besides it will be safer. If there is a war France might be overrun as she has been before. They say it is impossible, but they said the same thing in 1914.'

'The Germans never came to Paris in 1914.'

'No but they overran northern France. This time they might get further.'

Her father stood up abruptly and, from where she was looking at him, he seemed to have reached a greater height than was usual. He appeared to have a position, a stature and authority that she couldn't recall since she was a little girl. He gazed down at her and she remembered that expression that had once filled her with awe and struck fear into her heart.

'We don't want the children any longer, Hélène, and we don't want you. We want peace and quiet before we die.'

Hélène rose slowly to her feet. For a moment she stared at her father like the rebellious girl she had once been. She was a little taller than he was and once upright she seemed to see him

44

once again in proportion. She sighed. 'Good night, Father. Tomorrow I will make arrangements.'

As she walked towards the door she turned her back on him as though she were shutting out the past.

On the other side Stefanie Lighterman, who had spent the past few minutes with her ear pressed to the door, ran back to her own room, throwing herself onto the bed and covering her head with the bedclothes – weeping, weeping.

Charlotte, indignant at Alexei's treatment of her, would like to have given a home both to Hélène and her daughters. But to add a family of four to a family of four was stretching the resources of her home too much. She felt Bobby should do more and it was against Bobby that the full force of Ferov and, more importantly, Askham indignation was turned.

Ralph, who had troubles enough of his own, didn't hesitate when hearing of his cousin's predicament. As head of the family he sought an interview with Bobby at Lighterman House in Manchester Square which he had inherited on the recent death of his grandmother, the widow of Sir Robert. The house occupied the whole of one side of the square and in his lifetime Sir Robert had accumulated enough treasures to turn it into a virtual museum. Bobby was gradually completely doing it over though leaving most of the priceless ornaments, furniture and paintings where they were.

Bobby received him rather formally in the long, light drawing room overlooking the square, as though he were a business acquaintance rather than a close relation who had grown up with him, though he was seven years older than Ralph. Many years before, when Ralph married Cheryl and intended to return with her to Kenya, Bobby had advised Ralph to sell him most of the Askham assets. Ralph, besotted by love and anxious to return to what he regarded as his home in the British colony, trusted his cousin and had been only too willing. This was just one of the things the family could never forgive Bobby for; another was his treatment of his wife and daughters.

Throughout his life Bobby Lighterman, who had just had his fortieth birthday, had had a curious relationship with the rest of his family which would have defied analysis by even the most skilled disciple of Freud. Though born into wealth and related to the Askhams through his mother Lady Melanie, he had always carried a chip on his shoulder because of his father's side of the family. This had reached its eminence only in his grandfather's time and solely through trade and the manipulation of the greed, or otherwise, of his fellow men.

Bobby loved money but somehow the Lighterman origins always distressed him. When his then wife, Hélène, had taunted him for being the grandson of a grocer it had sealed her fate as much as her adultery, or her father's shady dealings in the armaments' world, which had brought notoriety to part of the Askham empire controlled by Bobby – Askham Armaments. Bobby's second marriage to the daughter of one of his foremen hadn't made either her or himself happy, but it had given him a son, David, his most precious, most priceless, most valued possession: David on whom was lavished all the love, the affection, the tenderness of which this rather hard, dour man was capable. It was a love that exceeded that for his mother, father, grandfather, grandmother and family combined. With David, Bobby was a different person, tender and indulgent, and he never ever regretted marrying beneath him to legitimize his son.

The men seated themselves in a corner of the elegant room while the butler, with a good deal of solemnity and ceremony, supervised the serving of coffee by two other servants: a maid and a footman. Ralph felt vaguely uncomfortable in Lighterman House because its opulent standards seemed out of step with the times, anachronistic. Half of Askham House in St James's Square had been closed down and the number of servants at the Hall reduced. It didn't help when one reflected that most of Bobby's fabulous wealth over the last ten years was due to his purchase, for much less than they were worth, of the assets of the Askham family who now, all of them, had to live on a very much reduced scale.

'How is David?' Ralph began conversationally knowing it was always a good way to get Bobby into a receptive mood. Bobby, however, shrugged, not looking too pleased on this occasion at the mention of the name of the apple of his eye.

'We all know David's no scholar,' he began.

'But I thought he was...'

'Well he *was* until I married his mother. Then everything changed. Harrow will take him, of course, but he'll have to pull his socks up. It wasn't a blow when he failed Common Entrance, but it shouldn't have happened. He has a first-class brain. I sometimes think that knowing the fortune he was in line for wasn't a good thing for David, whereas for me it was. It certainly was. It was a challenge. I wanted to improve on my inheritance. David seems to think all he has to do is spend his. Well, he'll have to wait.'

Bobby ran his hand over his blue jowl, fingering his trim moustache, a relatively new acquisition. It was difficult now, in his forty-first year, to believe that as a boy Bobby had ever been regarded as beautiful. Now he was a slightly corpulent man, due to the excess of City dinners, of which he partook a good many, and the comforts of the large limousine in which he always travelled. Apart from his business he had no interests, no sports or hobbies, no mistress. He ate, drank, slept, thought and talked business and, apart from David, he cared about very little else.

'He'll change,' Ralph said comfortingly. 'He'll grow up.'

'It's the change I don't like.' Bobby settled back in his chair and unbuttoned the lower button of his jacket. 'I wish he'd change back. He used to be very nice, once upon a time, waiting for me at that house in Harrow. Once he saw all this, knew how wealthy I really was ...' Bobby hunched his shoulders as if visualizing what might have been. He looked at his watch, checking it with the large clock on the wall close by the huge portrait by Sargent of his grandfather Sir Robert in Alderman's robes. Bobby frequently looked at his watch as though to remind people that they were in the presence of someone whose time was precious, whose time was worth money – pounds and pounds of it. 'Now what can I do for you, Ralph?'

Ralph got at once to the point. Younger than Bobby, he was also his opposite: tall, slim, boyish-looking with his straight fair hair close cropped in military fashion, piercing blue eyes and clean cut image. In his army uniform he looked like some hero from the *Boys Own* paper, the very salt of which England was made. 'I came about the girls,' Ralph said. 'Your girls.'

'Oh, I thought that would be it.' Bobby studied his carefully pared nails. 'Either that or money.'

'No, not a loan this time,' Ralph was conscious of the fact that the family was now in debt to Bobby for several thousand pounds. He half owned the stud Ralph managed at his farm in the country, and the Kenyan farm which Ralph never despaired of returning to, and which was now run by a tenant. 'In fact I think we are on a pretty level keel now that I've become a full-time soldier. Hugo is excellent on the farm and even Cheryl is cutting down on expenses.'

'That's good news.' Bobby frowned. 'Well, what about the girls?'

'Hélène is out of prison.'

'So I heard.' Bobby's frown turned to a scowl. 'So much for French justice or, rather, injustice. She should have been guillotined.'

Ralph winced at the brutal statement of a man about a woman to whom he had once been married.

'That's a very hard thing to say, Bobby,' Ralph said disapprovingly. 'Even for you.'

'What do you mean "even for me"?'

'Well, you're not a man to let sentiment cloud your judgement. You know all the family, including your mother, I believe, and mine think as I do that you have not done the right

48

thing by Stefanie, Olga and Natasha. They have lived in reduced circumstances with their grandparents, without even a servant I understand. Alexei now wishes that he and Irina should be on their own.'

'The girls will be well provided for eventually. They have enough. Those Russians don't know how to look after money. They never did.'

'Don't you feel *any* sense of responsibility for your own?' Ralph got up and started to pace the room, examining some of the many masterpieces of art which graced the walls, minutely inspecting them as if he hadn't seen them before, to hide his irritation.

Bobby also rose and, lighting a cigarette, moved to one of the windows which stood open onto the square.

'I put my daughters out of my life when I divorced Hélène,' Bobby said. 'I even have doubts if they are all mine. Stefanie, maybe, as there is a family resemblance to me, but what of Natasha? Don't you think she looks like an Askham, a Kitto?'

'You don't think she's *Jamie's* daughter?'

'Why not?' Bobby carelessly puffed smoke into the air. 'I don't think Hélène ever ceased to have relations with that man. She had them before we were married, during and after. Stefanie I am pretty certain *is* my daughter, and Olga is possibly mine too because, as far as I know, Jamie was in South America at the crucial time; but Natasha?' Bobby opened wide blue eyes and, briefly, it was possible once again to recall the striking boy and youth he had been. 'Natasha is almost certainly not my child because Hélène had resumed her relationship with Kitto by that time. But, really, they could all be bastards as far as I'm concerned and frankly, Ralph, since you ask me,' Bobby violently stubbed out his cigarette, 'I think I'm being remarkably generous in not instituting proceedings against Hélène to have their legitimacy investigated. That way I need give them nothing. As it is I have accepted them all and they are well provided for; *very* well provided for. As they get older and out of the clutches of the parasitical Ferovs they will

49

be even better provided for – it can't be too soon, for me. Their mother in any case should look after them now. It's her responsibility. Let her find work if it's difficult to make ends meet. The girls will be quite wealthy young women when they're in their twenties.'

Bobby glanced quickly at his watch and appeared to make some calculations.

'Now I really must go, Ralph. I have an important meeting in the City. If we are to have war, and you seem to think we will, and I must say I do too, we cannot be too well prepared. At the moment, thanks to that idiot Chamberlain, we are not. Hitler could overrun us tomorrow if he wanted to.' He looked Ralph up and down for a moment, smiling. 'You know, Ralph, you were an idiot to join up; there was no need for it. You'll be killed just like your father and brother – both fools to rush in where angels fear to tread. Neither of them need have fought, and neither do you – yet. There are plenty of younger men without your responsibilities. Had you not enlisted there would have been a place for you with Askham Armaments. A Lord Askham would once again have been at its head. You could have helped with the war effort and, if I'm not mistaken, you would have made a packet out of it. As I hope to. I can tell you, if there *is* a war it will be a very lucrative affair for me. Very lucrative indeed. Can I drop you anywhere?'

'No thank you,' Ralph said, not troubling to conceal the expression of disgust and distaste on his face. 'Quite frankly, Bobby, I prefer to walk.'

CHAPTER 3

When Hitler entered Poland, ostensibly in defence of the Port of Danzig and the Polish Corridor, on 1 September 1939, it was to find a world largely unprepared. Thus, despite the events that had happened since Munich, the inflammatory speeches, the aggressive acts, the remobilization, the air of unrest that permeated the world, debate after debate took place on whether Europe should sacrifice possibly millions of men – no one thought of civilians much in those days – for the sake of a port on the Baltic Sea whose population was largely German anyway.

After all, what did Poland matter to people whose cultural links with it were remote? The debate had gone on for months in the British press; but when Hitler marched into Poland and war was declared, it was stopped abruptly. The enthusiastic frenzy that had seized such a large proportion of the population for many months – those who had hated appeasement and wanted to teach Hitler a lesson – seemed to grip the whole nation. Thousands hastened to enlist and thousands more joined the civilian organizations: the WVS, ARP and Home Guard.

Rachel listened to Chamberlain solemnly declaring that Britain was at war with Germany, for the second time in her lifetime, with her brother Adam at their home Darley Manor in a very rural part of Hampshire. It had been a lovely August and they had spent a lot of the time in the garden watching with pleasure Adam's children Giles and Flora at play with Rachel's baby grandson, Paul, Freddie's child.

Paul's mother had been a German Jewess whose father and brother had disappeared in the mid-thirties when Hitler's persecution of the Jews gathered momentum. Watching her half-German grandson play on the lawn Rachel felt her heart turn over as, precisely at eleven o'clock, the momentous words were uttered: '... this country is now at war with Germany'.

Rachel groped for Adam's hand and the tears that had been welling there sprang to her eyes. Adam returned her clasp, trying to be reassuring, but how could one be reassuring when one had already fought in two wars? Adam had been at the famous charge of the 21st Lancers at Omdurman, and had nearly lost his life in 1915.

Adam was now sixty-three, a Judge of the High Court, and there would be no more battles for him. But the whole country would be involved and somehow, one could not help thinking, so would the entire world.

'It will be a world war,' Adam said. 'It will involve the globe. No one will escape. You mark my words.'

Rachel, who owned a newspaper and was in contact with her editor in London by phone several times a day, had no doubt that he was right. Tomorrow she would get up early to motor to the capital with Adam while the children stayed with their nurses, Giles and Flora being home for the holiday from school.

'If Russia had stayed out of it the extent might have been avoided.' Rachel looked at her brother with anxious eyes. 'But with their perfidy, in making an alliance with Hitler, who knows what will happen? You don't think they could possibly *win*, Adam, do you?'

Adam too looked anxious. He rose to switch off the wireless and the sound of martial music, and strolled to the window looking out upon that peculiarly English scene of beautifully kept lawn and garden, surrounded by the thick foliage of plane and chestnut trees.

'Of course they won't *win*.' Adam turned to look at Rachel. 'But how long will it take to defeat them and what will happen to ... those we love: Charlotte, Ralph? Susan says Sasha wants to enlist and yet he is only seventeen. I tell you I shall do all I can to forbid it!'

Sasha was his grandson Alexander at school in England.

'Ralph had no need to enlist,' Rachel said sadly. 'He's his father all over again, and Freddie...'

The family was indeed a worry. It was so dispersed – Charlotte and Bobby's daughters in France; Susan, Adam's eldest daughter, in Venice. Her son, Sasha, had only just returned in order to go back to school for his final year. Instead he wanted to join up.

'Mother said I should talk to you and Uncle Bobby about it,' he informed Rachel and Adam a few days after the declaration of war, having come straight down to see them upon arriving in London. 'I thought I'd speak to you first.'

'Don't think we can persuade him,' Adam said grumpily. 'Bobby would never listen to us.'

'But you're my grandfather,' Sasha insisted. 'Surely what you think is the most important?'

Even as he spoke he knew what Adam's answer would be. In many ways Bobby, with his wealth, experience and influence, was the head of the family; he held all the reins, more than Ralph, Adam, Rachel or his grandmother, Melanie, Adam's first wife who lived in Cannes. No one particularly liked Bobby but they listened to him, so that his word was a sort of family rendition of the law.

His grandfather, after considering the matter, confirmed what he knew they were both thinking.

'Bobby knows the ropes,' Adam said gruffly, stroking his chin. 'He will know what is best for you to do.'

'I think you should get your Higher School Certificate first,' Rachel sounded adamant. 'We don't know how long the war will last and you will need some qualifications. Personally...'

'Yes?' Sasha put down his coffee cup and looked up at her.

Rachel took a deep breath. 'Personally I think you should go on to university and wait until you're called up. Don't be in too much of a hurry to throw your life away ... darling Sasha.'

Tenderly Rachel put out a hand and touched his shoulder. 'It is too awful to be young at this moment.'

'I think it's marvellous: "Bliss was it in that dawn to be alive", Aunt, "but to be young was very heaven!"'

'Yes, but Wordsworth and the French Revolution are very remote compared to what is happening today.'

Rachel sat down and put on a large hat to shade her head from the sun. They seemed to spend a lot of time in the garden these days as if to postpone for as long as possible that evil day, if it should come, when they would be engulfed by war; as if a contemplation of the peaceful, fragrant countryside of England, with its qualities of endurance, would take their minds off the war raging in Poland.

Adam's legs were stretched out in the attitude he adopted for a snooze and everywhere was quiet except for the trees brushed by the wind, sighing and wafting backwards and forwards. There wasn't a cloud in the sky and Sasha, sighing contentedly, leaned back and stared into that vast space of cerulean blue.

'Bombers,' he said.

Adam grunted and Rachel stared up in alarm.

'What? Where?'

'I'd like to go into bombers. Fly them or something.'

'Oh there won't be any bombing.' Rachel settled down again. 'Whatever could we bomb? Not *people*, I hope.'

'Enemy installations, battle lines...'

'Sasha, dear, let's hope it won't come to that. A lot of people think that when Hitler overruns Poland he'll sue for peace.'

'You really don't believe that, Aunt, do you?' Sasha looked lazily at her as though somehow all this talk about the war and bombers was academic; the sort of philosophical discussion the family, when together, so enjoyed. Sasha, putting his arms behind his head, seemed completely at ease.

'I don't know what I think.' Rachel stared at him and saw that, his eyes half closed, his mind seemed very far away. For a long time she looked at him surreptitiously from under the brim of her hat, trying to banish from her mind the terrifying thoughts of what war might mean not only to Sasha, but to others like him.

Sasha was the one all the family loved. He was a gentle, charming boy with thick brown curly hair and a rather long, stooping gait making him slightly round-shouldered, blue eyes and the tanned complexion of the habitual sportsman. He did have the Slav looks of the Ferov family, the slightly slanted eyes with long, beautiful lashes, but he had the elusive attraction, also, of the Askhams – an indefinable insouciance that seemed to accept life with ease and assurance. He had been brought up in a curious family atmosphere, alone with his mother for many years before he met, for the first time, his father Kyril, then recently released from a Russian farm labour camp.

Soon after, Sasha was dispatched to school in England as if his parents wished to exclude him from the tenderness of their reunion. The birth of his sister Anna seemed to confirm this and, thereafter, Sasha always felt that his life was lived in comparative isolation; at boarding school, in trains or boats visiting various relations during the long school holidays.

He was fond of his cousins, the three Lighterman girls, sharing grandparents with them, but, as soon as he struck up any relationship or felt settled, it was time to move on again – to his mother in Venice, his maternal grandmother in the south of France, his father in Paris or the many relations scattered around England. Sasha Ferov, the boy who never quite belonged, whose home was always a suitcase in which were immaculately pressed clothes, clean underwear, toilet things and several books.

To celebrate Sasha's arrival and to hear news of Melanie, Susan and Anna and the Ferov family, particularly Hélène and the three girls, Rachel organized a family get-together to which Em was persuaded to bring Luis and the reluctant, sulky Felipe who hardly ever went anywhere but had pronounced views about the war which he liked to air. Luis was a grandson Rachel didn't see much of, a sturdy little toddler whom she hardly felt she knew.

Adam's son Christopher was there to discuss some business with his father and with him came his wife Sylvia and children, well brought up and well behaved paragons who were both down for select boarding schools.

Hugo drove over from his farm which he managed without Ralph. Since war had become a certainty he had longed to join up but, instead, was besieged by directives from various ministries telling him that his was a vital occupation, an important source of food and sustenance for the country.

Cheryl, who was always invited to family gatherings as Ralph's wife, seldom came. Her life apart from the family was meant to be a secret, but most of them knew it involved a lot of travel, socializing and spending what was left of Ralph's money on clothes and the interior decoration of both her houses.

The day the British Expeditionary Force under the command of Lord Gort had landed in France, 19 September, Hitler made a speech after his triumphal entry into Danzig which seemed to offer hope of conciliation to France and England, both of whom now had War Cabinets. When the family gathered at the Manor, a few days later, it was another lovely day with hardly a hint of autumn and wars and rumours of wars seemed very far away. The children played on the lawn, among the trees, the adults sat or walked about chatting, speculating, hoping, and the maids ran in and out with drinks, squashes for the children and, occasionally, a cloth to mop up a spill.

It was the kind of day the Askham and Bolingbroke families had seen, together, many times before. Rachel in particular always enjoyed them because there was a sameness and security now about them that, in the current uncertainty of war, was all the more reassuring.

Sasha had given them an account over lunch of his mother

and sister, grandparents, aunts and cousins on the continent and then talk turned to the war, the prospects of peace after the Danzig overtures. Em, who had lived for a long time in Germany was pessimistic, but Rachel wanted to believe the war would soon end and gave her reasons at some length.

Felipe sat with them on the terrace after lunch listening, glowering at the scene, the manifestation of English country society which he detested. He had tried not to come but Em, telling him it might be the last time they would be gathered together, persuaded him. Besides, just occasionally, Felipe liked to air his controversial views to a larger audience than the one provided by Em and the baby who couldn't understand a word except 'do', 'don't', 'Mama' and 'Dadda'. Felipe, arms crossed, eyes half closed, strong smelling cigarette burning in the corner of his mouth, listened to Rachel with a smirk of disbelief on his face.

'You are quite wrong, Lady Askham,' he announced in a pause. 'Hitler wants to dominate the world. He will never be satisfied with Danzig. He and Russia will divide Eastern Europe between them and go on to conquer the rest. The Russians will have succeeded in getting the defences they have wanted for centuries, to be surrounded by satellites.'

'You sound very sure of yourself,' Adam murmured, recumbent, like Hugo, in a long low-lying wicker chair. 'Have you parted company with your Communist friends? If so I'm glad to hear it.'

'Not at all.' Felipe sprang up nearly knocking over Em and the baby, who were sitting next to him. 'You make the mistake of many Fascists of thinking that one can only be a Communist *and* a supporter of Russia...'

'My brother is *not* a Fascist.' Rachel flushed and glared at Felipe. 'Please withdraw that remark.'

'He speaks like a Fascist,' Felipe said loftily, sitting down again. 'I don't withdraw it.'

'Maybe you meant capitalist?' Em ventured helpfully, dreading a scene, though, invariably, Felipe provoked one when she was with her family. She wondered now, as she usually did, why she was so keen for him to come unless it was to try and persuade the family, as well as herself, that some kind of bond existed between them in a relationship unsanctified by marriage.

'Capitalist, Fascist, they are the same.' Felipe appeared about to begin on one of his political monologues which Rachel so dreaded and resented. Only Hugo intervened, albeit with a yawn, as though to try and defuse the situation by pretending to be bored.

'They are *not* the same. Even an untutored fellow like me knows that. Uncle Adam is neither a Fascist nor a capitalist but an independent member of our judiciary of which we're very proud. Now why don't you shut up?'

'Hugo!' Em sprang up and Luis, who had peacefully been slumbering in her arms, his head on her chest, thumb in his mouth, woke to issue a cry of protest.

'It's absolutely true.' Hugo opened one eye and gazed at her. 'Your boyfriend is a pain in the neck, if you want the truth, Em. I don't think we've had a single meal here in the past year or a gathering at which he's been present that has been in any way pleasant.'

'Then why don't *you* stay away?' Em put Luis on the floor and, as he sat down with a bump, he began to scream again.

'Why should I?' Hugo looked aggrieved. 'I don't cause trouble.'

'Felipe has views that are very important to him.'

Hugo sat up and folded his arms, bronzed with haymaking. He looked so tanned, fit and altogether wholesome that Rachel gazed at him with all the pride of his real mother. And she did love him; she always had. Hugo the beloved; the child Bosco had wanted her to have before he died. There was something good and strong about Hugo; he was so principled and straight. How Bosco would have adored him.

'So do I,' Hugo said after a few moments of consideration. 'I have views that are very important to me and I think

58

politeness to my host and hostess is one of them. Yet when Felipe comes here after eating Adam's meat and drinking his wine, plenty of both I notice, he then starts to insult him; and Adam, being the saint he is, the perfect gentleman, sits there and takes it. Even when he's called a Fascist! Well, it so happens that we're fighting the Fascists and, by God, I wish I were fighting them too. Seeing that you hate them so much why don't *you* go and fight them, Felipe? I would have thought that after what they did to you and your country you would have been one of the first to volunteer. Don't tell me you're afraid?'

Before Hugo had finished Felipe stood up, the drooping cigarette in the corner of his mouth long spent.

'Come, Em,' he said, 'I don't have to put up with this. We will never come here again unless we have an apology. Come, bring the baby.' He pointed imperiously to the squawking Luis who was tired and wanted his afternoon sleep.

'Oh, Felipe,' Em began appealingly but his expression plainly cowed her and she turned to Rachel: 'I'll ring you, Mum.'

'Of course.' Rachel got up and put her arm around her daughter's shoulder, her hand squeezing it as though she were trying to impart some kind of message.

'Never again, Lady Askham, I can tell you,' Felipe said loudly. 'Don't think I shall readily forget this insult.'

'Don't forget she owns your house,' Hugo called out as Felipe, posturing, turned to lead the way back through the French windows into the house. 'If you're not very careful Rachel will give you your marching orders.'

Momentarily Felipe looked as though he were going to turn back, but Em firmly put her hand in the small of his back and pushed him through the door. Rachel followed.

'You did the right thing,' Sasha said after they had gone, but he looked abashed. Family rows made him nervous and the introduction of the subjects of Communism and Fascism even more so. His grandfather, Alexei, had a number of German friends who were openly Nazis and his father, Kyril, though once a Communist, had spent a lot of time in Spain before and during the war. Though his activities were secret everyone supposed he was there to help Franco. Whatever the truth they had taken him far too long away from home.

Consequently Sasha, who disliked extremes, who valued family life, had become apolitical, a neutral in a family that thrived on politics, discussion and controversy.

He had kept well out of the discussion and now he rose, stretched and invited Hugo, or anyone who would care to, to join him for a walk. No one wanted to. Sasha waved, said he wouldn't be long and walked off towards the paddock and the woods beyond.

Adam watched him go until he was out of sight; a detached, rather solitary young man who liked his own company. No longer a boy, he was not yet quite grown up. Adam sighed. Rachel's plans for the day had gone awry. He looked round for her but she was still probably trying to comfort Em. Telling her that, of course, it was absolutely all right. Rachel would.

Hugo appeared to go to sleep and Adam's eyes turned to his two younger children, animatedly talking to their cousins. Flora and Giles were the offspring of his second wife, Margaret, who had died at Flora's birth. His children spanned two complete generations; Susan was already twenty-five and a mother herself when Giles was born, and Christopher's children were about the same age as his.

He was a *paterfamilias*, but he had always been a shy, rather withdrawn man, not particularly ambitious and never very wealthy. All his life he had relied a good deal on his sister Rachel. Their lives were so entwined it was like a marriage. He needed Rachel near him and her counsels were invariably followed. Having children of two completely different generations, grandchildren who were older than one's youngest children, was not the easiest thing in the world and, for a man of Adam's temperament, the reassuring presence of Rachel, who always knew what to do, was essential. She would know what to do now with Em and Felipe. The row would blow over.

Adam almost fell into a doze like Hugo when Sylvia and Christopher appeared and demanded to know what the commotion had been about. Sylvia had walked up from the garden pausing to chat to Sasha on the way, but he had been non-committal. Christopher looked as though he had been having an afternoon sleep on the bed upstairs; his hair was tousled and his bland, blue eyes rather bleary. Christopher was the unexceptional member of the family, a true Bolingbroke, unimaginative but very well meaning. He was uxorious, loved his children and family life and ran a very successful solicitor's practice in Winchester.

His wife Sylvia, however, was a febrile, restless girl, blonde, pretty but her bad-tempered nature was reflected in a habitual pout. She had aspirations to be something better than she was, grand as the Askhams used to be; at one time she had been very friendly with Cheryl.

She closely cross-examined Adam and Hugo, who had now woken up, about the fracas and told the assembled company exactly what she thought about Felipe and about the tolerance of a country that gave such men a home.

'They should be sent back to where they came from,' she said.

'You mean deported?' Adam seemed to be seeking clarification rather than administering a reproof.

'Sylvia doesn't know what she's talking about.' Christopher scratched his arm and yawned. 'I'd have given him a good thump.'

'Oh I'd like to have seen *that*.' Sylvia looked critically at her slightly lazy, slightly overweight husband. What so irritated her about Christopher was his blandness; nothing ever seemed to move him very much so long as he had enough money to spend, his children were well and his physical needs were satisfied.

He yawned again, an amiable expression on his face and was

61

about to reply when Rachel returned from seeing Em and Felipe off with her grandson. She looked sad and preoccupied and Adam gave her a sympathetic smile.

'He'll get over it.'

'I'm not sure,' Rachel said. 'He's the sort of person one should take care not to provoke.'

'Why?' Hugo said. 'Am *I* meant to apologize because he's so rude?'

'You know better; he can't help it,' Rachel said beckoning to the butler who stood hesitating at the door of the French windows. 'He is, I think, slightly mad; so terribly carried away by his political views that he can't see reason. I only wish he were not Luis's father and that Em,' she sighed and cleared a space for the tea things, 'that Em were not so attached to him.' She moved her chair back: 'There, please Vance.'

The butler solemnly placed a large silver teapot on the table by the side of Rachel and then made way for the maid who had come behind him pushing a trolley on which there was an assortment of sandwiches, scones and cakes. Hugo opened his eyes wide.

'Tea already? My goodness,' he reached for a sandwich. 'Why I'm hungry I don't know, but I am.'

'It's all that hard physical work,' Rachel said, smiling and starting to pour. Gradually she was assuming control of herself again.

'I must be getting back.' Hugo looked at his watch.

'Oh, I hoped you'd stay for dinner.'

'Yes, do stay,' Sylvia said, getting up to help Rachel. She liked Hugo and would have flirted with him, given half the chance, even though she had known him a long time. Her restlessness made her attractive to, and attracted by, other men. But Hugo would never have entertained the idea of dalliance with his cousin's wife. He simply wasn't like that.

Like Sasha, only for different reasons, Sylvia felt an outsider in the family circle; never quite at ease, quite wanted or acceptable. The family didn't do it deliberately but they did seem to have this effect on a lot of people, as though theirs was a charmed circle to which hardly anyone ever gained admission. Sylvia had been trying for years; some never tried, like Felipe or Cheryl, and some were accepted immediately, without question, like Freddie's wife Marian whom Rachel had loved from the beginning.

Hugo, sensing Sylvia's need for friends, smiled at her in a way that had only warmth and understanding, no other meaning.

'All right, I'll stay and have dinner,' he said, 'seeing that I'm so popular.' He put his hands behind his head, squinting into the sun which was gradually sinking low in the valley. 'You know I feel utterly content here today. It's such a lovely day that I can't really believe the war is real. Can anyone? They discouraged me like anything from enlisting because, apart from the importance of the farm, the authorities seem sure it won't last. Hitler may occupy a few eastern European countries, as Felipe says, and then sue for peace.'

'But would we accept?' Adam, fully awake, lit a cigarette to have with his tea. 'Why should the rest of Europe be enslaved by the Communists and Fascists while we're free? No, I think that after months of appeasement the mood of this country is bellicose. If you ask me we're in for a long war and I can tell you one thing,' he stirred his tea thoughtfully, 'nothing will ever be the same again. When this war is over the world will be even more different than it was in 1918, believe you me.'

Looking at him Rachel felt suddenly anxious, sharing Adam's foreboding. As she passed a fresh cup of tea to Sylvia, her spine seemed to tingle with apprehension as though someone had walked on her grave.

They were just sitting down to dinner when, unannounced, unexpected, Cheryl Askham arrived, having driven herself over in her smart little Citroën roadster which she'd bought on one of her trips to France. The butler who opened the door had hardly time to announce her before she rushed in, the expression on her face betraying her extreme agitation. Rachel, in the act of taking her seat, stood up again.

'Is everything all right?' she asked, while everyone else remained standing too.

'Everything is decidedly not all right,' Cheryl said. 'Ralph rang to inform me he was being sent to France. Did you ever hear *anything* so ridiculous?'

'But there's no war in France. The force there's just a precaution.' Adam signalled for the butler to lay a further place, 'Lady Askham will be eating with us, Vance.' Then he said to the new arrival, 'Do sit down, Cheryl, we've got some excellent beef.'

Cheryl abruptly sat down. She looked beautiful and elegant in a tailored cotton dress with a wide blue bow, hatless, her dark hair smooth on top, a bunch of little curls behind caught by a blue bow to match her dress.

'There's no need for Ralph to have joined up at all. *He volunteered* to be sent to France! I really don't understand it. It's as though he won't be happy until he has the Channel between himself and me. Can't you do *anything* about it, Lady Askham?' She looked at her mother-in-law.

Cheryl had been married to Ralph for ten years, yet she had never got closer to Rachel than a formal peck on the cheek and she still called her Lady Askham.

'I can't influence Ralph, Cheryl, you know that.' Rachel signalled for Cheryl to be served. 'Besides, I wouldn't want to. He has decided to join the Army and he wants to feel useful.'

'You've *always* taken his side,' Cheryl cried. 'I don't suppose you'll ever change. You Askhams, you always stick together.'

Hugo, who had been watching her warily, didn't want to intervene. He and his sister-in-law had never got on. Yet once again the family was under attack from an outsider and, for the second time that day, Hugo rushed to its defence.

'*You* are an Askham too, Cheryl.'

'An outsider,' Cheryl said bluntly. 'Always was and always

will be. Not accepted by the family because I was not out of the top drawer.'

'You know that's quite untrue.' Rachel clenched her teeth. 'Please don't go over all that again.'

At the far side of the table Sasha turned pale.

Rachel felt her appetite had gone. 'Cheryl, dear, we've had rather a tiring day. I'm sure you have, too, and you're upset. *Please* try and relax and enjoy your meal. If the war goes on we might not often see beef like this.'

Cheryl flung up her hands in horror.

'Oh don't talk about the war going *on*,' she said. 'Someone told me that it was going to end because Hitler has got what he wants. Oh I do hope so.' She put her hand to her head swaying backwards and forwards. 'I can't *bear* to think of what will happen next.' Dramatically she looked round the table. 'Do you know, they want to turn Askham Hall into a reception place for evacuees? Dirty, horrible little children from the East End of London, full of bugs and lice. Can you imagine anything more *awful*? I shall leave if they do. I couldn't stand it. Imagine, my beautiful home, redecorated, furnished with such care at such expense, full of people like that? *That's* why I wanted Ralph here to oppose it. Don't you think it's a cowardly thing to go off and leave me all on my own?' Cheryl dabbed at her face with her napkin, careful not to smudge her mascara.

But the family with one accord had all stopped eating, looking first of all at Cheryl and then wide-eyed at one another.

Askham Hall, the family seat, sacrosanct for hundreds of years, a reception centre for evacuees? Was it possible? Could it happen? It seemed, at last, that the war had crossed the Channel and was threatening them on home ground. It had come very, very close indeed.

CHAPTER 4

The Russian church in Rue Darue was full and, in the lights of the hundreds of guttering candles, it was possible to see quite clearly the expressions of hope and anxiety, fear and piety on the faces of the worshippers. For the old who had seen war before, whose lives had been completely disrupted by it, who had suffered exile and poverty because of it there was a sort of resignation. On the faces of the middle-aged anxiety had already left its mark, uncertainty about the future, the burden and responsibility both for the very old and the very young.

Youth fared best, youth who had no forebodings about the future, no nightmares about the past. In the last days of 1939 and the early days of 1940 the celebration of the Orthodox Christmas and New Year was still a hopeful, joyful time for many.

For Ralph, on leave from the British Expeditionary Force centred on Lille, standing between Charlotte and Hélène, it was a time of relaxation. He and Charlotte had wanted to share the Orthodox devotions with the Ferov family, especially the three Lighterman girls. Yet the celebration of the liturgy seemed endless and the voices of the priests, the unaccompanied singing of the choir, induced in him a comatose feeling that made him fear that he would fall asleep. Maybe that was why so much of the time was spent standing? As he swayed on his feet Charlotte nudged him and Hélène, on the other side, murmured: 'It won't be long now.'

To keep himself awake Ralph moved away to take a little walk, as many of the worshippers did during the long ceremonies, blessing themselves in front of the family ikons or greeting friends. Many of them had quite long conversations. Ralph looked back at his own family and thought with nostalgia, as he always did at that time of the year, of those in England; of Mother and Em, Luis, Hugo, Adam, Flora, Giles, Bobby, Aileen and all the children gathered this year at Darley Manor for Christmas. All the family except Cheryl, who remained at the Hall which had been invaded by a small army of children evacuated from the East End of London. The very thought of it sent a smile to Ralph's face. It seemed like a quiet act of revenge, though he'd had nothing to do with it. Cheryl who had always hated children would now be surrounded by them. The amazing thing was that she was still there. Maybe, with the London house closed for the duration she had no alternative. Yet Rachel had written that Cheryl seemed to be enjoying herself. Could it be true?

Ralph dismissed from his mind the thought of his estranged wife, and strolled to the far end of the church from where he could better examine those he had just left. Next to Hélène was Natasha, the baby, a fair girl who resembled her mother with her ash blonde hair and thick dark eyebrows. Then there was Sasha Ferov who had come over for the Christmas holidays only to find that Susan had stayed in Venice because she was not well. His father was still in Paris and the two enjoyed a reunion after many months of separation. Next to Sasha was Stefanie, the most striking of the Lighterman girls, who had refused to leave her grandparents and move in with her mother, who was staying with Charlotte. Ralph couldn't help thinking that Sasha and Stefanie, first cousins on the Askham side, the children of Susan and Bobby, made an attractive couple. Stefanie had Olga's hand tightly in hers, presumably to try and keep her awake because, like Ralph a few minutes before, Olga was swaying on her feet. Except for inches Olga and Natasha looked like twins.

Next to Olga was Alexei, spruce as usual in a fur coat and a close fitting Cossak hat. He was singing lustily and making the responses, clearly enjoying himself in a familiar environment. Next to him, sitting most of the time in a chair specially brought for her, was Irina whose head was sunk on her chest as though she were either sleeping or thinking ... or was it dreaming? Dreaming, perhaps, of the past, of those Christmases and New Years spent at the court of the last Czar?

Although still alert and bright, enjoying Christmas with the family, Irina had certainly aged. She was no longer that bright bird-like woman, the devoted companion of his grandmother Dulcie who had spent so many happy months at Askham before she died.

Lastly, grave and unsmiling at the end of the row, nearest the sacristy, was Kyril, that enigmatic figure whose activities were still so mysterious. For Christmas there had been a big feast at the Ferov flat given by Kyril and Sasha and tonight they were all going back to Charlotte's who had been working for many days past with Hélène to prepare food suitable for the occasion.

Unobserved Ralph stared for a long time at Kyril wishing to divine something from his impassive face. Kyril made him nervous. It wasn't that he didn't like him. He didn't understand him – a man who had been a Communist and could become a Fascist. A man of extremes. Even among the community of Russian emigrés in Paris no one seemed to trust him. Some said it was because, while most of the Russians didn't like Communism, they didn't like Hitler either; they feared his extremism and his racial attacks on the Jews. There were still many Russian Jews in Paris of good families who had fled from the Bolsheviks.

When they got outside the church after the service it was dark and a voluntary curfew made them hurry home.

Irina clapped her hands with joy when she saw the decorations Charlotte and her maid had hung for the traditional Christmas; the huge tree in the hall glittering with lights, candles and coloured glass balls swinging gently to and fro, reflecting the myriad colours of the lights.

'Oh it is so pretty!' Irina exclaimed, the rapturous expression on her face recapturing the memory of so many happy festivals in the past.

Just to be away from her old musty apartment was sufficient to rejuvenate Irina and, in the short time since she left it to attend the church with her family for the New Year service, she seemed to have shed twenty years. Indeed the charm of her beautiful old apartment owed much to Charlotte's youth; to having grown up in circumstances of some style, comfort and even splendour, to a knowledge of antiques and a familiarity with possessions which, if not priceless, were certainly valuable. Here, Irina always told herself, birth and breeding showed.

A huge fire leapt in the grate of the main salon which was lit with candles to welcome the worshippers, a brightly lit candelabra hung from the ceiling and sconces flared on the walls. The sofas and armchairs were covered with soft Italian leather and on the gleaming parquet were scattered a few Persian and Afghan rugs. Interesting old masters, not priceless but valuable, hung on the panelled walls.

'It is all so pretty, so warm, so welcoming, Charlotte dear.' Impulsively Irina turned to hug her. 'How your dear grandmother would have loved to be with us. Ah! I loved her so much.'

'She loved *you*, Irina,' Ralph said, helping her off with her warm fur coat, the one that was so often pawned for a few francs, worth less and less all the time. 'You were very alike.'

'We were, we were!' Irina looked gratefully up at him. 'We were of the same generation, the same background. Do you know I wonder if those days will ever return, or if your poor King will be toppled, like ours was at the end of the last war?'

'Oh nothing like that will happen, Irina,' Ralph said hastily. 'We have no intention of letting Hitler invade England. But whether he will topple Stalin I can't say. It seems unlikely seeing that they're supposed to be friends.'

'Hitler would restore the Czar,' Alexei said confidently as Ralph passed him a glass of punch. 'That is why I have always supported him.'

'Why then did Hitler side with Stalin?' Ralph also accepted a glass of punch and moved towards the fire.

69

'It is only temporary.' Kyril who had been listening carefully moved towards the group by the fire. 'Believe me, Hitler has plans to invade Russia.'

'His ally? Do you mean it?' Ralph didn't hide his amazement.

'I know it, believe me. There are many things about this war I know that you don't.'

'I'm sure of that,' Ralph murmured, examining his glass. 'Why else should you stay in Paris?'

'I don't think I know what you mean.' As Kyril's eyes narrowed Charlotte interrupted, putting a hand on his arm.

'Do you think we could have a night without politics, boys? Without talk about the war? We are here to drink, eat and be merry.'

'We shall be all those things.' Kyril bowed at her and smiled gesturing with his hands. 'I will talk to you later Ralph, if you like. I could tell you many things of interest. As a member of the British Army there is a lot more you should know.'

Despite Charlotte's plea, it was difficult not to talk about the progress of the war or, rather, its lack, as food was served, buffet style, and wine followed the punch. Having dug themselves in behind the formidable Maginot Line the French, who at least at the beginning of the war had the strongest army in the world, imagined they were safe from invasion. The Germans were heavily engaged in a war in Finland which, surprisingly, had not gone all their way, and Hitler had made an important speech in the Reichstag appealing for peace. Between them Germany and Russia had carved up not only Poland but the tiny countries of Latvia, Estonia and Lithuania and Hitler invited the Western powers to recognize the status quo in Eastern Europe. In December the flower of the German navy, the *Admiral Graf Spee* had scuttled itself outside Montevideo.

It was a curious waiting period this Christmas, a mood summarized by George VI in his broadcast to the nation: 'A New Year is at hand ... if it brings peace how thankful we shall be. If it brings us continued struggle we shall remain undaunted.'

Ralph, huddled in a corner with Kyril and Alexei, learned that the Maginot Line was far from being impregnable and where its weakness was: in the wooded Ardennes which the French considered too dense to be penetrated.

From time to time Alexei chipped in with his reminiscences of the German perfidy in the First World War (fought largely by him in Poland). It seemed to have no relevance at all to what was currently going on in Poland, but still Ralph and Kyril listened politely.

Irina sat by the fire warmed by its flames, the wine, the luxury of Charlotte's house – one hand was extended towards the glow, in the other was a well-filled glass. Irina, who loved people but, best of all, to be surrounded by her family, felt at her happiest on this night of the Orthodox New Year. Dressed in her best court frock, the one with the purple flounces the Czarina used so to admire, her cheeks covered with powder, freshly rouged, her eyes sparkling just that little bit extra because she had drunk just that little bit too much. If only, she thought, Hélène and Alexei would make up...

Kyril kept looking at his watch and Ralph sensed a wary unease, maybe because of him.

Hélène, busying herself serving food and drink, nodded and smiled at her mother, but kept well out of the way of her father with whom she had not exchanged a word, not even the customary New Year greeting. She was followed around by Natasha and Olga, but ignored by Stefanie who tried to detach Sasha from eavesdropping on his father, grandfather and Ralph. Sasha had rather the attitude towards Kyril that the Lighterman girls had to their mother – that of cautious veneration, as if he were not quite sure what he would do next.

Stefanie listened too, but kept on tugging at Sasha's arm. She had always loved him and wished he had been a brother; yet, like her mother, he was a slightly remote, evasive person, scarcely ever there. Sasha had always seemed infinitely older and superior: a changeless, golden being. Now he was taller and his voice was deep – more awesome than ever.

Finally Sasha, perceiving that the adults didn't really want him, their voices getting lower as they spoke, reluctantly allowed himself to be dragged away by Stefanie, who had found a wind-up gramophone in the corner and a stack of English and American records.

'Can you do the jitterbug?' Stefanie whispered looking nervously over her shoulder towards her mother.

'I can but I'm not going to *here*.' Sasha smiled down at her anxious, mischievous face.

'Charlotte thinks it's shocking, or so she tells Angelica. Sometimes I think Charlotte is very old-fashioned, so does her daughter,' Stefanie sighed and began slowly winding up the gramophone. 'Angelica is really quite clever for a ten year old. She's always frightened of her mother finding out about things.'

'What kind of things?' Sasha bent his head conspiratorially.

'*Things*, you know. Angelica hides practically everything from her mother. You'd be surprised.' The detached, sophisticated Angelica was almost as revered a being as Sasha even though she was so much younger. 'When she lived over here, she would often put on her mother's lipstick when she was out. That kind of thing.' Energetically she finished winding the gramophone and began to sort through the stack of records. 'Do you like Glenn Miller?'

Sasha supposed she was going to ask him to dance. He thought that, for a girl of eleven, she was probably even more precocious than her cousin Angelica Verdi whom she obviously envied. Angelica was very beautiful, dark and swan-like and very much admired by grown-ups who thought that, as well as beautiful, she was good, such a help to Charlotte. Now with her brothers she was confined to England until the war was over, and they were spending Christmas with their grandmother Rachel at Darley Manor.

72

Sasha put his arms out in invitation as the music started up but Stefanie shook her head.

'Why not?' he asked.

'I'm too shy. Let's wait until the others start.'

'I can't see Grandpa and Grandma dancing! Father and Ralph are too busy.'

'Grandma *used* to love it. She told me she was the best dancer in Petersburg.'

'I think the dancing was different then.' Sasha put his arm round her waist and they began to sway together in the middle of the floor, the rug pushed back exposing the parquet.

The adults, various expressions registering on their faces, all stopped talking to look at them. Girls of Stefanie's age were usually thought of as scarcely out of the nursery. Now here she was dancing with her cousin, only a head shorter than he was, like a sophisticated teenager. Hélène frowned and was about to go over and stop the gramophone when Charlotte took her hand and shook her head.

'Don't spoil it.'

'But look how close they are!'

'It's just pretend,' Charlotte whispered back. 'They both like to think they're grown up.'

But in the far corner Kyril had stopped his conversation with Ralph and his father to look at the scene too.

'This is the kind of thing Hélène lets them do,' he said angrily, starting to get up.

'I don't think they're doing anything wrong.' Ralph was amused.

'They're *much* too close.'

'Miller writes that sort of music. Don't be silly, Kyril. Stefanie is only a child.'

'Is she? She doesn't look it. She's too like her mother.'

'What a strange lot you are.' Ralph put a restraining hand on Kyril's arm. 'They're related; they're like brother and sister. There's nothing wrong. Why is it, besides, that none of you Ferovs ever appreciate Hélène's good qualities?'

'Has she got any?' Kyril sounded sarcastic.

'She's beautiful for a start.' Ralph was studying her profile as she put food from dishes onto plates.

'That's not a quality. Qualities are ...' Kyril followed Ralph's gaze. '*You're* not smitten too are you?'

'Of course I'm not,' Ralph protested loudly. 'Once upon a time, though, I envied Bobby. I've always admired Hélène's looks.'

'But no longer?'

Ralph shrugged and shook his head. 'Well maybe not as much.'

'I must be going.' Kyril consulted his watch again.

'Have you an appointment? At *this* time?' Alexei looked indignant.

'I have someone to see...'

'Ahah, a lady friend ...' Alexei wagged a finger knowingly.

'Politics,' Kyril said briefly. 'One day I'll tell you about it. I'd better see if Sasha wants to come with me.'

Kyril started to cross the room when there was the sharp ringing of the doorbell. Charlotte stared and then left the room while Ralph, thinking it was late for anyone to call, followed quickly behind.

'Arthur, *darling*!' Charlotte was saying as he got to the hall. There was the sound of a loud kiss ... a smack on the cheek rather than anything more intimate.

Arthur, like Ralph, was in uniform, only he looked as though he had just landed by plane. His face was grimy and he looked tired. Arthur often made a habit of hopping over in his Spitfire, when he got the opportunity, on official business.

Ralph shook hands with him as the rest of the party gathered at the door of the lounge. Kyril had his coat on.

'I'm sorry, I'm just going,' he said turning to Arthur, then he kissed Charlotte. 'Please forgive me. There's someone I have to see.'

'At *this* time?' Charlotte looked at her watch. 'It's after midnight.'

74

'It can only be a tryst.' Hélène leaned against the door, her arms akimbo, but Kyril shook his head, smiling, and said nothing.

'I hope it's got nothing to do with me,' Arthur said, but he couldn't take his eyes off Charlotte.

Kyril shook his head. 'Sasha is going to escort his grandparents and Stefanie home. Olga and Natasha are apparently staying here for the night.'

'That's right.' Charlotte suddenly looked preoccupied. 'On second thoughts they'd better not. I'll need their room for Arthur. Unfortunately I only have three bedrooms. Do you mind, darlings?'

She turned to look at the girls who, crestfallen, had gathered beneath the protective arms of their mother.

'It won't be for long,' Hélène said. 'We'll soon have our own flat and all be together.'

'It's long after curfew.' Alexei peered anxiously outside. 'We really must be going. People abroad after midnight are likely to be asked questions.'

'I'll give you a lift in my car,' Arthur said. 'Why not? I can just about squeeze you all in. Not Sasha, I'm afraid. Too many.'

'I'll walk with Sasha.' Stefanie suddenly appeared at the doorway. 'Then there'll be plenty of room.'

'It *is* late.' Charlotte looked doubtful

'It's our New Year,' Sasha said. 'Surely the authorities will be a little bit lenient?'

With the reassuring arm of her cousin around her Stefanie felt utterly secure, completely at peace, a little bit in love. They would say it was a schoolgirl's crush and when she was old enough Sasha would be married to someone else. How could she tell him how she felt about him – this tall, eager young man who only wanted to leave school so that he could join up?

As they made their way along the deserted back streets towards the Gare du Nord it was a bit scary, but with Sasha

Stefanie couldn't possibly feel frightened. It did give her an excuse, though, for huddling against him. It was quite useful at times to pretend to be a little girl, even if one felt grown up inside as she had when they were dancing and she was aware that all the grown-ups, her mother, her grandparents, her uncle and Charlotte were looking at them with varying degrees of disapproval. 'Grandpa absolutely forbade me to leave school,' Sasha said. 'He and Uncle Bobby got together to stop it.'

'I'd hate you to join up,' Stefanie said.

'Why?' He looked down at her, amused.

'You might get killed.'

'Uncle Bobby thinks the war will end soon. He's quite gloomy although business is *very* good at the moment.' Sasha stopped, suddenly realizing he'd made a *faux pas*. 'Sorry.'

'Why are you sorry?' Despite the warmth of his body, the cold night air was making Stefanie tremble; at least she *thought* it was that.

'Because Uncle Bobby is your father. I keep on forgetting. You must feel quite unhappy and bitter about him.'

As they got nearer the station the number of people about on the streets increased. There were few cars but those there were crawled along in the dark, blacked-out streets with nothing to guide them but blue-painted mudguard lights.

'I very seldom think of my father,' Stefanie said. 'I think of him more than the other two do because I remember him better than they do, but I couldn't say I ever miss him. Now that we know why he behaved as he did I despise him, anyway.'

'How do you mean "behaved as he did"?' Sasha's voice was low although there was no one to hear them, not a soul to listen in.

'Because he wanted to marry someone else. He has a little boy.'

'David is quite a big boy now,' Sasha said, misunderstanding the extent of Stefanie's knowledge. 'He's older than you.'

'How can he be older than me?' Stefanie stopped, her arm dropping from around his waist.

'Oh ...' Sasha wanted to walk on but she stood her ground.

'How *can* he possibly be older than me?' she repeated.

'Then no one told you about that?'

'I don't understand.' Stefanie felt her heart starting to beat faster.

'Well you're old enough to know,' Sasha said as if almost to himself. 'I think you're older than people think. Your father had a girlfriend while he was married to your mother. He had a son by her but no one knew it, at the time...'

'Then my mother left my father ...' Stefanie thought she was beginning to understand, but his next words plunged her even deeper into confusion.

'Not quite ... oh dear. I am getting into a mess, aren't I?'

'I know quite a lot,' Stefanie said carefully, 'but not everything. There have been so many lies told to us that I wonder if we shall ever discover the truth. I know my mother went to prison for instance. Everyone pretended she had gone abroad but I *know* she went to prison. They lied there, all right. She killed someone, didn't she?'

'Oh dear.' Sasha put his arm through hers again and began to trudge on. Then on the spur of the moment and very quickly he decided to tell her everything he knew. 'Look,' he said, 'I think you're old enough to know what happened to your mother.' He took a deep breath.

'It's like this. She met a man, before she married Bobby, who was very attractive. His name was Jamie Kitto and he was related to the Askhams. He was a bit of a bounder, though, and eventually she left him to marry your father. Your mother was a very lovely woman, Stefanie, as she is now; but she had had an unhappy life, leaving her home, coming to Paris in poverty. The riches Bobby had must have seemed tantalizing and I think, everyone thinks, that she didn't love Bobby when she married him. There was something insincere about him too because he had this woman, Aileen, and a son by her. But Hélène was a princess and, at that time, Aileen wasn't quite good enough for Bobby.

'You see,' he put a hand on her arm as he saw her start, 'they never really had much of a chance, your mother and father, loving other people. After a while Hélène met up again with Jamie and they resumed their affair. But Jamie was a bounder. He always needed money and he sold some information to the English newspapers that put the Askhams in a bad light.'

'What information?' Stefanie sounded breathless.

'He told them that the Askhams sold arms to Hitler. Well this was a lie, but when Bobby found out the truth he also discovered – it is too roundabout to tell you how, but one day I will – about your mother and Jamie. He sent her away, divorced her. It was a very cruel thing to do because he treated you girls badly too.

'Your mother couldn't stand it and when she found out what Jamie had done she had a mental brainstorm. She killed him. In France it is called *crime passionel* – a crime caused by love – and she only got a few years in gaol. She did it all on the spur of the moment. She is a very good woman, a brave and kind woman, but, at that time, a very silly woman nevertheless.'

He was about to continue but stopped. Stefanie had flung her head on his chest, her shoulders shaking with sobs.

Suddenly Sasha bitterly regretted what he had done. It was a very hard thing for such a young girl to learn about her parents. He put his arms right round her to comfort her, and they stood like that for some time – like two lovers in the dark.

Arthur said: 'I really got very worried when you told me I was to sleep in the room reserved for Olga and Natasha.'

Charlotte giggled in the deep, warm bed. It was very cold and she was grateful for the heat of Arthur's body.

'I didn't want the girls to know that we shared a bed.'

'You don't want *anyone* to know do you, Charlotte?' When she didn't reply he asked her again.

'I'd prefer they didn't,' Charlotte admitted.

'Even your mother.'

'I feel nervous about discussing these things with my mother. She is old-fashioned, you know.'

'That's not what I heard.' Arthur's voice sounded sly.

'Well, her lover *was* my father, if that's what you mean. He made it all right in the end.'

'But I want to make it all right in the end,' Arthur whispered. 'I want to make it all right now. I want us to go back to England together and get married. I want you to be safe at home with your family during the war.'

'Even if it finishes in the spring?'

'It won't finish in the spring. Anyone who thinks that is deceiving themselves. From all the preparations that are going on it will get worse.'

'Ralph said they're having a lovely time in Lille,' Charlotte protested. 'It's like a holiday.'

'Well, it won't last.'

Charlotte suddenly found she was trembling.

'Do stop, you're frightening me. What on earth will happen to the Ferovs and the girls if what you say is true?'

'They should all come to England, and Hélène. They should come as soon as they can and not hesitate. Sometimes ...' Arthur paused and Charlotte realized he was beginning to tremble too. 'Sometimes I think you don't really love me, Charlotte.'

'You know I do.' Even in the dark she wouldn't look at him, but kept her eyes closed, her face resting on the pillow.

'Then marry me.'

'You don't just *marry* people to prove you love them, Arthur.' She turned over on her back putting one arm under her head. Her eyes were open now, staring at the ceiling. 'I have been a widow for so long, nearly eight years since Paolo died. I'm a woman of independent means...'

'You could still be with me.'

She shook her head. 'You really don't understand, darling.'

'Chanel has closed her business. You have nothing to do,'

79

Arthur persisted. 'You stay on here in Paris, as if hoping for something to happen.'

'Yes I do,' Charlotte nodded. 'Yes, you're right, I want something to happen, but not marriage. Not yet.' She turned towards him and flung her arms passionately round his neck pushing him down on the bed. 'Oh Arthur, I do love you, in a way. Please believe that.'

In the lounge amid the debris of the party Ralph had put the gramophone on again. Hélène sitting down at last, a drink in her hand, watched him. All evening, she knew, Ralph had been looking at her, trying to catch her eye, smiling in her direction. She had always liked Ralph – who wouldn't? He was an attractive man but, above all, he was kind. She was sure of that. No Bobby or Jamie here. Both her lover and her husband had only had one thought – themselves. Ralph thought of everybody.

Hélène was very lonely – a lonely woman racked not only by guilt but by remorse. How nice it would be to feel loved again, to lose oneself in those strong, protective, comforting arms. As she smiled at him he held out his arms and Hélène rose and walked into them resting her cheek against his. Slowly they began to dance to the music of Ambrose.

'It was a funny sort of evening,' Ralph said, keenly aware of her lithe slim body pressed closely against his.

'In what way?' Hélène felt the firm clasp of his hand on her hip.

They continued to dance round and round on the tiny patch of floor, cheek to cheek. When the record stopped Ralph turned it over and wound the machine up again. He and Hélène resumed, this time drawing a little closer.

'You didn't answer my question,' she murmured, 'about it being a funny sort of evening.'

'It was, very funny. Your brother is an odd sort of bloke.' He stopped for a moment and looked at her. 'Do you actually know what he does, what way his allegiances lie?'

'What allegiances?' she opened her eyes in a question.

'Does he support Hitler? Stalin?'

'Oh no, neither. He is definitely on our side in the war, the side of France and England.'

'He doesn't give me that impression. He seems to have a lot of information on what I would have thought were rather secret things, like the disposition of the French troops all along the Maginot Line. That surprised me a great deal. How does he come by that sort of knowledge?'

'He was a bit drunk tonight, I thought,' Hélène said, trying to explain a man she hardly understood herself, or was she making excuses for him?

'I didn't think he was drunk at all,' Ralph said.

'He drinks a lot, but no one can tell it. Besides, if he knows all about the French forces surely he is on the side of France?'

But did she believe it herself? Did Ralph?

'*Does* he have a mistress?' Ralph looked into her eyes. He had often thought they were blue but in this dim light they were almost violet. Her pale face, her blonde hair and those enigmatic violet eyes made her the most enticing woman he could imagine and, as she lifted her head, he kissed her.

'Who cares about my brother?' she said at last, trying to break away.

But Ralph, having tasted heaven, wanted more and, for a long time, they stood in the middle of the room while the record on the gramophone went round and round, the needle in the final groove soundlessly playing.

CHAPTER 5

It was a mild, late spring day and already the little groups were forming on the lawn, their neatly combed heads fresh, scrubbed shining faces bent over their books. Occasionally the voice of one of the teachers would become audible and, inevitably, was followed a second or two later by laughter. Gazing at the clusters of small children on the perfectly mown turf of Askham Hall from the window of her sitting room on the first floor, Cheryl found herself sighing with satisfaction. She turned to Em who was standing next to her:

'It's a far cry from what it was six months ago.'

'You've done marvels. I'd never have believed...' Em stopped and looked awkwardly at her sister-in-law.

'That I had it in me?' Cheryl arched a perfectly shaped, quizzical eyebrow. 'I must say, neither did I. When I saw the hordes of little horrors all standing in the drive by the porch with their runny noses, their gas-mask boxes, their names on labels round their necks and their abject expressions of misery I could have wept. Like them. My instinct was to shut the door and run; but it was a government order. What could one do?'

What indeed? Privately the family, expecting the worst, that Rachel would be speedily sent for to take charge, were amazed by the change that had come over Cheryl. She had not only taken charge and assumed command of fifty evacuees from Stepney, aged from five to twelve, and their teachers, but she had appeared to relish it. In the two weeks' notice she'd had after she received the government order she'd had anything of value removed to the bank or the store, had closed the main reception rooms with her beautiful furniture, the best that mid-thirties Art Deco had to offer, had bunk beds moved into the vacated and cleaned bedrooms and a dining hall made of the former servants' room. Many of the men had been called up, and the women who were left took to the task of mothering the homeless charges with as much, if not more, enthusiasm than their mistress. To Cheryl it became a patriotic task to be accepted and performed with dignity, as the wife of one of England's premier earls who was on active service in France. To the maidservants who remained, many whose menfolk were also at the war, it was a welcome relief from worry. It gave them something else to think about.

The previous September Cheryl had planned to go back to Kenya. The thought of war terrified her and she would be safe there. Also London and Askham Hall were no longer the fine prizes she had risked her marriage to stay in England for. She had also lost the love of her husband and the regard of his family. When Ralph went overseas with the BEF without saying goodbye to her; when no one came to call; when all her society friends also retreated to the country or, some of them, the Colonies or America, she felt lost, cut off, abandoned every bit as much as those poor children who had been forced to leave their homes.

The transformation in Cheryl had, of course, not happened overnight. There was no pity for the refugees on her doorstep. It was just a job to be done: to feed them, make them comfortable, see that their lessons continued in as normal a manner as possible and keep them warm and out of trouble. At first some of them roamed about the village and there were cases of pilfering; there were petty acts of vandalism to the Hall and outbuildings. Many of the children were abusive and most of them homesick. She could hardly understand their raucous Cockney accents and most of them had nits. Yet Cheryl, although she had emerged as a countess, had been brought up on a farm in a remote part of the huge American State of Wyoming. Watching the young evacuees from a distance gradually becoming acclimatized and settling down to the kind of gracious living they had never in their lives imagined, let alone experienced, she saw sometimes herself when young.

Her family had been refugees from Poland in the middle of the nineteenth century, and in her youth she had roughed it with the farmhands and worked side by side in her mother's kitchen with the maids even though her father had become an affluent farmer.

For many weeks it had been for Cheryl an exercise in organization and logistics, a way of planning diets, feeding fifty young mouths and five extra adult ones, and seeing that they were all safe and well looked after. There were those who tried to run away, and there were the parents who came to visit and either complained or were so impressed by what they saw – their children's sojourn in a stately home – that they would like to have stayed too.

Cheryl, not surprisingly, found her unusual and unwelcome task an easy one. Had she not completely redecorated and refurbished two large houses? She was good at her job and she enjoyed it to the extent that she started rejecting the social invitations that did come her way as people gradually recovered from the shock of the declaration of war, panic subsided, and life got more or less back to normal. Moreover she found herself unwinding, talking to the young people, literally finding out how the other half lived. Many of them were unused to proper beds or meals off tables. All of them had no idea of table manners or the politeness, deference and courtesy she had come to expect. Yet, as she stopped to talk to them or sought them out while they were at recreation she came gradually to know young working-class England, the underprivileged poor; and she realized they were not some species of animal but people, though they were not too keen on hot water and spoke in a way she could hardly understand. They were impulsive, warm and friendly, anxious after a while to please; grateful though not subservient, and she found that they had their own integrity, their own patriotism that was, after all, just like hers. Their fathers had gone to war just like Ralph; many of their grandfathers had fought in the 1914/18 war and, like Ralph's father, had failed to return. Death, after all, was the great leveller, of rich as well as poor.

Cheryl and Em strolled through the, by now, cavernous house which had developed echoes Em never remembered from when they were children.

'It *is* rather like a barracks,' she said smiling. 'Not the gracious home you wanted at all Cheryl?'

'Nothing turned out as I expected,' Cheryl began and called sharply to a young boy scampering over the resonant tiles of the hall.

'Jimmy, where are you off to?'

'I'm going to the toilet, Miss.' Jimmy abruptly pulled himself up, looking furtive.

'The lavatory is the *other* way, Jimmy.' Cheryl firmly pinioned his arms with her hands and a half eaten chocolate bar fell to the floor.

'I see.' Cheryl stared at it with an expression of distaste as if she somehow expected it to spring to life, complete with fleas. 'Stealing again, are we, Jimmy?'

'It's only a bit o' chocolate, Miss,' Jimmy whined.

'Yes, but it didn't belong to you, did it?'

'I *found* it, Miss.'

'Doubtless. Well, I'm sure the person you stole it from won't want it back in that state. Your punishment, Jimmy, will be to forgo your personal ration of chocolate for two weeks. Is that clear?'

'Yes, Miss.' Jimmy's eyes looked haunted.

'And if I find you stealing again I will ask for you to be removed. I cannot tolerate thieves in my house.'

'No, Miss.' Jimmy looked at his feet.

'Go back to your class, Jimmy, or your recreation period or whatever it is and remember what I told you. And remember to call me "your ladyship". How *many* times must I tell you?'

'Yes, Miss. Thank you, Miss.' As Jimmy scampered away Cheryl looked after him and Em saw a glint of triumph in her eyes.

'He was the worst. The very worst. I thought I couldn't keep him here. He pinched things in the village, from the maids, everywhere he could. He once tried to break into my main salon which still has a few priceless *objets d'art*, not that Jimmy would know what they were. But you know, we've worked on him and it has been very rewarding. His father is always in prison. His mother takes in lodgers which I believe is some kind of euphemism for prostitution. What kind of chance had Jimmy?'

'What, indeed,' Em said softly, impressed. 'It makes one very grateful doesn't it?'

'It certainly does.'

By now they stood on the steps of the fine Doric portico of Askham Hall that had been built in the eighteenth century by the 6th Earl of Askham from designs by James Wyatt. As the women strolled outside Cheryl slipped an arm through Em's, the first sign of chumminess Em could recall from her sister-in-law ever since she'd known her. Cheryl hadn't approved of Em having a baby by a man to whom she wasn't married, living openly with him only a stone's throw away from the Hall. Cheryl yearned for order, symmetry, conformity, respectability, and yet the more she yearned for it the harder it was to find. By marrying into the aristocratic family of the Earls of Askham who had served the reigning monarch for generation after generation it would be imagined that she would have achieved her goal, yet it had proved elusive.

The Askhams were, unfortunately, always doing odd, unconventional things of which Cheryl disapproved. They had a propensity for surrounding themselves with notoriety, like Ralph's Aunt Melanie who had been married three times and had numerous affairs. There was his Aunt Flora who had lived openly with Adam Bolingbroke and then committed suicide when he married another woman; the preposterous Em who had wandered abroad as a newspaper correspondent getting herself arrested on the personal orders of Hitler. There was Em's twin Freddie who had quite needlessly sacrificed his life in the Spanish Civil War, and the elegant Charlotte who had married a racing driver. Then there was Hugo, Bosco's son by his Egyptian mistress who was not only tolerated but loved by his father's wife and his half brothers and sisters. Finally, there was Rachel herself who, at the age of sixty-two, was not content to sit at home in the country looking after her orphaned grandson, nephew and niece; but had resumed active editorship of the newspaper she owned and had plagued the government with her inflammatory articles. Some said that her attacks on Chamberlain were primarily responsible for his resignation and the elevation of Winston Churchill, a close friend, and also an outsider, to the premiership. People said that Rachel Askham had too much influence in the counsels of government, and memories of the 'Red Countess' of the twenties were recalled.

'Your mother was in the news again,' Cheryl said with a sniff as they rounded the house and started to walk down towards the lake where a sketching party – two groups of children seated in punts – was in progress.

'You don't approve of Mummy much, do you?'

'Some people think she interferes too much...'

'Do you mean in the government, or in your life?' Em never minced words.

'I think Ralph and I would have got on better if it hadn't been for your mother, I must be frank, Em.' Cheryl removed her arm from her sister-in-law's as though to distance herself again. 'She never liked *me* from the start.'

'Maybe it was a difficult position for her?'

'And it was *very* difficult for me,' Cheryl looked indignant. 'After all *I* was the stranger. *I* was new to the family. Your mother made it quite clear she resented me and wanted us to go back to Kenya.'

'I know Mummy only wanted Ralph to be happy,' Em said softly. 'I'm sure she didn't resent you.' But even as Em spoke she remembered how Rachel had seemed instinctively to dislike her new daughter-in-law whereas all the family had, at

87

first, liked Cheryl. Hélène and Charlotte had doted on her and she, Em, couldn't quite fathom the reason for her mother's dislike. Was she so perceptive, or was it instinctive, brought about by jealousy of the new Lady Askham, a woman who, because of her position as Ralph's wife, had in fact supplanted her?

It didn't really seem like Rachel, a person synonymous with generosity and forgiveness. Yet she had also done little to make Felipe welcome when he had come as a refugee from the Spanish war. Em knew that Felipe was prickly and could be very disagreeable, but he had tried without success to charm her mother. No, Felipe remained a refugee, unwanted and unloved by Rachel; maybe because he did not believe in marriage, or maybe because he didn't seem right for her daughter.

This attitude had drawn Em and Cheryl together. Soon after the evacuees arrived Em got into the habit of popping over to the Hall to see if she could be useful. For their part the young evacuees from London, used to being surrounded, most of them, by masses of brothers and sisters, immediately adored Luis and took it in turns to look after him. Cheryl had been worried that the new arrivals were not fit to look after the child; but Em trusted them and they responded to her trust. Em with her natural, unaffected ways was a great hit with the wartime guests, and had done much to bridge the gap between them, their teachers and the haughty and, at first, remote and condescending Lady Askham.

Cheryl stopped abruptly before they got to the lake and plopped onto the grass idly plucking a few overgrown daisies and buttercups. Ralph had wanted to keep cattle in the field to help the war effort, but Cheryl wouldn't allow it. She patted the ground beside her and looked up at Em.

'Sit down,' she invited. 'I want to ask you what you think about me.'

'Me?' Em looked puzzled.

'We haven't always got on, you and I.'

'We do now,' Em said judiciously. 'That's the main thing.'

'I was pretty terrible, wasn't I? Greedy and ambitious. I never made Ralph happy.'

'Oh yes you did.' Em's instinctive sympathy went out to someone in the grip of remorse. 'He was quite potty about you. *That* made him happy, to start with anyway. I have never seen a man so in love as Ralph during those first days after you came back.'

'But it didn't last, did it?' Cheryl grimaced and began making a daisy chain. 'Ralph wanted to go back to Kenya, to farm. That was his life's ambition. I wanted to play the Lady of the Manor and I thwarted it. When we married I had no idea of the extent of his wealth or property. We had a lot of titled people in Kenya who were flat broke. When I came to England and saw this, the Hall, I was astounded. Fancy wanting to give it up! I think also that Ralph knew his mother would resent me. She was still a young woman and she enjoyed having her home and being the mistress of it. I virtually kicked her out, made her an exile. I was beastly to his grandmother. Ralph wanted children. I refused to have them.'

'Yes, why did you?' Em looked puzzled. Sitting there in a dirndl skirt and blouse, sandals on her bare feet, her fair hair, which had never been her glory, cut rather short and a lock of it hanging over her face, Em seemed the epitome of the healthy young womanhood that the war posters wanted to encourage.

Cheryl looked at her and then away from her.

'I can't explain it, really. I hated having babies, the physical thing. It was *so* awful. I guess I was afraid to have any more.'

'Did you tell Ralph you were afraid? You could have been helped, perhaps?'

'No, I didn't.' Cheryl's voice changed. 'I wasn't very nice to him. I made out it was his fault, that he was not ... quite a man, you know ...' Em observed a blush slowly creeping up Cheryl's cheek.

'Maybe it was his fault then, if you tried to have children and couldn't. After all, you'd had two.'

'Yes, I don't know why. I was just grateful, that's all, that it didn't happen. But I didn't want it to happen. I wasn't at all nice to Ralph. Not as nice as a wife should be. Not understanding. We grew very much apart. I taunted him and I have regretted it. I have, truthfully, since he went away very much regretted the way I behaved with Ralph. I often think if he is killed I'll have a lot on my conscience. And the war news isn't very good is it?'

'No, it's awful,' Em agreed. 'And it's ages since we heard from Ralph; since Hitler invaded France. We haven't heard from Charlotte either.'

Em's hand went out to cover Cheryl's which lay on the grass, but she hesitated and then withdrew it. Even now Cheryl remained slightly forbidding. As always Cheryl was beautifully turned out in a soft belted green moygashel dress with white revers. One never saw her casual or anything but immaculately groomed, never without make-up or a hair out of place. Her lips were always crimson and her even teeth like a toothpaste smile when she opened her mouth.

'I've enjoyed this talk,' Em said rather briskly. 'I'm glad we had it. I'm sure Ralph will be all right and, maybe, when he comes home you can begin again.'

'I'd like to.' Cheryl sounded sincere. 'I would like to make it up with all your family, really. I'd like to fit in.'

'Poor Cherry,' Em said kindly, using the diminutive of her name, something hardly anyone ever did. 'I didn't know how isolated we made you feel. I should have guessed.'

'The Askhams together *are* pretty formidable,' Cheryl said shakily. 'I tried to fight them, because I didn't think I would fit in. I never ever thought they wanted me.'

In a way, Em thought, Cheryl was as much a casualty of her upbringing as these young evacuees who had never slept in a bed with sheets or eaten from a table laid with knives and forks in their lives. Both were in a sense, and for different reasons and in different ways, deprived.

Some of the children in one of the berthed punts were

waving cheerily to Cheryl, whom they persisted in calling 'Miss', and begged her to come and see their drawings. Eagerly Cheryl got up with Em to go over and inspect them but they were diverted by one of the maids calling from the terrace, bellowing from it, her mouth cupped between her capable hands.

'In the old days a servant would never have dared to behave like that,' Cheryl said disapprovingly. 'She would have run all the way down, not shouted from the terrace. What *is* the world coming to? Have *all* the old standards disappeared? The servants will be calling me by my Christian name next.' Cheryl cupped a hand to her ear. 'Can you tell what she's saying, Em?'

'She wants you to go up,' Em said. 'You have a visitor.'

As they started back towards the house Em took her sister-in-law by the arm and pressed her close. She had a feeling of foreboding. She hoped it wasn't someone from the War Office with bad news about Ralph.

When they got over the brow of the hill that formed the tip of the meadow they saw a young woman standing behind Doris, the maid who had hailed them. She was a slim young woman and she shielded her eyes against the morning sun as Em and Cheryl reached the top. Then she looked nervously from one to the other as though uncertain as to whom it was she sought. But the answer wasn't hard to find as Cheryl, who resembled the young woman she was staring at, suddenly flew towards her.

'It is ...' she cried. 'It is ... oh Amelia.'

'It *is* Amelia, Mummy.' The young woman clasped her mother, breaking into a broad smile. 'I wondered if you'd recognise me after all these years.'

'Oh *Amelia*,' Cheryl said and with the strain of it all – everything that she and Em had spoken about that morning, the bad news from Europe with the collapse of Belgium and Holland and, now, to cap it all the arrival of a daughter she had virtually abandoned eleven years before – she broke down and, uncharacteristically, wept.

Amelia Lee had been nine when Cheryl met the young earl of Askham in 1929. Now she was just twenty. Her mother, expecting to return to Kenya after her marriage trip to England, said no final farewells to her two young daughters. But Cheryl had never returned, never even gone for a holiday in case Ralph, who loved Kenya, refused to leave again; in case, having got her there, he refused to go back.

So the long-promised visit never materialized and letters were few. But there were snapshots of the girls growing up on her ex-husband George Lee's farm where he had stayed on, made possible by a handsome settlement from Ralph. George, who never wanted to divorce Cheryl, had intended to sell up and go back to Chicago. But there was nothing much there to attract a disappointed man with two young daughters who had, anyway, nearly been ruined in the Depression.

Amelia and her sister Kathleen had grown up in Kenya without a mother it is true, but in no way neglected or deprived. Kenya Colony was a fine place for settlers in the thirties and a good place for young people, men and women, to grow up in. Both Kathleen and Amelia, who was a year older than her sister, had a good schooling, with as rich and varied a social life as any growing girl or young woman could wish for. George Lee had prospered after Cheryl left him and though he had not remarried he enjoyed the company of women friends, the life in Happy Valley which some found scandalous but others good fun.

Amelia and Kathleen thus grew up in a rather freer atmosphere than many of their counterparts in boarding schools in England. When Amelia, in the spring of 1939, thought she would like to travel abroad her father didn't demur. The plan was that she would go through Africa on Safari, then the Middle East and Europe to end up, maybe in a year's time, with her mother. It was to be a surprise.

But what was meant to be a holiday turned into an adventure, almost a nightmare as Amelia just made it to Boulogne before Hitler swept into France.

All these adventures, and many more, were told and retold in the days of happy reunion after Amelia Lee arrived at her mother's erstwhile gracious home to find it turned into a school for evacuees.

As for Cheryl, it was not only a considerable surprise, but a shock to see her grown-up daughter on the terrace of Askham Hall that day in the dark month of May 1940 when fears were rife that Hitler would not stop with the collapse of France. He would want to invade England as well.

It was a shock, but it soon became a pleasure. It was most exciting to find oneself the mother of a fully mature, grown-up young woman with as many pretensions to beauty as her mother had when her age.

Cheryl and Amelia talked for days; then Cheryl wanted to share her happiness and Em was invited to bring Felipe for dinner because it was important to have people to show her daughter to. Cheryl even tried to call Rachel, but she was in London and too busy at that critical time even to talk on the phone. Cheryl would even have liked to have Adam, Sylvia and Christopher for dinner, maybe even Bobby and Aileen, but everyone seemed too busy or preoccupied to be able to come.

The extent of Cheryl's isolation was revealed to her most clearly at this time, when she couldn't get enough people together to provide a dinner party of welcome for her daughter.

There was Hugo, of course, Ralph's half brother; but Hugo was the last person Cheryl would have invited. Hugo and Cheryl had never got on since their first meeting many years before at Askham House when Cheryl greeted Hugo as an interloper and treated him as one, even when she heard who he was.

No, even if one were desperate one would *never* invite Hugo.

Hugo came, nevertheless. Not in the way that Cheryl would have intended even if she had invited him. It hadn't been the most sparkling or successful of dinner parties. Felipe was his usual argumentative self and Em, the instinctive journalist, was preoccupied by the bad news from France. Amelia, though, was one of those gifted people who seem to have an instinctive ability to appraise situations and make the best of them. Moreover, as the elder of her father's daughters, she had acted as his hostess from quite early on. Now, much travelled as well, she was adept at putting people at their ease. So she took it upon herself to entertain her mother and her guests with stories of travel in Africa, particularly in the wilder parts of the southern Sudan and her exploration of the sources of the Nile.

She had reached Italy from Palestine just as Hitler invaded Poland, but Mussolini had not yet involved himself actively on the Führer's side so Italy, for the time being, was safe. Germany, of course, was avoided but not Switzerland where she spent Christmas, and then it was time to go to France.

She was in Paris when Hitler invaded Holland and Belgium, and lingered even when the Germans broke through the Ardennes to penetrate the indestructible Maginot Line, and France was on the verge of collapse. Then it was time to flee.

'You look as though you'd enjoyed it all.' Em looked at the excited face above the candlelight. Amelia was very like her mother to look at: dark, clear-eyed, good bone structure with high cheekbones, well groomed. She had that indefinable poise and allure that attracted men. She gazed at Em and, elbows on the table, joined her hands.

'I can't say I was *ever* frightened; but it was nice to think that Mummy was here if I needed her.'

'And I'd no idea ...' Cheryl began when Doris, dressed in housemaid black with a white apron, opened the door, poked her face around it and said:

'Mr Down is here, Madam.'

So like Doris to ignore the proper convention, she hadn't the slightest idea, but Cheryl's butler had enlisted soon after Ralph. More than anything Cheryl wanted the war to end so that she could dismiss the insolent Doris.

'*Mr* ...' Cheryl, thunderstruck, was about to rise but Hugo, pushing past Doris, forestalled her.

'Sorry to burst in on you, Cheryl.'

'I ... this is my daughter,' Cheryl managed to say but, clearly, Hugo wasn't very interested. He nodded at Amelia, briefly kissed Em on the cheek and, grabbing a chair, sat down next to Felipe.

'There's the most frightful news from France,' Hugo spoke rapidly. 'The British forces have been pushed to the beach at Dunkirk and are trapped. There's a call for everyone with a boat to go and rescue them. Ralph's there somewhere. I'm going ...'

Em jumped up and seized him by the arm. 'Is there news of Ralph?'

'No news. Rachel, naturally, is frantic with worry; but the situation in France is chaotic. Ralph is sure to be with his regiment and they were last heard of trying to stop the German advance at Lille. Ralph, if he is OK, might be on the beach with his men waiting to be rescued. I'm going.'

'But Hugo, you won't find *Ralph* among so many thousands,' Em protested.

'Don't you see, Em, I *must* go?' Hugo said. 'The war has made me powerless because I work on the land and now here is something I *can* do. Willy Hamble, who I sometimes go sailing with, has a boat at Portsmouth all ready to go this very night. I wondered if Felipe would come too because...'

'I know nothing at all about boats,' Felipe said equably, gazing at the tip of his small, freshly lit cigar.

'But darling, *can't* you ...' Em leaned towards him.

'I'd be no good,' Felipe pushed her hand away. 'Anyway I get seasick. Believe me, if I thought I could help I would.'

'We'd like an extra man,' Hugo said grimly, 'to help haul in the wounded. That's why I came. I thought with your experience of war...'

'I'd be useless.' Felipe avoided Hugo's eyes, those of everyone in the room which seemed riveted upon him, and went on studying the tip of the cigar as though it mesmerized him. 'I'd be seasick. I can't speak English, or French, very well. I'd be a liability. If there's anything else I could do ...' He gestured hopefully with an expressive hand. 'Besides, if the Germans found me they'd shoot me. In Spain I was a wanted man.'

'Oh darling, that *is* far-fetched ...' Em felt herself redden with shame and humiliation as her lover piled excuse upon excuse. What had happened to the daredevil fighter of the Spanish Civil War?

'*I*'d like to come,' Em said, 'but...'

'You can't possibly come,' Hugo replied. 'You have Luis. Besides, we want strong men.'

'I'm not a particularly strong man.' Felipe made the remark to no one in particular. 'My chief strength was here,' and he tapped his head. Em looked away.

'I'm *awfully* strong.' Jumping up Amelia flexed her muscles. 'I'd love it. I was terribly good on my father's farm mucking out and that kind of thing. I can ride bareback, if that's any use.'

'Don't be absurd,' Cheryl said sharply, reaching out to tug her down.

'I'm afraid we're not taking women.' Hugo seemed to see Amelia for the first time. 'It's frightfully decent of you to offer.' His tone was respectful.

'But I *want* to come.' Amelia shook her mother's hand away. 'I went across the African desert in a convoy and I was the only girl.'

'No girls,' Hugo said firmly, reluctantly turning his eyes from her. 'But, I say, I do admire your spunk. I must go now...'

96

'I'll come with you.' Em got up and took hold of his hand. 'I want to see you off.'

'We'll all come.' Amelia brightly led the way through the door and Hugo had a fleeting impression of life, energy, beauty, a slip of a girl who was a full grown woman. He followed her quite forgetful of Em, trying to catch up with her; but she outpaced him, like a sprite. In the hall there were kisses, handshakes, words of encouragement. Even Cheryl's cold lips brushed his cheek. There were a few tears from Em. No one glanced again at Felipe, standing well back in the hall almost out of sight as Hugo's friend Willy Hamble honked the horn of the car that stood with its engine ticking over in the drive.

And as he closed the door and leaned his head out of the window Amelia sprang forward, away from the others. Suddenly, incredibly, her warm lips were on his. He could taste the wine on her tongue.

'Come back, won't you?' she said clasping his hand. 'I'll be waiting for you.'

'Yes, please wait for me,' he called.

But he never knew if she heard him as the engine roared into life, Amelia stepped quickly back and the car rushed off down the drive.

CHAPTER 6

Ralph had neither the time nor the opportunity to visit his father's grave. Although the family had been there, together and separately, several times since Bosco's death in 1915, Ralph had promised himself that he would visit it as a soldier, fighting as his father had fought against the same enemy, over the same ground, twenty-five years before.

But before this could come about, as Kyril had prophesied, the Maginot Line broke just at its most vulnerable spot near the Ardennes Forest. Von Rundstedt's Army Group A, with over 1,800 tanks and supported by 325 *Stuka* divebombers, came hurtling into France on a route that was to cut off the French and British armies and drive them to the sea.

In Belgium General von Bock's Army Group B steadily pushed the British forces back and, with the total surrender of Belgium on 28 May, the rout was complete. The entire British Expeditionary Force, together with remnants of the French Army and those of the Belgians who did not wish to surrender, foregathered on the beachhead near Dunkirk in an area known as 'the perimeter'.

Crouched among the dunes on the beach west of La Panne at Zuydcoote Ralph tried to snatch some sleep for, with his brigade, he had been on the march for nine days alternately falling back, digging in, and falling back again. The German *Stuka* divebombers screeched out of the sky as they launched their fifth attack on the destroyer *Keith*, now crippled and lying low in the water. Around her in the sea survivors, coated with oil, half-blind and choking, sought desperately for a hold on floating wreckage as they trod water to try and stay alive.

There seemed no end to the carnage, the chaos, as the screaming *Stukas* filled the sky, undeterred by the valiant

British Spitfires which tore in and out of them like a swarm of angry bees.

To the east the French destroyer *Fourdroyant* was foundering and the destroyers *Ivanhoe* and *Havant* were sustaining fierce attacks. The minesweeper *Saltash* approached the *Havant* and began to unload survivors, many of whom had been on *Ivanhoe*.

Suddenly in front of them an ME 109 dived straight into the sea leaving a trail of black smoke and Ralph's men gave a feeble cheer.

'This is hopeless, Sir.' Sergeant Boff tapped Ralph on the shoulder and Ralph, who had briefly sought refuge in sleep – although he wondered whether it was really sleep or unconsciousness brought about by fatigue and a suppurating wound in his leg – jerked himself awake again.

'We're stuck here, Sir,' Sergeant Boff said. 'The whole beach from Dunkirk to La Panne shelves gradually so that even at High Tide the destroyers can't get closer. We shall have to go towards Dunkirk.'

Ralph sat up, surveyed the scene, clasped his hands together and nodded.

'I order you to move with the men towards Dunkirk, Sergeant. I'm absolutely done for. I'll slow you down too much.'

His men gathered round him looking anxiously at their captain who had already led them heroically through weeks of fierce fighting without any regard for his own safety. The small group of men who had been detached in the confusion from the rest of the Brigade felt not only that they couldn't leave him but they needed him. It was known that the Germans were only a few miles away and any wounded comrades left on the beach would undoubtedly be bayoneted.

Suddenly Corporal Brown pointed to the sea and, on the water, miraculously bobbing up and down, was a dinghy with one oar trailing into the water.

'Look,' the corporal shouted. 'It's probably floated ashore

from one of the boats. If we put the captain into it we can row to England.'

'Don't be so daft, Corporal,' Sergeant Boff said sternly. 'Use your wits, man.'

'I think he's got an idea,' Ralph managed a weak smile. 'Five or six of you might well row out to sea and be picked up by one of the boats. If you leave now you can do it before nightfall.'

'If we leave now, Sir,' Sergeant Boff corrected his commanding officer, 'we are not leaving you.'

'You've had your orders, Sergeant.'

'I'm afraid this is one of those times, Sir, when orders are not meant to be obeyed,' and, without more ado, Sergeant Boff grasped Ralph tenderly by the feet while Private Parkinson took his shoulders and, struggling over the dunes and the tough grass, they lumbered towards the floating dinghy, which reminded Ralph of the story of Moses in the bulrushes, and gently lowered him into it.

'Parkinson, Jones, Pudsey,' Sergeant Boff sharply barked his commands, 'you accompany the captain out to sea, and take care of him mind. We'll make our way towards Dunkirk...'

From the bottom of the boat, where he felt he was about to lapse into unconsciousness again, Ralph managed to wave two suggestive fingers at the man he no longer thought of as a subordinate but a friend.

'Wait until I get you in civvies, Sergeant.'

'I'll look forward to that, Sir.' The sergeant saluted smartly and looked on as the men commanded to go with Ralph stepped gingerly into the frail craft which was quickly pushed out from the shore by willing hands. Then Parkinson and Jones grasped the oars and began to pull strongly for the open sea.

Boff looked at the small craft, wondering for a moment if he had sent the captain to his death as the sky once again came alive with aircraft of all description: Heinkels, ME 109s, 110s, *Stukas* and Spitfires. Smoke and flames mingled with the rapid action of machine-gun fire and the ominous thud of bombs dropping on the harbour of Dunkirk towards which they were heading.

But for Ralph it suddenly seemed very tranquil. The sea was calm though there was a good breeze and the men pulling on the oars seemed to have discovered reserves of strength they thought they'd lost. Resting his head on the lap of Private Parkinson, Ralph said:

'I feel a right softie.'

'You'll be all right sir.' Parkinson gave his head a paternal pat, and Ralph recalled his old nanny who would sit beside his bed stroking his head to lull him to sleep. He'd had a very privileged life, but in the last few months he'd made up for it. He realized how privileged it had been, how isolated when he got to know, as intimately as he now had, the men he commanded – the ordinary working man, many of whom had come through the thirties without a job. The army had seemed like paradise after years of unemployment – until now.

But if atonement had to be made for a life of ease, Ralph had atoned. He couldn't recall when he'd last changed his underclothes, had a proper period of sleep or eaten a decent meal. Several times he and his men had become detached from the main body of troops and found themselves behind enemy lines. On countless occasions he thought the end had come, especially when, with a bullet in his leg, he had found himself enmeshed in barbed wire. Then he remembered how his father had died, rescuing Uncle Adam also stuck fast on barbed wire, and he thought that his number was up. But his only concern then had been for his mother, losing a husband and her two sons in war.

But he survived, and he'd survive now. It was strangely eerie lying in the bottom of the boat, lulled by the gentle sound of the sea in the few intervals between the noises from the sky. In the silence one could imagine oneself on the lake at Askham.

'I think I see a boat, Sir,' Jones called, 'quite low in the water. A small boat she is, not sinking.'

'Thank God for that,' Ralph murmured. 'I hardly think we'd make it to England in this.'

Jones stood up to hail the small craft passing about two hundred yards in front of their bow and, as he did, something screamed towards them out of the sky. There was a mighty thud, a torrent of water, and the watchers on the deck of the boat that had turned towards them saw the small craft disappear from sight. From the shore his men, about to set off for Dunkirk, looked at one another in dismay.

The *Mary Anne* was a fifty-foot power cruiser that Willy Hamble, who was a neighbour of Hugo's and a fellow farmer, kept at Portsmouth where he spent every weekend. Willy had been intended for a naval career but rheumatic fever had made him unfit and he had taken to farming instead. He was an enthusiastic weekend and holiday sailor and Hugo often used to go with him. Sailing had become a favourite hobby, a way of relaxing away from the farm.

On the morning of 26 May, Willy had responded to the many calls that came mysteriously through the night to owners of small craft from Admiral Ramsay's office at Dover to proceed with his *Mary Anne* to Ramsgate. First he telephoned Hugo to come along as crew. Hugo had suggested Felipe as an additional hand thinking that he might actually like to have this opportunity of having a go at the Boche.

By 1 June the whole of England knew what hitherto had been a closely guarded secret: that the British Army was drawing out of France. There were still thousands of men waiting at Dunkirk and all along the beach as far as Nieuport Bains, although the Germans were closing in all the time. The *Mary Anne* could take up to seventy tightly-packed soldiers; at one time it had taken over a hundred though then it only just made Ramsgate harbour. Hugo and Willy, taking it in turns to captain the ship, had had very little sleep since their first crossing four days before.

The rumour was, however, that the war against the

Germans had been lost. The battle now was to bring home all the troops, and slowly, tenaciously, thousands not only of British but also allied troops were being ferried across the sea to safety.

On 2 June Admiral Ramsay signalled the whole of his command: 'The final evacuation is staged for tonight...' Once again Hugo and Willy found themselves crossing the by now familiar stretch of Channel marked with its wrecks, its debris and sometimes, alas, the all too familiar sight of floating, bloated bodies.

Willy had wanted Hugo to stay behind because on the previous two trips he had had no rest at all but Hugo, fearing that this would be his first and only taste of war, had wanted to stick it out to the end, identifying with the exhausted fighting troops. Every time they came up against the eastern pier in Dunkirk harbour known as the Mole, which was ably commanded by members of the Royal Navy acting as harbour masters, he anxiously scanned the orderly lines waiting to embark. Now, as they crossed on what was perhaps to be their last journey, Willy, his hands on the wheel, his keen sailor's eyes peering ahead, removed his pipe from his mouth and said:

'I know what's on your mind, Hugo lad. Ralph. He's probably safe in England by now, you know.'

'No one from the Grenadiers I spoke to seemed to know,' Hugo replied. 'They're all over the place. No, I'm not especially thinking about Ralph...'

'Aren't you though?' Willy clasped the younger man's shoulder. 'You're a good lad, Hugo, I'm proud to work with you. Better than that brother-in-law of yours, I'll say. Actually it was just as well he didn't come. We didn't need a third. Room for one more soldier.'

'I bet my sister's not too pleased.' Hugo thought of Em's face as Felipe refused to be conscripted. 'I bet there are a few rows going on in that department. That was a smashing girl who offered to come though.' Hugo's face was reflective.

'Who was that?' Willy nimbly moved the wheel to avoid

collision with a ship of about their size passing on the starboard side. 'Bloody fool! Lay off man. Lay off!' He angrily motioned with his hand and sounded a few blasts on the siren.

'Cheryl's daughter! I'd never met her.'

'That's not Ralph's...'

'No, she was married before. She left two little girls in Kenya. Well, well...'

Further conversation suddenly stopped as the familiar sight of the bombed harbour came into view with the obedient queue of ships forming up against the Mole to load the remaining soldiers.

At the seaward end of the eastern Mole, Commander Guy Maund, who had appointed himself a kind of superior traffic cop, was directing the ships of all shapes and sizes through a loud hailer as they berthed alongside. By now there was a strong tide running and it was difficult for some of the vessels to position themselves correctly against the pilings. At the base of the Mole two officers monitored the line of troops on to the walkway, and the Green Howards, with fixed bayonets, kept an eye on the queues. It was now getting dark, but beyond them the fires from the ruins of Dunkirk still blazed brightly as the *Mary Anne*, slightly dipping into the water, began to take on her load.

'Do you mind if I try and find out about Ralph?' Hugo said pointing to a small group of Grenadiers who stood chatting on the pier. 'I shan't be a tick.'

'Don't,' Willy warned good-humouredly, reaching out a hand to a soldier with his arm in a sling. 'I'll go without you. Here, give me a hand, my man's barmy,' he said to an able-bodied soldier who willingly took Hugo's place at the side of the deck.

Hugo jumped onto the wooden jetty and, as he did, he saw the Grenadiers disappearing out of sight onto the deck of one of the boats anchored at the other side. The Mole now was teeming with troops, many of whom were wounded because a couple of hospital ships had been hurriedly called up to save

104

the wounded, who were the last to go. The orders had been to leave the wounded behind; but too many companies felt unable to abandon their comrades and disobeyed orders. Desperately Hugo sought out the Grenadiers but, in the encroaching dark, he realized he had missed them and, simultaneously, what a stupid thing he'd done leaving his boat which was anchored on the very outer perimeter of the pier.

He was about to return when he saw a fresh party of Grenadiers, their faces blackened, their eyes red-rimmed with exhaustion. Running after them he stopped in front of a man with a sergeant's stripes on his sleeve.

'Have you any news of Captain Askham?'

'Ralph Askham, is it?' The man looked at him keenly. The place was alive with spies of all kinds, fifth columnists who had been dropped by the enemy to mislead the fleeing British.

'Yes, he's my brother.'

'I thought his brother was dead ...' the sergeant began suspiciously, but Hugo's face in the gloom lit up with joy.

'You *do* know him? That's Freddie who was killed in Spain. I'm Hugo, the youngest...'

'Oh aye, the farmer.' Sergeant Boff's eyes grew more friendly. 'We left the captain on the beach by La Panne. He was wounded...'

'Seriously?' Hugo found himself choking.

'Only in the leg, but he was very, very tired. He told us to go ahead, but we were able to put him in a small dinghy which set out to sea...'

'Then he *is* safe?' Hugo said, aware that he was holding up the tired troops who were eyeing one another anxiously.

'We must get on, Sergeant,' Corporal Morley tugged at the NCO's sleeve.

'I'm coming, I'm coming,' the sergeant said impatiently. 'The fact is, Mr Askham, that the captain's boat was shot out of the water when a Messerschmitt came out of the blue and machine-gunned her. There was a small boat standing by, about to come to their rescue. We couldn't tell what happened.

We couldn't wait. I'm sorry but ... you know there are many people in this situation. It's absolute chaos here, a wilderness...'

'Whereabouts in La Panne?' Hugo demanded. 'Do you think he might have crawled back to the beach?'

'He might, if the other boat didn't get to them. They were very near the shore. Or ... he might be dead, Mr Askham. I'd get back to your boat if I were you.'

'*Whereabouts* at La Panne?' Hugo shouted, seizing his arm and shaking him.

'I tell you it's useless, Sir. By the small town of Zuydcoote. But it's like looking for a needle in a haystack. You should go back to your boat.'

Hugo looked along the pier to where he could see the *Mary Anne* about to weigh anchor. It was too late to tell Willy, too late to do anything. He must know. How could he ever face Rachel again, or the family, if he had come so near Ralph and failed to find him, perhaps save his life?

By dawn the following day Hugo knew that his task was hopeless. The beach at La Panne was strewn with bodies, the dead and the dying, and, as he looked towards Dunkirk, he realized that the enemy were preparing for a final assault. He felt lost and surrounded and knew that, by his foolhardiness, he had put his own life in considerable danger. He had been able to do nothing for the dead, little for the wounded, besides a few words of comfort, and he had not found Ralph. He spent the hour before dawn nursing a man who died in his arms: an unknown soldier. It was a bitter experience, and it was going on all around him.

By now the *Mary Anne* would be safely back in Ramsgate and Willy would have the thankless task of telling Rachel he was missing. His one chance was to try and get on a boat going back but, from the sound of gunfire, he guessed that the enemy was very near and the evacuation was complete. Those who had not got away were trapped.

Dressed in navy serge slacks, high wader boots and a thick jersey Hugo, with his dark curly hair and olive complexion, his stubble of beard, could pass for a French fisherman. He knew that if he kept his head and spoke as little as possible, because his French was very weak, he might hole out in Dunkirk for a few days and then by some means get back to England in a small craft. Somehow he still thought that if he stayed on the beach he might find Ralph, or what had happened to him.

However, as the day advanced Hugo, picking his way among the bodies, knew that it was impossible. If Ralph had been wounded, and yet had managed to come ashore, he might by now be dead; yet he wasn't among the many corpses that Hugo had, in the most gruesome task of his life, turned over time and time again to stare at, his heart pounding in his breast.

By nightfall on 4 June Hugo knew that Dunkirk had fallen. The German troops had streamed onto the beach and stood looking out to sea, congratulating one another on the terrible disaster they had inflicted on the British.

Hugo made his way to the battle-scarred outskirts of La Panne and, having no money, was forced to steal from an unoccupied house whose owners had fled from the bombardment. There he also spent his second night wrapped up in a rug against the cold.

By 5 June the Germans were in complete command of the coastline, and Hugo knew that escape by sea was impossible. It was then that he thought of his sister Charlotte in Paris. But would she be there, or would she too have fled south with the Ferovs as the German army threatened to occupy the whole of France?

As he set out keeping to the fields, the tracks through the sand dunes, and the ruins that surrounded Dunkirk, Hugo wanted to put as much distance as he could between himself and the hated place that had perhaps claimed the life of his brother. Despite the streams of refugees who poured along the road with him, many clasping all the worldly possessions that remained to them in pathetic bundles, or trundling them along in carts, Hugo felt abandoned and alone. Rachel had found him as a little boy cast off, abandoned, about to be taken to an orphanage. Maybe this feeling had never left him, remaining buried in his subconscious, because that sense of isolation and desolation quickly returned, as though it had never been very far away.

Now it was each one for himself, though families clung together, children carried in their mothers' arms or hanging onto coat tails, perched on top of carts with the family dog or pet. Once Hugo saw a little girl hugging a cage in which there was her pet rabbit, every bit as frightened as herself.

It was a scene of desolation: Armageddon. The fires still rising from the town and villages round about; what sun there was obscured by smoke. The blackened wrecks of British vehicles were strewn along the highway.

Slowly, perilously, with his fellow refugees occasionally sharing a crust of bread with him, Hugo made his way south.

High up above Ludgate Circus Rachel sat at her desk in the bare office that had been part of her life for almost thirty years. Shortly after Bosco had bought the paper she had started to write for it, one of the emerging breed of women whose means of self-expression was the Suffragette movement. Rachel used to write on women's issues and, after Bosco's death, she took over the editorship of the paper. In the twenties it rose to prominence because of its left-wing, anti-establishment views.

It had been one of the first to warn the British public against Hitler even though, in time, Rachel found herself siding with Chamberlain in his efforts to avoid war. But, once war came, she turned against Chamberlain and campaigned for Churchill. Now England had been at war for nine months and Churchill was Prime Minister. Already his speeches were stirring the nation. The period known as 'the phoney war', when life seemed to go on almost as normal, had been shattered when the might of the German Armies A and B invaded Holland, Belgium and Luxembourg on 10 May. Knowing that Ralph was somewhere involved in the fighting, almost exactly where her husband Bosco had perished, had filled her with foreboding. It had almost been impossible to continue with her work, to prevent her mind from fragmenting as the allied armies disintegrated in Europe beneath the onslaught of the resurgent Hun.

Yet that will to survive that had kept her going for so many years, that had made her such a tower of strength and support to her family, did not desert her now. Every day she went resolutely into the office, climbed the stairs to the top and pounded out her daily leader on the same typewriter upon which she had first learned to type before the Great War.

Rachel paused in her task and gazed out of the window at the familiar scene which had provided her with many inspirational moments in the days that had gone: the dome of St Paul's outlined against a brilliant blue sky. The gleam of its golden cross seemed, as it had so often, to send out a message of hope. A pigeon landed on her windowsill and began to strut along, peering hopefully at her as it passed. Surely its parents, and grandparents, had done the same thing for years – city pigeons, at home among the historic buildings of London? Rachel smiled and, going over to the bag of crumbs she kept on a shelf, sprinkled some on the sill. It was a signal for many more to fly onto the ledge, fighting for position. Some fell off, but some succeeded in maintaining their positions and gobbling up the crumbs. It was like a battle – a recurring symbol of war.

There were some good moments in life, Rachel thought, sprinkling a fresh layer of crumbs, casting some onto a lower ledge for those who had been defeated, or for the sparrows who waited high above the Fleet Street traffic. Funnily enough it was always when things seemed very bad that these moments of tranquillity came to her; as though the basic fundamentals of life, like eating to survive, overcame the dark realities of death and deprivation.

She hadn't heard the door open and the tap on her shoulder made her jump.

'Em! You startled me!'

'Sorry, Mum, I didn't mean to. I thought you'd be hard at work, not feeding the birds.'

'They depend on me,' Rachel said defensively. 'I think I knew some of their grandparents.' She screwed up the top of the bag and tucked it away on the shelf. Em threw her arms round her and hugged her, leaning her head on her breast.

'Oh Mum. I do love you...'

'Em ... Em, darling? This isn't like you.' Detecting a tearful note in her daughter's voice Rachel gently led her to the old battered leather sofa that had come from Bosco's study at Askham House when Cheryl took over. Em was the sturdiest, the least emotional of her children. Em hadn't even cried, or not in public, when Freddie, the twin with whom she had such a deep bond, had been killed. Em hardly ever shed tears however much she grieved.

Em didn't cry now. She sat on the sofa with her mother, tightly holding her hand.

'Any news?' she said at last, her eyes just a little brighter as she lifted her head to study Rachel's face.

Rachel shook her head.

'There's every chance that he's been taken prisoner.'

'But why wouldn't he have gone back to his ship. I can't understand it.'

'He went to look for Ralph, that much we know. He'd heard Ralph had been wounded. It must have been like looking for a needle in a haystack. But how like Hugo!' Rachel clasped her hands together and then dabbed at her own eyes. 'I'm so proud of him, Em ... yet so sad. How ironical that Ralph is safe and Hugo is lost.'

It was indeed a miracle that Ralph and his men were rescued from the dinghy sunk by machine-gun fire that had missed them. The small boat coming to their rescue had taken them on board and landed safely home within a few hours. Now

Ralph was recovering from his wounds and the effect of inhaling the fumes of oil on the sea in hospital. Yet, like all the family, he too was worried about Hugo.

'I think he must be dead, Mum. Hugo, of all people, would have found his way back.'

'Shortly after Ralph was rescued the Germans invaded the beaches of Dunkirk and took all those who were left prisoner. There would have been no chance to escape by sea, but I still feel Hugo is safe.'

Rachel pressed her heart and Em seized her hand.

'You always loved him best...'

'I loved him. I *do* love him, but not best. I love you all equally...'

'But in your heart you loved the little stray,' Em teased, thinking of the story Rachel told about the way she had found him playing in the back garden of a run-down house in Streatham. Because of this Rachel's children had always felt Hugo had a very special place in their mother's heart and, when they were younger, they had been jealous.

'It shows how much Hugo loved Ralph.' Rachel sighed heavily. 'Oh, but I wish he hadn't done it. To think he could be safe on the farm...'

'He wanted to go to the war. It was his way.' Em got up and started to pace about the room, her expression scornful. 'How he shows up Felipe! Mum, I am *so* ashamed...'

'*That's* why you're here,' Rachel said gently. 'I did wonder. You wanted Felipe to be a war hero too.'

'Don't be so cruel.'

'But you did, you do. It's understandable.' Rachel walked slowly over to where Em stood by the window making little mounds of the few crumbs that remained. Bright, hopeful eyes looked at her from the surrounding windowsills, short necks craned eagerly forward. 'But, Em, don't you see, it's not Felipe's war. He's fought his war, and fought it very bravely, I understand, and he lost. He feels embittered.'

'I feel ashamed. *His* war was mine. Why isn't mine, *ours*, his?'

' I don't know.' Rachel shook her head. 'Well, yes, I think I do. I think we've never made him feel welcome. He doesn't like us. We are a cliquey family; people have said so before. We don't realize it, but sometimes those who join us are not really made to feel welcome. Like Cheryl...'

'That was largely her fault ... But we *all* loved Marian...'

'Yes ...' Rachel sighed, thinking of that slight, elusive creature, the mother of Paul, who had so briefly been her daughter-in-law. It was true, they had all loved her.

'Well, if they conform to what we want we do; but if they don't ... it's rather horrible of us really. I should have been more aware of it because I was an outsider too. Your grandmother simply loathed me for so long. Yet when I became assimilated into the family I quickly forgot what it was like not to be inside. Now that I am aware of this attitude I will take more care in future, because the family is growing and expanding and I shan't always like the friends my children, grandchildren, nieces and nephews choose. You see, we all like Arthur because he's one of us...'

'If only Charlotte had married Arthur she'd be here now.'

Charlotte was another worry, still in Paris refusing to leave. Happily her three children were safe with Cheryl, helping to look after the evacuees during the holidays. By all accounts they were having a marvellous time, though rapidly acquiring cockney accents, to Cheryl's horror.

'I'm going to try and get Charlotte on the phone today.' Rachel sounded suddenly distraught, her defences down. 'She simply *must* come or I'll go and get her, as I got you from Berlin ...' As she gazed at Em, her daughter burst out laughing.

'I do *adore* you, Mum! And I want you to give me a job. I want to go to war again as a correspondent. I must. I simply must.'

'Felipe has made you fidgety, hasn't he?'

'He helped, but it's been in my mind for ages. I don't want to sit the war out in the country and, yes, I do want to get away from Felipe. If he hadn't let Hugo down, Hugo might be here.'

'Willy Hamble says nothing could have stopped Hugo. He saw some men from the Grenadiers and he was gone. *They* told Willy what they'd told Hugo, otherwise none of us would have known what had happened to him. I think, Em, you must not use it as an excuse to leave Felipe...'

'I'm not *leaving* him...'

'Getting away then.'

'Well?' Em looked at her. 'Does it matter? You don't like him; oh, not because he doesn't fit in, but because you've seen through him all along, just as you saw through Cheryl.'

'I was prejudiced against Cheryl...'

'No.' Vigorously Em shook her head. 'You saw what she was after and you were right. She may have come good now, but ten years ago it was a different story. She didn't make Ralph happy. I think you knew Felipe wouldn't make me happy...'

'He's so *male*,' Rachel said gently. 'Not in the nice way your father was; but he's pig-headed. He really has an idea of women as something inferior and that's why I found him hard to take. I hated the way he gave orders and expected to be instantly obeyed. I couldn't understand when you obeyed him, unless it was to keep the peace. An expensive way to do it, if you ask me. But Em, he *is* the father of Luis and your common-law husband. You don't want to get rid of him do you?'

'I shan't fling him out,' Em said loftily. 'He can stay at the Grange and write his definitive history of the Spanish war. It may even be very good. But I wondered if *you'd* have Luis, Mum? I know it's a hard thing...'

'Darling, I can't *possibly* have Luis!' Rachel exclaimed. 'I'm not even able to give full time to the charges I do have.'

'Yes, but with Flora, Giles and Paul he'd be in good company.'

113

'But he'd be my responsibility. Besides, now I'm in London most of the time. I couldn't take him, Em. It wouldn't be fair.'

'I can't leave him with Felipe...'

'Then you mustn't go. I don't think you should anyway. It's very dangerous and there are quite enough war correspondents who don't have your responsibilities. Don't you think that, with one daughter in Paris and a son missing, I have enough on my mind?'

'But you know mine's made up, Mum,' Em said. 'Don't blackmail me. I want to go, and I shall – even if you don't employ me.'

Rachel sighed. She knew that when Em spoke in that tone of voice nothing would shift her.

The brief, happy mood of the morning when feeding the pigeons had suddenly passed. No happy moments lasted for very long these days.

CHAPTER 7

Stefanie's face was appealing:

'Can't I come with you, Charlotte?'

'Oh, my dear.' Charlotte knelt and embraced her small cousin. 'I wish you could. But it's *much* too dangerous. The ports are closed; it's impossible by air and I have to go as best I can via Spain. Believe me, you'll be safer here...'

'But I don't *want* to see the Germans in Paris.'

'They may still be stopped.' Charlotte looked doubtful. After the Allied defeat at Dunkirk it was impossible to believe that the French Army would prevent the Germans from reaching Paris.

'But why are *you* going?'

'Because I'm English, Stefanie, and we are at war with Germany.'

'I'm English too.'

'Yes, but they won't know that. You live with your grandparents, who are Russian. If we can get you out safely we will. But as neither your mother or your grandparents want to go I can't take you.'

Stefanie felt very isolated and alone. As an intelligent, sensitive child she was more awake to the realities and implications of the war than her sisters. For in Paris, remarkably, life went on as usual. There was rationing, there had been one or two air-raids, the government was clearly in disorder, with some wanting to surrender and others, led by the premier, Paul Reynaud, wanting to fight on. Many of the French thought that the English had let them down; that they had been deserted, betrayed by them. Others knew that what had happened to France was inevitable, caused by the lack of preparation during the years of the thirties, the refusal by the populist party to modernize France's weapons and Air Force and train her troops as Hitler was training his. In the numerical strength of her forces France had been smug, and when Hitler had struck and France had thrown her huge army into the field it was to fight a war on the principles of 1914, not 1939, when the real power was in mechanization, superior tanks, guns and planes.

It was too late now for recriminations, but those who could get out of Paris went, and those who couldn't put up their shutters and kept their animals off the streets.

The Ferovs had never wanted to leave Paris. They had nowhere to go. They didn't think of themselves as English, nor would they feel welcome in England. They clung to the shredded remnants of their pride, and would not ask the Lighterman or Askham families for help. Bobby had not sent for his daughters even though Stefanie was supposed now to go to school in England. The attack on France had been so sudden that Bobby was as much surprised by the rapid advances of the German armies as anyone else. For the time being the Lighterman girls would stay in Paris.

There was, however, to be one important change. The Ferovs were to move in with Hélène. For her it would be more secure. For them it would be more comfortable. It would get them away from the cold, damp apartment behind the Gare du Nord; it would reunite Hélène with her daughters and it might lead to a reconciliation with her father. At first Hélène was not enthusiastic and offered to move elsewhere, but where should she go? She had no money, being dependent on the goodwill of Charlotte. There were many anxious moments as the discussions proceeded. It was difficult to get Hélène and Alexei even to agree to talk to each other, let alone to live together. But, finally, good sense prevailed, good sense cemented by the exigencies of war: together they felt safe.

As for Alexei and Irina it was possible to think that, yet again, their fortunes were on the turn; that the good times might be about to come back again. Besides, Alexei had so many useful connections in Berlin, who could say that it might not be quite agreeable to have the German Army occupying Paris? This idea however he kept very carefully to himself but, as the German troops began to advance along the Meuse and cut off the rest of France from Paris, he busied himself having his suits cleaned, applying an extra coat of pomade to his hair and generally paying close attention to his personal appearance in order to look his best when they arrived.

The Ferovs were, thus, well settled in as Charlotte prepared to leave. She was travelling with two other English couples, friends of Arthur's, who still had some petrol and a large car in which they hoped to get to Bordeaux. It was true that the Germans were advancing along the Meuse, but the French still held the Loire and the West of France. From Bordeaux they hoped to find a plane to take them home.

The wireless was on all day long blaring out the latest news, a list of continual disasters. At one time a French victory had been hailed, but that seemed so long ago and was, in any event, unsure. The government didn't seem now even to be trying to keep up morale. An air of fatalism prevailed in the doomed City as the ordinary Parisian preferred to keep up his or her daily routine. Already two million men had been enlisted in the Forces and hardly a family remained unaffected by the war.

It was the night of 8 June, four days after Dunkirk had officially fallen. Irina paradoxically felt happier than she had for years – she had, after all, lived through an upheaval much greater than this – and was making bortsch in the kitchen with some scraps she had managed to get from the market. Charlotte's maid had left to return to her home in the country, but old Marie, the concierge, liked nothing better than a princess and had already ingratiated herself with Irina. Hélène she liked less, though she was chic. Hélène was sharp and critical. She did not fawn on her as it was necessary now to fawn upon servants in wartime. But on the whole Marie was happy to have this family in place of beloved Madame

Charlotte; and Madame Charlotte's little dog Flic and her cat Zero to look after for as long as the war would last.

At the same time as Irina, humming a little tune of happiness, stirred the thick red soup she had only learned to make after she came to France, Marie, muttering to herself, hastened out of her little apartment by the gate to answer the persistent ringing of the doorbell.

As soon as she opened the door she wanted to shut it again; but the man on the other side pushed against it with his hand saying, in his poor French, heavily accented:

'Please let me in.'

The stranger had several days' growth of beard; he was haggard, he looked as though he'd lived in his clothes and he smelt. Marie's immediate thought was that he was a prisoner on the run. She was about to try and shut the door again with a firm shake of her head; but then she saw the look in his eyes and she became afraid.

Running ahead she knocked on Madame's door and was thankful when Charlotte opened it herself and first of all looked at her, a question in her eyes. But when she saw the man behind Marie she uttered one word: 'Hugo!' in a voice so full of emotion that Marie was pleased she hadn't sent the man away. Not, she thought, that he'd have gone that easily. Instead she smiled ingratiatingly at Madame and Madame's curious friend as he fell into Charlotte's arms: and then, still clutching him, she drew him into the dining room where Stefanie and Olga were laying the table.

'It's Hugo! He's all right. Oh, I must try and get a message to Mummy!'

'You knew I was missing?' Hugo still looked dazed at his good fortune in finding Charlotte. He thought she might have been among the thousands leaving Paris.

'The family have all been in a terrible state. Mummy managed to get a message through to me via Reuters. It's almost impossible to communicate in any other way. Oh Hugo, *how* did you make it and what happened?'

'First he looks as though he must sleep.' Irina, who, hearing the noise, had bustled in, studied him with concern. 'Did you walk *all* the way from Dunkirk?'

Hugo nodded, slumping in a chair. The once sturdy soles of his fisherman's boots were holed in places and his clothes were covered with dirt and caked with blood. For a moment such was the extent of his relief that his head fell onto his chest and he appeared to go to sleep. Then he jerked himself awake again.

'Ralph...'

'Ralph is *safe*!' Charlotte knelt by the side of his chair and put her arm round him. 'Isn't it marvellous? His boat was overturned by machine-gun fire, but none of them were hurt and they were hauled out of the water by men from a nearby boat. Within hours Ralph was in hospital at Ramsgate. His lungs, however, were damaged by inhalation of oil fumes from the water, and the wound in his leg is quite serious. He'll live, he'll live! It will take time, but he'll live.'

'Thank God ...' Hugo said, closing his eyes.

'Everyone is very worried about you,' Charlotte added reprovingly, as Irina came over to him, a large bowl tenderly clasped between her still long and beautiful hands.

'Have a little bortsch,' she crooned, 'it will restore you to life ...'

'A little whisky first if there is any,' Hugo opened his eyes, 'or brandy. I haven't slept for four nights. The German Army is advancing on Paris and I had to be always just a little ahead of them. You have no idea of the things I have seen on the way...'

'We have *some* idea,' Hélène said gravely, entering after her mother and standing quietly listening. She took the bowl of soup from Irina and put it on the table while Charlotte put a glass half filled with brandy into Hugo's hand, murmuring:

'There, drink some of this ... but only a little. The journey isn't finished, Hugo. We can't stay here. I'm about to leave.'

'Not tonight. I can't move...'

'Not tonight, but tomorrow ... first thing. We have a car, we have some petrol, and our only hope is to go to Bordeaux where we'll try and get a boat or a plane.'

'God knows what would have happened to me if I hadn't found you. The Germans were just behind me.' Hugo glanced towards the door as though expecting at any moment to see one of them come in.

'We know. They say the government is about to leave Paris and the Germans are at Rouen. It's been the most frightful collapse, hasn't it Hugo? Totally unexpected.'

Hugo shrugged. His energy, activated by fear, had lasted just long enough. Now he felt drained, too numb to think.

After Hugo had gone to bed they sat at the table at what was to be their last meal together, who knew for how long? Alexei and Irina were extremely cheerful, as though on the verge of a new life, whereas Hélène was resigned and also, somehow, resentful that she had to share Charlotte's elegant, beautiful flat with her parents. Her daughters were something else. Maybe she would like to have been alone with Olga and Natasha, the compliant ones – and the difficult, nervous, trouble-making Stefanie could have stayed with her grandparents. Hélène spent a lot of time during the meal uttering deep sighs punctuated with gloomy forebodings. She was ill at ease.

'How will we live while you're away?' she said yet again. 'How will Bobby's money get through?'

'Well, you know that I've left money for you in the bank.' Charlotte was the practical one. 'You have no rent to pay or other household expenses and the children will, presumably, go on receiving their education on the State.'

'But supposing there is inflation as there was in Germany in the twenties?' Hélène persisted. 'What will happen to the value of the franc?'

'I don't know,' Charlotte impatiently shook her head, 'but there will certainly be enough to keep you all for the time being. We shan't forget you, Hélène, and, if the opportunity comes for you and the girls, or just the girls if you prefer it, to go to London we shall take it, providing Hitler doesn't invade England too.'

'It *is* all rather frightening.' Stefanie excitedly spooned her thick, nourishing soup made of beetroot and little pieces of meat. 'I'm quite looking forward to it.'

'Are you, darling?' Charlotte tenderly stroked her smooth, dark head. 'It *is* rather an adventure isn't it? I must say I feel quite excited too.'

It seemed important to Charlotte to hide the terror that she really felt. It was important, for everyone's sake, to keep up morale. This is what her mother would have wanted her to do, would be doing now, even before she knew Hugo was safe. All her life Charlotte recalled her mother's stoicism in adversity. It was an example, but a difficult one to live up to. To be terrified, yet to smile ... At Freddie's memorial service Rachel went around cheering everyone up. It was impossible to say whether she broke down when she was alone.

'Madame,' Marie, who had shuffled into the dining room almost unnoticed, whispered into her ear, 'there is yet *another* visitor.' Marie sounded excited. She had lived through the war in Paris in 1914-18 when they even used to eat dogs who were unwise enough to stray on the streets, and the situation held no terrors for her.

'Who is it, Marie?' Charlotte began to rise.

'He won't say, Madame. He wishes to see you in private.' Marie's eyes shone.

'How mysterious. Do excuse me.'

Charlotte followed the concierge to the door, and saw in the hall a man she didn't know. He was short and fairly nondescript and wore a raincoat tightly fastened even though the night was warm.

'You don't know me, Lady Charlotte,' the man said rapidly in French. 'I wonder if we could have a word in private?'

'Certainly.' Charlotte pointed to the door of the sitting room. 'You just caught me. I'm leaving the country.'

'I know, that's why I'm here,' the man murmured behind her as she led the way into the drawing room and shut the door after them.

'Really? Will you have a drink?'

Charlotte went over to the drinks table, but the man shook his head.

'I have no time, thank you. I wondered ...' he put his hand into the inner pocket of his raincoat and produced a long thin envelope. 'I wondered if you would deliver this for me to an address in London? It's very important and very secret.'

'Really?' Doubtfully Charlotte looked at it. 'But not illegal I hope.'

'Not at all.' The man laughed and produced his identity card from his wallet. 'I am Colonel Charles Leroux of French Military Intelligence. You see, for a long time we have known that if the Germans did invade France it would all be over very quickly. France was unprepared for war. The Popular Front did not believe that Germany would ever be in a position to make war again and opted for disarmament. Those of us in Military Intelligence knew that if we were cut off we should have to make arrangements to channel information to our allies in London.' He held out the document. 'This is very secret. It contains the names of all the agents in France we can rely on. We want to establish a secret network of resistance to the German enemy and the man that you will give this to in London will be expecting it. Please give it to him personally, and no one else and, please, if you think you might not complete your journey destroy it at once. A lot of lives may depend on you.'

Charlotte took the envelope and studied it for a few seconds. It was addressed to a Captain Sharples at an address in Whitehall.

'How do you know you can trust me?'

'I know you're the daughter of a hero, and the sister of a serving British soldier, Captain Ralph Askham. I'm sure you are heroic yourself, making this dangerous journey to the frontiers of freedom. I know your brother, Ralph, very slightly and he will know me. If I can rely on anyone, Lady Charlotte, surely it is you?' Colonel Leroux glanced at his watch; he was, obviously, a very brusque, punctilious man. Charlotte liked him. A moment later he held out his hand and Charlotte saw him to the door and out into the silent street. Not even a cat was abroad and the eerie darkness caused by the blackout was all-enveloping.

'Good luck,' she whispered, clasping Leroux's arm. 'May we meet again in free France.'

'*Bonne chance*, Lady Charlotte,' the colonel said. 'To Victory.' And then he was gone, swallowed up in the dark.

Thoughtfully Charlotte turned back into the apartment tapping the envelope with her fingers. Names of all the agents in France. Suddenly she seemed part of something very big and despite her fears, exciting, as though she were on the verge of a new and important experience.

'Who was the man?' Hélène said later that night after everyone was in bed. Charlotte and Hélène were too tense to sleep and sat up over cigarettes, a pot of coffee between them.

'He was someone from the French Army. He wants me to deliver a document to someone in London. I know nothing more.'

'How exciting.' Hélène rubbed her arms but she was trembling. 'I will miss you terribly, Charlotte.'

'And I will miss you.' A lock of Charlotte's modishly cut hair fell over her brow. 'I will miss you so terribly you won't believe it. I will miss France and, above all, I will miss Paris.' She touched Hélène's hand. 'For you it is a time to get to know your daughters, to make friends with them and with your father now you are to be together.'

'Is *that* why you offered us your flat?'

'It is partly why,' Charlotte acknowledged. 'But also it is much nicer than your parents' flat behind the railway and also, I think, much safer. They always bomb railway stations first, though God forbid they should bomb Paris on a wide scale. They didn't in the last war and I hope they won't again.'

'I will go mad here with Father, Mother, and the girls,' Hélène burst out. 'I dread it.'

'Then come with me,' Charlotte said suddenly, 'and leave the children with your mother.'

'Oh, I can't do that,' Hélène shook her head vigorously. 'I've thought of it, but I can't. It will be another desertion. The girls will feel it too keenly. As you say, I must make friends with them. Natasha and Olga I find easy, I love them very much, but I find Stefanie difficult because she is so hostile. But I must try. I must find something to do...'

'Go and see Chanel,' Charlotte said suddenly. 'The business is closed, but the shop is open. She knows everyone.'

'Who will be wearing couture clothes in wartime Paris?'

'Some people will, you'll see,' Charlotte said. 'Some people will also fraternize with the enemy...'

'I shan't be one of them.'

'No, but you can still model clothes. But why do we talk so gloomily?' Charlotte poured coffee from the jug and lit another cigarette, glancing, as she did, at the clock. 'It's not a very cheerful note on which to pass our last night.'

'Because we're being realistic,' Hélène murmured. 'There's nothing to be cheerful about.' For a moment she leaned her head back against the chair, closing her eyes as if, in the dark, she could see into the future. 'All I can see is gloom – gloom, and disaster. Why pretend otherwise?' She opened her eyes and stared at Charlotte. 'And there are times, I'll confess to you, I feel I may not live to see the end of it. But that won't be a disaster. In many ways it will be a release.'

'You mustn't say that.' Charlotte leaned forward anxiously. 'That's a terrible thing to say.'

'It's true.' Hélène put her hands behind her head. 'I have completely ruined my life – a divorced woman, a convicted murderess. Who can forgive me, or forget? Do you think my children forget? My parents certainly do not. Even my mother always has a sad expression when she looks at me.' She gazed around her, at Charlotte's antique furniture, the few old masters hung on the wall – not very rare or valuable old masters, but with a style and charm of their own. There was nothing to compare here with the pictures that graced the walls of Lighterman House, or of Askham Hall in the old days, before Cheryl embraced *art deco*. But, because Charlotte loved them and had chosen them, because it was she who liked them, they seemed even more valuable. Charlotte had unique taste, and always put her own exquisite touch on everything she bought.

'I think you overdramatize things.' Charlotte had followed the sweep of Hélène's gaze.

'How can one overdramatize murder? Isn't it dramatic in itself?'

'The court thought you were not responsible. If the law can be lenient with you, why can't you be lenient with yourself? You must try and give yourself a chance, Hélène.'

Gazing at the wan, rapt face, beautiful but in a rather faded, old-fashioned way, Charlotte felt more remorse at leaving her than anything else.

But that she didn't tell her.

Bobby paced up and down, not troubling to try to conceal his annoyance.

'There's absolutely no need for you to volunteer at all. You should get your degree and then see. You're still a boy. I could get you an exemption on the grounds that ...'

Bobby stared at the beautiful ceiling of his study in Lighterman House as though seeking grounds for exemption from war service of a fit, intelligent young man who had recently had his eighteenth birthday. His brow puckered. 'Let me see...'

'You don't appear to understand, Uncle Bobby,' Sasha said patiently. 'I have already volunteered. I'm telling you, not

125

asking permission. I've told grandfather, too. I certainly don't want an exemption either.'

'Throwing it all away are you?' Bobby said with pretended resignation. He sat on one of the Chippendale chairs bought by his own grandfather in the previous century, crossed his legs and lit a cigarette. 'Your upbringing, your education...'

'Just what is being thrown away?'

'All that. The war has taken a very serious turn. Have you thought you might be killed?'

'Yes.'

'That the life expectancy of a combat pilot is about six weeks.'

'Is it as much as that?'

'Don't be insolent, Alexander.'

Bobby always called his nephew 'Alexander' when he was displeased with him, which was quite often. There were too many aspects, inherited and acquired, of Sasha that Bobby disliked. One half of him was Ferov and the other was Bolingbroke. Bobby had no time at all for the Ferovs, and the middle-class Bolingbrokes – except for Sasha's mother – were so ordinary. When had a Bolingbroke ever shone, ever achieved anything? Never, as far as Bobby knew. Adam had some sort of success as a judge, but there was none of the sparkle, the entrepreneurial flair that had made the boy from Brixton so successful, that would make his grandson even more so. Sasha, in Bobby's opinion, had a poor inheritance.

Sasha was much closer to Bobby than a nephew. He was almost a son, but an irritating son. He had spent many of his holidays with him. He was not naughty at school; Bobby didn't have to visit the headmaster several times a year as he did David's, but he was individualistic and he was disobedient. He was also iconoclastic. He liked to have his own way. Clearly he meant to have it now though, technically, he was still a minor.

'Your mother would be frightfully disappointed with you,

Sasha,' Bobby went on more gently. 'She had such hopes for you.'

Sasha got up and paced restlessly to the window. He gazed up at the sky, listening for the telltale jug-jug of the German bombers coming on another wave of attacks over London. Since August London had been bombarded day and night, and the heroism of the Spitfires of the RAF in resisting these attacks had inspired many young men like Sasha.

Sasha came back into the room more familiar than his own home. He had never really thought of his mother's grandiose apartment in Paris, or her sumptuous Venetian palazzo or even her comfortable villa on the Lido as 'home'. Home had never been Susan and Kyril, but Bobby and, first of all, Hélène, and now Aileen. Of the two he preferred the latter to the vain, detached, cold young woman who had ended up in prison for murdering her lover.

Bobby sat gazing at his nephew through the smoke of his cigarette.

'Uncle, you're killing me off already. I am absolutely determined to join the RAF. I would like your support.'

'And if I don't give it?'

'I shall still go. But I would rather go with your blessing than without it.'

'I can't bless you,' he said with a smile of mockery, 'but I will support you. The Air Force it will be. I only hope that when it's over, that's if you survive, you'll come into my business. I need young men of spirit and determination.'

'Thanks, Uncle Bobby.' Sasha became a young boy again and clasped his uncle round the neck. Despite everything he was someone of whom he was fond. He knew he was about the only member of the family who *was* fond of Bobby. Those who had once loved Bobby ceased to do so when his various underhand activities were discovered – as, invariably, they were.

But Sasha trusted Bobby. In business, he knew, he was a hard man, and in his personal life he had been hard too. His behaviour to his daughters had been unspeakable. But five years ago Sasha had been in no position to make a protest and, he had heard, Uncle Bobby did have his reasons. Rightly or wrongly he suspected the children might not be his.

'There's a call for you, Bobby, from some Ministry or the other.' Aileen came in looking very smart in a calf-length check skirt with a tie silk blouse. Over her shoulders a cardigan was casually slung; on the edge of her nose perched half-moon glasses, and in her hands she had a sheaf of papers. Aileen, for so long in the shadow of her powerful and domineering husband, had found herself at last in the war. As Mrs Bobby Lighterman she had been invited to serve on any number of committees; to be secretary of this and chairman of that. She was now almost as busy as Bobby, in her way almost as powerful. She loved it.

She peered over her glasses towards the window to which Sasha had returned when Bobby went out.

'Sorry, Sasha, I didn't see you. Are you expecting a raid gazing at the sky like that? I must say that one last night terrified me. The most frightful damage was done in the City. It's a wonder your aunt's newspaper escaped.'

'I believe the building's just standing, but all the windows have gone. Aunt Rachel was there all night with Em. If I'd known I'd have been there too. They've got a lot of guts.'

'Your Aunt Rachel has always had a lot of guts.' Aileen glanced surreptitiously at her papers. Sitting down and taking the lid off the coffee pot she peered inside. 'We must get more coffee. But to stay in that building when the City was going up in flames seems to me foolhardy. Em has a young son to consider. Anyway, they're all right and that's the main thing. Now, Sash, where are you off to today?'

'I'm going to the RAF headquarters to enlist. Uncle Bobby has agreed. I wanted him to be behind me, in case Mother or anyone asks questions.'

'Oh, Sasha ...' Aileen's eyes unexpectedly filled with tears and, putting the papers and spectacles on a nearby table, she got up and came over to him. 'Oh, *must* you? There are so many fatalities among fliers. Sash, you're only eighteen...'

'A lot of them are only eighteen, Aunt. Don't worry, I won't be in the air for ages. There's a long training. By that time the blasted war might be over.'

'If only I thought it would,' Aileen gulped. 'I dread that it will last long enough for David to be involved as of course he wants to be, like you. But, oh Sasha, we are so fond of you. You're like our son. Please, wouldn't you think about it? Have a year at Oxford...'

'I couldn't, Aunt, thank you. We've been through all this.' Sasha put his hands on her shoulders and lightly kissed her cheeks. For a boy who had grown up with singularly little affection from his parents he had a loving and gentle disposition.

The fresh coffee had arrived and, with it, Bobby rubbing his hands.

'Good news, good news,' he said. 'A big contract for ammunitions, and government aid to expand the plant. Askham Armaments will soon be one of the biggest suppliers of ammunitions in the world.'

'Don't you ever feel *awful*, Uncle, about manufacturing weapons of destruction?'

'Not at all,' Bobby said sharply. 'Where would we be if it were not for people like Askham Armaments and our expertise? I tell you, we were inadequately prepared for this war as it was, thanks to Chamberlain, appeasement and all those softies of the left who wanted disarmament. Some of them got their way and, in France, we know with what disastrous results. The French Army, ill prepared and ill equipped, went down like a pack of cards, nearly taking us with them. Well they didn't, and let me tell you young man, when you're in the air you will be very glad to have in your plane guns manufactured by Askham Armaments with tested bullets, also made by us, to fire from it. If you are behind one

129

I hope you pat the barrel of your gun as you go into attack and say: "Thank you Uncle Bobby."'

Bobby's good humour had been restored by the call from the Ministry. 'Now, young man,' he said, jovially, 'now we must set about getting you a commission. I know all the right people for Cranwell.'

'I want to enlist in the ranks, Uncle.'

'Nonsense.'

'Nevertheless, I do.'

'What are you, socialist or something?' Bobby's brief good humour had rapidly evaporated. 'Have your father's early communist ideas infiltrated you too?'

'I don't believe in having a commission unless I earn it.'

'That's rubbish. You're a member of the governing classes.'

'I think that's rubbish too...'

As Bobby made a threatening move towards Sasha, Aileen stepped forward and firmly took hold of her husband's arm.

'Please stop this nonsense,' she said in the crisp, authoritative voice she would never have dreamed of using to him ten years before. 'There are far more important things to discuss than stupid family quarrels. Personally I think Sasha is a very brave young man to want to join the ranks. I admire him for it. Now look here, Bobby,' she shook a piece of paper under his nose, 'this should please you. The Queen is delighted that Robertswood is being used as a convalescent home and would like to visit it as a sign of Royal approval.'

Bobby raised his hands in the air and clasped them over his head, shaking them like a prize fighter.

'That's absolutely *marvellous*.' He stepped sideways to kiss his wife on the cheek. 'That should make a knighthood a certainty.'

'Oh, Uncle!' Sasha looked disgusted. 'What a horrible thing to say.'

'What's wrong with it?' Bobby looked annoyed. 'Don't you think I deserve one? I am among the first not only to give my country home, full of priceless antiques, to the nation as a

130

convalescent home but I also endow it. It's cost a bloody fortune to refit Robertswood as a hospital. Don't I deserve some reward? I think so.'

Bobby patted his pockets and glanced at himself in the huge mirror which, placed over the marble mantelpiece, made the room, already large, seem twice its size.

'What about Askham Hall being a school for evacuees? Cheryl's made a great success of that,' Aileen smiled conspiratorially at Sasha.

'Yes, but she didn't volunteer it, did she? Not quite the same thing,' Bobby said sanctimoniously. '*Nor* has the Queen asked to visit it.' Bobby buffed his nails against the soft woollen barathea of his striped, double-breasted suit and glanced approvingly at them. 'Just you wait until you see all the publicity in the newspapers.'

Bobby's optimism proved well founded:

> Mr Robert Lighterman, public benefactor to the nation. Visit by HM Queen Elizabeth.
>
> Mr and Mrs Bobby Lighterman were hosts to Her Majesty the Queen when she visited Robertswood, Mr Lighterman's vast country home on the banks of the Thames which he inherited from his grandfather, the industrialist Sir Robert. This has recently been turned into a convalescent home for our gallant soldiers. Mr Lighterman was one of the first in the country, not only to offer his home but also to equip it at his own expense, and some one hundred and fifty officers can be accommodated there of whom, at present, half are from the Colonies, including many veterans from Dunkirk. Pictured on the right are Mr and Mrs Lighterman with Her Majesty and a cousin of Mr Lighterman, Captain the Earl of Askham who was seriously wounded at Dunkirk and is convalescing there himself.

Ralph read the article, studied the picture and chuckled. Then he threw the newspaper on his bed and gazed out of the window. It was very odd, it still felt odd, to be convalescing in a place one had known since childhood. But when he had been sent there from hospital no one had realized his connection

131

with it. But this was the room, overlooking the river, which old Sir Robert had used as a study and Ralph could vividly remember coming here with his mother to see the old man shortly before he died.

Ralph got his stick and, opening the French windows, went into the small garden where he had chatted with the Queen only the day before. It was she who had reminded him of his family's connection with the Royal family – long years of service which had somehow petered out after the Great War, mainly because of Melanie's divorce from Adam and Dulcie's decision to retire from the Court. Up to then there had always been an Askham at the Court since records of the family connection with the monarchy had begun in the sixteenth century.

Ralph had thanked Her Majesty for her graciousness in recalling his grandmother, who was a friend of her mother-in-law, Queen Mary. He reported on Charlotte's successful escape from France, after a hazardous journey to Spain, and Em's new accreditation as a war correspondent. What was more, his young cousin Sasha was training with the RAF, in the ranks.

The Queen had said it was a fine tradition and invited him to tour round with them as she inspected the premises and had lunch with the family and the senior members of the medical staff who ran the home.

Ralph took a deep breath of air and coughed. There was a nip of autumn about and the chief damage, after immersion in the water and the inhalation of oil, had been to his lungs, one of which had collapsed. He knew there were plans to give him a desk job, but he was determined to go back to a fighting unit, even though his mother, remembering his father, had begged him not to. Bosco had insisted on going back to the war after being wounded even though he was nearly forty. Rachel always thought he was insufficiently recovered when he died.

Ralph flopped gratefully onto a wooden bench and coughed again. His lungs worried him because he knew that, until they

132

were clear, he wouldn't be allowed back, and the threat of being useless and idle worried him. He turned his head at a step behind him and a cup of coffee was put into his hands.

'Isn't it too cold out here for you?'

'Why, Sister, I thought fresh air was what the doctor ordered.'

'Not *too* fresh, Captain Askham,' the girl behind him laughed, and as he patted the bench she looked behind and then sat gingerly down. 'I suppose I might, just for a moment. I've been on duty since six.'

'Caught fraternizing with an officer. Black mark.' Ralph pretended to smack her hand and then briefly his palm touched the back of hers and rested on it.

'Oh Ralph ...' Jennifer Tandem took her hand away and again looked round. 'Anyone might see...'

'Who cares?'

'I do.' Jenny lowered her voice. 'You should too. You're a married man.'

'I don't feel married,' Ralph said, gazing at her. 'I don't recall my wife coming to see me since I arrived here. Do you?'

'That's not the point.'

'It *is* the point. Cheryl and I are separated. To all intents and purposes we no longer live together. I want a divorce but she won't divorce me...'

'Oh, I'm not talking about that,' Jenny said quickly.

'Then what *are* you talking about. Don't we love each other?' Ralph's hand closed over hers again and stayed there. 'Let's go back into my room,' Ralph whispered.

'If matron saw me going back with you to your room I'd probably be dismissed the service.'

'If matron saw you doing the other thing you'd be shot at dawn.'

'Oh Ralph!' Jenny blushed and, not for the first time since he had woken up to find her gazing at him several weeks before, Ralph's heart turned over.

By any standards Jenny was pretty. She was of medium

height, medium build with a trim waist, a neat but full bust and, in her Queen Alexandra's nursing uniform, she looked stunning. Jenny had straight fair hair which, when she was on duty, she wore pinned at the back in a soft bun. She had full, firm lips and a stubborn dent in her chin, very blue eyes.

Like Cheryl, Jenny was a farmer's daughter, but unlike that fragile beauty she was strong and robust. She looked what she was: a practical, good-natured girl from the chilly fells of Cumberland who had been a nurse since she was in her teens. She had trained at St Thomas's in London and volunteered for Queen Alexandra's at the outbreak of war. She was twenty-six. Jenny, like many modern girls, was uninhibited about love. She had not been a virgin, and at first Ralph wondered if she were just continuing the reputation that nurses had among the military.

But during the ensuing weeks of their affair Ralph had begun to feel something more enduring in his relationship with Jenny. Soon, it was obvious to them both, it was mutual – not just attraction, carnal satisfaction; it was love.

Rachel, approaching from the lawn, saw them from quite a distance and, as Jenny had, she too looked nervously up at the house to be sure no one else was observing them. They were doing nothing incorrect, not even holding hands, but Rachel wondered if it was quite in order for her son and a nurse to be sitting so closely together, obviously engrossed in each other. Not wishing to appear to be snooping she hailed them quite loudly when she was still a distance away, and Ralph jumped up, seized his stick and came forward to greet her while Jenny vanished inside.

'Hello, darling.' Rachel leaned up to kiss him, anxiously noting the pallor of his face. 'You seem short of breath.'

'It's just time, Mother.' Ralph took her arm. 'I'm absolutely fit.'

'And the leg?' Rachel took the stick from him as they sat down.

'That only gives me the occasional twinge. I'm right as rain, Mother.'

'Who was that pretty girl I saw you with?'

'That's no pretty girl, Mother, that's a nursing sister,' Ralph said, laughing. But he couldn't conceal his excitement as he gazed at Rachel. 'She's terrific, isn't she?'

'I could hardly see her.' Rachel's tone was cool.

'You will. Her name's Jenny. She's a farmer's daughter from Cumberland.'

'Nothing serious, I hope, Ralph?' Rachel's eyes were anxious as she looked at him.

'Why do you "hope", Mother? I would have thought you might "hope" it was serious…'

'No. I still hope that you and Cheryl will get together again. She *is* your wife and she has enormously improved over this past year. If only you'd go and see her, you'd know. I can't tell you how well she has run those evacuees. They adore her.'

'That's something.'

'Ralph, I'm serious,' Rachel said primly. 'She is much *nicer*.'

'Then why doesn't she come and see *me*?'

'I think she's too nervous because of the row you had when you left. She wants you to make the first move. I think she *does* want a reconciliation, Ralph.'

'Well *I* don't.' Ralph removed his hand and his mulish expression was one with which Rachel was quite familiar. 'I'm no longer in love with Cheryl and I want a divorce…'

'But surely this girl …' Rachel looked towards the house in dismay, 'surely it can't be anything serious?'

'Why not?'

'Well, darling, the war, you've been ill…'

'It's not just a wartime romance, Mother. I'm quite serious about her. She's serious about me.'

'That's your trouble, Ralph.' Rachel began to peel off her gloves. 'You're too serious. I believe you've never had a flirtation in your life. Well, darling, I don't mind you falling in love but it needn't be forever.'

'Wait until you meet Jenny,' Ralph said. 'You'll see.'

'I'm not sure I want to meet her,' Rachel said stiffly, looking at her watch. 'I can't stay long today anyway. I've been to the manor and was on my way back to London. We now have all the windows replaced in the office and are fully functioning again. I just wanted to bring you these.' Rachel put a bag of grapes on the bench beside him. 'They came from the greenhouse. Adam is particularly proud of them.'

'Thanks.' Ralph's tone was terse and he didn't smile.

'Oh *Ralph*.' Rachel leaned towards him. 'Don't let's fall out, *please*. I just don't want you to think that every time you fall in love it's for life. You've never had a lot of girlfriends, Ralph, as some young men do. Your father was a well known flirt in his early twenties. Sometimes I wish you were more like him...'

'Oh, do you?' Ralph said, his voice heavy with sarcasm. 'I'm no longer in my twenties. I'm well into my thirties. Besides, look what Father got up to.'

'Oh, Ralph,' Rachel flushed and put her hands to her face, 'I didn't mean *that*. I meant in his younger days, before he met me...'

'Yes, but *after* he met you too, Mother, he nearly broke your heart didn't he? You nearly split up. Is that the sort of fellow you want me to be? If I no longer love Cheryl it's not because I wanted to be unfaithful. *She* rejected *me*.'

'Oh, it's only that ...' Rachel struggled to find the right words. 'I just...'

'You just want me to go back to Cheryl who hasn't been a proper wife to me for *years*. You've no idea the degrading things that went on in our bedroom, Mother...'

'Whereas I suppose there's *nothing* degrading about that with the nurse,' Rachel said hotly, tossing her head towards the house. 'They say they take it all in their stride, these women. I wonder how many convalescent officers she's comforted this year? She must have thought it was really her lucky day when the Earl of Askham was wheeled in.'

Ralph jumped up, seized his stick from where it was leaning against the bench and thumped it on the ground.

'I *hate* you for saying that, Mother. You'd better go now. You said you were in a hurry. I should hate to do something I'd regret all my life ... and hit you.'

Turning round, Ralph walked rapidly back to the house. From the window, anxiously watching the scene, Jenny quickly stepped back so that he shouldn't see her.

She saw Lady Askham stand up, look down at the bag of grapes, as though wondering what do with them, and then, without a backward look at the house, walk slowly down the path the way she had come. Jenny wondered if she were weeping.

CHAPTER 8

Very soon, even in wartime Paris, Hélène found herself gradually continuing the aimless, peripatetic way of life she had followed after her divorce from Bobby and before she went to prison. For even in Paris under the Nazis, at least in the early days of the occupation, it was possible to exist in a kind of normality. The children went to school, gradually restaurants and shops reopened, although their fare was very limited, and businesses continued very much as they had before. As in every country in every age some people did well out of war and some did badly: it was only gradually that the term 'collaborateur' came to be used. The German army, moreover, was not full of boors and butchers. Quite a large number of the officers were cultured, civilized men who, before the war, had been lawyers, civil servants and businessmen.

Men like this loved Paris and the company of artists and intellectuals; they liked men of the world such as Prince Alexei Ferov who knew their way about. Soon his elegant home, formerly the hôtel of a *grande horizontale* of France, became a meeting place for those officers of the Wehrmacht stationed in Paris fortunate enough to make his acquaintance. And eagerly, like a butterfly emerging from the chrysalis in which she had for so long been entombed, Irina began to entertain for them, acquiring food and drink on the Black Market to impress the conquerors of France.

It was strange how quickly one could throw off the lethargy, apathy and hypochondria of years, ever since she had left the service of Dulcie Askham, banished because of a quarrel with Cheryl. The sparkle had returned to Irina's eyes, the artificial blush of not too skilfully applied rouge to her cheeks. The ersatz Ferov jewels appeared from a forgotten box in the attic, and the creations of the twenties and early thirties were shaken out of mothballs. Once again Princess Irina of the noble house of Ferov was in her element, this time as an entertainer of the Nazis rather than the aristocracy of England. Well, what did it matter? As an exile, uprooted and unwanted, one found one's friends where one could.

Her daughter Hélène, however, was very different. Rootless, stateless, a woman with a past she might be, but she hated the *boche*. She hated the way they had trampled over Europe driving the British into the sea. For a while in the autumn, while rumours persisted that England was to be invaded, she had sat with her ear to the clandestine wireless in her room listening to the BBC. Hélène hadn't realized she was a patriot; and indeed she wasn't. Patriot for what country? She had good reason to hate the British, to hate the nation that had spawned someone as ignoble and detestable as Bobby, yet she did not. Her daughters were British, so part of her was British. Many of those in the Askham family – particularly Charlotte and Rachel – had been gracious to her. Since Churchill, that epitome of the bulldog breed, had become leader, she loved them more than ever. She would have liked nothing better than to resume her place in London society as Mrs Robert Lighterman, daughter of one noble house, allied by marriage to another, now even in wartime having lunches for good causes, patron of this and that, talked about, written about, envied and admired. Yes, she would have loved it all. More than ever had she cause to regret the past.

Instead, as soon as she could leave the house in the morning, after taking the children to school, she wandered from one café to another drinking coffee, smoking endless cigarettes, chatting aimlessly to the waiters and waitresses, passing the time at this bar or that where she had been known in the past.

She could hardly bear the sight of her father pomaded and spruce, a flower in his buttonhole, on the telephone as soon as he decently could to invite Oberleutnant this or Colonel that to drinks and dinner or coffee, a game of bridge afterwards. Irina would be busy in the kitchen helped by a newly acquired maid who, somehow, the Ferovs could now afford. Suddenly there was money where there had not been before. But Hélène always took good care not to be around when the Nazis were there, not to be tainted by their presence. It was obvious to Hélène that her father was up to his old tricks again, accepting graft, selling knowledge, know-how, anything illegal for gain.

One night in the winter of 1940/41, when the news about the progress of the war was mainly from Greece and North and East Africa, after the last of the Nazis had gone, Alexei was sitting alone over a brandy when there was a knock at the door. Thinking Colonel Schwarz had forgotten something, Alexei went affably to the door and opened it. Standing on the threshold was a man he didn't know.

'Prince Ferov?' the man said looking instinctively to right and left.

'Yes.' Alexei screwed his monocle tightly to his eye and peered at him.

'May I come in? I'm a friend of Lady Charlotte's.'

'Lady Charlotte is not here I'm afraid,' Alexei said nervously, thinking of his recently departed guests.

'I know that, but I wonder if I may come in. Quickly please.' Before Alexei had time to react the man gently tapped him on the chest and pushed past him. 'Please close the door,' he said. 'Bolt it.'

'I think you've made some mistake,' Alexei began, but the man impatiently pushed him aside and bolted the door. Then he extinguished the light and stood in the dark, listening.

'This is preposterous!' Alexei said turning to the light switch, but the man grasped his hand.

'Don't put it on! If you do I may shoot you.'

'I assure you Lady Charlotte took all her valuable possessions with her.' Alexei began to feel genuine fear. 'There is not a thing in the house...'

'I'm not a burglar, my friend.' The stranger crouched listening then he went to a side window and peered out. 'I think

140

it's all right now. You can put on the light. Sorry to frighten you. Look, I badly need your help. As I know you are related to Lady Charlotte...'

'We are *not* related,' Alexei said stiffly. 'My daughter was formerly married to her cousin, but is so no longer...'

'But she has lent you her apartment. You must be close. She must trust you.'

'Mmmm,' Alexei's mouth curled up into an expression of disdain. 'Trust yes, close no. I think that about sums it up.'

'Oh dear, that's a pity,' the man said. Then he extended his hand. 'Charles Leroux. Please forgive this intrusion, Prince Alexei.'

'You seem to know all about me anyway.' Alexei, rarely ruffled, led the way back to the room where he had been ruminatively sipping brandy before being disturbed.

'All I know is that this apartment belonged to Lady Charlotte, that you, or your family, are related to her and obviously she trusts you. I wondered if I, in turn, could trust you?'

'Trust me? Of course,' Alexei said magnanimously. 'What can I do for you? Cognac?'

'Thank you.' Colonel Leroux unbelted his coat and rubbed his hands together extending them towards the embers of the fire which still glowed in the grate. He took the balloon glass from Alexei's hand and appreciatively sniffed the contents. 'I thought I could trust you. I know your wife was a friend of the old Lady Askham.'

'A very close friend, a confidante,' Alexei said grandly. 'Alas, she's dead.'

'Still it is a good recommendation for us.'

'Us?' Alexei looked surprised.

'Well, the people I'm associated with. I must tell you that I was being chased through the streets when I sought refuge with you. Even now the police are looking for me with bloodhounds.'

'Whatever have you done?' Alexei's monocle nearly fell from his eye with astonishment.

'I had with me an English airman. He was found in a field near where his plane had crashed returning from a bombing raid. The rest of his crew are dead but he is alive.'

'Good gracious!' Alexei said in alarm. 'Where is he?'

'He's at a safe house that, after tonight, will be a safe house no more because I think I was seen coming from there.'

'And you ran to me? But that's terrible!'

'Oh, no one saw me, Prince Alexei. Don't worry.' Colonel Leroux smiled. 'But would it disturb you very much if, from time to time...'

'If what?' Alexei said sharply.

'We used this apartment belonging to Lady Charlotte as a safe house, should we require it. With your connections with the British aristocracy you are surely utterly reliable?'

'I would prefer to have nothing to do with it,' Alexei said. 'I can't possibly risk the lives of my wife, my grandchildren, my daughter...'

'No one would think of looking here in the house of a Russian emigré,' Colonel Leroux said. 'Not for one moment would they think of looking in your house for an escaped airman or a wireless transmitter.'

'Out of the question,' Alexei said, but a quiet voice behind him intervened.

'What a good idea. No one would suspect. That way, Papa, you can keep irons in both fires and, whichever side wins, you will be sure to be on the winning side.'

As Hélène came into the room tightly fastening her dressing gown around her, the sleep still in her eyes, Colonel Leroux got to his feet, extending a hand.

'Princess Hélène? How do you do?'

'You appear to know an awful lot about us,' Hélène said.

'I have to know what I can about those whom we ask to help us. You see, we don't know whom we can trust. There are spies

142

everywhere, friends of the *boche*. As yet our organization is in its infancy.'

'What organization is that?' Nervously Alexei put a cigarette to his mouth and lit it with a hand that shook slightly.

'Broadly speaking our organization is to help people to escape, primarily Jews and those trapped in France who are still in hiding. But now we are more and more able to aid English airmen shot down or captured over northern Europe. We have a line that stretches from Germany through Holland and Belgium as far as...'

'You had better be very careful what you say in front of my father,' Hélène said sarcastically. 'He had three German officers for dinner here tonight.'

'I know that the Prince is on good terms with the enemy,' Colonel Leroux said quietly. 'And I *hoped* the reason was that, in order to help some Allied cause, he could gain their confidence. I didn't think that Lady Charlotte, with her close relationship to the illustrious Askham family, would ever let her apartment be used by a Nazi sympathizer.'

'I'm not *exactly* a sympathizer,' Alexei replied, speaking slowly, 'but I cannot possibly help you. I would be putting my entire existence and that of my family at risk. You can be sure I will say absolutely nothing about this conversation. But I can't help you.'

'I see I have made a mistake.' The Colonel coloured. 'This puts me in a very awkward position because of what I have told you.'

'Oh, my father will say nothing if you threaten him,' Hélène said cheerfully. 'Tell him you'll shoot him if your organization is discovered. He is such a coward he will do anything for a peaceful life.'

'I see.' Colonel Leroux bit his lip. 'Well, certainly we have to close the mouths of traitors.'

'I am no traitor,' Alexei said indignantly. 'Please believe that. Why, my grandchildren are British citizens. If the Nazis knew that, heaven knows what would happen. They might take them away, intern them. I assure you, Colonel, if you leave me and my household in peace I will never breathe a word.' With a sweeping movement of his arm he brought a finger to his lips. 'From this day onwards, all recollection of our conversation is obliterated from my memory.'

'Let me show you out,' Hélène said coldly. 'I need to breathe some fresh air after sharing the same room with a man like this.'

She gazed at her father for a moment then, abruptly turning her back on him, led Colonel Leroux into the hall, carefully shutting the door of the salon.

'Quick,' she whispered, 'tell me where I can contact you. I can help you, and I want to. You can be sure I'm completely trustworthy, but he is not.'

Leroux looked at her carefully in the dim light of the hall.

'I feel certain I can trust you, Princess,' he said, 'but we must talk again. Can you meet me at five tomorrow at the Café aux Yeux Bleus at the corner of the Place Malarmé. Five in the afternoon. Is that all right?'

'Five in the afternoon. Tomorrow.' Opening the outer door Hélène nodded, her eyes shining with excitement.

Meanwhile in the salon Alexei poured more brandy into his glass and stared lugubriously into its amber depths before drinking the entire contents. Even then he found he was still trembling.

Arthur Crewe seemed to have led a charmed life. By the spring of 1941 he was one of the acknowledged aces of the war in the air, one of those who had saved Britain the previous summer, twice decorated with the DFC and bar. One of Churchill's 'Few'. From being dull, kind old Arthur, he had become a hero, and it was part of the Askham character to admire heroes.

Arthur had lost weight since those pre-war days and a large moustache coupled with a certain inconsequential swagger he'd developed, the jauntiness of the fictional Pilot Officer

Kite, had improved both his appearance and his image. Charlotte began to see dull old Arthur Crewe, that faithful swain, provider of champagne and roses, in a new light.

Since her escape from France with Hugo, a long and dangerous trek to the Spanish frontier after having to abandon the car because of lack of petrol, Charlotte had found it impossible to resume any kind of normal life. She was at home but she felt she had no home. All the children were at boarding school; Rachel was busy on the paper; Em, a fully accredited, uniformed war correspondent, was somewhere in North Africa, and Ralph, his convalescence over, had returned to duty. Her restlessness wasn't helped by the fact that the family, that anchor of her childhood and youth, that bulwark upon which one could always rely in times of stress, had changed.

Askham Hall was a boarding school for evacuees; Askham House was closed for the duration, except for one or two rooms the family could use if necessary; Robertswood was a convalescent home, and Bobby lived on the ground floor of Lighterman House which he had converted into a virtual air-raid shelter, the rest of the house being closed, the valuables all removed for safe keeping to the country. Charlotte lived with her mother and Adam in Bedford Row though even this wasn't considered safe due to its proximity to the East End and the City, and most nights were spent in Chancery Lane Underground Station together with hundreds of other people, as soon as the air-raid warnings sounded.

Rachel wanted Charlotte to go to the country; but Charlotte felt more useless there than she did in the city where, at least, she could share in the suffering of the London people who gathered nightly in the shelters away from the German bombs. And night after night the others came to value the presence of Charlotte who was so good with the children, so comforting to women whose husbands were serving overseas. In her way Charlotte did her bit, but it wasn't enough.

'If you married me,' Arthur said, 'you'd have the anchor you're looking for.'

145

'What anchor is that?' Charlotte replied, amused. 'I thought I was an anchor already?' Arthur had a *pied à terre* just round the corner from Askham House. It had a bedroom, a sitting room and a small kitchen but, in its way, it was dangerous being on the top floor right in the path of the German bombers.

Arthur turned to her, his moustache tickling her cheek. Arthur had even improved as a lover since the war began. Maybe it was because they saw each other infrequently and, when they did, the added danger gave an extra edge to their encounters.

'You *are* the anchor. But I want that ring on your finger.'

'Oh, the sign that I belong to you.' Charlotte reached out for a cigarette from the pack by the bed. Yes, she felt content. She enjoyed being with Arthur and, here in this little room under the eaves, there was somehow an air of sin, of wickedness, as though it were a place of assignation. She and Arthur had eaten at Pruniers in St James's where a special 'Blackout' dinner with oysters could be had for 10/6d, but when the air-raid warning sounded they were in bed. Silently they listened to the menacing chug-chug of the advancing German bombers and the searchlights that suddenly stabbed the sky made the room seem like day.

'You do belong to me, Charlotte. I love you,' Arthur said after a long, thoughtful silence. 'We've been engaged for three years. Isn't it long enough? We could be married tomorrow by special licence. Hell!' Arthur sat up and leaned across her to help himself to a cigarette, 'we really don't know what tomorrow will bring. I may be sent abroad.'

'You never said.' Charlotte unbelievingly blew smoke into the air.

'It's only a rumour.'

'There are a lot of them about.'

'I don't really think you care. I would also like to have a child and, although you're not old, it doesn't get any easier.'

'Oh Arthur, you never told me about children!' Charlotte

146

looked reproachfully at him in the dark. 'I can't go through all that business again, even to please you.'

'But I thought you *liked* being a mother?'

'I do, but babies ... all that was a long, long time ago.' Charlotte fell silent. Babies! It was nearly ten years since her husband Paolo had been killed. Paolo, babies and the water mill outside Paris. All seemed to go together in a moment of acutely poignant nostalgia for the past. Blissful days when she had grown chubby with happiness, her frame filling out, loose frocks billowing because she didn't care. After the death of Paolo she had lost nearly three stones and then become a model. Everything had changed, even her nature. 'I'm a different person,' she said at length. 'I don't want another baby, even for you.'

And then Charlotte realized that, after all, she didn't love him. Not in the way she had loved Paolo; not with that special love that wanted to give life. But Arthur was so deserving; so utterly good and unselfish. Abruptly she sat up and swung her legs over the bed.

'I've been very self-absorbed, haven't I?' she said. 'I *will* marry you, Arthur. When?'

As she looked at him there was a crash and the whole building shook. Arthur jumped out of bed and ran to the window.

'My God that was near. Where's your mother tonight?'

'In the shelter, I hope. Oh my giddy aunt, Arthur. What on earth are we doing *here* while the whole of London is falling?'

'We're getting *married*,' Arthur shouted. '*Married*. I can't believe it. Oh Charlotte.'

He took her, naked, in his arms but then the building shook again, and a probing searchlight seemed to peer pruriently right into the room.

'Quick, the shelter,' he said. 'I don't want to lose my bride.'

Most of the people had been in the Piccadilly Underground for hours. Reluctantly they made way for the two latecomers mainly because the man wore the uniform of a Wing Commander and he had two lines of medal ribbons on his chest.

'Move up for the Wing Commander,' a gruff cockney voice shouted. 'One of our 'eroes with his pretty lady. Move up then.'

'Thanks,' Arthur said, squatting down and pulling Charlotte beside him. 'We're getting married tomorrow.' He put his arm round her. 'She's just said "yes".'

'Congratulations,' the cockney boomed and then in a loud voice announced, 'the Wing Commander and 'is lady are getting wed tomorrow. Who's for three cheers then?'

A rousing three cheers that echoed along the entire length of the platform was followed by two choruses of *For they are jolly good fellows.* Only the density prevented a knees up.

At last, crimson and laughing, Charlotte fell into Arthur's arms, snuggling up to him as the crowd, suddenly quiet again, strained their ears to listen to what was happening overhead.

'I sometimes think that to die underground would be worse than being bombed,' a man in the uniform of the Free French said next to them. Another latecomer, he had squeezed in while the singing was going on. He extended a hand to Arthur. 'I understand I must congratulate you.'

'Thank you.' Arthur's arm round Charlotte tightened. 'I'm a very lucky man.'

'You are, monsieur, you are,' the French officer said, staring admiringly at Charlotte. 'I have a feeling I have seen you, mademoiselle, somewhere before.'

'Maybe from the pages of a magazine,' Arthur volunteered proudly. 'Charlotte was a model for Chanel until the war.'

'You lived in Paris, mademoiselle?'

'Yes.' Charlotte's expression changed. 'I had to leave when Paris was invaded. As an Englishwoman it seemed foolish to stay.'

'I think quite a lot of English people stayed in Paris. As far as I know the Germans do not harm them.'

'My brother is in the Army. We are a very military family. It didn't seem wise.'

'I see.' The officer nodded and then he leaned his head back against the shiny walls of the tube and wearily closed his eyes. Charlotte realized that he was very tired.

'Have you come from France?' she whispered, but he was asleep. She nudged Arthur to move up, they were so squeezed together, and, as he did, the Frenchman fell sideways, his head resting on Charlotte's shoulder, his hand clasping her waist. Seeing the indignation on Arthur's face Charlotte shook her head.

'He's dead tired,' she whispered. 'There's nothing personal in this. I bet he's been on some mission to France. See how worn out he looks.'

She gazed down at his face again and briefly, as if in a moment of hallucination, she saw Paolo there, leaning on her breast as he would before settling down to sleep. The man had a long, thin cavernous face like Paolo and deeply recessed eyes like a man of the Italian Renaissance. His sculpted mouth was curved, his cheeks slightly concave. His black, straight hair sprang back from his forehead as Paolo's had. They could have been brothers. The Frenchman sighed and a little smile suddenly played on those stern lips as though, in his dreams, he was – like her – remembering happier times. His hand tightened round Charlotte's waist as his face snuggled deeper into her shoulder. Charlotte found herself clasping him on the other side or he would have fallen completely onto her lap. She felt strangely, unexpectedly content.

The next day she had promised to marry Arthur.

'There's a letter for you,' Rachel said, her face drawn and anxious when at last they got home. Spending the night in the Chancery Lane tube shelter herself she'd been constantly worried about the whereabouts of Charlotte and Arthur. '*And* his unit wants Arthur to ring them urgently.'

'We're getting married, Mummy.'

'Good,' Rachel said, scarcely appearing to hear what was being said. 'St Paul's took a direct hit last night. Paternoster Row is in ruins. A lot of publishing firms will be in ruins too. The windows have all gone from the office again. God knows how we escaped a direct hit.'

'I hope you weren't there,' Charlotte said reprovingly, her long nails sliding under the gummed flap of the official-looking envelope, while Arthur went off to phone.

'We went to Chancery Lane, but on our way we could see the planes silhouetted in the sky by the searchlights above St Paul's. God, how I hate them! When are you getting married?' Rachel was also opening her post, pointing to coffee and toast which had suddenly appeared from the kitchen. 'Did you want bacon and eggs or something? I brought both from the country, thanks to Hugo.'

'I think Arthur would rather like that.' From the normality of their conversation one would never imagine that none of them had had a wink of sleep. Charlotte was reading the letter. Her brow creased. 'I'm so whacked that I'd like a few hours' sleep before my wedding.'

'You're not *serious*?' Rachel glanced up at her, half smiling.

Charlotte raised her eyes from her letter. 'Arthur *does* want to get married, Mummy. I feel mean that I've kept him waiting so long ... he wants babies, that sort of thing. I didn't know. I'm getting a bit long in the tooth.'

'Well of course he wants babies, darling. Every man does.' Rachel looked at the door through which Arthur had gone to the phone. 'I didn't think *you* did though.'

'Well I thought a lot about it last night. Arthur thinks he might have to go abroad. Life is so uncertain and – he *is* a brick, Mummy.'

'Oh he *is* darling, and I'm *very* glad.' Rachel rose to embrace her daughter but then the look in Charlotte's eyes surprised her and, as she bent down to kiss her, she paused. 'You *do* want to, Charlotte, don't you?'

'Of course I do,' Charlotte tossed back her hair. 'I mean, it will be a change in my life, but so what? Maybe a new family will give me a purpose. I feel so *useless*.'

'But, darling, a baby in wartime ... at your age.'

'Mummy I'm *only* thirty-four. Weren't you quite old when you had Freddie and Em?'

'Not *quite* as old, Charlotte.' Then Rachel smiled. 'But, seriously, it's not *old* and it would be nice to have babies about again. At one time everyone was having them – you, Hélène, Margaret, Sylvia, then suddenly everyone stopped. This is the new generation. By the way, Sasha's got his Gunner's wings. He's to be a sergeant.' Rachel paused for a moment to let the news sink in. Sasha had refused to apply for a commission and had trained in the ranks. The family admired him but, all the same, it was strange. He was surely the first member of the family ever to hold non-commissioned rank in one of the British forces. But Sasha was proving his individuality, and successfully.

'Sergeant Ferov!' Charlotte's face broke into a smile. 'Well done. Isn't that splendid?' She turned to Arthur as he came slowly through the door. 'Arthur, Sasha's got his Gunner's wings. Isn't that spiffing?'

'In record time. He was first in his class or something ... Arthur, is anything the matter?'

'I have to go to the base immediately,' Arthur said. 'I have to report by tonight.'

'Oh Arthur, that *is* tough.' Rachel stared at him. 'Did you tell them about the wedding?'

'I asked for another forty-eight hours but I have to report back at once. There's something brewing. I fear we're going abroad. There were all these rumours.'

Rachel glanced at Charlotte, but her daughter's expression gave her no clue as to her feelings. Had she hazarded a guess, though, she would have said Charlotte looked relieved. Somehow it didn't surprise her. Her mother's instinct had already told her that Charlotte's reaction to her marriage was all wrong.

151

Charlotte however was studying again the letter she'd received. It was a typewritten letter with an address in Whitehall, also typewritten. It had come in the sort of buff envelope ministries used and there was something definitely official about it.

'Someone wants to see me,' she said.

'Who is it?' Rachel leaned over, glad of the chance to talk about something other than the delayed wedding. Arthur must already be hurt by Charlotte's lack of response to his phone call. She'd glanced at him but continued to study the letter. Sometimes Charlotte, who found it hard to conceal her true feelings, was a very bad actress indeed.

'A David Masters. Anyone know David Masters?'

Rachel shook her head. Arthur continued to look hurt as well as miserable and sat down silently drinking coffee. He didn't seem to take in the fact of the letter at all. Charlotte passed her mother the letter and then she got up very deliberately, as though she'd planned her action, and sat down next to Arthur, taking his hand.

'In the very next leave, I promise,' she said. 'I'll be there in a white dress, carrying a posy when you get off the plane.'

'Promise?' Arthur wrinkled his brow trying hard to smile.

'Promise,' Charlotte said kissing him. 'Hope to die if I tell a lie.'

Mr Masters was a man in his late thirties, maybe early forties, with the inscrutable expression of the experienced civil servant. Charlotte doubted if she would ever recognize him again unless he were pointed out to her, or they met in the same place. There seemed to be lots of Mr Masters scattered about the offices of Whitehall, and the room in which they sat was as impersonal as the man who had written to her. It had a deal table with Mr Masters at one side and Charlotte at the other. He had a pad with yellowish paper in front of him, faintly ruled, and with the Royal crest at the top. In the small room there was a tall filing cabinet, an easy chair in front of a two-bar electric fire and a calendar for the year 1940. A single window looked over another grey stone building, similar to this, at the side of St James's station. It was a depressing place. At first Charlotte thought it was something to do with the Ferovs because, after introducing himself and thanking her for coming, Mr Masters began to talk about France.

Did she know it well? Did she know Paris well? How long had she lived there? Did she speak fluent French? Without accent? Could she pass as a Frenchwoman? Slowly, gradually, the realization dawned on Charlotte that the focus of interest was her.

'We are training agents to send into France, Lady Charlotte. A special organization has been set up with money from the government to assist the Resistance in France. It is highly secret, of course. We were reluctant to approach women but the few whom we have recruited have proved very good indeed. Your work would be largely as a courier going between England and France. You would be dropped by plane and possibly brought back the same way. But I must tell you: it is extremely dangerous work. We can't guarantee your safety.' He sat back and joined his hands in a steeple before him. 'I know you have a family.'

'Yes I see.' Charlotte realized her heart was beating too quickly. She thought of the bombs that had been falling on London all that week; of Birmingham, Coventry and Plymouth, which had been devastated. Bombs didn't frighten her but the idea of this silent, secret war frightened her very much indeed. 'You mean you want me to be a spy?' she said at last.

Mr Masters cleared his throat. He produced a pair of gold-rimmed glasses from a steel spectacle case and placed them carefully on his nose. Then he peered at the pad in front of him beside which there was a folder. Out of this he drew a single sheet of paper on which there were a lot of typewritten words. He leaned over and studied it.

'We do not call it "spying", Lady Charlotte, we call it intelligence. But, technically, spying is what it is and if you are

153

caught you are likely to be shot after being tortured. We leave those we recruit, men and women, in no doubt as to what to expect; but we train them very carefully. What's really important is the fact that you are so familiar with France, speak the language fluently. You will not, for instance, be expected to go to France tomorrow. You will receive training in armed and unarmed combat, parachuting, the use of guns, the planting of explosives, all kinds of things.' He leaned back and smiled. 'Some people love it.'

'But will I be any *good*? I've *never* done anything...'

'Oh I know you were a mannequin, Lady Charlotte; but I believe you are also a horsewoman. You like sports. Your husband was a racing driver. Your fiancé is an RAF squash rackets champion. Your family is well known ...' Mr Masters paused. 'I know I needn't go on but really, Lady Charlotte, you are just the sort of person we're looking for. A patriot whose loyalty is unquestioned, a linguist, a brave woman who coped well with her husband's death. Your family have for generations given service to this country and continue to do so today. I can't help thinking you'll agree.'

Charlotte thought of her three children, her mother, Arthur who wanted to be married, and babies ... how old would she be when this was all over? Would she, indeed, survive?

'You will have time to think it over, Lady Charlotte, of course,' Mr Masters went on, though the expression on his face left one in no doubt as to what he thought her answer would be, 'but I would ask you to discuss it with no one, not your mother or your brother, not even your fiancé. If you come with us you will be engaged in top secret work. No one must know.'

'But they'll know if I go away ...' Charlotte protested.

'You will be attached to the armed forces. Probably an officer in FANY or the WAAF. It sounds innocuous but most of our agents have a rank in the armed services. You can tell your family you've decided to join up.'

'How can I suddenly explain why I've joined up? I was on

154

the verge of getting married. If my fiancé hadn't been recalled to his squadron, by today I should have been.'

'Isn't that fortunate?' Mr Masters said, then, hastily correcting himself: 'I mean, for us? Unfortunate for you and Wing Commander Crewe. I'm sure you'll be able to explain to him that you wanted to do your bit for the country. After the war you can have a grand society wedding at St Margaret's; just the sort your family have always had. Think how happy you'll be then that you served your country. But,' Mr Masters closed his pad and rose, 'think it over, Lady Charlotte, the pros, and cons, your children, your family, Wing Commander Crewe. Then when you have...'

'There's no need.' Charlotte, who was dressed in a black Chanel two-piece costume, a double choker of pearls at her throat, drew on her long gloves. 'You already knew I'd accept, didn't you? Well I have. There is no need to think anything over.'

Mr Masters inclined his head. 'Thank you, Lady Charlotte,' he said. 'I knew my instinct would not let me down, or an Askham fail in the service of her country.'

They shook hands and Charlotte went down the stone stairs, out through the door of the ministry nodding to the uniformed official who had let her in, after consulting a list. He saluted and she smiled.

She walked down Caxton Street, past the tube station into Queen Anne's Gate and into Birdcage Walk. The trees in St James's Park were cautiously burgeoning into leaf and the ducks on the lake swam up and down, enviably ignorant of the fact that London was at war. It was a peaceful scene, the loiterers in the park containing a fair sprinkling of uniforms. Some sat on benches, eyes closed, their faces raised to the sun. To the left was the Palace where the Royal Family remained at home leading the nation by their example. Behind was Whitehall, where opposing parties had united in a coalition to preside over the war. To the right was Downing Street where that doughty old man was inspiring England's spirit to resist.

These were dark days and there were doubtless darker ones ahead.

And she, Charlotte, had also been called. She sat down and removed her little pill-box hat, running her fingers through her hair, tossing back her head, closing her eyes to the sun like the others. There were no doubts now: whether to marry Arthur, whether to have babies, whether to live in London or the country. Her country had called her and, Askham that she was, naturally she would obey.

In a way she was glad that generations of her family before her had made the decision so easy.

PART 2

'...we shall never surrender'

Winston Churchill: speech in the
House of Commons, 4 June 1940

Spring 1942–Summer 1943

CHAPTER 9

'You should come to Cannes more often, Kyril,' Melanie said nervously touching his arm, though she was a little frightened of her son-in-law. He was a person who came and went – one never knew for how long, or why. He never explained himself or the reasons for doing what he did.

He had never seemed part of the family, and yet he had been married to Susan for over twenty years. He was Sasha and Anna's father. Not a person one knew very easily, she thought, squinting at him through the sun, even after twenty years. 'I miss my family, you know,' Melanie continued. 'There are so few of them left.'

'Scattered, rather, Lady Melanie.' Kyril gave her that cold, appraising glance, one of the reasons, she realized, why it had been so difficult to get close to him. Still 'Lady Melanie' too, after all these years, as though they had just met.

He was a detached, forbidding, somehow rather menacing man. Of course he *was* Russian and he *was* dour, but they weren't all like that. There was his mother Irina whose gaiety and laughter had filled the rooms of Askham Hall in the early thirties making her mother, Dulcie, smile again. And there was his father, Alexei, whose cosmopolitan charm and affability had made him so many friends.

'Shall you be staying *long*, Kyril?'

'I have only come for a few days, Lady Melanie. My "*Ausweis*" is only stamped until the end of the week.'

'Oh dear those permits. So uncivilized.' Melanie fanned herself with her handkerchief. It was nearly noon and the sun was already high so that there was a heat haze between her house on the hills behind Cannes and the sea. 'Fancy having to get permission to go from one part of France to another.

However, we've been lucky,' she sighed again. 'The war has scarcely touched us. For all we know there could hardly *be* a war! Is Paris like that, Kyril?'

'Oh no.' Kyril gave his short, mirthless laugh and shifted in his chair. 'There is no doubt when one is in Paris that the country is in the hands of an occupying power.'

'That's what Hélène said. I tried to get her to move down here with the girls, but she refuses.'

'My mother is very fond of her grandchildren,' Kyril said. 'I think that's the reason.'

'Hélène does worry me, though.' Melanie sank back in her wicker chair and put her elegant feet on a wicker stool.

'Why?' Kyril looked surprised. 'Do you care very much what happens to Hélène?'

'Of *course* I care!' Melanie looked indignant. 'She was married to my son. Her daughters are my grandchildren. Of course I care.'

'She didn't treat your son very well.'

'And he didn't treat *her* very well, or *them*.' Melanie fanned herself vigorously; the folds of her organdie day dress wafted about as though caught by a strong breeze. 'They were incompatible and should never have married. Bobby always felt jealous, you know, of his Askham cousins, so ridiculous really. He always thought they were thoroughbreds and he, as it were, was a half breed, which was quite absurd. You must know what I mean, Kyril?'

Kyril was looking ahead, his eyes fastened on the sea, and Melanie wasn't even sure he was listening. She tapped his knee.

'Go on,' Kyril said.

'Well you, as a Russian prince through and through, must know how poor Bobby felt to have a grandfather who was a grocer! Ridiculous to think of it these days, that it should matter so much, I mean; but in those days it did.'

'Without the grocer's money, though, Bobby wouldn't be where he is now would he?' Kyril gave one of his rare smiles and Melanie thought that, at times, in moments rarely seen, he was quite an attractive man. She hadn't known him when he captivated her under-age daughter in Russia in 1921. When he reappeared seven years later, his hair receding and his sunken cheeks testimony to years of malnutrition and deprivation in his state farm prison, he looked about the same as he did now – dour, unsmiling, unforgiving, haunted by the past. Only then he had been a Communist and now, she squinted at him again, what was he now? Did he support Hitler? Could one possibly ask?

'Bobby is a businessman,' Melanie said sharply. 'He has the instinct that his grandfather had, and I must say I'm proud of him. Very.' She looked keenly at Kyril. 'Do you know, he is something like the *twelfth* richest man in England? It's not all inherited – by no means. At least half of his fortune he's made himself. Isn't that something to be proud of then?'

'Yes I suppose it is.' Kyril shifted in his chair. 'Really, the twelfth richest? I didn't know that. Yet for quite a long time he allowed his daughters to live in squalor.'

'Oh no, Kyril, that's not fair,' Melanie said firmly. 'There *was* the money, Bobby assured me of that, but it was misused by Hélène and, I'm afraid, your parents. Your mother has always been good at spending money, but not at saving it, or using it wisely. Maybe that was Bobby's mistake – he was too generous and too trusting. Besides, when the girls are independent, when they have *nobody* after their money, they will be quite wealthy.'

'I see, bread today and jam tomorrow. Besides, it is insulting to imply my parents were after the pittance Bobby made available for the girls – *his* daughters.'

Melanie didn't reply. She put a hand to her head and closed her eyes. It was going to be another tiring day with Kyril who had arrived unexpectedly the day before yesterday. He seemed to thrive on discord and arguments. With her large house overlooking the bay at Cannes and only herself, her husband Denton, Jordan and a few servants occupying it one could hardly not offer him hospitality.

Also he was still married to Susan though it was a marriage in name only. They hadn't met since the war began, and now Susan and Anna had decided to remain permanently in Venice even after Mussolini declared war on the Allies. She had the odd letter smuggled out from Susan who assured her that in Venice one wouldn't know there was a war on, except that there were an awful lot of top Nazi officers hogging the best tables at the best restaurants and the best seats at the Fenice.

From the corner of the terrace Jordan, hands in his pockets, leaned against the wall. For some time he had been watching his mother and brother-in-law. They were an extremely ill-assorted pair, he thought gleefully. Lady Melanie, three times married, with a string of lovers and admirers in between; even now, at the age of sixty-five she was never lacking for a companion to dine and wine her, partner her at bridge or take her to the opera at Monte Carlo or the theatre at Nice.

It was difficult to be dispassionate about one's own mother, Jordan knew that; but even on her worst days Melanie didn't look much more than fifty. Her auburn hair was a rich, burnished copper with barely a streak of grey, and her famous peaches-and-cream complexion as flawless as that of a woman half her age. But then his grandmother had been a beauty at seventy; one of those elegant, graceful women whom very few people could call old.

It was probably the way his mother and grandmother had looked after themselves, Jordan thought. They were both selfish people, though the mothers of numerous children, and took care to put themselves first. And although over the years Melanie had suffered, there was no doubt of that, she had always taken care to distance herself from the sting of immediate grief. She had moved to the South of France where, at least, one had the sun and sea and endless entertainment and none of the family too close at hand except for visits. Yet when he, Jordan, had had to leave Germany in fear of his life to spend months in a private nursing home suffering from acute fear and anxiety, no one had been closer or more understand-

162

ing than his mother. No one more supportive or forgiving. And now no one demanded less. She protected him at the age of thirty-three as she had ever since he was a boy. He was a prisoner, though his place of incarceration was his own choice.

'Oh Jordan, darling,' Melanie called with relief, sensing a movement by the terrace. 'How long have you been there?'

'I just arrived, Mother. Morning,' he nodded at Kyril and slumped in his chair, legs outstretched, a man who was tired even before the day began.

'Just got up?' Kyril said.

'Do you mind?' Jordan stared rudely at him.

'Not at all.' Kyril glanced at his watch. 'Only it is nearly lunch time.'

'Jordan doesn't sleep well,' Melanie said indulgently, moving towards the edge of her chair. 'He has never quite got over his breakdown.' She instinctively lowered her voice. 'He has to be very careful because his nerves are *so* fragile. Aren't they, darling?'

Jordan ignored his mother and stared out to sea, his chin resting on his hand. It was a stance he quite deliberately adopted when the twitterings of his mother annoyed him more than usual. He needed her but she irritated him and he made life hard for her. Often he wished he could make that break, but he didn't dare. He nearly died of fright when the Germans occupied the north of France but they had left the south undisturbed, in the control, ostensibly anyway, of the Vichy government.

'Oh well, I'll see to lunch, and maybe you'd like a drink, Kyril?' Melanie's hands fluttered to her hair, to her dress, smoothing its diaphanous folds as she got to her feet, teetering on her very high-heeled shoes. Helping her as she got up, Kyril thought she would not be out of place in a fashionable pre-war restaurant or salon in London or Paris. She still dressed as she always had; still kept the standards of an aristocratic English-woman of whom much was expected.

'A beer would be very nice,' Kyril said, stretching – not quite knowing what to do.

'Oh, don't disturb yourself. Stay and chat to Jordan. He always longs for someone to talk to...'

Melanie fled, sensing a reprimand from Jordan, whose pale, aquiline face with its permanently disagreeable expression had turned sharply towards her.

Kyril put his hands in his pockets and began to pace up and down, his head on his chest as though he were lost in thought. Then he sat down again, folded his arms and closed his eyes. That done he nodded to himself as though he had made up his mind about something and turned deliberately to the younger man beside him.

'Would you like to come to Paris?'

'Paris?' Jordan stared at him.

'Come and stay with me.'

'Oh I *couldn't* go to Paris.' Jordan looked fearfully back at the house as though expecting to see an armed member of the Gestapo come round the corner.

'Why not? Don't you like Paris? I could do with some company too.'

'How do you mean "too"?' Jordan's tone was insolent.

'I think you're a lonely man. Don't you think it's abnormal that you should live here with your mother and stepfather from one end of the year to the other?'

'No I don't,' Jordan replied. 'And I don't see what business it is of yours.'

Kyril smiled to himself as if finding the situation genuinely amusing and shook his head.

'Maybe I feel it is my business when I see an able young man, a relation of mine, my wife's brother, who is content to let life slip by. Yet once upon a time you were very active. I hear you were an early champion of Hitler.'

'I was an early champion of Nazism but I backed the wrong man,' Jordan scowled. 'Röhm, whom Hitler had murdered.'

'You supplied Röhm with arms.' Kyril said it as a statement rather than a question.

'Only a few. They couldn't possibly have made any difference.'

'Why were you so nervous then?'

'In those days one was.' Jordan's voice sounded tired. 'You've no idea of the atmosphere of suspicion in Berlin in 1934. I felt for a long time that my life was in danger. I suppose your father told you about all this.'

'About the arms part, yes,' Kyril said carefully. 'It was certainly a very silly, dangerous thing to do, to supply one faction of the Nazi party with arms they were not supposed to have.'

'I know that now,' Jordan said bitterly. 'He would have used them to kill Hitler. My God,' Jordan's hands ran over his drawn face, 'it's a wonder I'm still alive.'

'But you are *still* afraid?' As Kyril leaned forward to stare closely at him one of the maids emerged onto the terrace with a tray. On it was a large glass of chilled beer, and a cup with a filter over it and, by its side, a piece of darkish coloured bread and a pot of jam.

'Your breakfast, Monsieur Jordan,' the woman said in French, handing the glass to Kyril who thanked her.

Jordan peered at the filter to see how far the thick black coffee had dripped into his cup. Melanie patronized the Black Market, as did most of those citizens of Nice who could afford it, and so in this household there was no shortage of real coffee, or real anything. Anything could be got for a price.

'The Nazis never forget, you know,' Jordan murmured, his eyes on his cup. 'I am probably on some sort of list. I keep a very low profile here and never go out.'

'Never to the town, never to the beach?'

'Never,' Jordan shook his head, 'never, ever since June 1940. For two years I have not ventured out of the gates of this house.'

'That really is an awful life.'

'One gets used to it, but you see why I can't go to Paris?'

'On the contrary. Eight years is a very long time to expiate a minor sin. You were probably never on any black list at all you know, Jordan. I can easily find out anyway.'

'How?' Jordan stared at him, fear once again showing on his dark, aesthetic, tormented face.

'Well, I am not without friends in the high ranks of the Nazi Party.'

'Oh, it *is* true then.' Jordan studied his rope-soled sandals.

'What's true?'

'Hélène told us you were a fervent Nazi. She said you were horrified when Hitler signed a pact with Stalin, but when he invaded Russia you became more of a fan than ever. You realized how clever he'd been, to fool the Russians into a false sense of security.'

'He played a very clever game. He *is* a very clever man. Of course I don't know him personally; but no one can help admiring him and all he's done.'

'So what is your position in Paris exactly?'

'I have no position,' Kyril looked vague. 'I have a little business here and there. I lead a modest life in the apartment. It *is* rather a lonely life at times and that's why I wondered if you'd like to come and stay.'

'I would like to but I can't.' The sudden burst of animation on Jordan's face faded. 'I'd be found with my throat cut.'

'I assure you, you won't be. At last you will feel free. Wouldn't you like to be friends with the Nazis again? Wouldn't you *like* to feel safe?'

'Yes I would.'

'Then I can arrange it all.' Kyril sat back, smiling.

Suddenly Jordan, breakfast forgotten, stretched his arms as though, wholly and unexpectedly, he had been vouchsafed a vision of the Promised Land which, for so long, had eluded him.

* * *

Melanie was very excited that at last Jordan was to break away from home, and in the company of his brother-in-law.

'I *know* you will look after him,' she confided to Kyril the night before they were due to leave.

'But he's thirty-three, Lady Melanie!' Kyril got as near to an expostulation as he ever got.

'Yes, but you know,' Melanie tapped her brow, 'not really quite normal. He had the most frightful nervous breakdown thinking the Nazis were after him in '34. I'm really surprised he has agreed to go with you to a town swarming with them.'

'He is under my protection.'

Once again they were on the terrace, only looking at the moon rather than shaded from the sun. Jordan had gone to bed and Denton was spending the evening in Monte Carlo at the casino, a favourite haunt. Melanie was a little nervous, but still quite excited at the departure of the son who had, much as she loved him, been something of a millstone round her neck for the past eight years.

'You *are* a Nazi then?' Melanie crossed her arms. 'I did wonder. Hélène said you were.'

'Hélène? Why did you talk about me?'

'Oh we talked about everybody,' Melanie said frankly. 'You know, family and friends, a good old gossip. Hélène actually said that we must be *careful* of you...'

'Indeed?' Kyril was aware of a feeling of anxiety. 'Why would she say that? I'm her brother.'

'She doesn't trust you.'

'But *why*? What about? She isn't involved in politics is she?'

'Oh not *politics*,' Melanie tugged at her pearls. 'But I am a *bit* worried about her.'

'But Hélène does nothing all day except wander about and drink coffee. She tried to get a job as a mannequin but no one wanted her.'

'Oh she does quite a lot *I* can tell you.' Melanie smiled mysteriously. 'Well I can't really because what she did tell me when she was here with the girls was a secret.'

'But you can tell me, I'm her brother.'

'Ah but she doesn't trust *you*!' Melanie wagged a finger at him. 'I do though and, quite frankly, I don't really see what is wrong with supporting Hitler. Denton and I spoke out quite openly for him before the war. Now of course we can't. He has done *marvels* for Germany, brought her right up from the bottom. He hates those Communists whom we all hate and, personally, *my* wish is that he and England make friends and we can all live in harmony again.'

'That's exactly my wish, Lady Melanie,' Kyril said with as much emotion in his voice as Melanie had ever detected. 'You remember that for so many years I was a prisoner of the Bolsheviks, a witness, if one were needed – there are so many hundreds of thousands – to their ruthlessness and greed. I think Hitler has the right ideas too and he has been misunderstood by the democracies. His back has been pushed to the wall. Why, in France he has done all he can to conciliate people he has conquered. Look,' Kyril spread his arms towards the town of Cannes, the line of coastal villages, 'he could have swarmed all over here if he wanted. But did he? No. He wisely let the French govern themselves. Marshal Pétain is a fervent admirer of Hitler.'

'And *he* should know,' Melanie said, 'the hero of Verdun.'

'Quite, *un vrai français* if ever there was one. A loyal patriot, no one can doubt that. The Germans have behaved impeccably in France, an example to the world of the humanity of a conquering nation. In Paris the French police the streets and there is only the minimum German presence, I assure you. Why, France is even allowed a small army of her own.' Kyril laughed. 'It's quite absurd how good the Germans have been. I don't quite understand it.'

'I don't understand it either,' Melanie shook her head in bewilderment. '*I* don't understand why everyone doesn't think as you and I and Denton. Why should Hélène for instance ... oh I shouldn't say.' She put a hand to her mouth as if biting her tongue.

'But *do* say, I'm her brother ...' Kyril prompted, leaning forward.

'Well I know you wouldn't do her any harm, and you *may*, just, help to stop her doing anything foolish, as I fear she is.'

'Of course I will.' Kyril's face was creased with brotherly concern.

'I really think she may get into serious trouble, and maybe a word from you now...'

'Then you have to tell me, don't you?' Kyril looked severe, 'or I can't help her.'

'Exactly, that's what I told Denton. I said I wanted to tell you and he said he didn't think I should; but I'm sure that if he were here he would.' Melanie drew her chair closer to Kyril's. 'I still feel I should be discreet though, and so must you.'

'Yes, yes,' Kyril said impatiently.

'Well I don't know *how* involved she is or really what she's up to – and you'd think, by the way, that with three young children she'd be more careful – but she did ask *me* if I could possibly put up, just for a few days, escaped English airmen, Jews – Jews mind you! – people who were fleeing from the regime.'

'How could you put them up?' Kyril looked genuinely astonished.

'Exactly. I ask you?'

'But I mean where would they come from?'

'As far as I understand it,' Melanie's head was practically touching his, 'from Paris or even further north. Of course for English airmen I would do anything – I am, after all, English – but their best bet, in my opinion anyway and Denton's, would be to give themselves up to the Germans who would be sure to look after them and treat them properly. As for the Jews ...' she briskly dusted her hands, 'what has happened to them they have brought on themselves. I wouldn't lift a finger to help them. Everyone knows the Jews control most of the world's big financial institutions. Anyway I told Hélène no quite firmly and begged her to have nothing to do with it either.'

'What did she say?'

'I think she was rather surprised by my reaction, to tell you the truth. She asked me to forget completely what she'd said. I did actually,' Melanie looked around, 'until tonight and my conversation with you has reminded me again. But I'm glad I spoke. I should hate Hélène to get into any trouble.'

'So should I,' Kyril said grimly and, in the dark, he savagely dug the nails of one hand into the palm of the other.

It was odd to be entering one's own home as though one were a stranger. Cap in hand Ralph stood in the huge hall of Askham Hall and looked around. Nothing had changed, though he could hear the sound of many childish voices from different parts of the huge, cavernous house. He'd hardly reached the hall when Cheryl, arms outstretched, a big smile of welcome on her face, ran down the stairs to greet him.

'Ralph, it's been so long!'

She put her cheek up to him and, nervously, Ralph bent and pecked it. This was not quite the welcome that, arriving unannounced, he'd expected.

'Yes it has,' he said. 'Er...'

'Come, let me show you round.' She tugged at his arm as if to lead him through the door that had once been the small reception room where unexpected callers, like himself just now, were asked to wait until someone was sent for to see them. Estate workers and obvious menials were taken round to the back, but anyone calling dressed in collar and tie was asked to sit in the parlour, as it had been known when Ralph was small.

'Cheryl ...' Ralph stood his ground and Cheryl stopped, turned and gazed at him. It was odd he thought how beautiful she still was and yet what little appeal she now held for him. Was it *possible* he had ever been so helplessly in love with her?

'Cheryl, I've come to talk...'

170

'I can sense that Ralph ... but...'

'I *would* like just to have a few words with you in private and at once,' Ralph persisted. 'Hugo is waiting for me in the car outside.'

'Oh, you brought him, did you? For protection?' It was significant how easily the bitterness returned, the old 'barbed' Cheryl.

'Of course not. He's giving me a lift to London where he has ministry business.'

'He must be one of the few people in the neighbourhood to have any petrol,' Cheryl observed sulkily. 'I finished my ration ages ago. I'm learning to ride a bicycle.'

Despite himself Ralph smiled.

'I wish you luck. Hugo has an allowance as a farmer and I have too as a serving officer. I've been down to have a look at the farm. I may be sent abroad...'

'Oh?' Cheryl succeeded in propelling him, at last, into the small parlour. 'Have tea anyway?' she said.

'I'd like that.' Ralph smiled as Cheryl rang the bell.

'We still have a few servants left,' she said. 'I wish I'd known you were coming.'

'I really didn't have time. Hugo wanted me urgently to discuss business and ... I'm expecting to hear in London that I'm being sent overseas.'

'Do you know where?'

'If I did I couldn't tell you, I'm afraid. Anyway I don't.'

'Oh Ralph.' Cheryl, in the act of lighting a cigarette, put her hands onto her lap instead. 'It *has* been a long time hasn't it? Too long. No trust left is there?'

'I couldn't tell anyone, Cheryl, not even my mother.'

'Oh well.' Cheryl gave the fey laugh that, Ralph recalled, had once made his heart thump, but now left him completely unmoved. What he had told Jenny was quite true. He had fallen completely out of love with his wife. Not a spark was left.

'If you can't tell your mother it *must* be serious.' Cheryl

171

finally lit the cigarette and blew out the match. 'Now what is it you want to see me about, or did you just come to say hello?'

'I wanted to ask you for a divorce.'

'My dear! Not again.' Cheryl sounded exaggeratedly bored.

'The last time was three years ago Cheryl, in 1939...'

'I said "no" then and I say "no" now. Anyway it wasn't the last time. Your lawyers have written me dozens of letters on the subject...'

'No, but the last time I asked you, personally.'

'Ralph, I remain married to you,' Cheryl humped her shoulders. 'You can come back here any time you wish and resume our married life together. It's what I want. This is your home.'

'But I don't want to, Cheryl, and it isn't.' This was going to be even more difficult than he had expected and, getting up, Ralph paced restlessly towards the window where he could see Hugo waiting for him by the side of the car smoking a cigarette. In the distance an attractive young woman in uniform was walking up the drive with two dogs on leads. Ralph turned to Cheryl.

'I want to get married again.'

'Ahah. I *see*.'

'I can give you grounds for divorce.'

'I dare say you can. Bully for you.' The brittleness that Ralph could now recall so well had returned to Cheryl's voice. At one time, towards the end, it was the only way she spoke to him ... remorselessly brittle and sharp. 'I should have expected it I suppose; but I don't mind. Sin away. I shan't divorce you.'

'But why *not*, Cheryl?' Ralph shouted. He hadn't expected to lose his temper so quickly.

'Because I have everything I want, Ralph,' Cheryl answered sweetly, pausing to greet the maid who had brought in tea. '*I* want to be Lady Askham...'

'You will be Lady Askham...'

'Yes but not the *ex* Lady Askham. I want to be *the* Lady Askham. I want to keep this house.'

172

'Cheryl, you will have everything that you have now; the house, your title, the money you want...'

'But I want you, Ralph.' Cheryl began to pour tea into porcelain cups, only a tiny tremor of her hand betraying her nervousness. 'You may not believe it but I do. I've changed. I realize now I was very silly.' She approached him rather timidly handing him the cup, his large khaki-clad form contrasting with her slim, almost fragile figure in pastel colours. 'I would like to be a wife to you again. I know I wasn't a very good one, but I would like to try once more. I know you want a family...'

'You said I couldn't have children,' Ralph said caustically. 'You said it was my fault...'

'Well, maybe we could do something about it. See a doctor.'

'Cheryl, I don't want to be married to you.' Ralph put down the cup untouched. 'Please understand that.'

'The marriage vows said for better or worse, Ralph.'

'That was twelve years ago and we have had the worst of each other. I have now met a woman whom I love very much, and I'd like to marry again.'

'I suppose she's someone you met in the Army?'

'She's a nurse.'

'Yes, I thought as much.' Cheryl showed her gleaming, even teeth and offered him a plate of biscuits. Neither of them had yet sat down. 'It doesn't last you know.'

'Ours didn't last either.'

'There were reasons for that. Your family, especially your mother...'

'Your greed...'

'Oh Ralph *please*, don't be insulting! I was *never* greedy. All I did I wanted to do for you, as your wife...'

'Ah Cheryl, what *is* the use?' Ralph looked at his watch and then out of the window where the girl, much closer now, was within hailing distance of Hugo. 'I can see it's no use talking to you.'

'Anyway, if you're going abroad there won't be much time

173

for married bliss, will there? With anyone? Oh Ralph,' Cheryl's carefully controlled voice broke at last, 'I *did* hope we could start again. Maybe when you come home you'll see I'm doing the best thing. Stopping you making a disastrous marriage with someone who is just after your title and wealth ... well what wealth you have left. Not much, from what I hear.'

'She's not like that!' To his dismay Ralph found himself shouting again.

'I'm sure she doesn't appear to be *now*. Ralph, to change the subject, would you like to see round my little school? You would never have believed the things I've done. I'm so proud...'

But Ralph swallowed his tea, grabbed his cap, and made for the door.

*

Hugo had been watching the young woman dressed in uniform, with two strong red setters running on long leashes in front of her, walk up the drive. As she got nearer he realized that they'd met before. The girl stopped and, smiling, put out her hand, recognizing him too.

'Hello! I'm so glad you got back safely. Last time I was here you were lost in France.'

'My goodness, that was two years ago.' Hugo smiled and shook hands. 'You're Cheryl's daughter, aren't you?'

'Amelia. Amelia Lee.'

'Whatever happened to you?' Hugo indicated the uniform.

'Well as soon as America entered the war I went home and joined up. We've always kept our American nationality. I've been sent over here which is very nice. I'm a wireless operator.'

'That's very responsible.'

'Luckily I'm stationed not far away, so I can see quite a lot of Mummy. She's doing the most wonderful job here.'

'So I've heard.' Hugo was guarded.

'You don't like her much, do you?' Amelia looked at him closely.

'She doesn't like me. We never got on.'

'I don't know why. I think you're kind of nice.'

Hugo was aware once again of the feeling he'd had about the girl the first time he saw her. He'd thought about her quite a bit after that, even when toiling along the refugee-strewn roads of Northern France. But then so much had happened and the image of Amelia had fled. In her uniform she looked even more attractive than before.

'My mother had a very bad time with the Askham family,' Amelia said solemnly. 'They never liked her.'

'I think it was six of one and half a dozen of the other,' Hugo said. 'It's a very long, complicated story.'

Amelia considered him gravely for a minute, the bottom of her lip caught in between her even white teeth. Like Cheryl, she was dark, trim, neat. Her beautiful breasts were enhanced by the severe lines of her uniform jacket and Hugo could imagine taking her to bed. He wondered if the desire showed on his face. Guiltily he looked away.

'Would you like to come in and have a cup of tea? Are you waiting for someone?' Amelia pointed towards the Hall.

'Ralph.' Hugo swallowed.

'Lord Askham?'

'Cheryl's husband.'

'Oh my! Did she know he was coming?'

'I don't think so.'

'She sure missed him. She does love him, you know.'

Hugo looked at the ground. 'Could I see you sometime? I could try and explain it all to you.'

'Of course.' Amelia looked delighted, and bending down unleashed the dogs and let them scamper away towards the meadow.

'Your mother won't be very pleased, I warn you.'

'Then I won't tell her.' For a moment there was rather a naughty look in Amelia's eye. She reached under the flap of her uniform pocket and took out a pad and a gold pencil. Her tongue once again between her teeth she scribbled something on it, tore out the small sheet, and gave it to him.

'You can call me here.'

'Thanks. I...'

But at that moment he saw Ralph coming quickly from the house making towards the car.

'This is Ralph,' Hugo began, as if explanations were necessary. 'Ralph, this is...'

'Please, I've no time for introductions, Hugo. Take me away from this place. Do forgive me,' he said politely to Amelia who had stepped back, her pleasant expression replaced by one of concern.

Ralph abruptly turned his back on her and climbed into the car. After a second Hugo followed him and got into the driver's seat. He leaned out of the window to give Amelia a wink.

'See you,' he said and he looked towards the house.

But of Cheryl, ominously, there was no sign.

CHAPTER 10

Stefanie Lighterman leaned against the door of the bedroom she shared with her sisters. Her eyes were tightly closed and her breathing irregular. In a house, a life, so full of mysteries, she was continually creeping along darkened corridors to listen at doors and scampering back again. The curiosity that pervaded Stefanie's life seemed absent in that of her sisters who were content, once in bed, to go to sleep. But not Stefanie. She would lie there for a long time watching the shadows on the ceiling and reviewing in her mind the events of the day.

Usually, not always, they seemed to revolve round her mother. Since they had come to live in cousin Charlotte's apartment the tensions between her grandparents and her mother had grown acute. Living alone with Charlotte it was quite clear that her mother hadn't wanted them there. There was a state of war between Hélène and Prince Alexei whose origins Stefanie didn't know; but there was so much she didn't know, could hardly guess at. This seemed part of the price they had to pay for living with their mother again.

Had her mother wanted them, the children? She said she had, but she didn't behave as though she meant it. She was out a lot. Sometimes she took them to school but mostly, now that Stefanie was older, fourteen in this third year of the war, she took the smaller ones with her. She was big enough now to go on the streets by herself, to do some light shopping at the boucherie, the boulangerie or the alimentation for grandma. She was always told to go and come back as quickly as she could. Not to speak to *anybody* but, if someone stopped her, to run as quickly as she could back home.

But what her sad, bored, preoccupied mother did during the day Stefanie didn't know. Sometimes she ate with the family at lunch time or in the evening, but mostly she didn't. It was like not having a mother at all; as though she were just visiting, or a paying guest. Uncomfortable.

But occasionally Stefanie, a light sleeper, was woken by movement at night. At first she was frightened, then she got used to it and, gradually, she grew curious enough to peep out into the darkened hall. Still she saw nothing, but tonight she had ventured to stop outside her mother's room, put her ear to the door and, finally, nervously, her eye to the keyhole.

What she saw shocked her. A man was lying on her mother's bed, fully clothed, but her mother was sitting by his side whispering. They were both smoking. After a while her mother got up and seemed to come to the door, and petrified, thinking she was discovered, Stefanie raced back to her room. Now here she was, back pressed against the door while it sounded as though her heart were going from back to front, side to side, knocking at it.

Not long after, when Stefanie had crawled back into her bed, as exhausted as if she had run a hundred miles, she heard her mother's door open and softly, very softly, a person, or was it two? crept down the corridor, past Stefanie's room and into the hall.

Her mother had men in her room. Why? Stefanie thought of the women one sometimes saw on the street: attractive, nicely dressed women like her mother, who paced up and down smoking – her mother smoked a lot – until they were approached by a man, or men. Some earnest talking would take place and then the woman and the man went off together. Sometimes they linked arms. Stefanie was quite ingenuous about the ways of the world and neither her mother nor her grandmother would have dreamed of telling her the facts of life; but she did have an idea about why those ladies paced up and down the streets and what they were called. She guessed what happened in her mother's bedroom when the men came.

Dry-eyed she stared at the ceiling. Her mother was a *poule*.

* * *

The Café aux Yeux Bleus was not one of those smart cafés where people, even in wartime, foregathered to drink ersatz coffee on the pavements, to see and be seen. It was a local café where the men mostly met to drink what they could, to drown their sorrows and play cards. There was a lot of talk, of course, about the war and the occupation. But in the two years since the Nazis had come most of the inhabitants of Paris had settled down to life as an occupied nation.

It was known there was a Resistance movement but not who belonged or how many. There was the occasional shooting on the street, talk of executions at Mont Valerian, and the Gestapo had a grim building on the Avenue Foch where all sorts of unpleasant things were supposed to happen. If one were wise one kept well away from opposition to the regime and then one was left in peace.

In Paris, as elsewhere in occupied Europe, the efficient German war machine tried to propagate and, where possible, implement the concept of *Gleichschaltung* – in other words the conformity principle. Everyone must do what they were told for the common well-being and all would be well.

This suited the majority of Frenchmen, most of whom were glad to see the end to hostilities, to the return to their homes of some of the two million men who had been called up. Of those who escaped to England most opted to be repatriated rather than join the Free French Forces. For most French men and women, as for those in Belgium and the Netherlands, the war was over.

But for a few it was not. It became intensified. It was helped by an organization in England which had been set up especially to help and encourage the resistance movements in France and other occupied countries. A system of *réseaux*, or circuits, had been established, each of which had a leader and a means of communication with the headquarters in England: the Special Operations Executive. It was from here that planes were sent with wirelesses and supplies, including guns and bombs, and new operatives to help and encourage those in the field. The toll in lives was high.

In retrospect Hélène seemed made for the Resistance. From the day that Charles Leroux called to see her up to this moment when, in the Parisian sun on an August day, she sat waiting for him outside the Café aux Yeux Bleus, she had not only carried out valuable work for the organization, but she had helped to rescue half a dozen Jews and at least as many British and Allied airmen. These had been found wandering in France after their crippled planes had failed to make it across the Channel after returning from a mission.

Hélène was used to the secrecy from her affair with Jamie Kitto and, indeed, she rather enjoyed it. She had found that the excitement of that illicit affair and the excitement of operating against the German occupiers aroused in her very similar emotions. She felt more alive, more eager for life. She moved around in a kind of high fever of activity, of sensitivity that supercharged her existence and suddenly made it, from being singularly drab, worthwhile. She had been accepted as an agent in the field by London. She had become an official statistic which might be useful after the war when accounts came to be settled between those who had collaborated and those who had not.

Of course when she had been married to Bobby she had had the stimulation of an open bank balance for whatever she wished to buy. She could go where she liked, within reason, but when Bobby called she had to obey. She shared her life with a man she didn't love, and this in itself was a kind of prison. Her affair with Jamie momentarily released her from it until she was put inside a real prison for years and life became normalized again – the sort of existence she had endured, on and off, ever since she had left Russia.

Now it was all excitement again. The dreariness of the routine of living with her mother and father, seeing to the needs of the children, was forgotten in the thrill of secrecy, danger, flirtation with death.

The locals were quite used to her waiting on the pavement or in the back drinking the black coffee or, occasionally, a glass of wine, until the man she always waited for joined her. It was always the same man and it was assumed they were lovers meeting clandestinely. As such they were treated with respect and left alone.

Hélène stirred her coffee and lit a Gauloise. She could always see Charles coming out of the road opposite, move quickly across the square and approach the café without looking to right or left. He would have made quite sure, several blocks away, that he wasn't being followed. She realized that she was waiting for him with an even sharper sense of anticipation than usual because they hadn't met for a month. He'd been in England. One or two of the regulars commented on the fact they hadn't been seen for some time and she smiled. Now he was here.

'*Le voilà!*' one of the men said, pointing with his finger in the direction of the small street and Hélène felt herself tremble and stubbed out her cigarette.

They always kissed on the cheek to encourage the idea that they were lovers. Then, her hand tucked into his, he leaned forward and began rapidly to talk.

Today was no exception but, before sitting next to her, he gazed at her for a moment or two. The peck on the cheek seemed more intimate than usual and the clasp of his hand especially warm. Then, as usual, they moved inside, taking seats at the back and the players inside at the table, the stragglers at the little dark bar in the corner, averted their eyes, pretending they weren't interested.

'How was it?' Hélène whispered, her lips brushing his cheek.

'I missed you.'

Was it a game? He looked into her eyes and she knew it was not.

'I missed you too,' she said.

'Really?'

'Really.' The pressure of his hand was comforting.

Briefly, speaking in rapid French, he began to tell her about his visit, about his complaints that the sprawling *réseau*, of which he was in charge, was too fragmented, had not enough supplies or wireless operators. Paris was too large he had told them. He must have help. Charles was also able to tell her about the progress of the war and here the news was not good. Greece and Crete were in Nazi hands, Tobruk had fallen and the whole of the British future in North Africa threatened.

'These are very dark days for the Allies,' he concluded. 'While I was there the Prime Minister was criticized in the House of Commons for the defeats in the war. The Axis powers for the moment are completely victorious. But I do have good news, some good news for us.' He squeezed her hand. 'We are to have an extra pianist' (a pianist was slang for a wireless operator) 'and a courier dropped from England. I have asked for a woman because they are more inconspicuous.'

'They have women working for them?' Hélène put a cigarette in her mouth and he lit it for her.

'They have a lot of women. They are mostly half French, or speak fluent French. Now the other thing, Hélène, concerns you.' He put his hand over hers and kept it there. 'Do you know your brother is not trusted?'

'Kyril?'

'Yes.'

'I know he is not to be trusted, but I didn't know it was known by the British authorities.'

'Yes, it is known by them. You see they know so many things in London – your association with the Askhams, with Bobby Lighterman and so on. There is a complete dossier on you. I saw a very senior man in counter-espionage who said they had been alerted by the fact that Kyril is your brother and *his* brother-in-law, who was a well known Nazi supporter in the thirties, is staying with him.'

'That will be Jordan Bolingbroke.' Hélène nodded. 'I knew

he had come, but I haven't seen him. He's apparently afraid to go out.'

'Why is that?'

'He's afraid the Nazis are still looking for him because he supplied Röhm with arms. It appears he so exaggerates his own importance in something that happened many years ago that some people think he is mentally ill. Kyril brought him back to Paris a few weeks ago, shortly after I was there with the girls.'

'And that was when you asked Lady Melanie if she would help with the line?'

Hélène bit her lip.

'It was very silly of me, shortsighted; but she *is* English, a member of a great patriotic family. I did ask her not to mention it to anyone.'

'Might she have mentioned it to Jordan?' Charles looked perturbed.

'Oh no. She would never talk about anything like that with him. He's too frightened, too nervous.'

'And she wouldn't say anything to Kyril?'

'I'm sure not.' Here Hélène was on shakier ground but she tried not to show it. After being accepted by London she didn't want, now, to be put on the list of those with a question mark by their names – unless she had one already because she was a Ferov?

'I hope she didn't,' Charles said. 'If Kyril's name is on the list of the British counter-espionage authorities you can be sure things are pretty serious.'

'How serious?'

'He is thought to be a Nazi stooge, planted in Paris to see what is going on, to inform.'

'Then they must think that I am a stooge too.'

'On the contrary,' his handclasp grew firmer, 'they *know* you are not. You have done too much good work in the year you have worked with me. They know that it has been invaluable for you to hide escapees in your father's home where, as he is

183

a White Russian of pro-fascist leanings, they are undetected. Many of them have spoken personally to the colonel, my contact, of your bravery, regardless of your own safety. There is no doubt about that, or you; but there is worry about Kyril. How often does he visit your home?'

'About once a month. Usually my father and mother go to him, because he seems to have no shortage of money or food and entertains very well. They meet all the top Nazis and collaborationist French there. He gives quite big parties. I never go. I'm never asked.'

'Still I, we, the authorities, don't think it is safe for you to continue to receive the airmen in your home.'

'Why not?'

'It has gone on for too long. People might have noticed and become suspicious. You never know.'

'Then my work is finished? Is it because I am not trusted by the British?' Hélène felt close to tears, but spontaneously he brushed her cheek with his lips.

'My dear, you are trusted, believe me. I have told them my life, and the lives of many others, are in your hands. I want to give you even more important work but for this you must be mobile.'

'What work is that?' The fear suddenly left Hélène's eyes and she looked like an excited child.

'You know we have what we call "passers", people who travel with the escapees down the line? We also can't use them for too long because the authorities recognize them, petty officials like ticket collectors and guards on trains a few of whom are quite eager to betray their fellow countrymen for a few francs and a pat on the shoulders from the *Boche*. A "passer" is thus in considerable danger. They have been arrested, imprisoned, tortured and shot. I am asking a lot from you, Hélène...'

'I will do it.'

'I knew you would.' His hand closed over hers again. 'As the sister of a friend of the Nazis you are not suspected by them. But what will your family say if you start to be away at night?'

Hélène bit her lip. 'They will come to the wrong conclusion.'

'That is?'

'That I have a lover.'

'Then why not let them think that?' Charles's eyes were close to hers so that their lips almost touched. 'Is it so wrong for a beautiful woman to have a lover?'

'I have had a lover before,' Hélène said. 'It led me to disaster.'

'I know.' Charles looked into her eyes. 'It will not do so this time.'

Stefanie knew when her mother moved out of the apartment that it was for good. There had been an enormous row between her mother and grandfather during which the words 'Kyril', 'Jordan' and '*boche*' flew round and around until at last the door of the salon slammed and her mother tore into her bedroom and began to throw some things in her case. The three girls stood outside the door watching their mother, Natasha with her finger in her mouth.

'It's only for a while,' Hélène told them, seeing them at the door and drawing them into her bedroom. 'Grandpapa and I have never got on. I must have some relaxation away from him.'

'Can't we come with you?' Natasha cuddled appealingly up to her mother.

'You want to go back to that old flat by the Gare du Nord? That's where I'm going.'

'To be with you, yes,' Natasha said. Natasha, the youngest, loved her mother the best, seemed to need her most.

'It is too dangerous, my darling.' Hélène's voice was close to breaking.

'Then why do you go?'

'Because I have nowhere else. No money, no other place.'

'I don't like to think of you being in danger, Mama.' Olga

began to weep and, as she put her arms round her to embrace her too Hélène looked at Stefanie, standing a little way back from the others.

'And you, Stefanie? Will you miss me?'

Stefanie said nothing, neither shaking her head nor nodding. She just stood there gazing at her mother, an enigmatic, distant expression in her eyes that Hélène couldn't fathom. Then she said, sadly: 'I can see you won't.'

Stefanie still didn't answer.

Later that evening when Olga and Natasha had gone, weeping, to bed she went to the outside door to watch her mother walk away carrying her suitcase, her bag slung over her shoulder. Her blonde hair was tucked into a ribbon round her head and she wore a short tweed jacket over her dress. She looked a solitary, lonely figure – anyone, going anywhere.

Stefanie, slowly closing the door, watched her until she vanished around a corner. Neither waved. Without a twinge of remorse or pity she banged the door shut as upon a stranger. Anyone, going anywhere. Not her mother.

Those first days in the flat alone with Charles were like the very first heady days with Jamie, when she used to sneak away from Bobby's elegant apartment in the Champs Elysées and climb the hundreds of stairs to her lover's sordid little *pied à terre* in Montmartre. Jamie had considered it rather Bohemian, romantic, but Hélène was quite certain what it was: sordid, and exciting.

The old Ferov flat, with its peeling wallpaper, behind the Gare du Nord, with the perpetual sound of trains running in and out all day and all night, had a similar air of intrigue and excitement. It was the perfect place from which to spy, and also the perfect love nest; the perfect place for her and Charles, who had been attracted from the very beginning, to make love. They had not been lovers before Hélène moved into the flat, but became so soon afterwards. It really had just been a matter of time, and occasion. Charles often wondered how much

186

they'd created the occasion to find the time: how much they decided she should leave her parents' flat in order, not to save others' lives, but to be alone together?

In peacetime Charles had been a prosperous Parisian lawyer with a large practice. He had joined the army before the outbreak of war and was immediately seconded to intelligence. Rather than join General de Gaulle in England he had asked to stay in Paris where he felt he was more useful, resuming his legal career as a subterfuge for what he did for most of the day and night. Yet to be a lawyer in Nazi-occupied Paris wasn't easy. He spent most of his time immersed in frustrating bits of paper, wallowing in masses of documents. But he took great care to keep away from the Germans, never to get into any argument with a Nazi. Never to draw attention to himself.

Charles Leroux was forty years old when Hélène met him. She was the same age. Had they met before the war it is not to be doubted that they would have found the very same attraction that they did in those much grimmer days. But it was not the danger that brought them together; they would have come together anyway.

For a number of years Charles had lived apart from his wife. There was no question of divorce because they were both Catholic. But Charles hadn't particularly wanted a divorce because he hadn't intended to marry again. They had two children who were aged fifteen and thirteen at the outbreak of war. Then they had been sent to their grandparents who lived close to the border with Spain; a part of the world that was to become very useful when Charles became head of that Paris *réseau* which specialized in sending escapees down the line to Spain. Unlike the Ferov family Charles had no doubt about the loyalty of his mother and father, their passionate commitment to freedom and de Gaulle.

Since he separated from his wife Charles had lived alone, but he had girlfriends. When he first met Hélène he had a girlfriend and, although he liked Hélène, he thought her life was too complicated with her parents and her children. But as he got to know her he became seriously attracted. He also knew about her past, as London did. As a lawyer it was not difficult to look up that celebrated case in 1935 when the divorced wife of the fabulously wealthy English businessman had murdered her lover. It made Hélène more intriguing, even more attractive, and also someone dangerous to know: a woman who had lived fully and taken risks. There were elements of the adventurer in both their natures. Charles hadn't even kissed her fully until they were alone in the Ferov flat where they had just set up a wireless in the next room which was waiting for the 'pianist'. Hélène was not much of a cook and never had been but Charles, who had for many years looked after himself, was very good. He was also good at improvising, making quite enticing dishes out of the meagre provisions that were now available in the Paris food stores. In the country it was quite different and sometimes, after he had been to Normandy to meet members of other *réseaux* and plan the drops from London, he would return with some sausages or a fat chicken and cook something really delicious.

Following her departure from the flat, Hélène often found it necessary to talk compulsively about her children. Charles, a father himself, was very understanding.

'She will miss her mother.' Charles poured wine into their glasses. Even in wartime there was always plenty of wine.

'No, she doesn't miss me. She hates me.' Almost always Stefanie dominated the conversation.

'How can anyone hate you?' Charles put down the bottle and, gently drawing back her gown, kissed the nape of her neck. They made love quite naturally and, in the French way, usually before the meal. They made love and then, still in their dressing gowns, they talked while Charles cooked and Hélène, maybe, made the salad.

'I wish I *knew* why she hates me so much. She always has.'

'It is to do with love.'

'How do you mean?' Hélène sipped her wine.

'She loves you so much. It's quite obvious. Yet you do not come up to expectations...'

'She's a very intelligent girl. She always has been. But I often wonder if she heard anything ... you know, when I had people in my room, or even saw anything. Maybe that's why she's so hostile.'

Charles looked alarmed. 'Would she say anything?'

'I don't think so. She would brood on it.'

'Maybe it's just as well you got away.' Charles began cutting up the bread. 'I can tell you that teenage children are very difficult. I was not exactly sorry when I sent both of mine to my parents. What I can't understand is why your girls were never sent to England?'

'Well.' Hélène slumped into a chair. Her gown fell open so that Charles could see her bare thighs. He got a lot of pleasure looking at her like that because it was a factor in possession. 'We left it too late. It all happened so quickly, the fall of France. When Charlotte left it was too dangerous. Besides, did we not think then that England would be invaded too? After a while we began to see that it was no more dangerous for them in Paris than anywhere else. Besides, my mother has always been especially fond of the children, and good to them. They know France. She looked after them when I was in prison. Bobby didn't want them then, nor did his family, the famous Askhams. You would have thought they would have done more, but they did nothing. I'm not sorry we didn't fling ourselves on their charity. We had enough of that when I was married to Bobby.'

'Surely that wasn't a charity,' Charles smiled at her. 'It was a privilege to be married to you.'

'Ha! Bobby didn't think that. He was a vain man. It was a privilege for me, a penniless Russian emigré, to be married to him. The rest of his family thought that too, though they didn't say it. Then my mother was taken up by the grandmother of the present Lord Askham and they patronized *her*...'

'I see you're very bitter about that family.'

'Not Charlotte,' Hélène said softly. 'I am not bitter about her. She was not one of them; married to an Italian and a Latin by temperament.'

'I liked her too,' Charles said, 'the brief time I met her. I wonder what happened to her?'

But just at that moment the 'pianist' Henri arrived, and their minds flew to business, to the reason for which, ostensibly, they were here. They offered him a good meal before setting him to work on the latest messages for London.

CHAPTER 11

During the first leave they shared Ralph showed Jenny the city sprawling below them from the parapet of the Citadel, and recalled that it was in Cairo that his father and mother had first met. Somehow the city seemed part of his heritage, like Askham or St James's Square; his brother Hugo was half-Egyptian by blood, not just by association.

From the parapet the Nile could be seen shimmering in the distance, a broad band of water three thousand miles long from its source in Lake Victoria to the Mediterranean. It was by the Nile that his father had fought in 1898 at the Battle of Omdurman alongside his Uncle Adam and Bobby's father, Harry, who lay buried beside it. Aunt Flora had drowned in the Nile and was buried here in the British cemetery. Ralph was the first of his family to visit her grave and to lay a wreath there.

To the west the pyramids shimmered through the heat haze and, nearer still, the slim minarets of the Mosque of Mehemet Ali, founder of the present ruling dynasty – or rather the dynasty that ruled under the British – gleamed in the sun.

Below them stretched the City of the Dead – thirteen miles of streets filled with roofless houses, the burial places of the Muslims. It was eerie to look upon that lifeless city in a metropolis otherwise teeming with life, for Cairo was severely overcrowded.

'Mother had come over to see Uncle Adam,' Ralph explained. 'He was in the Lancers with my father and Bobby's father Harry. Harry was killed in the battle. He and Aunt Melanie had only been married three months.'

'It seems awfully long ago, doesn't it?' Jenny moved closer to him.

'Aeons,' Ralph replied, comforted by her presence, for even after all this time some events, especially Aunt Flora's tragic death, seemed very close at hand. 'Compare Omdurman, fought with spears and rifles, to the battles of today. And yet I'm not an old man. It's all happened in an incredibly short space of time – just over forty years.'

It was hard now though even to think of the present war because the sky above Cairo was always blue and here, on the parapet, the atmosphere one of almost immeasurable tranquillity. Ralph glanced around and, seeing themselves to be almost alone, he kissed Jenny full on the mouth.

'People might see ...' Jenny murmured, pushing him away.

'You mean I'd be reported to the colonel?' Ralph linked his arm through hers and they resumed their walk round the castle built by Salah Din which still had British guns trained over the city, as it had in the days of Lords Cromer and Kitchener to stifle any possible insurrection against the British.

Jenny looked anxiously around her. It was hard to have to try and pretend not to be in love.

'Someone might see,' she said, glancing round.

'I don't care. If it's any of their business I can tell them that I haven't lived with my wife as man and wife for years and I've several times asked her for a divorce. Had she given me one you probably wouldn't be here, and maybe we would never have seen Egypt together.'

'So perhaps it wasn't such a bad thing.' Jenny laughed shakily, but she removed his arm from hers. 'Your mother and father didn't marry at once then,' she wanted to change the subject away from themselves, 'if you were born eight years after they met?'

'No. My grandmother opposed it.'

'On what grounds?' Jenny looked at him closely and he lowered his gaze.

'Well, in those days, as you say another world ...'

'She wasn't good enough ..?'

'Well the Askhams *were* frightfully self-important then.

They thought they ran the world. My grandfather was one of the old imperialists. I can't remember him very well because he died when I was five. But my father was a great chap. He loved my mother and he stuck out for her whatever the family said. And he made a jolly good choice.'

Jenny made no comment, she didn't want to argue; but, later when they separated after an ice cream at the fashionable Groppi's – Ralph to go to the Army HQ on business and Jenny to lie down in the heat of the afternoon at their hotel – she thought over their conversation on the Citadel in the morning.

Sometimes she wondered what she was doing as the girlfriend of the Earl of Askham. Neither family nor friends knew Ralph was a lord, and for most of the time it was quite easy for Jenny to forget that he was. Ralph was such a natural, good-natured, unaffected person that the inequalities in their backgrounds never worried either of them. But one day it might. Ralph made no secret of the fact that his feeling for her, as hers for him, was permanent rather than transitory. One day, Ralph promised, they were going to marry.

But how easy would that be when all the families became involved – her small and very humble one and Ralph's extensive family; his powerful cousin Bobby; above all, his mother? It was important for the women around a man to get on, but Jenny and Ralph's mother hadn't clicked. It was quite obvious to Jenny that Rachel didn't approve of her. They had met only once, in London the previous winter, before Jenny left Robertswood for North Africa. It had been a stilted, awkward meeting; tea at the Savoy. Very inappropriate for a girl from Cumberland who scarcely knew London and had certainly never been to the Savoy. She had known, moreover, that Rachel didn't want to meet her, that she regarded Ralph as being married to Cheryl – which he was. It was a very strange situation and one that both women found uncomfortable. Tea together hadn't taken long and soon after Jenny had sailed for Tobruk.

Now Tobruk had fallen, but long before it fell Jenny was

evacuated to a hospital in the desert which, had they not been in the middle of a bitter war, would have been quite an attractive place on a promontory not far from Alexandria looking towards the sea.

Ralph was among the new shipment of troops who had been sped out to Egypt after the fall of Tobruk to reinforce Auchinlek's forces. Soon after his arrival Churchill had come for a top level conference and the 'Auk', much loved by his men but considered now an ineffective commander, had been dismissed and replaced by Alexander. A series of reverses not only in the Western Desert but all over the world had induced a mood of gloom among the Allies in the year 1942. Was it really possible we might lose the war? But the Japanese attack on Pearl Harbor in December 1941 had brought the Americans in and, for the first time, their troops, planes, guns and tanks were in the desert too, reinforcing the beleaguered Allied troops exhausted from so many weeks of fighting.

But General Erwin Rommel's men were also tired. They were so tired that he was unable to take advantage of the fall of Tobruk and press on to Alexandria and Cairo. Instead both sides regrouped along a line forty miles long between the Quattara Depression, deep in the desert, and a tiny railway station called El Alamein set amid salt lakes close by the sea.

The Quattara Depression was a long hollow broken up into cliffs through which it was very difficult to get armed vehicles other than by laying wire mesh on the ground. The alternative was to go round the Depression which meant going out into open desert and exposing one's troops to attack from the air.

Thus it suited the Allies to make their stand at El Alamein which forced a kind of bottleneck, excellent for defending Alexandria.

Tobruk had fallen on 21 June and for a while there was chaos. Not realizing that the Axis powers were literally dead beat it was expected that Rommel would press on to Alexandria and Cairo. Many Egyptians actually went out to welcome him, regarding the British, who had been so long in

Egypt, as oppressors – rather as Mehemet Ali had regarded the Turks nearly a century before. The British had subsequently defeated Mehemet Ali at the Battle of Alexandria and had stayed, adding first Egypt and then the Sudan to the Crown.

Many of the indigenous population wanted Egypt to be ruled by Egyptians and they were not alone in this for, throughout the world, rumblings of nationalism coincided with the upheaval of world war.

Because of his injuries at Dunkirk, especially of the effects of inhalation of oil on his lungs, Ralph came close to being invalided out of the Army. In the end he had been given a staff post, and the chance to go to Egypt and be near Jenny that came with it made it hard to resist. But he wasn't a staff man and he wanted to get back to the regiment. When General Bernard Montgomery was put in charge of the Eighth Army he quickly reduced the number of staff officers, sending some of them home and others to service units. Ralph was quick to volunteer for the latter, and was attached to a Guards Armoured Division as liaison officer with the veteran 9th Australian Division. With this went promotion to Major.

As his father had been before him, Major Askham MC, was popular with the troops. No one knew he was an earl, a peer of the United Kingdom, and few would have guessed. He had a standard English accent, a confident but modest manner, a good war record and a way of getting on with the men. Moreover, Ralph liked life in the desert, 'the blue' as it was called, despite the flies and the heat, the poor rations and lack of modern comforts. He liked the rough, tough life, the enforced discipline that was part of it. More than that he loved the desert and its beauty, the pristine mornings and unforgettable sunsets. But he liked coming to Cairo for a few days' leave and, if he could, squeezing a night or two at Shepheard's with Jenny.

Ralph often thought these were the happiest days of his life – days broken by sporadic skirmishes but, above all, re-equipping and training for the day they all knew must come:

flushing Rommel out and sending him and his men falling back into open desert.

By early October it was clear that something was brewing. The artillery were moving up and there was change in the air. It was hot but the intense heat of the summer was passing, and sometimes the nights were so cold it was necessary to wear greatcoats. It was less easy to get leave, to arrange to see Jenny. Ralph knew how Jenny felt, how his mother felt and he certainly knew how Cheryl felt. Unless she changed her mind he would have to stay married to her, but only in name. He would never ever go back to her again. From now on his life, wed or unwed, would be with Jenny.

Jenny was a frank, natural, open girl with the tone in her voice of her native Cumberland. She was good-natured and possessed of a kind of innocence that had nothing to do with lack of sensual experience. She had had plenty of that. She had never hidden her past from Ralph; but it was not a disgraceful past, nothing of which to be ashamed in an age more enlightened than when his parents were young – though Ralph knew that his parents had lived together for a number of years before being married: an outrageous thing for those days. Jenny had known a few men, had been in love once or twice, but for her, as for Ralph, this was the real thing. There were only two major drawbacks: the first was that he was married and the second was the attitude of his mother. This was ironic when one thought of the number of years Rachel had spent hating Cheryl.

It was important in the short time they were able to spend in each other's company, the brief leaves they were able to snatch, not to brood on possibilities that involved a future which might never happen. They were both quite well aware by now of the realities of war and also its fatalities. Ralph had already escaped death and Jenny and her nursing colleagues were surrounded all day by dying men.

And Jenny and Ralph were happy. It was hard not to be

because, apart from their contentment with each other, Cairo was a city of fun. There were many luxurious restaurants where menus were quite untouched by the shortages that affected England and the rest of Europe; one could dine in the open and by candlelight – on terraces by the river or on the very edge of the desert itself. There was the Muski Bazaar to explore, prices to haggle over and a thousand and one churches, mosques and museums to see. There was sailing on the Nile and swimming and sunbathing by the pool at the Gezira Club. There were drinks at the Turf Club, though here it was important also to be seen with other people and not just alone, as it was full of officers newly arrived from England. Ralph played polo against the RAF and Jenny was just one of the many pretty, appreciative women in the crowd of onlookers.

And then it was nearly time for the leave to end, both to return to their posts in the desert where everyone was sure a new battle would soon be fought. Ralph wondered if the atmosphere were not a little like that before Omdurman as he and Jenny strolled, late one afternoon, in the comparative safety and anonymity of the Ezbekiah Gardens which was empty except for other courting couples like themselves also trying to be discreet. Ralph had returned again to the subject of the part Cairo had played in the lives of so many members of his family and had told Jenny, at last, about his father and his mistress, Nimet – about Hugo their son.

'You see,' he said, 'we have a lot of skeletons in the family cupboard.'

'That's not unusual,' Jenny replied. 'Have you ever met Nimet?'

'No. That part of Hugo's life he has always kept very much to himself. When he met her again he went to live with her – he was so overjoyed to find a blood relative *and* a mother at that. Our mother didn't want us to go and see him there, quite naturally. Or here,' Ralph indicated the vast city outside the

197

gardens. 'She's supposed to have returned here when France was overrun. I wouldn't *dream* of trying to see her.'

'Naturally,' Jenny's voice was sarcastic, 'you always defend your mother, Ralph.'

'Well, why shouldn't I? She was *very* badly treated by my father.'

'But why would he want to have an affair if she was so perfect? Did you ever think of that?'

'I never said she was *perfect*.' Ralph sounded annoyed.

'Maybe there were some flaws in her character.'

'Maybe there were.' Ralph looked hard at her. 'We've all got faults, haven't we?'

'We certainly have,' Jenny agreed. 'I didn't mean to be insulting about your mother, Ralph.'

'I think you did,' Ralph said. 'I know you don't like her and it hurts me. My mother is a wholly admirable, wonderful woman. If you only knew ...'

He stopped and looked at her and, as had often happened before, like a mirage in the desert, when he looked at Jenny he saw Rachel. They were physically very alike. In her duty uniform of khaki skirt and blouse, her fair hair tucked under her peaked cap, sunglasses over her blue eyes, Ralph thought this was very much how his mother might have looked in uniform when young.

'I don't want to quarrel with you about your mother, Ralph. I understand her feelings about me.'

'What feelings? She likes you.'

'Are you sure?' Jenny's sidewise glance at him was sceptical. 'Did you ask her?'

'I wouldn't ask Mother that sort of thing,' Ralph said stiffly.

'And she wouldn't tell you the truth either.'

'I think you're being very devious, if I may say so.'

'Oh *certainly* you may, Lord Askham!' Jenny laughed mockingly. 'Isn't it time we peasants were put in our place?'

'That's an absolutely disgusting thing to say.'

'True, though.'

'Not true. I don't want to go on with this conversation, Jenny.'

'Neither do I, except to say one thing more.' Jenny grasped her shoulder-bag firmly by the strap and gazed at Ralph. 'I think your mother *is* possessive, Ralph. I think she's possessive and she's jealous. She doesn't want you to be happy with any woman but her.'

'That's ...' Ralph began but Jenny held up a hand.

'Please let me finish. You told me that for years she disliked Cheryl; now she doesn't want you to leave her! You tell me that she's never had the "airs" of a lady; that she's a democrat, even a socialist, but it's quite clear to me that she thinks I'm not good enough for you. Too rough: a peasant. Or, maybe, she simply doesn't want you to have any other woman but herself. Work that out ... if you can!'

Ralph, beside himself with fury, tried to grasp her arm but she tugged herself away and ran off between the trees before he could stop her. One moment she was there and then she wasn't.

For a while Ralph was glad that she'd gone. He was very angry. He and his mother enjoyed a warm relationship, but there was nothing abnormal about it. It was true she had never liked Cheryl, but he attributed that to her instinct that subsequently proved to be right. He felt that she and Jenny merely had to have time to get to know each other. In many ways they were very alike.

Ralph took a cab back to the hotel and by the time he reached it he half expected to find Jenny there waiting for him. After all, this was their last day of leave, too precious to lose; certainly too precious to quarrel. He felt frustrated and annoyed that she wasn't there and, after visiting their room, he went downstairs to leave a message with the desk clerk and then wandered out onto the terrace for a drink. The sun was setting over Cairo and soon it would be dusk. It seemed terrible to think of spending his last night of leave on his own.

Gradually his anger changed to concern and he began to

fret. There were many ruffians on the Cairo streets, maybe lurking among the trees in the Ezbekiah Gardens. He should have run after her. They should never have had the quarrel. Jenny was too sensitive, too proud. He ordered a drink and gazed moodily at the masses of people still promenading the street. If anything it was busier than ever.

Ever since he had come to Cairo Ralph had been conscious of its association with his parents, the place of their meeting all those years before, of the consequences for them, his family, not least himself. It was because of that momentous encounter that he was sitting on the same terrace where Bosco and Rachel had been introduced to each other, when his mother had first met the formidable Lady Askham, his grandmother Dulcie.

The City of Cairo was founded in the seventh century A.D. by the Arab conquerors who called it *al Fustat*. The material to build the magnificent mosques was plundered from the remains of the temples, pyramids and tombs of ancient Egypt. Before that the capital of Egypt had been the City of Memphis, a few miles further south. Now all that remained of that once great city were a few dusty palms and stones surrounded by desert. It seemed unlikely, Ralph thought as he surveyed the contemporary scene, that a similar fate would overtake the bustling, frenetic metropolis with its contrasts of luxury and squalor.

The street upon which his parents had once looked and at which he was gazing now could have changed very little over the centuries, with its throngs of colourfully clad Bedouin in their striped *kufeihs* jostling with blue-clad black-veiled women, street vendors, barefoot children, innumerable beggars, hands outstretched for the *baksheesh* that Lord Cromer, Consul-General of Egypt at the time of Ralph's parents, had tried in vain to ban. Begging in Egypt was endemic and no amount of legislation could prevent it. Europeans and Cairenes in normal everyday clothes, open shirt, jacket and trousers, going about their business, mixed with the blue, khaki and navy of service personnel. Here and there a Bedouin pulled along a sleepy donkey, sometimes trailing a small wooden cart containing produce from the fruitful banks of the Nile.

But the greatest change since the days when his parents, grandmother and aunts were here was the loud roar of motor traffic jostling its way through the masses, and the strident blare of taxi horns. This and the planes that flew overhead, mostly bound to reinforce and equip the Allied troops in the desert, were the main, perhaps the only, differences between present-day Cairo and the city built by the conquering Arabs twelve hundred years before. The busy scene below him almost had the normality and jollity of pre-war days.

Since the Allies had regrouped at El Alamein the Cairenes had settled down again to the idea of continuing British rule. King Farouk was still in the Khedival Palace and the British presence was as strong as ever. Stronger because more and more troops had arrived to swell the First and Eighth Armies out in the desert. Those Egyptians who had gone out to welcome the Germans, and those who had fled the City altogether, mainly the Jews and those to whom the thought of German occupation was more odious than the British, had long ago slunk back.

The cosmopolitan Cairo of 1898 was not so very different from now, Ralph thought, thanking the waiter who had brought his whisky, except for the dress of the Europeans and the uniforms of many different nationalities. He was staring at the street when suddenly he became aware of someone in a skirt hovering by the side of his table. Thinking it was Jenny his gaze didn't waver, but his heart lifted at the thought that she had sought him out. But maybe the muscles of his face relaxed and his hand shook slightly as he lifted his glass for a familiar voice suddenly said: 'Aren't you going to offer me a drink and ask me to sit down ... you slob.'

Ralph looked up, startled, amazed. A familiar face was smiling down at him and, by her side another familiar face, but one he couldn't at first place.

'Em!' Ralph shouted. 'Em! How in God's name did you get here?'

Rising, he threw his arms around her and hugged her. 'Oh Em, it's *so* good to see ...' He stopped and looked at the man by her side, also in uniform, with the familiar slouched hat of the Australian 'digger'.

'Ralph, you remember Randy Tucker don't you?' Em said.

'How do you do, Major?' The tall man with the weather-beaten face and sergeant's stripes on his rolled-back shirt sleeves stepped forward, saluted and shook hands.

'Tucker! Sergeant Tucker!' Ralph exclaimed. 'What a small world it is. Please sit down.'

Randy looked rather doubtfully around him but Ralph pointed firmly to the chair.

'We're not standing on rank here. We're both on leave.'

'Thank you, Sir.' Randy sat down. Although he was tall he was neat and his movements were economical. He was a self-effacing kind of man, and Ralph recalled quite clearly the occasion when they'd met before.

'Freddie's memorial service,' he said. 'My goodness, that was in 1937. What have you been doing with yourself, Sergeant?'

'Oh this and that, Sir.' Randy spoke carefully, as if reluctant to give anything away. 'I was always a soldier of fortune you know, but I never went back to Spain after what happened to Freddie. It was a dirty war.'

'Well.' Ralph paused to order drinks for Em and Randy. 'All war is dirty from what I can see.'

'It is, Sir.' Randy lit a cigarette and, as he did, one could see the deep furrows on his face. 'You been out here long, Sir?'

'Not as long as I'd like.'

'He was badly wounded at Dunkirk,' Em said, pointing to the ribbon of the MC. 'And then he was nearly drowned in oil which practically destroyed one of his lungs. He shouldn't in fact be here, but he is.' She touched his hand. 'Where's Jenny? I expected to find her with you.'

'She's, oh ...' Ralph looked uncomfortable. 'She'll be here shortly, I expect. Can you explain how *you* come to be here?'

'I'm an accredited war correspondent,' Em pointed to the flashes on her shoulder, 'sent now to cover the campaign in North Africa. As a matter of fact,' she smiled tantalizingly at Ralph, 'if you want the truth, Mum asked me to keep an eye on you ...'

As Ralph made a threatening gesture Randy smiled.

'I don't expect your sister meant that seriously, Sir.'

'Of course she didn't,' Ralph grimaced. 'My sister has ever mocked me. Please don't call me "Sir", Randy. We're not on the field now. I'm going to invite you to dinner and I want you to think of us as friends. We think of you as one, a great friend of the family to whom we owe a debt.'

Randy was the last person they knew to have seen Freddie before he fell at Brunete in the Spanish Civil War. He had brought Freddie's last letter to his mother and his effects, arriving just in time for his memorial service.

'Well, thank you, Ralph,' Randy said awkwardly. 'I'm a rough man, you know, not really used to eating with the officers.'

'Oh please don't talk like that,' Em said. 'We hate it.'

Em was dressed in uniform, khaki skirt and shirt with the green-and-gold tabs on her shoulder. She wore no hat but carried a shoulder bag from which a bulky note-pad could be seen protruding. Em had been in Greece and was sun-tanned despite the bitterness of the fighting going on there. With a true newspaper woman's eye she kept on looking around her as they talked.

'Freddie was like that,' Randy said, accepting his drink from the waiter. 'I'd never have known he was a lord if I hadn't seen the letter addressed to his mother – Lady Askham. We all just knew him as "Freddie". He was completely one of the lads.'

'Ralph is too,' Em said, 'despite that thing on his shoulder.' She pointed to the crown on Ralph's epaulettes, then jerked up her arm and looked at her watch. 'I'm going to see if I can get a room at this place, Ralph, and have a nap before dinner. I haven't slept for twenty-four hours. Can you and Randy amuse each other?'

'I hope so, ' Ralph said, taking her hand. 'It *is* good to see you. It's a wonderful surprise. Don't be long.'

'Dinner at eight,' Em said. 'Don't be late – and do try and bring Jenny. She's the one I really want to see.'

But there was no Jenny when they met in the restaurant of the hotel at eight having dismissed the idea of eating in one of the more fashionable restaurants with French cuisine. Ralph hoped that if Jenny came to the hotel she'd look for him here.

Em knew there was a mystery, but she didn't probe. As brother and sister they had always respected each other's secrets. It was a point of honour in the family not to ask questions unless sympathy seemed indicated and just now, in the case of Ralph, Em didn't think it was. When she came down and saw Ralph and Randy alone at the table chatting and smoking she just slid into her seat without asking why they were three instead of four.

Em had changed into a white linen frock. She wore no stockings and sling-back open-toed sandals. Her freckled, brown face had only a touch of peach-coloured lipstick, no other make-up. Em had straight fair hair and the good looks which were shared by most of her family, except that Charlotte's had been refined into beauty and Em's hadn't. Em looked what she was: a good sort, a strong, practical woman who, without lacking sympathy and compassion, was hard enough to withstand the horrors she had already experienced of the war. Dressed in uniform, like a man, in trousers and military-style shirt, Em was one of the very few women correspondents to have covered the war mainly, so far, in the Aegean. To keep the respect of their colleagues and to be tolerated by the military forces, many correspondents engaged in active combat: it was necessary to act like men were expected to act; not to get in the way, to be dispassionate, discreet and, above all, fearless. Apparently fearless; no one lacked fear completely. But it was important not to show it.

Em loved her world: the travel, the hardship, the uncertainty, the excitement, the fun. It was important to file reports as quickly after the event she had described as possible, and all kinds of dodges were employed to get to the cable offices first – first past the censor, first onto the wire.

It was necessary to move quickly all the time, be on the alert and able to do without sleep. Sometimes Em averaged about two hours a night for nights on end. Some nights, especially when the army was retreating, there was no sleep at all. So far the war hadn't gone well for the Allies and it showed in the weariness of the war correspondents as well as the fighting men. But after a few days' leave, sleep, a bath and a change of clothes, things took on a rosier hue: there was even optimism about the future, now that the enemy had been prevented from capitalizing on the disaster at Tobruk and falling on Cairo and Alexandria as well.

'You'd never think you'd seen a war.' Ralph looked at her admiringly as she sat down.

'Do I look as though I'd just been presented at court?' Em shook out her napkin and gave him a sarcastic smile.

'Well, not quite.' Ralph remembered how Em had flatly refused to join the debutantes who lined up before the Royal Family in their satin gowns and ostrich plumes. It seemed a very daring thing to do in the heyday of the twenties, when Em was seventeen – 1925. Even then she was a rebel, a bluestocking, planning to go to Oxford. Charlotte had been presented though, the year before she met Paolo. How long ago *that* all seemed.

'Did you meet the King and Queen?' Randy stared at her with open-mouthed interest.

'I *have* met them,' Em said matter-of-factly. 'But I was never presented at court. I didn't agree with it.'

'Still doesn't,' Ralph said. 'She'd like a Republic.'

'Let's not get political.' Em leaned over and tweaked his ear before remembering where they were and the fact he was in Service uniform. 'Sorry about that.' She laughed and began to study the menu.

Then as though she'd suddenly remembered something she put the menu flat on the table, joined her hands and stared gravely at Ralph.

'Did you hear that Sasha was missing? I should have told you first thing, but meeting Randy put it out of my mind.' She bent her head. 'I feel awful.'

'That's *terrible*.' Ralph abruptly put down the glass containing his pre-dinner cocktail. 'No, I hadn't heard.'

'I thought you mightn't have. It just came over the wire. A raid on Hamburg. He failed to return with his crew. Everyone's keeping fingers crossed. He hasn't been reported killed.'

'*Poor* Susan,' Ralph murmured. 'As if Kyril wasn't enough.'

'Kyril, at least, is still alive. That we do know. Mummy can't get through to Susan. Bobby is trying too. Apparently he has more power than Reuters and the United Press put together.

'Sasha's our cousin,' Em explained to Randy. 'He's a lovely young man, only twenty. An air gunner in the RAF. The last thing we wanted him to be, but what can you do? He's a sergeant, by the way, too.'

'That really is bad news,' Randy grimaced sympathetically. 'I guess your family sure make their marks in a war. You must feel proud.'

'Our father was out here,' Em said. With her hair loose she looked quite pretty, most unlike her usual self: the practical, hard drinking war correspondent. For the time being she was enjoying being a woman who liked dining at a smart place in the company of men.

'In Egypt?' Randy looked puzzled. 'I thought he was dead.'

'Our father was out here in 1898. Now, what do you think of *that*?' Em stabbed a finger at him. 'You must have heard of Omdurman.'

'Your father was killed at Omdurman?' Randy looked puzzled.

'Don't be silly! We're not that old.' Em and Ralph began to laugh, but suddenly Ralph looked sad. 'Father was killed in 1915 and as you know our brother Freddie was killed in Spain.' For a moment there was silence.

'You know,' Randy lit a cigarette and began to comb the tablecloth with his fork, making narrow little lines like railway tracks on the starched linen, 'I always did think there was something funny about your brother's death.'

'Funny?' Ralph and Em stopped laughing and Em said, 'How do you mean "funny?"'

'He was shot in the back.' Randy looked up to see her reaction.

Ralph and Em looked at each other.

'Oh, not running away or anything, I don't mean that.' Randy hastily corrected himself. 'I don't mean to imply that he was a coward. Didn't mean that at all. No. He was a very brave man. You see,' Randy settled down in his chair and began sketching with his fork as he spoke. Ralph and Em stared at the table. ' Here were the enemy, the Nats in front, here the mountains. There,' Randy drew a little mound behind the front line, 'were a group of farm buildings. They'd been shelled to pieces and were a complete ruin. Now we were all running, here,' Randy gestured again with his fork, 'towards the hills where the enemy were firing *at* us. It was a bit of a foolhardy thing to do, but we were sick of the bastards and wanted at them. We'd got them on the run anyway.' Randy spoke as though he were reliving something that had happened a short time ago. He could have been talking about recent skirmishes in the desert. He'd been with the Australians in North Africa since the opening of the campaign in 1940. Maybe the desert reminded him of that arid plain at Brunete outside Madrid five years before.

'So there was me, here, and there was Freddie, just a bit behind. Freddie called something to me in the din and I didn't hear so I moved a bit closer, waited for him to catch up. I saw Freddie glance behind and, at that moment, he fell back. The

207

rest of us went on running, but I stopped and slithered back on my belly to Freddie, looking at the ruins behind us. I could swear I saw some movement there.'

'An enemy sniper?'

'I suppose so. Yes, a sniper, who got Freddie in the back. Yes a sniper,' Randy banged the table. 'That would be it. Why didn't I think of that? One of the Nats who had got left behind.'

'But why did you think it was anything else?' Ralph felt his flesh crawling the way it had at Dunkirk when one was perpetually one step in front of the enemy, who were pushing from behind. 'Anyone other than a sniper?'

'I guess it was my imagination,' Randy said. 'But you remember that fellow I told you about? The one who Freddie met the night before he died?'

'No, I don't remember,' Ralph appeared to search his memory.

'I do,' Em said, 'because I remember that Randy seemed a bit puzzled by who this person was. I don't know why I remember it so vividly, because it was a long time ago, but I do. Of course we were all so upset about Freddie, and I knew too that I had to tell Mummy about me being pregnant, and she didn't even *know* about Felipe. I guess we all forgot that. But I do remember it now.'

'Anyway, I don't see the connection.' Ralph glanced at his watch. Maybe Jenny would still come even though it was getting late? Maybe she was waiting for him in his room. Surely on the last night she wouldn't be so petty ... but maybe he'd hurt her pretty badly.

'Sorry.' He turned his eyes away from the door.

'Expecting someone?' Em raised her eyebrows.

'I thought ... Jenny. Never mind.' Ralph looked at his guest. 'I think you're trying to tell us something, Randy, but either we're too thick or we can't understand what it is.'

'Well, you weren't there, Ralph. You can't realize the mood. Maybe you can better now because of this stinking war; but the Spanish Civil War was very different, very personal. I feel that

208

Freddie's death was a personal thing – not an accident of war. That he was killed by someone who knew him, and I've never got that feeling out of my mind from that day to this.' Randy slapped the table with his fork and stared at brother and sister. 'I feel *he* knew who killed him and that person was something to do with his past. In other words he knew him long before the war began. Don't ask me why I have that feeling,' Randy paused as though to get the full dramatic effect, 'but I do.'

That night, sweating and alone in the large double bed he had reserved for what he had hoped was to be a night of love, Ralph couldn't sleep, or if he slept his dreams were crowded with vivid moments, so vivid he couldn't tell whether he were asleep or awake. All the memories of the past seemed to crowd in on him, memories connected with Cairo, with the heat – always with the heat – with Spain. Dad and Nimet, Mother and Hugo … passion, love, remorse. But more than anything else was the thought of his brother racing along the torrid Spanish plain in a war he didn't have to fight for a cause which didn't really concern him. Freddie alone, running … running from someone in the past, until he got a bullet in the back?

When fitfully, fretfully, Ralph finally completely woke up he found he was still alone. Jenny hadn't come and the dreams, the bad dreams, still wouldn't go away.

A few days later, Ralph came across Randy again during one of his routine visits to the veteran 9th Australian Division. He thought it was remarkable he hadn't seen him before they'd met in Cairo. Rumours of impending action were rife and the men were keen to get going, restless and polishing their bits and pieces over and over again, oiling their guns and tidying out their tents.

Randy hailed Ralph from a distance, this time with more respect, and the two men saluted as Randy, wiping his hands on a rag, came towards him.

'I thought it was you, Sir. Thank you very much for the other evening.'

'Em and I very much enjoyed it.' Ralph squinted at his new-found friend in the hot sun. 'We must do it again. Em is here to cover the campaign.'

'Doesn't seem like a job for a sheila,' Randy shook his head and scratched his nose. 'She sure is a competent girl, though, eh?'

'She'd be flattered to hear you say that.' Ralph paused and mopped his brow. 'There's *one* thing I was going to ask you.' Ralph tucked his cane under his arm and sat on a tin can in front of Randy's tent. With the cane he began drawing in the sandy desert rather as Randy had drawn on the tablecloth in the restaurant. 'I can't get it out of my mind about this man you thought Freddie knew.'

'Yes, Sir.' Randy remained standing, gazing at the ground.

'Just why do you think he was from the past? That he wasn't a Spaniard, someone, perhaps, Freddie had known in Madrid?'

'Oh he wasn't Spanish, Sir. That's why I thought it was so singular.'

'English then?'

'No, Sir.' Randy scratched his head, the stub of a cigarette hanging permanently from his lips. 'He was foreign; not Spanish, not English, not French. Something like mid-European, you know, Czech or Hungarian, something like that. Russian maybe?' He brightened. 'Come to think, it could be Russian. He looked rather Russian too, rather Slav with high cheekbones. I didn't see him clearly, mind. The only time I saw him it was getting dark. We had a lot of Russians there, you know. They were supposed to be on our side.' Randy laughed.

'Russian?' Suddenly Ralph felt that crawling sensation again; the awareness, the apprehension of danger, the unknown.

'Yes, Balkan. Russian. Something like that.' Randy brightened as if with the effort of remembering he was producing results and slowly he traced a line down his face with a nicotine-stained finger. 'He had a deep scar on his chin, I seem to recall,' he said at last. 'Maybe it's my imagination but, come to think, I'm pretty sure of it now. I think if ever I were to see him again I'd know him. Know him by that scar.'

CHAPTER 12

Sasha Ferov crouched low under the bale of hay that covered him. His heart made such a racket that he was sure it could be heard by whoever it was coming up the steps to the loft. From the viewpoint of the farmhouse they had seen the car begin to crawl up the valley and the farmer's wife had quickly taken him to the loft, as planned, and covered him carefully with the coarse hay gathered the previous summer. The hay provided much needed food for the cattle because cattle food, formerly imported from abroad, was hard to come by.

Yet here in the Ardennes where the Germans had struck through in May 1940, before the fall of France, there was plenty of everything even though the enemy presence was quite widely felt. When a line was drawn dividing occupied and unoccupied France the Ardennes was supposed to be free of troops but, because of its importance, quite a number remained there to keep an eye on the border where the German Panzer divisions had first attacked.

Now it was February 1943 and it was very cold. But Sasha wasn't cold. Heated by fear he waited, wondering if these months on the run after his Lancaster had come down on its way back from a raid on Hamburg had, after all, been worthwhile. If he'd given himself up he would probably now have been in safety, if not comfort, in a prison camp awaiting the end of hostilities, instead of enduring the cold and damp, the uncertainty of capture. By the way things were going, it had seemed that the end of the war would not be too far off. In 1942 Germany had appeared to be winning. Cut off from news since the crash, Sasha knew very little about what was happening in the world beyond the remote farmhouse in the shadow of the Ardennes forest where he had been since painstakingly making his way across Germany, hiding by day and travelling by night, stealing to keep alive, always on the run. Luckily Sasha spoke reasonably good German so, in the times when he was exposed, he could get by.

French Sasha spoke fluently, having been half brought up there, and when he crossed the border into France he immediately felt at home. He also felt at the end of his tether. He was exhausted, he was cold and he was starving. He stopped at the first farm he came to and threw himself on the mercy of the farmer, saying that he was a fugitive from the Germans in Paris, a native Frenchman. By chance as well as good fortune – because there were many who collaborated with the enemy – he had come to the right place. The Viollets were no friends of the *Boche* who had driven them out of their farm, killing all their cattle and overrunning the land during the invasion of France. It was with difficulty they had got started again and they welcomed a deserter to their home, even though they might be punished for hiding him. When they discovered that he was a British airman on the run they knew the penalty for concealment was death.

The Viollets had two sons who worked on the farm and a daughter still at school, Christiane. Christiane had been warned not to talk but that day when they saw the car sneak through the valley below they wondered if, by chance, she had inadvertently given him away.

Now lying in the sweet-smelling hay – as long as he lived harvest time would have nostalgic associations for Sasha – he wondered if his kind friends would pay the penalty for helping him. He thought of Claude and Marie Viollet and their three children; of the farm animals, the dogs and the cats he regarded as his friendly companions during the considerable amount of time he spent on his own, out of sight in the attic, reading.

'Sasha!' He jumped as his name was whispered loudly, but still he didn't move in case it was a trick. It was some time since he had heard the car drawing up in the farmyard and all the hens squawking with interest because people in cars were few and far between, unless they were officials come to check up on one's papers and permits.

'Sasha!' The voice spoke again quite normally. 'It is I, Georges. Come on. I know where you are. It's quite safe to come out.'

Sasha moved the straw and peeked above it and there, standing over him, was Georges, the eldest Viollet boy, who the day before had set off for the town to buy provisions and spare parts in the horse and cart the Viollets used for transport, yet had failed to return at night.

'Georges!' Sasha threw back the hay as, his face transformed by a smile of relief, he stood up and shook himself. 'You gave me such a fright. Was it you in the car?'

'Yes, but not only me. I have contacted the local Maquis who will arrange to send you to safety. That's why I didn't come home.'

'The Maquis?'

'The Resistance. Those who refuse to work for the Germans.' Georges spat savagely on the floor. 'They live in the forests of the Ardennes, brave men and women prepared to rise up with arms when the liberation begins.'

'Is the war news as good as that?' Sasha began to pick the pieces of straw out of the thick sweater that had belonged to François Violett, the younger son who was Sasha's age.

'In Europe there is nothing new, but in Africa the British are pushing back the *boche*. Now, look, Sasha, my friend can help you to return to your country. It is what you want?'

'Of course!' Sasha's worn face glowed with happiness.

'It *is* dangerous,' Georges warned.

'But it is dangerous staying here, and for you too. Believe me I died a thousand deaths when your mother and I saw the car sneaking up the road. I don't think a car has passed that way for a week.'

'Longer,' Georges agreed. 'To tell you the truth I have been trying to contact the Maquis for ages, but they have to be very

214

careful. It is not easy to find out who and where they are. It took me some time.'

'It is very good of you.' Sasha put his hand on his friend's shoulder and realized he would miss him.

'It is not only for you, but for me,' Georges assured him. 'François and I too wish to join the Resistance, to carry out acts of sabotage against the enemy of France, to be ready when the liberation begins. And it will. Already the war is turning. They expected the Allies would be pushed into the sea at El Alamein, but they were not. They had a marvellous victory instead and have changed the course of the war.'

'My cousin Ralph was there,' Sasha said thoughtfully. 'He was also at Dunkirk. He would not like to have been ditched in the sea twice.' It was rather as though Sasha felt that Ralph's preferences would have determined the course of the war.

'You must be proud of your family.' Georges smiled at him. 'I am proud of you too, and of knowing you. Don't forget us after the war, old fellow.' Sasha too felt sad at the thought of the parting, at the use of the past tense, but Georges gripped his shoulder manfully. 'Come now. We haven't got very long. My friend is anxious to be gone.'

When Hélène got back to the apartment behind the Gare du Nord she felt, as usual, a profound sense of relief. It was regarded as such a safe house that it was used extensively by the local Resistance and Henri, the 'pianist', had set up his wireless there more or less permanently although each time, after transmission, he disassembled it and hid it beneath some floorboards. In Nazi-occupied Paris one could not take chances. Too many good men and women were being captured because of lack of care. The existence of the Resistance was known and its growing strength feared by the authorities. There had already been many betrayals, followed by shootings and summary executions. It was never safe to assume that anyone was a friend until it had been proved over many weeks; even then one could not be sure. The rewards for

215

betrayal were large and many Frenchmen, too many, thought that the *boche* were there for the duration of the thousand-year Reich promised by Hitler.

As Hélène carefully let herself into the blacked-out apartment Charles Leroux looked up from the table at which he was writing. His customary initial expression of anxiety and fear was quickly replaced by a more special one: tenderness, relief that she was back.

Getting up he quickly crossed the room to her so that they met half-way and she leaned on him as one who, exhausted, is glad and relieved to be enfolded in a friendly embrace.

'Was it all right?' He looked at her anxiously, and she nodded, her face still pressed against his chest.

'Did they meet the plane?'

'The plane was late so we were worried. It was too near Rouen and we are to ask London to arrange another position for a drop.'

Hélène put her head up for a kiss then moved away from Charles, dropping wearily into a chair.

'Does Henri come tonight?'

'Not tonight.'

'Good, then we can sleep.'

'Have you eaten?'

Hélène shook her head. 'I'm too tired for food. The long wait made me very anxious and the train both to Rouen and back was full of Germans. That airman Gordon didn't understand one word of French. It was nerve-racking.'

'Would you like to go back to England for a rest?'

'Go back?' Hélène jerked her head up indignantly. 'Are you crazy? I haven't lived in England since 1936. It's not exactly my home. No, I am happy here and I like my work here. Besides I am with you. That's the best part of all.'

Charles dropped to his knees beside her and kissed her hand.

'I do love you very much,' he said. 'For me it is the best part too.'

'No, for you getting rid of the *boche* is the best part. The rest comes a long way down.'

Charles laughed and got to his feet. 'I'll go and make coffee.'

In a way Hélène was right. Charles hated the people who had occupied his country, who behaved towards patriotic Frenchmen with such ferocity. Above all he hated those of his fellow countrymen who collaborated with the enemy: a militia of Frenchmen had recently been set up called the *Milice*, specifically to act against the Resistance. But there were aspects of his work that were important and rewarding and it would always take precedence over his private life. Yet his relationship with Hélène was important too and he told her so later in bed where they huddled together for warmth.

'After the war I'll get a divorce.'

'Oh, don't talk about that, yet anyway.'

'Don't you want me to?' He tried to see into her fine sad eyes in the moonlight, but it was wintry and feeble. He couldn't see her face at all, only trace the contours with his fingers and feel the impress of her body against his.

'I don't want to think about the future,' Hélène said. 'I don't see the point.'

'Your past has made you too bitter. There *is* hope you know, my darling.' He waited for her to reply and when she didn't he went on, 'You don't feel much hope do you? You are too marked by the past.'

'If one doesn't hope one isn't disappointed,' Hélène replied. 'If the war ends and we're alive, let's think about it then.'

Shortly after that she could hear Charles's regular breathing and knew that he was asleep. But, in the dark, the tears trickled down her face. Had she spoken too hastily? Was she too frightened of the possibility of happiness? Was happiness possible even with someone like him? Was it not just because they were comrades in arms that they were so happy? Would it not prove to be a wartime romance doomed to finish like so many others?

Charles wasn't remotely like Bobby or Jamie. In Charles she

217

had met the man she had always been looking for, someone strong but not a bully, someone who valued her as an equal – an equal in love and in danger. Both her husband and lover had in their own ways patronized her: treated her as a woman there mainly for their pleasure. And, for their pleasure, she had played up to this image even taking care to dress and behave as she did to enhance Bobby's prestige. Charles had completely different expectations ... but to see a future together, was it possible?

The next morning they discussed the programme for the day. Usually when she came back from a trip escorting escapees down the line she went to pick the children up from school and spent some time with her mother, though always trying to avoid her father. It was impossible to trust him, to let him have any idea of the nature of the work she was doing.

Charles wrote a weekly bulletin for circulation to his members and this he and Hélène would deliver personally in whatever part of Paris they happened to be. It was important to give this information, yet for it to contain nothing that would cause any danger to his people if it fell into the wrong hands. They agreed to meet that night at a café after Hélène had seen the children and her mother, and Charles had delivered his bulletin and spoken personally to some members of his circuit. First, of course, he had to spend the day in his office because to be away too often and too long would invite suspicion. That night too he would spend in his own flat for the same reason.

Hélène hated the nights when she was alone, prey to all kinds of fears and bad dreams. That was the worst part of her existence; worse than the danger, the suspicious glances of German soldiers, of French policemen when she was taking an escapee on public transport or along the street; worse than the fear when the plane landed that they would be surrounded and captured. For she knew that what she was doing merited only one punishment: torture and inevitable death.

It was still quite dark when they breakfasted because even

with late nights they rose early; there was such a lot to do. Hélène might go back to bed, but she would have coffee with Charles while he dressed and got ready for work putting his precious bulletins in his briefcase among the legal documents.

She was sitting at the table, her hands round her mug of hot coffee, and Charles was still in the bathroom when the doorbell rang.

It was very unusual for the doorbell to ring. Members of the organization usually tapped on the door or gave a prearranged whistle or signal outside the window so that no one would hear them go in.

Hélène thought of what Charles had said the night before about the future and, as he came out of the bathroom, still with some shaving soap on his face, she gave him a long, loving, sad look as though it might be the last.

Then she went swiftly to the door and leaned against it.

'Who is it?' she said in a low voice.

'It's a surprise,' the voice said in French, and there was something about the tone that was familiar.

'Who is it?' she repeated, fearing a trap.

'Open the door, Aunt Hélène,' the voice called. 'It's freezing to death out here.'

Oh joy.

'Sasha!' she cried, opening the door wide and flinging her arms round him. 'Oh my God, they said you were dead.'

She started to weep as, gently, Sasha drew her into the room, his arm round her waist. He smiled at the man who had accompanied him, standing in the shadows by the door.

'Frederic, you're very naughty,' Charles said, shaking his finger at Sasha's companion. 'We thought you were the Germans.'

'I'm sorry,' Frederic said contritely, but still smiling. 'He told me he wanted to surprise his aunt and I forgot to tell him that we never rang the bell. I knew you would be frightened. Hélène, forgive me.'

219

Hélène, smiling now, her arm round her nephew's shoulder, shook her head.

'What does it matter? He's here. That is the marvellous thing. What happened?'

Sasha suddenly grew serious.

'I was thrown clear from my gun turret. In the air it may be considered exposed, more dangerous, but believe me on the ground it's the quickest way to escape. Then the plane started to burn. Another man was thrown with me and he died. I buried him so that his body would not be found. That it might be supposed we had all been killed. Then, very quickly, I got away.'

As Charles prepared coffee, Hélène, not taking her eyes from Sasha, heard about his adventures: of the tortuous journey through Germany where often only the fact he spoke the language so well saved him. Then the stay with the Viollets who had looked after him and helped him to recover. How Georges Viollet had contacted the Maquis and how, again after a long dangerous journey across occupied France – he had even spent a few days in a sewer alone with the smells and the rats ('enough to drive a man mad') – finally, they had brought him to Paris.

'I wanted to go to Father...'

'Oh no!' Hélène said instinctively, putting her hands to her face, and she saw a cloud come over Sasha's as the happy, relieved expression vanished.

'You don't think I would have been safe with my own father?'

'Well, you would have been safe, sure.' Charles glanced at Hélène as he handed Sasha and Frederic mugs of hot coffee. 'But he would not have known how to get you out of Paris. We do.'

'But Father would have come to you...' Sasha looked at them, his voice faltering. 'Are you being diplomatic? Father isn't a sympathizer, is he, a supporter of the Nazis? How *can* he be?'

'Sasha.' Hélène took his hand and led him to the old horsehair settee that some said was the only antique in the apartment, but that didn't make it very comfortable. How did one tell a man, a patriot who had already suffered in the war, unpleasant things about his father? She gripped his hand hard. 'You know that your father had a very bad time in Russia with the Communists? When he left he was attracted to the opposite side.'

'Quite understandably,' Charles concurred. '*Then* of course one didn't know about Hitler...'

'You *are* trying to tell me that father is a Nazi, aren't you?' Sasha said bitterly. 'They told me my grandmother Melanie was too and, maybe, my mother a supporter of Mussolini. Well, I don't believe it. I'm going to see Father and ask him.'

'No, no, no you *must* not see your father.' Hélène's voice was adamant. 'After all, he's my brother, don't forget. I love him like a brother, naturally, but I don't share his views...'

'In France there are many like that,' Frederic intervened sympathetically. 'Families divided, one unable to trust the other...'

'But my father would *never* betray me.'

'Of course he would not; but we wouldn't like him to know,' Hélène looked at Charles, 'about us. That we operate a *réseau* of the Resistance. That I am instrumental in helping Allied airmen to escape. I would hate him to know all that. He might be tempted to pass it on.'

'Then what does Father think you do?'

Hélène shrugged. 'Does he wonder ... does he care? None of my family have a very high opinion of me, you know that. They think I spend my days in cafés, and my nights,' she blinked, 'who knows?'

'But Frederic told me you were a heroine, that you defy death all the time.'

'What is a heroine?' Hélène looked wanly at him. 'It is a word that may have a meaning to someone, but, for me, it has none. I do what I have to do and that is that. No, Sasha, as soon as we can we will get you out of here. Sometimes we are lucky enough to get a plane straight to England, but more often it involves another long and even more dangerous journey to Spain which means crossing the Pyrenees. Looking at you,' she said scrutinizing him closely, 'I think we will try for the plane. Not only have you had a long journey already, but I can't wait for your family to know you're alive.'

After Frederic and Charles had gone Hélène spoke frankly to Sasha about her past and her life. She didn't know her nephew very well because latterly their paths had not often crossed. But when he was small, living with his mother in her luxurious Paris apartment before he went to school in England, she had seen him often and he, for his part, retained an almost awesome memory of this very beautiful and elegant aunt who smelled delicious and looked so marvellous, but seemed to keep everyone at a distance – including her daughters. Then when the bad times came upon her – the divorce and the murder of her lover – he was a rather gauche boy at public school in England and no one had talked of Aunt Hélène very much. The little cousins, too, had gone back to France.

Immediately he saw her he knew how much Hélène had changed. She was a different woman – no longer remote or detached and not at all sophisticated in her blue woollen turtle-neck jersey and skirt. Of course she was beautiful – surely nothing could ever change that? – but her beauty now was tempered by something else, something that had been quite absent when Sasha had gone in awe of her ten years before. After they had talked for some time he knew what that something else was: suffering. Her life had been full of suffering in recent years, experiences which made the departure from Russia in 1920 seem quite trivial. For three years this elegant woman, a Russian princess, had been inside a tough woman's prison and what she had not experienced herself she had lived through in the experiences of others. Nothing now in the human condition could ever surprise her.

222

He saw that Hélène now smoked quite heavily; but those deeply etched lines by the sides of her mouth, particularly round her eyes and on her forehead, seemed richer and more meaningful than any amount of lost poise or sophistication when she was at her peak as a young society gadfly.

In those hours after Charles had gone Sasha felt a tightening of the bond with the woman to whom he was doubly related – his father was her brother and her ex-husband, Bobby, had been his mother's brother. He felt so close, so loving, he could have taken her in his arms, not for any carnal reasons, but just to comfort her: to tell her that he understood and knew what she'd been through.

Yet the most astonishing part of it all was how she had overcome all these disasters to emerge somehow triumphant. She was a woman whose past was suffering, yet who seemed to look with such serenity into the future.

Eventually he felt bold enough to ask her why and, gazing at him without smiling, she replied:

'It's Charles. I never knew a really good man before. Everyone I knew wanted something I could give them, even my father when I married Bobby. Charles only wants me for what I am. We are united, not only by this and our love for each other, but by this cause that we're engaged in: we are fighting for the freedom of France and the liberation of our country and all the occupied countries of Europe from the *boche*.' Leaning towards him – they had been sitting in facing armchairs close to the fire – she squeezed his hand. 'I know you're upset about your father, Sasha, but, believe me, he is a man who if he too had a cause would be much happier. His only cause now is somehow to get by.' She stood up suddenly and straightened her skirt, tugged tighter the belt around her narrow waist: 'Sometimes I think he would have been happier if he'd stayed in Russia.'

'Why is that?' Sasha rose too, feeling stiff although he was used to cramped circumstances and staying for hours in the same position. He rubbed his cramped leg.

'He might have remained a Communist. I think he didn't want to come to the west. Bobby did some sort of deal with Stalin and Kyril was released. We all thought at the time how unhappy he seemed to be home, but then he appeared to settle down and, gradually, he was drawn to Hitler and admiration of right-wing causes. I know you love your father, Sasha, but right now he is a dangerous man to know. Maybe after the war everything will be different, but now is not the time to see him.'

Sasha stuck his hands in his pockets, averting his eyes from hers. He was glad that she didn't seem to expect a reply.

Hélène, instead, after looking at the clock and uttering an exclamation, took up her overcoat which had been lying over a chair and crammed her blonde hair under a blue beret. This simple tactic succeeded in making her look quite anonymous, like any other woman, housewife or worker, whom one might see on the street: passably attractive but nothing to make a man turn his head. There were many such now in Nazi-occupied France; busy, harassed women, sometimes with a man or men who had gone underground rather than be sent to work in Germany, wondering how they could make ends meet.

'I must go and meet the children.' Hélène tucked the final few strands of hair under her beret and looked critically at herself. 'I like to see them as soon as I can after I've been away. It's important for them to see me as often as possible.'

'Where do they think you go?'

Hélène shrugged her shoulders and tied the belt of her coat. 'They don't know. I tell them I go to the country to see a friend.' For a moment she looked solemnly at him, again without smiling. 'These girls, you know, my poor little ones, have grown up with so much mystery in their lives, so many unanswered questions. What is one more?'

Sasha also crossed the room to get his coat and shrugged himself into it.

'Let me come with you.'

'Oh no!' Hélène shook her head vigorously. 'It's *much* too dangerous.'

'But they would love to see me and I them. Why is it dangerous?'

'They may talk, not meaning to give you away, but they are very young. They will be so excited they might want to tell their school friends about you. They won't be able to resist telling their grandparents.'

Sasha turned abruptly and looked at her. 'Your *parents* don't even know what you do?'

'Of course they don't know! *Mustn't* know! I staged a row – it wasn't hard – with my father and found an excuse to leave. Before that I was hiding airmen in my room.' Hélène smiled grimly. 'It seemed to fit in with my reputation.'

'Which is what?' Sasha came over to her and held her by her wrists.

'That I'm a whore. Haven't you heard it?'

'Of course I haven't!'

'Bobby always said I was a whore. I'm sure the family think it.'

'Because you once had a lover...'

'They think if you have one you must have many. You are "that kind of woman"! Maybe it suits me. Anyway at the moment I don't much care.' She gave a little shrug which made him release her wrists, and lit a cigarette. 'Well, I must be off. You stay here and don't go out.'

'But for how long?' Sasha went to the window with its rather grubby net curtains and gazed moodily into the street.

'Maybe weeks.' Hélène went to the mirror and put lipstick on. To be too drab when one was considered, she knew in all modesty, a beautiful woman would attract attention too. 'We must tell London you are here. And then we must arrange to get you out. It all takes time.' Looking at herself once more she pulled her beret over her forehead. 'It all takes time.'

Time was something, Sasha thought, he had plenty of and yet on the other hand he didn't. It irked him very much to be cooped up in the flat, to know he was in the same city as his

225

father and grandparents yet he couldn't see them. He felt especially indignant about his father because he was a man he didn't know very well. Yet he had always admired and loved him with that special and often irrational veneration children, largely brought up by one parent, have for the other.

Kyril was almost a stranger to him and yet he was his flesh and blood; he had engendered him long ago in Russia when he and Sasha's mother were on their honeymoon. Susan used to talk a lot about that Caucasian holiday in the days before his father came home; about the romance of the Ferov house near Batum and the history of the Ferov family, the pride of Russia. She told him that he must never be ashamed of his ancestry, but proud of it, because what had happened to them had happened to a lot of people.

Sasha grew up feeling very Russian, yet very English too – proud of being both a Ferov and a Bolingbroke and, through his grandmother Lady Melanie, a member of the Askham family. It was because he was British he was fighting a war against tyranny: more than ever, now, he was proud of his part in it.

As the days passed and Hélène and Charles went about their dangerous business, leaving Sasha alone for much of the time, he grew restless and bored. The weather was bad and there was nothing for him to do. There was little fuel in Nazi-occupied Paris so it was bitterly cold in the flat, and sometimes he used to slip out in the afternoons and go to a cinema where at least it was warm. As he spoke flawless French it was considered that there was little danger so long as he took care.

One afternoon, after the cinema, Sasha popped into a café for a beer and sat there thinking about the film and about the newsreel, carefully edited by the Nazis to give a favourable view of the war. According to them it was all gloom for the Allies and victory for the Germans. There were lots of pictures of the Führer and of the fighting in the Far East, where Japan was made out to be victorious, and Russia where the Germans, after their defeat at Stalingrad, had at last taken Kharkov and Belgorod.

Seeing pictures of the Russian front made Sasha think of that country where he had been conceived but which he had never visited. It made him think of his father. He longed desperately to see his father again, that man he loved so much and who thought he was dead. How pleased Kyril would be to see *him*.

He looked at the telephone in the corner and then down at the glass in his hand. He took a deep draught and finished the beer. Then he went to the phone, put a jeton in and dialled.

'Hello?' his father said at the other end, 'who's speaking please?'

'Of *course* I'm pleased to see you.' Kyril had tears in his eyes as he drew Sasha into the long room with its beautiful view of the Seine. 'Oh my Sasha, we thought you were dead.'

Kyril folded his son in his arms and then Sasha, grown man, now, and an RAF gunner, wept too. Sasha could never remember weeping since he had enlisted; not when he was shot down, not in the cold, not when he was afraid, not when he had seen his aunt and she had cried. But now he wept.

Man to man they wept. Father and son, together at last.

CHAPTER 13

At the airfield near Tempsford in Bedfordshire Charlotte waited for the man she was going to drop with. She only knew that he was French, that he had been in France on several missions and that he was to liaise with the Paris circuits that took escapees down the line to Spain. She was to be the courier and it was her first trip. For some time now Charlotte had been ready to drop into France but no suitable occasion had arisen. Many men didn't like working with women; they felt they were a liability. But in this case it was thought that a woman would be suitable because women were more inconspicuous. This particular woman spoke French well and, with her chestnut hair and slim figure, could pass for a Frenchwoman. Some thought at first that she was too good looking and that a mistake had been made: besides, her face was known in France when she had been a top mannequin.

Many were the debates that went on in SOE headquarters in Baker Street about using Lady Charlotte Verdi at all. Maybe a mistake had been made in recruiting her. But those who had been with her during the extensive and difficult training – that included learning how to shoot and prime ammunition, sabotage, hand-to-hand combat, long marches and dropping by parachute into rough, unmarked territory – had no doubt at all. She had come out of every test with top marks. And, despite her flawless bone structure, that rather fine, imperious air that was inherited from generations of Askham forebears, she could look quite nondescript too when without make-up.

The family thought she had joined up: that, after Arthur was sent to the Far East, she decided to do her bit too, guilty perhaps because Arthur had left without being married. It seemed quite logical, because of Arthur, that she should join the WAAF. During those hard months of training, some of them spent in a rugged part of Scotland, she told no one, not even Rachel, what was happening to her.

Now it was all over and Charlotte, perfectly drilled, well-equipped, waited in the house by the side of the airfield. She had not met her fellow agent because he had only just returned from an important mission and had been urgently recalled after giving his report to his superiors. She only knew him by his code name 'Plus Fort', strongest. Maybe it was apposite. After much deliberation she herself had asked for and been given permission to use the one name that had a sentimental association for her: Rachel, her mother's name. She hoped it would bring her safe home.

For a while they had wondered whether the Lysander would be able to go because although it was a time of full moon, one of the requisites for a drop, there was cloud on the other side of the Channel. Already one of the aircraft had returned, with a full complement of people to be dropped in the massif central; but when it got there there was no one to receive it, no lights, no signals – a dangerous sign. Occasionally members of the Resistance arrived to find the Germans there too. Charlotte had been warned that sometimes they went like this night after night and then the mission had to be postponed until the next full moon. Often an agent who had to get there quickly went by boat. This would be what would happen to Plus Fort if the mission proved abortive. Plus Fort was obviously someone very important indeed.

The plane was already on the runway, the engine running, the propellers turning, and then a car drew up by the side of the house and someone already clad in a flying suit, like Charlotte, from which all identification or personal effects would have been removed, got out. There was a hurried discussion and, without even coming into the house, the man was taken towards the plane. Charlotte, hastily saying 'goodbye' to those with her, hurried out to meet him.

'This is Plus Fort,' Squadron Leader Richmond in whose charge she had been, said, 'Plus Fort meet Rachel.'

'How do you do?' Plus Fort proffered his hand and then, in the flares from the runway, their eyes met.

Charlotte had last seen Plus Fort when, briefly while he slept, his head rested on her breast in Piccadilly Underground during the blitz fourteen months before.

The recognition was mutual. He smiled.

'*Quelle coincidence*,' he said. '*Bonjour Rachel. Bienvenu à France.*'

All during dinner Irina could scarcely take her eyes off Sasha. Sasha, a Russian conceived in Russia if not born there, so Slav in his looks, his mannerisms, his gestures, so like Kyril. And Kyril, smiling too across the table, rather nervous and edgy as if at any moment the door might open to admit someone who would betray his son.

Of course it was very dangerous, not only for Sasha. They were all in great danger. Kyril had gone personally to his parents' home rather than risk a message or telephone call. And here they were: Irina, Alexei, Kyril and Sasha, beloved Sasha in the bosom of his family, not dead at all.

Although Sasha had an English mother, had received his secondary education in England and spoke perfect, unaccented English, the Ferov family had always been inclined to consider him as one of themselves. They saw in Sasha the inheritor of that Russian ancestry he would pass on to his children.

For, to them, Sasha was a prince – son of a prince, and the thought of Prince Alexander Ferov being a sergeant in the British Air Force seemed to them incongruous. Thirty years before, in the old country, Sasha would have been an officer, like his grandfather, in the Preobrazhensky Guard, the heir to the estates of his father and grandfather.

But the Revolution had put paid to that logical sequence of events. For a time they hoped it was temporary but by now everyone knew it was not – even those who had hopes that Germany might conquer Russia, as the Ferovs certainly had.

Yet, curiously, they avoided talking about the war. It meant too much to them in different ways. For Sasha there was the suspicion that, much as he loved them, they might support Hitler; for them there was the fear of giving too much away: the dinners, the parties, the entertainments involving senior Nazis.

But all that seemed as far away as the St Petersburg of the Czars as the family gathered around Kyril's table laid in Russian style with the heavy embossed Ferov cutlery, the ornamental crystal glasses and the heavy damask linen that Irina had insisted, all those years ago, on packing in order to take something of permanence with them.

There was grace before the meal in Russian, a blessing given by Alexei, and there was a Russian meal – as far as that was possible in the circumstances although the Ferovs, through their friendship with the conquerors, found it easier to procure scarce goods than most of the population. Even Kyril, also unused to doing without, was astonished by the proliferation and extent of the Russian dishes, prepared by Irina all day in his kitchen with only the aid of her Russian maid: various *zakuski*, Russian hors d'oeuvres eaten with small glasses of neat vodka, followed by *bortsch*, red beetroot soup, *blini*, hot pastry pancakes, *sylopka*, salted herring with plenty of soured cream, and *pulmany*, noodles cut into pieces and soaked with minced meat. To accompany these there was endless red or white Caucasian wine brought by the Germans who had occupied the south of Russia.

During the Russian meal the family spoke Russian, and it was with an air of contentment that Sasha, who had not eaten so much for months, looked round the table at the end of the meal. He had to pretend not to know where his aunt was. All he had told his father was that he was being sheltered by friends, he could not say who or where. Kyril had professed to

231

understand the need for this secrecy and had not asked questions.

'How's Aunt Hélène?'

After Sasha's question there was an awkward silence broken at last by Alexei: 'Your aunt doesn't live with us any more. We didn't get on. There was a big scene.' Alexei opened his arms as though to show just how wide and on what a scale the scene was.

'I thought you might ask her just for this evening.' Sasha imagined he was helping to cover his tracks, and Hélène's, by deceiving the family.

'Oh no!' Alexei pursed his lips. 'It was too dangerous to ask her or, alas, the girls. Not that they would not all love to see you; they would. But the fewer people who know…' Alexei put his finger to his mouth as if sealing his lips.

From what he'd heard, what he knew, the gesture made Sasha feel only contempt for his grandfather – a loving contempt, because how could one cease to love such a well meaning but stupid old man? Yet he knew what they were risking by this meeting with him, a risk minimized by holding the dinner in Kyril's well protected apartment high up and isolated from sudden surprises and unexpected visits.

Sasha felt he was able to suspend all criticism of his family for the time he was with them, all doubts he might have had about their cooperation with the sworn enemies of the country he, and Hélène, were fighting for – free France.

As a boy who had grown up with no close feelings of belonging, either to a person or people or a country, both France and his relations, however flawed, meant a great deal to him.

He thought it was unwise to continue to ask questions about Hélène because he knew that the feud with her father went very deep, and back a long way to events he knew little about.

For the rest of the evening Sasha sat next to his grandmother, her hand in his. He noted with pain the deep lines of suffering scored in her face not only by her life in exile but also

232

by so many unkind acts, both wittingly and unwittingly performed by the Askham and Lighterman families over the years.

Soon it was time for the family to go, in a car provided by Kyril who used his manservant as chauffeur. But Irina wanted to cling to the beloved grandchild who had come back from the dead. Her eyes filled with tears as she hugged him, cascaded down her face, interfering with her profuse and carefully applied make-up – the layers of rouge, powder and mascara, the latter making her eyelashes resemble spiders' legs which now created feathery runnels down her parchment-like cheeks. With a trembling hand she stroked his face, looking into his eyes.

'I don't feel I will see you again, Sasha mine.'

'You will, Baba, you will,' Sasha answered in Russian. 'I am not going to die for a very long time.'

'Then you won't fly again?' Irina's eyes lit up hopefully.

'As soon as I can; but I won't be killed.'

'You have my prayers,' Irina raised her heavily ringed eyes to heaven piously, 'and those of all the family ... those who still pray.' She looked reproachfully at Kyril, but he was gazing anxiously out of the window.

'Mama, remember the curfew. If you are stopped you will be asked where you were...'

'With my son.'

'It isn't wise, Mama. Go now so that I can talk to Sasha some more. Remember, precious as he is to you he is my son. My only son.'

Sorrowfully Irina allowed herself to be parted from Sasha who, with his arm tenderly around her waist, saw her down the stairs and to the car waiting silently in the darkness outside.

'I wish you would stay the night. One night,' Kyril said after his parents had gone. 'It might be years before I see you again. Never maybe.'

'Why do you say that, Father?' Each man now had a brandy and they sat side by side on the deep leather sofa.

'Well, this life is so short, so dangerous.' Kyril waved his hands. 'We all thought you dead already. This is a bonus.' Kyril reached diffidently for his hand; he was not a man who showed emotion, but the sight of his newly resurrected son had moved him beyond words. Nobody in the family meant as much to Kyril as Sasha – his first-born, his only son, and if anything made him feel guilty it was the realization not only of how much he had neglected him, but how he had deceived him. Above all things he wanted Sasha to love him. 'You know, I often feel I don't know you, my son. It *is* my fault…'

'It isn't your fault, Father! You couldn't help being sent to Siberia. From what I've heard it was very unfair.'

'Oh no, the State had its reasons.' Kyril's eyes narrowed as he blew smoke from the large Havana.

'You always defend them. I can't think why.' Sasha stared at him conscious, as he always was when he saw his father, of how they resembled each other.

'Do I?'

'One would have thought you hated them. I understood you did hate them. That that was why you went to Spain, to fight against the Republic.'

'I didn't fight. I never fought. That was a misunderstanding,' Kyril said firmly. 'It was purely business.'

'Why did you stay so long?'

'It is very hard to get out of a country at war,' Kyril replied, 'as you know. Yes, I admit, I *am* right-wing, but it doesn't always help. I supported the Nationalists in Spain, and they won. The Germans might not be so lucky.'

Sasha hadn't wanted to ask this question but nevertheless he asked it.

'Tell me, Father, do you *actively* support the *boche*?'

Kyril, who had anticipated being interrogated, studied the glowing tip of his cigar. 'Of course not. In this war I am a neutral. If you like, I can see both sides.'

'But you do have friends who are Nazis?'

'Not *friends*, not friends in any way,' Kyril didn't appear in the least perturbed, 'but I know a few. I know lots of Frenchmen too and, before the war, lots of English. Don't think, my dearest Sasha, that I have any plans to betray you.'

'I don't think that for a moment, Father. Of course, in a war like this we see only black and white not shades of grey.' He looked around. 'Gran told me you had Jordan Bolingbroke staying with you. Now I always heard *he* was a fervent Nazi.'

Kyril should have expected this question, but he hadn't. He appeared taken by surprise and laughed awkwardly. 'Oh that! That was nearly ten years ago. We have all changed a lot from what we were in our youth. I used to be a member of the Communist Party and I was rather older then than Jordan.'

'But why is he staying with you?'

Kyril's face grew solemn. He had let his cigar go out. 'He is my brother-in-law. He has been a very sick man. He has come here to see some doctors, because he suffers from a psychological illness that makes him live in a permanent state of fear: acute anxiety. Was it not charitable of me to do that for my brother-in-law?'

'Yes, I suppose so.' Sasha seemed doubtful. Kyril looked sorrowfully at him.

'Really Sasha, you make me sad. You don't appear to believe anything I say.'

'But why wasn't Jordan here tonight?'

'Because he doesn't know you're here. I would prefer he doesn't know because, as you say, the fewer people who know the better. He has gone for two or three days to friends in Cherbourg. It was very convenient. Really, Sasha, I can see the suspicion in your eyes.' His voice faltered. 'What have I done that my own son doesn't trust me?'

'Oh Father.' Impulsively Sasha leaned towards him. 'Of *course* I trust you...'

'Then why don't you stay here with me just for a while?'

'Because I can't.' Sasha moved away as though the brief

235

moment of contact now embarrassed him. 'I gave a promise to the people who were sheltering me that I wouldn't contact my family.'

'Then they thought your family would betray you?' Kyril's question, delivered in a low voice, was almost rhetorical. He rose and began to walk about.

'They certainly knew that Grandfather was friendly with the Nazis.'

'I wonder what they said about me?'

Kyril, staring intently at Sasha, suddenly remembered Freddie, slightly older than Sasha but still youthful and full of life when he had been killed; indeed, eagerly anticipating life when he, Kyril, had shot him in the back to save himself from betrayal.

Kyril Ferov was a strange, complicated man brought up in a mould, first of privilege as a Russian prince and then as a favoured member of the newly fledged Bolshevik Party. He had little time for other loyalties and even his marriage to Susan was an uncharacteristic impulse which he had had many years to regret.

The Party had generously given him those in a prison farm in Siberia. Yet, instead of resentment, all Kyril had felt was gratitude to the Party for giving him the chance to examine himself in a way that was not open to everyone. To establish his loyalties and beliefs.

He had emerged from prison more dedicated than before, even more sure that the cause was the right one and yet he had been sent to the West against his will. Even there, in its wisdom, the Party was able to use him, deploy his talents in intelligence and subversion.

Yet when it came to killing a young man who was related to his wife – Freddie, Susan's cousin – even Kyril had a moment of apprehension, of revulsion, until the many years of his training in absolute obedience to a higher dictate made him stifle his doubts and pull the trigger. He only waited to see Freddie fall, to be sure that he was dead, before he turned away and ran swiftly to the command post in the village where he had been in charge of directing the advance of the Republican brigade.

The necessary deed done, Kyril never had another moment of anxiety about Freddie's death. He hardly ever saw the family, except for Freddie's sister Charlotte, and he had yet to face Freddie's mother. But if called upon to do so he would, without flinching. He knew that. Freddie's death was an act of war.

Yet, supposing Sasha were to discover his double life and betray him? Would he try and prevent it? Could he do the same to his son? He thought of Abraham taking his son Isaac up to the mountain and lifting his sword ready to sacrifice him in obedience to the Lord.

It was many years since Kyril had been instructed in religious knowledge, yet he still remembered the obedience of Abraham, and the willingness of Isaac to be sacrificed. Would Sasha be such a willing sacrificial lamb? For Kyril his god was, and always would be, the cause of Communism. He had already killed one innocent young man. How much could he, and would he, do in obedience to a higher end? He began to tremble.

'Father?' Sasha said anxiously coming up behind him; and, turning, Kyril fell upon his shoulder, buried his face in his chest and began to weep.

Sasha, bewildered, gently put his arms around him, relishing the close contact. Even when he was a small child he could never recall being held by Kyril, nor Susan. Any brief embraces he had came from his nurse.

'Oh Father,' he said emotionally, 'I do love you.'

But this statement, instead of assuaging Kyril's grief, strangely had the opposite effect. This hard, dour, even ruthless man, who had practised treachery and deceit for most of his adult life, felt completely helpless; consumed by guilt, in the face of the innocence of his only son.

* * *

Hélène looked at him oddly. 'Wherever have you been? We've been so worried.'

'You said I could go to the cinema.'

'But you have been such a *long* time. We must move very quickly because, tonight, the plane is coming to an airfield close to Paris. We have hardly any time to get there.'

'Tonight? Already?' Sasha was overjoyed. His heart sang. He was completely content for, not only was he going home where he would rejoin the war effort, but he had seen his family again, come closer to his father than ever before in his life.

'Quick,' Hélène, forgetting her annoyance, bundled him into his room. 'Get your things and don't lose a minute. Charles is outside in the car.'

Charles drove the car carefully through the streets of Paris. There were not many about and it would be dreadful to be stopped with an RAF flyer in the back. That would mean the firing squad for them all. Sasha lay on the floor covered with a blanket and Hélène sat beside Charles. They were all tense, and the conversation was desultory.

Once they were clear of the streets of the city Sasha was allowed to sit up, though with orders to duck if they saw anyone or were stopped. There was a gun loaded and primed in the glove compartment ready for a shoot-out on the spot, if necessary. Only if necessary. Better for them all to die in a fight than wait for the executioner's step.

Sasha began to feel guilty about going to see his family. He had deceived Hélène, who was risking her life for him. He had also disobeyed instructions for his, and their, safety. Yet what man could resist the chance to see his own father, grandparents who might not be alive when the war was over? In a subdued voice from the back of the car, he said:

'How did you know it was tonight?'

'We got a message from the BBC. It was a signal we were waiting for. We are expecting the man who controls all the circuits in the north of France and his courier.'

'Is he French?'

'Oh yes. He has been operating since the fall of France. He is very brave and has had numerous escapes. They are also sending us arms and equipment because we are preparing all the time for the invasion of France, to extend acts of sabotage against the *boche*.'

'I wish I could stay and help you,' Sasha said fervently.

'It's your job to fly in bombers,' Hélène said gently. 'You are much needed too. Here, we're near the field.' Hélène looked nervously at Charles. 'It is too near Paris for my liking.'

'If it were further away we should never have got your nephew out.' Charles still sounded annoyed. He felt Sasha had acted unprofessionally by his long absence and wondered if, indeed, he had told them the truth? 'It would have taken him weeks and months, maybe longer, to go via Spain.'

'You're very lucky,' Hélène assured Sasha over her shoulder. 'You'll be having bacon and eggs for breakfast.' He put out a hand and she took it.

'I wish you were coming with me,' Sasha said. 'Oh I wish ...' he sat back and sighed.

'Yes?'

'So many things. That the war hadn't begun...'

'Well, we all wish that.' Charles stopped the car and flashed his headlights in a prearranged signal. After a minute figures stole out of the hedgerows in the leafy lane and surrounded the car.

'All right?'

'No problems.' Charles looked over his shoulder. 'This is our airman.'

The man who appeared to be in charge nodded and told Hélène and Sasha to get out of the car. Then he showed Charles where he should leave it.

'You're *very* late.' The man was annoyed too.

'Our friend went to the cinema.' Charles jerked his head bad-humouredly. 'We nearly came without him.'

Just then there was a drone of a plane approaching, and the crowd of men with them began to spread out onto the field.

Hélène watched them anxiously. She didn't see how a plane could possibly land, but the Lysanders which were used for this kind of work were very manoeuvrable.

A flare was lit at one end of the field and, now, in the light of the moon the plane could be seen flying low. Fear clutched at Hélène's heart, as it always did at moments like this. Fear it might miss its mark and crash, or disappear altogether, or that, once it had landed, they would be surrounded by armed troops. There were always several minutes of nerve-racking suspense on occasions like this. Somehow one never got used to them.

But now it was safely down and coasting towards them. The side door in the fuselage opened almost before it stopped. A ladder was thrown down and two people got out dressed in flying clothes. Then they turned towards the plane to catch the bags thrown at them. Those who had waited on the ground swooped forward and more bags were thrown out. Quite a large crate was lowered on ropes. It was not difficult to guess what that contained. 'Careful,' somebody hissed, even though the handlers were being extra cautious – dynamite and bombs maybe, nitro glycerine ... Hélène shuddered and took Sasha's arm. She hugged him to her for a moment, her flesh and blood – who knew when they would meet again?

'I'm sorry about your father,' she said. 'But *please* take care.'

Sasha swallowed guiltily and hugged her. He couldn't speak. She saw his eyes glistening with tears.

'*You* take care,' he said and, 'thank you.' Then she pushed him away and he was bundled towards the plane whose propeller had never stopped.

On his way to the plane Sasha passed the couple who had left it and briefly they waved. Then he climbed aboard. The ladder was drawn up and the chocks removed. Silently everyone drew back into the shadows except a solitary man at the far end of the field signalling with his torch. The plane turned and then began its run down the field. Everyone instinctively held their breaths, eyes closed. Suddenly the plane rose into the air, narrowly topping the hedge at the end of the field, and then it was airborne.

Sergeant Ferov, RAF, was on his way home.

Then the bustle recommenced. The large crate would be hidden in the undergrowth until a lorry could be brought to fetch it. Some of the bags and parcels were carefully stowed in the car. Bicycles appeared and some men immediately set off with bundles. It was better to leave the scene as soon as possible, especially one as dangerous as this, so near Paris. It was a well organized, well rehearsed, operation.

Charles and Hélène shook hands with the man they knew as Plus Fort and then they turned to his companion who they saw, to their surprise, was a woman.

'This is Rachel,' Plus Fort said, leading her forward. 'This is Patissier,' he indicated Charles, 'and . . . ' but he didn't get as far as saying Hélène's codename because the two women each spontaneously gave a gasp and fell into each other's arms.

'Oh!' Hélène said, her voice thick with emotion. 'I should have known you would come back.'

It was dawn when the men left, but the two women still sat together talking in the kitchen. They could sleep all day because nothing was scheduled until the following evening when Plus Fort would be back with instructions for his new courier. Charles was going to Bordeaux on legal business and would be away for a few days. It was very important to keep this normal aspect of his life going.

'You look as though you haven't slept for a week.' Hélène tenderly touched the smudges under Charlotte's eyes.

'Well I was nervous; my first trip, understandable. I didn't sleep much,' Charlotte confessed. 'The funny thing is I have met Plus Fort before. Talk about coincidences! We sat next to each other by chance in Piccadilly Underground during an air raid. He was so tired that he went to sleep with his head on my breast. That was the day I'd agreed to marry Arthur!' Charlotte's expression was wry. 'It was rather amusing. Later

241

that day Arthur received orders to join his squadron.' Charlotte had already told her about the wedding being postponed.

'Where is Arthur now?'

'He's in the Far East. For a while he was in Singapore until it fell and he narrowly got out. We're not sure where he is now, but he seems to have a charmed life.'

Hélène gazed for a moment at her friend.

'Does he?'

'What do you mean?'

'Well, he hasn't married you. He's been trying for a long time, poor man.'

'He will when the war is over,' Charlotte said. 'I promised him that. Whatever happens I will marry Arthur – that is, if both of us are still alive.'

They had talked about the family, and the further astonishing coincidence that Sasha and Charlotte had passed in the dark without knowing about each other. There was a lot that Charlotte had to tell Hélène to bring her up to date. Em was still covering the successful Allied advance in the desert, and Ralph was with the victorious Eighth Army. Bobby was making a lot of money helping the war effort. He was an acknowledged wizard at getting every ounce of effort from his workers, and toured all the factories with famous stars urging them to renewed efforts. Hélène didn't particularly want to hear about Bobby except to have a grumble about his failure in his duties to the girls.

'Oh Bobby *is* very worried about the girls,' Charlotte assured her as they were washing up the dishes from the meal they'd had in the small hours of the morning. 'He feels terribly guilty about not getting them out in time. Aileen is always rubbing it in too. She really is an awfully nice person.' She stopped realizing how tactless she'd been.

'Let's drop the subject,' Hélène suggested, 'though it's not something that can hurt me now.' She passed Charlotte a plate

242

to dry, and Charlotte thought how changed Hélène was – how much more mature, practical and, strangely, happy.

The two days they spent together were fun, curiously devoid of tension or fear. Hélène and Charlotte had always been close, the unconventional members of the family. Charlotte had visited her in prison more than any of them and Hélène loved her unreservedly. They had, moreover, always confided, shared secrets, and it was good to do so again. They liked to sneak out shopping for food, queueing with the rest of Paris for what few scraps came up from the country and managed to bypass the Black Market to get into the shops.

Charlotte wore a dress bought in Paris with her sensible shoes and coat also made in France, a beret like Hélène's over her hair. She wore scarcely any make-up and had, amazingly, transformed herself into the average Parisian housewife. Few would have recognized her as Chanel's most famous manne-quin whose face had so frequently graced the covers of the leading fashion magazines. They were careful all the time to talk in French, both scarcely with accent. To the few people she knew Hélène introduced Charlotte as a friend who had come up from the country. It was strange how the two, formerly elegant, beautiful women whose faces had in the past so often been seen in the pages of society magazines, and in places where people of importance gathered, could pass quite comfortably in a crowd. The transformation to secret agent was magically, wondrously complete.

Seeing them together, whether in the street or in the apartment sharing chores, the casual bystander, supposing he or she had known them in the past, might have had difficulty recognizing the elegant daughter of the Earl of Askham, first the wife of a world-celebrated racing driver and then one of the foremost mannequins in a city renowned for its beautiful women. Or who would have placed the famous Mrs Bobby Lighterman, princess of the House of Ferov, who had slid so easily into the role of the rich society wife because it enabled her to lead the kind of life she had been born to? Princess Hélène, whom Bobby had married for her looks, for her connections, for her heritage rather than for love?

Was it possible that both women, drawn together by so many years of friendship that was also marked by suffering, could be happier now than at any other stage in their lives? Was it possible that shared danger, a new purpose, gave their lives a form of enhancement it had lacked before? Could these two attractive but quite ordinary youngish women walking about the streets of Paris, standing in queues, chatting with the crowd or peeling potatoes over the big stone sink in the old-fashioned flat behind the Gare du Nord finally have found something that their lives hitherto lacked?

It was possible that only time and the progress of the war would tell.

Then the two happy, almost carefree days had passed and Plus Fort came back with instructions. Henri the 'pianist' turned up to transmit some fresh messages to England, and Charles's bulletin had to be written and distributed with more care than usual because there had been much activity in Paris on the part of the detested *Milice* and a number of arrests had been made.

Plus Fort told Charlotte that he was unhappy with her based in Paris and would rather she went to Rouen or Amiens. Charlotte pointed out that it was useful to know someone in Paris; she was passed off as a friend of Hélène's, which she was.

'You can't stay here forever,' Plus Fort said testily. Hélène realized how dangerous it would be to disobey the orders of this man. She was rather frightened of him and suspected that Charlotte was beginning to be too.

There seemed to be a feeling that Charlotte might be trying to stay in Paris to be with Hélène; might be putting her duties as a secret agent in second place rather than first. So Charlotte immediately agreed to go wherever he sent her and do what he wished as she was under his command. Plus Fort calmed down and they made new plans, after rather a jolly meal with fresh pork and plenty of wine brought by Charles from the country.

That night after the men had gone Hélène and Charlotte sat over the fire for a long time, drinking hot cocoa – the powder brought from England by Charlotte as a treat.

'He's very fierce, isn't he?'

'Who? Plus Fort?'

'Yes.'

'He doesn't frighten me, though.'

'That's good. Don't let him. He's a bit of a bully but very good, very brave. He is quite fearless and he will expect you to be fearless too.'

'I hope I shall be,' Charlotte whispered. 'I'm afraid, you know. Sometimes I feel quite chicken.'

'We all do.'

'You mean you're afraid?'

'Every minute of my life,' Hélène said frankly, 'and now that I love Charles I am afraid for him. When Sasha was here I was terrified. Thank God that we got him away. I was always frightened something would happen.' They had heard only that night after listening to the BBC that Sasha had, indeed, arrived:

Tell Penelope that Ulysses has come home and sends love. This was the message they had arranged before he left.

'I was so frightened while Sasha was here that he would want to see his father.'

'With Jordan staying with him? I should think so.' Charlotte looked alarmed.

'Oh you know about that?'

'Aunt Melanie still manages to communicate with Mother. Unfortunately she is quite thick with the local German Commander who posts her letters as a favour! Trust Aunt Mel. Mother is quite disgusted but enjoys the letters nevertheless. She also writes to Bobby of course, but, as Bobby can't stand Jordan, his mother might not have mentioned it to him.'

'Few people *could* stand Jordan, if I remember,' Hélène said.

'It would have been quite disastrous if he and Sasha had met. You're *sure* they didn't?'

'Who, Sasha and Jordan?' Hélène looked puzzled.

'Or Sasha and Kyril?'

'Oh no. They never met. He promised me. I had to tell him Kyril was dangerous and it upset him.'

'Naturally. Kyril is such a mystery,' Charlotte went on.

'Why do you say that?'

'Well he is, isn't he? Where does he go to when he disappears? Is he really a Fascist? When Em and Freddie met him in Spain in the war they wondered what he was doing in Madrid at all.'

'But why shouldn't he have been in Madrid?' Hélène showed that the conversation was puzzling as well as disturbing her.

'Because the Nationalists hadn't arrived in Madrid. It was Republican, and remained so for a long time. It only fell towards the end of the war, yet Kyril seemed quite at home and was walking about openly.'

Hélène gave a grunt and it was a moment or two before she spoke. 'Kyril and I were never especially close, you know, but I hated the Communists. Even now in Paris they completely disrupt the united Resistance effort. There are so many factions and groups and we have to be as careful of them as we do of the *boche*. They are always juggling for power. Nothing they ever do is disinterested.'

'How does this link up with Kyril?' Now Charlotte sounded mystified.

'Well, he's like that, isn't he? Devious? Don't you think he's devious?'

'I don't know him all that well,' Charlotte said carefully. 'I thought he was a Communist who had seen the light. Susan certainly thought so. But I didn't think he was as right-wing as your father.'

Hélène seemed suddenly to get excited, to make up her mind

246

about something, and when she spoke her voice was rather breathless. 'You know, there was always something that quite puzzled me about Father and Kyril and I shall never know the truth.'

'What's that?'

'I haven't told a soul.'

'I shan't either.'

'You promise?'

'Word of a British spy.' Charlotte's solemn expression belied her frivolousness.

'It concerns something Jamie said just before I...'

'Yes, go on,' Charlotte's voice was gentle.

'Jamie said it was *Kyril* who betrayed me, not my father. Jamie ... just before he died, you know,' Hélène faltered but Charlotte gave an encouraging nod of her head. 'Well, Jamie told me that it was *Kyril* who bribed him to sell the story about Askham Armaments to the papers.'

'You mean Alexei?'

'That's the point,' Hélène said. 'We all thought it was my father, and when I tried to correct him Jamie gave an irritating smile as if to say it might not be true. Of course I was in such a state ... If it *was* Kyril, don't you see, and not my father it makes him more devious than ever, more inclined to be a full blown supporter of the Nazis. The point is that with Kyril we simply don't know.'

'Anyway it's a *very* good thing that Sasha didn't see him, because if he has betrayed the family once he'd do it again, even though Sasha is his son and you're his sister.'

'Oh, Kyril could never betray *family*.' Hélène looked quite horrified as though entering a plea on his behalf. Charlotte was reminded just how close and irrational blood ties could be. She would defend the family too ... though would she defend Jordan, her first cousin?

How twisted loyalties became in war, Charlotte thought, and, whether because of the emotion or whether it was late, she

247

suddenly became overwhelmed with tiredness. She put out a hand to pull up Hélène who was also yawning.

'You're very brave,' she said when Hélène was upright on her feet. 'Do you know that?'

'I think I have to make up for the past.' Hélène began to move restlessly around the room straightening the furniture, puffing up the cushions. Pausing she stared at Charlotte. 'I am very ashamed of the past, you know.'

'We've all things to be ashamed of.'

'Not like me! I'd just like to know what *you've* got to be ashamed of, Charlotte Verdi? You've always seemed to me to be a most upright character.'

'I treated Arthur badly. I led him on. I don't love him, you know.'

'I guessed.' Hélène perched on the frayed arm of a chair.

'I don't love him and yet I'm going to marry him.'

'But that's rather noble, isn't it?'

'Isn't it a form of deception?'

'It's not murdering anyone,' Hélène said in an emotionless voice.

Hurriedly Charlotte crossed the room and took her friend by the shoulders, tempted to shake her.

'Hélène, once and for all you *must* get what happened in 1935 out of your mind. You have paid the price; you have expiated your crime. Jamie was a very worthless character. I can hardly think of anyone more despicable – the way he treated you, the family. In a way...'

Charlotte paused and let her arms fall to her sides. She was about to say that, in a way, Jamie deserved to die. But could anyone, really, say that of a man whose chief crime was weakness of character... Did anyone, really, deserve to die for that?

CHAPTER 14

A lot was said, sung and written about Paris in the spring and there was some justification in it, Jordan Bolingbroke thought as he sauntered along the *quai* on the way to the flat that was occupied by Irina and Alexei Ferov and their granddaughters. He had promised to take the girls for a stroll and an ice cream, if such a thing could be found, and even as he walked and the waters of the Seine sparkled in the May sun and the birds sang in the heavy trees, it was hard not to feel joyful, even to feel safe. Safe at last.

Kyril had been true to his promise and had introduced him to all the important Nazis in Paris, to the Military Commander himself. There seemed not the slightest reason to think that anyone could recall those far-off days when a very young, insecure man had followed Röhm around rather than the Führer and, against his instructions, supplied the then favourite with arms.

Even today the memory of that massacre in 1934, known as the night of the long knives, when Hitler coolly had most of the opposition killed off, made Jordan's blood run cold. To think he had been there, one of them, and now Hitler had grown to be one of the most powerful, the most ruthless men in the world and he, Jordan, had defied him.

The goose pimples came up on Jordan's arm even in the warm spring sunshine and he hurried on finding the sunshine not quite so warm.

The three Lighterman girls were especially fond of their young uncle who had arrived from their grandmother's home a few months before.

There was little enough to brighten their lives in those dark wartime days of austerity, and the inevitable quality of fear and tension that life in a big city under enemy control brought to the occupants. There were no visits to the country or Granny's in Cannes, that glamorous grandmother Melanie whose lifestyle was so superior to theirs with servants and cars and a complete absence of austerity – no penny-pinching needed there. Not that life under the Nazis hadn't vastly improved for the Ferov family living in Charlotte's flat. There was a servant, there was no obvious lack of money and there was plenty of food. There were also lots of dinner parties with men in beautiful uniforms, with Grandmother Irina presiding at table and looking quite young again; but the little girls didn't attend these grand occasions, of course. They just peeped through the door as the guests came in, faces pressed to the window when they left.

Stefanie, who was the eldest, the most grown-up of the girls, who understood more about the war, hated the *boche*. Attitudes towards the conquerors varied, and much of it depended on what one's parents thought. If they were tolerated then the children tended to tolerate them; if they were hated so did the children. Very few would admit to open admiration of the enemy because sometimes those who dared were found in a back street with their throats cut. On the other hand a majority of the French people – many of them parents of the school friends of the Lighterman girls – cooperated with the enemy, tacitly if not actively. They wanted to let sleeping dogs lie.

But the Ferovs were Russians. They were not considered in any way native and they had few French friends. Those that they'd had had fled, most of them, to their houses in the country or abroad, if they could get there, to Switzerland or Spain. The rest of the White Russian colony, like the Ferovs, tolerated the *boche* as being the lesser of two evils – the swastika was preferred to the hammer and sickle any day of the week.

In the summer of 1943 Stefanie Lighterman was a girl of

fifteen who looked eighteen, or nineteen. Some thought she could pass for twenty. In mind and stature she was a young woman and the circumstances of her life, the hardship she'd endured, the relationship with her mother, had made her mature much more quickly than many of her contemporaries, some of whom continued to look and behave childishly.

But not Stefanie, she of the bold looks, the dark hair and flashing eyes who some people whispered could be Jewish because she was so dark. Hands were raised and rumours passed, but those who knew said she had her dark looks from her English father whose antecedents were well known. No trace of semitism there. Such gossip spared Stefanie much ignominy in school where Jewish girls went in fear of their lives.

Because she opposed everything that the adults did Stefanie hated the *boche* whom her grandparents fawned upon. She was ashamed of them and used to pull faces at them through the window when they left in their high polished boots, their bright shiny peaked caps. Much as she loved her grandparents she was ashamed of them too; ashamed of the family for taking the side of Hitler rather than Churchill.

All they knew of their Uncle Jordan was that he'd been ill. He was a highly strung young man of a nervous disposition whom Uncle Kyril had brought from the South of France to see doctors in Paris. And indeed once he was in Paris Jordan's health seemed to improve, perhaps because now he was away from the all-enveloping, smothering protectiveness of his mother.

To the girls, especially Stefanie who talked to him quite a lot about serious things, Jordan seemed equivocal about the Nazis. He preferred not to talk about them at all but, instead, went with the girls to the few cultural events that continued in Paris – the odd exhibition; a muscular show of German modern art was carefully viewed and discussed – and the usual galleries and places of interest that stayed open. Jordan was a great cultural enthusiast and in his flowing cloak and large hat, with his tall thin figure and chalk-white, interesting face, he was a delightful companion, a knowledgeable amateur. His hobby over the past years had been reading about art. His young nieces knew nothing about Ernest Röhm and the night of the long knives in 1934.

That day they looked forward to Jordan's visit because there was to be a picnic by the Seine, maybe a ride in a boat. Used to little in the way of entertainment Stefanie, Olga and Natasha were grateful for any kind of diversion in their humdrum lives. It was nice to get out of the apartment, away from their grandparents and spend time in the company of an amiable, interesting man, their uncle.

They liked to get Jordan to talk about the family: the Askhams, the Bolingbrokes and Lightermans. They loved to hear about the large parties that went on before the war. Jordan however was at pains to explain that he had lived for so long with his mother and stepfather in France that he could hardly remember England at all. There were, however, some visits to his grandmother, and he could tell them about the glories of Askham Hall before Cheryl had pulled it to pieces and redecorated it in a modern style he quite liked, but which he didn't think went with the period of the house. The rest of the family hated it, but Jordan was decidedly *avant-garde*, always had been, even if his cloak and wide-brimmed black hat were a little dated now.

Then they asked him about Cheryl, and Ralph and Em and poor Freddie who had been killed in Spain. They wanted to know about other cousins – Giles and Flora and baby Paul, the Bolingbroke children and the vast company of Kittos related to them through great-grandmother Dulcie.

Jordan was surprised, rather touched, by how much the girls wanted to hear stories about the family. He was surprised and saddened too because he wondered if anything could ever compensate them for their loss. Despite his self-preoccupation Jordan was not altogether lacking in tenderness and he cared quite deeply for his young nieces. Sometimes their situation reminded him of his own unloved childhood, similarly neglected by mother and father.

But today Stefanie was obviously bursting with something that she wished to tell him, and him alone. But she had to wait until Olga and Natasha, having met someone they knew in the Tuileries Gardens, had gone to play with them and she was alone with Uncle Jordan. She never called him 'uncle'; she called him Jordan because, although he was in his thirties, his youthful air made him seem like a contemporary. Despite his experiences of the dark and dissolute side of life he retained a quality of innocence that made the girls trust him.

'What is it?' He smiled. 'I can see you're dying to tell me something!'

'Oh yes,' Stefanie hesitated, looked on both sides to make sure that the younger ones were out of earshot. She and Jordan were sitting together on a bench and, as she leaned closer to him, he instinctively put his head nearer to hers to listen.

After he had gone it was not surprising that Princess Irina, so proud of her grandson Sasha and relieved to know he was alive, had felt unable to keep this secret to herself. It was not the kind of thing one could tell a neighbour, even a friend. She had been sworn to secrecy as much for the safety of the Ferovs left in Paris as for Sasha. One day however on an impulse she confided the joyful news to her eldest grandchild who was so responsible that it was like having a young woman in the house and not a child at all.

But instead of feeling elated, privileged, Stefanie Lighterman felt crushed. Here she was, taller than Grandma and nearly as tall as Grandpa, someone whom all the family now referred to as a young woman, and no one had told her that Sasha, the beloved brilliant Sasha, her first cousin, had been in France, had actually had dinner with them at Uncle Kyril's. She, Stefanie, in whom was placed so much responsibility, the care of taking her younger sisters backwards and forwards to school, of seeing to their welfare, had not been trusted with this

253

information; had not been invited even to see a cousin she adored, on whom she had had a crush ever since she could remember.

She'd been treated like a little girl and, instead of being pleased that Sasha was safe, Stefanie felt resentment. She was still simmering as she told the tale to Jordan sitting on the bench with the picnic between them, her sisters and their friends still in sight.

Jordan was quite stunned by the news. He too had been excluded but in his case for a different reason. Even Kyril didn't trust him. By the time the story came to an end he was quite flushed with rage. Stefanie, who had never seen him with any colour in his face, looked at him with concern. She remembered that he was supposed to be a semi-invalid.

'Did *you* know he was here?'

'No,' Jordan raised his head. 'You say they had a dinner party at Kyril's?'

Stefanie nodded, slightly mollified that she was not the only grown-up to be excluded. 'Maybe it was lunch; but the meal was at Uncle Kyril's.'

'I was away for a few days.' Jordan rubbed his nose. 'It must have been then. I wonder why he didn't tell me?'

'Well it *is* a secret.' Stefanie began to wonder about the wisdom of this confidence and if she was, after all, quite as grown-up as she thought. Grandma had absolutely *sworn* her to secrecy; but she never thought that Jordan ... Maybe it was because of his nerves they hadn't told him? Perhaps his illness made him unreliable? It was true that anything sudden or unexpected startled him, the backfire of a car in the street; the sudden appearance of someone round a corner made him jump for his life. Now she looked at him gravely. She felt worried. 'I don't think I should have told you,' she said. Too late.

'Why?' He looked at her sharply.

'Because ... it was *supposed* to be a secret; but I thought that meant from my sisters, not the rest of the family...'

'Does your mother know?'

'I don't *think* my mother knows.' Stefanie pretended the indifference she always tried to show when her mother was mentioned. 'I didn't ask Gran and I certainly wouldn't ask *her*.'

'I guess it's not so important,' Jordan said, but from the expression on his face Stefanie didn't think he meant it. The impression she had was that it had made him feel very angry indeed.

Now they had a bond. No one trusted them. She slipped her hand into his but instead of being cold as it usually was it was clammy and warm, rather unpleasant.

Although he was a convinced Communist Kyril liked to live well. He always said he could do without things, that, while he was in prison, he lived on practically nothing. But he hadn't been put to the test for many years; marriage to a wealthy wife had seen to that. So, even with Susan living in Venice and a virtual separation between them in operation – friendly but distant – Kyril was able, through Susan's generosity, to maintain the way of life she had accustomed him to.

Accordingly at an elegantly laid, well-stocked breakfast table while Kyril read the morning paper, Jordan sat glowering at him until, apparently unnerved by the intensity of his smouldering gaze, Kyril looked up, turning the sheet.

'Is something not to your liking?' He looked at the toast and crisp kidneys, the full-scale English breakfast Jordan liked because it was the way he had lived with his mother. Denton liked an English breakfast even if Melanie didn't.

'Why didn't you tell me that Sasha had been here? Here in this room, I understand? Didn't you trust me?'

Kyril, used to controlling himself for so many years, didn't even start but carefully continued to turn the pages of the paper.

'It wasn't a question of trust, but of caution.' He gazed at Jordan through the lenses of his half-moon reading glasses.

'Sasha was an escaped British airman. The fewer people who knew about it the better.'

'I could have been told. Irina and Alexei knew. Hélène knew ...'

'Did she?' Kyril's expression now briefly betrayed surprise. 'That I didn't know. I didn't tell her.'

'I think Irina has told everyone except me.'

Kyril put down his paper and raised his coffee cup to his lips. Behind them Paris basked in such a beautiful June sun that one would be hard put to imagine that France was a country flanked by the most terrible fighting and savagery the world had ever seen. No echoes of guns or thud of bombs, no scream of divebombers and the thump of anti-aircraft fire in Paris on this beautiful morning.

'Then how did *you* know?'

'Irina told Stefanie. Stefanie told me.'

'Ah. I should have known Mother wouldn't keep a secret. I was foolish to invite her; but Sasha so wanted to see his grandmother. He feels he has very little family, you know, with Susan and Anna in Venice and me here.' For a moment Kyril looked sad. 'Bobby and the rest don't make up for the close blood tie. Askham Hall is now a school! Lighterman House is only partly occupied until the war is over, and Robertswood a convalescent home. Sasha misses those family gatherings.'

'I'm family,' Jordan said severely. 'His mother is my sister. Had you forgotten that?'

'Not at all.' Kyril pushed back his chair, crossed his legs and lit a cigarette. 'Anyway you weren't here.'

'But you never *told* me.' Jordan thumped the table and Kyril could perceive that one of his outbursts of temper was coming on. 'That means you didn't trust me. Did you think I'd tell Colonel Weiss?'

Colonel Weiss was Jordan's main contact with the occupation forces. He had only had coffee with Colonel and Frau Weiss in their elegant apartment – belonging to Jews who had fled to America – near the Bourse the day before.

'I just didn't think about it, Jordan,' Kyril said placatingly. 'You must forgive me.'

'Who got him away? Did you?'

'Certainly not,' Kyril looked up sharply. 'How could I?'

'Sometimes I think you're playing a double game. Even the Nazis don't trust you completely.'

'There's no reason for them to trust me.' Kyril was at pains not to show his anger. 'In this war I am uncommitted to either side.'

'Except, maybe, the side of Russia?'

'What on earth makes you say that?' The normally imperturbable Kyril noticed that, as he tapped the ash off his cigarette, his hand shook. 'I have had nothing to do with Russia since I left it in 1929.'

'Yet the Germans *say* half the stories you told them about your pre-war links with Berlin are false. You are hardly known there. They think you might be a double agent – a communist spy. You always gave me the impression you knew most of the top Nazis in Berlin.'

'I did.' Kyril carefully brought his cigarette to his lips again so as not to betray himself by the tremor. He knew the best thing to do, when cornered, was to bluff.

'Who?'

'Why should I tell you? Didn't I introduce you to Weiss? Frankly this interrogation is ridiculous, and uncalled for.'

'Why *did* you bring me here, Kyril? You've told the family I'm seeing doctors, but that's not true. Instead you've introduced me to all the Nazis you know in Paris.'

Kyril ground out his cigarette and cracked the knuckles of both hands together.

'My dear boy, you're becoming paranoid. What *I* am doing for you was done for your own good. I did it for your mother too. I wanted you to realize that you were not in danger from the Nazis. That you could live life fully again. Your mother was extremely worried about your mental health. This is much better, is it not, than spending hours on a couch talking to a psychiatrist?'

'I've done enough of that,' Jordan said bitterly.

'Quite, that's what I thought. It happens that I do know quite a few members of the occupying power. I get on well with them and I thought if I could reassure you you were not in danger it would restore you completely to health, banish those dreams that torment you. You were a very frightened man, you know Jordan. Please don't try, now, to frighten me.'

With that Jordan got up and left the table, firmly shutting the door behind him to show his displeasure.

But Kyril *was* frightened. He stared at the door after Jordan had gone and let his breakfast coffee grow cold. Those who knew him for his calm and *sang froid*, his detachment and urbanity, might have been hard put to recognize him at that instant. For those few minutes he felt engulfed by an emotion almost strange to him: real, paralyzing fear. For so many years Kyril, who had got by on his wits ever since he could remember, even before the Revolution when he had to deceive his parents as to where his real allegiances lay, had played the double game. He had been a wholly political animal and moments of doubt there had never been, not once in the twenty-five years since, as a young man of twenty-one, he had embraced Revolution.

A Revolutionary he had remained even after being incarcerated by his own party in a prison farm in Siberia. He believed even then. This sense of certainty gave one security. One very seldom felt fear, since what one was doing was right. Even the unbeliever, who had no faith in God, had a certain sense of immortality; after him the Revolution would continue. Death had no sting.

Now Jordan had introduced this unwelcome emotion to a life dedicated to a cause: the service of Russia and the bringing about of world revolution. Jordan had made him wonder if all his double bluff of recent years, the assiduous presentation of himself as a right-wing White Russian, like his father truly was, had not been successful after all? How, if it had, had the Germans seen through him? Where had he gone wrong?

Over the years since he had lived in Paris, since he had first come there from Russia in 1929, Kyril had had the same meeting place with those who controlled him from Moscow: the Tuileries Gardens in the shadow of the Louvre. It might seem rather stupid to keep the same meeting place year after year and, as he sat there waiting for the man whose name he did not know to come, he wondered if that had been the mistake. If his presence there had been noticed, particularly by the new authorities who had occupied France three years before. But Susan's apartment was near the Tuileries Gardens and he often walked there, whether he was meeting his control or not. It had seemed rather a good idea, not to interrupt one's routine. Occasionally he sat down on a bench and was joined by a man formerly from the Embassy but, since Hitler and Stalin had become enemies, by someone else.

Even a dedicated Communist like Kyril had been shocked by the Nazi-Soviet pact in 1939. He wondered if he were about to be betrayed by his own side to the other. But he had been given even more important duties: to remain in Paris and continue his cultivation of the small units of Communist cells to organize the ultimate Revolution that the end of the war might facilitate.

To Kyril it had been quite obvious that Hitler and Stalin were playing a game of bluff when the Nazi-Soviet pact was signed, that it was just a matter of time before one betrayed the other. In that world of mistrust Kyril had felt eminently at home and, seeing that he was at home too in Berlin, he had wished very much to be given a more active part to play when, temporarily, Russia and Nazi Germany were allies. But when, finally, Germany stormed across the Russian frontiers in June 1941 in Operation Barbarossa, prepared, some said, the year before, Kyril was glad he had stayed where he was. Maybe it had saved his skin.

Until Germany attacked Russia the role of the Communists in the French Resistance had been equivocal; they hardly wanted to oppose an ally, even a Fascist one. For a year the Communist groups, many of them assiduously cultivated by Kyril, dithered; but when the German army invaded Russia it was as though a whistle had been blown in France. The various Communist cells, ideal for guerrilla warfare, came together to try and muscle out the others in preparation for the ultimate victory of the Revolution.

This part of his life had continued its clandestine operations; meetings in cellars, rooms where the blinds were drawn, issuing directives. It was a bit like the Spanish Civil War all over again, in besieged Madrid. But the other part continued to fraternize with the Germans, to cultivate that image of the patrician White Russian emigré who hated the people who had overthrown the Czar, and incarcerated him for several years.

And, because Kyril never did anything without a purpose, he had invited his brother-in-law who all his life had been a Nazi sympathizer to stay with him, to give credence to this connection with the people who ran Nazi Germany and its new empire from the Reich Chancellery in Berlin.

Kyril had known about the intention of the Germans to occupy the whole of France before they did it the previous year, thus helping some important Communist agents who would otherwise have been trapped in parts of unoccupied France to escape before the German hordes swept south. He had known through his Nazi contacts in Paris of the abandonment of the plan to invade England, and had warned Moscow of the German determination to concentrate on the eastern front long before it was invaded.

When a Communist spy network had been set up in Switzerland – activated after being prepared well before the war – Kyril was part of that; but he covered his tracks so carefully that when it was blown he remained safe. He was a master in the art of cross and double cross, bluff and double bluff.

Yet today he no longer felt secure. The fear that had assailed him after his confrontation with Jordan still seemed to lurk beneath the surface of his skin, making his flesh crawl. He rubbed his arms as a man in an open-necked shirt smoking a cigarette appeared to examine the grass at his feet with interest, then sat down beside him.

'You took a risk in calling me, Comrade,' the man said without preliminaries, the usual exchange of password. 'You were asked not to. Only in an emergency.'

'There is an emergency.'

'What is it?' The vacuous blue eyes looked appraisingly at him and not for the first time Kyril, who had been for so long in the service of his country, wondered what one had to do to be so trusted? To be in such a position of command? 'What is the emergency?'

'I believe the German High Command may be on to me.'

'Why is that?' The man's tone altered but not the expression in eyes trained to give nothing away.

'I have my brother-in-law staying with me.'

'Jordan Bolingbroke, yes I know. Is he not the useful cover you thought he would be?'

'I think he is either undermining me or knows something I don't know. He told me this morning at breakfast that the German High Command has certain reservations about me.'

'Mmmmm.' The blue eyes stared at the passing population. 'Are you sure he isn't bluffing?'

'He isn't that kind. He's a vicious man and I'm sorry I had anything to do with bringing him here. I made a grave mistake.'

Control looked away, his face impassive. It was not wise for an agent of Kyril's long experience to admit a mistake. Mistakes endangered other people. 'He knows nothing for sure? There's nothing in your apartment he could have found?'

'Nothing.'

'I see. Well it was a gamble and maybe he did you a service. If they are on to you then you must take more care.'

'Comrade,' Kyril's voice was pleading. 'May I not return home? I was told many years ago, when I asked to be sent back, that I was needed here. Now that I have fulfilled my tasks may I not be sent home again, maybe to fight in the war as an active soldier?'

'You would like that?' The blue eyes showed surprise.

'Nothing better. It would take me back to my youth when I was active in the Revolution.'

For a moment Control seemed amused. 'You *are* nostalgic, Comrade. I would never have thought it. I will get orders and relay them to you; but please let me contact you. In the meantime find out all you can. We may have to eliminate this Jordan before you go.'

He got up and without another word walked away. Kyril stared after him realizing that his fears had not been allayed; he felt more afraid than ever.

He had already killed one member of the Askham family in the line of duty. It hadn't been a pleasant experience and he hoped he wouldn't have to do it again: even kill a man he now feared and mistrusted.

Charlotte was an excellent courier. Plus Fort liked and trusted her though he had been opposed to having a woman work with him in the first place. In his way he was chauvinistic, and would really have liked women not to have had anything to do with special operations at all. He had been against them being recruited into the SOE.

Plus Fort had been quite dismayed when he saw the beautiful Charlotte Verdi – a woman he well remembered from his brief encounter with her in the tube station – on the tarmac at the secret aerodrome at Tempsford. For a few days he had been taciturn, demanding and even unpleasant; and how unfortunate it had been that one of their contacts in Paris was also a woman and related to her. He had felt so disgusted at this coincidence that he had signalled London to have

Charlotte brought home, but he was curtly ordered to get on with his work.

Soon Plus Fort came to realize that, although Charlotte, naturally, because of her inexperience, was a greenhorn in intelligence work compared with himself, she was a dedicated professional and eager to learn.

When he suggested she move away from Hélène she did without question and then some time later he saw the advantage of her moving back. For once he had made a mistake. Hélène had so merged herself with the landscape of that seedy working-class area of Paris, where the noise of trains could be heard all day long, that it seemed quite natural for her to have her friend from Nantes visiting her.

He realized then that Hélène, much longer in the game than Charlotte, was a professional too. Despite her relationship with Leroux, one couldn't criticize her. Plus Fort didn't approve of sexual relationships among people who worked together in the network, but he knew that Hélène and Leroux were not singular. There were quite a few and, occasionally, they led to disaster through jealousy or betrayal. At least Leroux wasn't married or, rather, he didn't live with his wife. Besides Hélène and Leroux were discreet.

During the summer of 1943 Charlotte went quietly and efficiently about her duties, learning all the time. The main thing she learned was how to control fear; not to let it dominate one's life because, of course, one was almost always afraid. One had to live with fear and let it work for one because it sharpened the senses, alerted one to hidden dangers by making one constantly suspicious. And, although Charlotte didn't like Plus Fort very much, had grown to dislike him because of the way he treated her, she could see that there was a method in what he did and a reason for it. She respected him and did as she was told.

Much of her work was dangerous, checking on the activities of all those in the circuits controlled by Plus Fort. She had to ensure that everyone had the supplies they needed, that the wireless operators were concealed and moved often enough so as not to give themselves away. The Germans had patrol cars that were capable of detecting the wirelesses and many an operator had had to abandon his set and run, leaving the Germans to take over and start transmitting false information. This happened not only in Paris, but throughout Nazi-occupied territory, in Holland and Belgium as well as France. There were many betrayals and much treachery, and the bigger the group the greater was the danger. Charlotte had to be constantly on the alert for treachery, for the beckoning from behind a window or the whisper in the dark. And then the knock at the door; one always dreaded that.

Charlotte threaded her way through the streets she knew and the environs of Paris she knew less well, anonymous in her plain coat and dress or blouse and skirt, her hair usually tucked into a beret, little make-up on. Practically nothing remained of her glamour. She had ceased to be an eagle and had become a Parisian sparrow.

Plus Fort soon realized that Charlotte's greatest asset was this gift for anonymity – she would have made a good actress and, indeed, had once wanted to be one before she fell in love with Paolo Verdi – and also her intelligence. She was sharp, accurate and her memory was so good that she could commit almost everything to the safe recesses of her mind. It was scarcely necessary for her to write anything down and so there were no tell-tale bits of paper to give her, or others, away.

'Your work's good,' Plus Fort admitted after they had been working together for three months. 'I find it hard to fault you.' He looked rather disappointed, as though he enjoyed picking holes.

'Thank you,' Charlotte smiled in an impersonal way. Although she didn't like him she admired his work and his praise was important to her. She knew what a high opinion they had of him in London. For once they were having dinner together at a brasserie in Montparnasse where the food was still passable. Plus Fort seldom came to the flat behind Gare du Nord and they communicated mostly by means of 'letter-boxes', people whom they could trust. In fact, for safety, she didn't even know where Plus Fort lived except that he changed his address every few days. She thought he looked tired again, as he had when they'd first met. He noticed her expression.

'Is anything wrong?'

'You look very tired,' Charlotte said, then laughed. 'I realize I must sound rather like my mother. Well I *am* a mother and I suppose that makes me feel maternal.'

'Really? You're a mother?' Plus Fort realized then how little he knew about her. 'I understood the night I first met you in the tube station that you were about to be married.'

Charlotte had never discussed anything personal with Plus Fort and she didn't much want to now. It was really going against the rules; the private rules she knew that she and he instinctively shared. She knew nothing about him, and never asked. She felt that Hélène and Charles would be safer if they were not involved with each other. She certainly didn't want any sort of similar relationship while she was at work on such dangerous and serious business.

'That would have been my second marriage,' she said reluctantly.

'I see.' Plus Fort looked thoughtful. 'Would have. It didn't take place after all?'

'My fiancé was recalled to his squadron and sent to the Far East. He's now a prisoner,' she said impassively. 'I only heard it the other day.'

'I'm sorry. And your first marriage, the one that produced the children?'

'That was many years ago.' Charlotte still had difficulty in talking about it, especially to strangers. 'My husband was killed. He was a racing driver...'

'Oh, *that* Paolo Verdi?' Plus Fort's face became animated. 'Of course, I knew him. I think you and I must have met many years ago, before the tube station.'

'*You* were a racing driver?' Charlotte looked at him in

amazement, realizing that this revelation had given them an unwanted intimacy.

'No, I was an engineer making racing cars. I won't tell you the name because you don't know my name and it is best like that.'

'But you didn't know my name either.'

'I did.' Plus Fort studied the table, a modest gesture that seemed alien to him. 'I was suspicious of you and I wanted to check up on you. I wondered why you'd lived in France and knew French so well. I found out that you were connected to the Askham family.' Plus Fort kept his eyes on the table.

'So you didn't *really* trust me?'

'I had to be sure. I had set up a network here that was almost unique in that we had never yet been betrayed or had anyone we couldn't trust. I was a little angry with London for giving you to me. Maybe that's why I wasn't always very nice to you. I don't really like women for this kind of work. I'm sorry.'

'That's all right,' Charlotte said offhandedly, though she felt annoyed. She looked at her watch as though the personal part of the conversation had become unpleasant. 'Do you think we should go soon?'

'You didn't tell me about your children.' Plus Fort seemed inclined to linger.

'Have *you* children?' Charlotte stared at him quite rudely.

'No, I'm not married.'

'Sorry, maybe I sounded rude.' Charlotte twiddled with her glass. 'Yes, I do miss my children. I have three – twin boys and a daughter, all at boarding school.'

'Don't you think that what you're doing is very dangerous with young children to consider?'

'They're not young. When they were very young I gave them every minute of my life. After Paolo died I had to work. Whatever you've heard about the Askhams we're not rich, or rather I certainly wasn't rich. My children got used to the idea of a working mother. I am a working mother now.' Charlotte

266

groped on the floor for her bag. 'They think I'm in the WAAF and I believe they're rather proud of me.'

'With every reason,' Plus Fort said quickly and got up to signal the waiter to pay the bill.

'Well, well,' a familiar voice broke in, making them start. 'If it isn't my cousin Charlotte. What in the *world* are you doing here?'

In the very brief time that elapsed Charlotte could see that Plus Fort's first instinct was to run, but she knew that would be fatal. Signalling a warning to him she stood up, holding out her hand, a smile of welcome on her face.

'Jordan, how lovely.' Speaking in French, she held up her cheek as Jordan bent to peck it as though, for all the world, they were meeting at some acceptable social gathering in pre-war France or England. Charlotte hadn't seen Jordan since their grandmother's funeral – he had been too ill to attend Freddie's memorial service – but he had scarcely changed at all. He was blessed, or cursed, according to one's viewpoint, with a boyish complexion, a sort of agelessness which meant that he could be twenty-four, or thirty-four as he was now. He still affected the same guilty Bohemian air, the same clothes, the rather raffish haughty manner. Next to him was a tall blond man dressed casually, but unmistakably German.

'This is my friend Horst,' Jordan edged the man next to him forward. 'My cousin, Charlotte Verdi.' Both Horst and Jordan looked expectantly towards Plus Fort who immediately stretched out his hand.

'Pierre Tournier. How do you do?'

Charlotte gulped. Was it his real name? She hoped not. At least he'd saved the situation for the moment.

'We were just about to leave.' Charlotte stooped to retrieve her bag from the floor. 'Have our table.'

'Oh don't go.' Jordan looked at them appealingly, then around him. The room was crammed full of those twilight people, whose sex was indeterminate in the half light. Charlotte and Plus Fort had only taken the risk of coming here because it was so anonymous. They were quite sure they would be safe in such a throng. Charlotte, though, now regretted the impulse that had made them want to dine outside instead of at a safe house. Yet occasionally one did want to get away, go out and try to recapture the time when life was normal and one could eat at leisure where one wished.

'Yes, stay and have a drink.' Horst was already indicating to them that they should sit down again. He had a faintly inquisitive expression that sent a shiver along Charlotte's back. She looked at Plus Fort – she could think of him as nothing else – and, as he nodded, she sat down again. Jordan signalled for the waiter.

'I didn't think you were in Paris any more, Charlotte? Someone told me you'd left.'

He turned to Horst and spoke rapidly in German and all the time Horst nodded, unsmiling, gazing at Charlotte from beneath drawn brows. Charlotte caught her name 'Lady Charlotte Verdi' in English and the name of Paolo. At the end Horst shook his head. Then Jordan said:

'I was telling Horst who you were. I thought he might have heard of Paolo but he hadn't.'

'Too young, I expect.' Charlotte's mouth felt dry and she looked up with relief when the bottle of wine arrived and Jordan started to pour.

'I can get whisky,' he said, 'but it's safer not to ask for it with Horst. He doesn't speak any English, by the way, in case you're worried.'

'I'm not worried,' Charlotte said. 'Why should I be?'

'I thought you looked amazed to see me,' Jordan explained. 'The last thing I heard you were in the WAAF.'

Jordan carefully didn't look at Plus Fort as he spoke. Charlotte began to feel that at any moment her hair would stand on end.

Jordan continued rapidly. 'Do you speak any German?' When Charlotte shook her head Jordan said: 'That's a pity.'

'We can't stay long, anyway. We were just off.'

'I have to get a train back to Bordeaux,' Plus Fort extemporized.

'Oh, you come from Bordeaux?' As Plus Fort nodded Jordan translated for Horst who also nodded.

'Is he with the occupying forces?' Charlotte's gaze went from Horst to Jordan.

'Of course. He should be in uniform but, occasionally, we come out like this. He'd get into trouble if anyone found out, which is why he's a bit nervous.'

'I didn't think he was nervous,' Charlotte said.

'Maybe he thinks *you're* a bit nervous Charlotte?' Jordan lit a cigarette, offering his case first to her and then to Plus Fort.

'Why do you insist I should be nervous? I live here, don't I? Paris is my home.'

On second thoughts Charlotte accepted a cigarette hoping her hand wouldn't shake.

'I thought you'd left for the war. Most people can't commute between Paris and London. There are some English here, but they've been here since the outbreak. Do the Ferovs know you're here?' Jordan's monologue had begun to seem like an interrogation. 'I think not.'

'Then you know they don't know.' Charlotte glanced at Plus Fort and, leaning over, said quietly to Jordan: 'I am here to see Pierre.' She hoped she was being sufficiently mysterious to indicate a love affair.

'Ah, clandestine is it?' Jordan nodded understandingly.

'Only in the sense,' Charlotte paused, 'that Pierre is married.'

'And you're engaged to the worthy Arthur who is at the war?'

'Yes.' Charlotte's voice dropped to a guilty whisper.

'Naughty Charlotte,' Jordan wagged a finger. 'I shan't tell Horst that.'

'Maybe you'd better.' Plus Fort was obviously trying to keep his voice noncommittal. 'He might think something else.'

Charlotte realized that Jordan was playing with them. That

he obviously knew far more than he was letting on. She had never liked him, remembering how he had treated her mother, who had helped him escape from Germany in 1934. Yet there was no gratitude or magnanimity in Jordan, and the cousins, since Melanie lived in the South of France, only infrequently met.

'The fact that your cousin is here without her family knowing certainly seems strange.'

'Yes, but how did Charlotte *get* here? That's what seems strange to me. Aren't we at war with the British?'

Both Charlotte and Plus Fort noted the 'we'.

'I am Italian.' Charlotte was suddenly inspired. 'Don't forget that by my marriage to Paolo I'm an ally.' She smiled in a friendly manner at Horst as if greeting a buddy and Jordan, obviously relieved to be able to relay something of the conversation to his friend, translated for her and Charlotte heard the word 'Paolo' and 'Verdi' twice. Then 'Italia'. Horst nodded.

'And now we really must go,' Charlotte got up, leaving her wine untouched. 'I'm sure you understand.'

'Perfectly,' Jordan leaned over for another kiss. 'We must meet again. Shall you be in Paris long?'

'I don't know,' Charlotte looked vague.

'Then give us a ring. I'm staying with Kyril, but I'm sure the Ferovs would love to see you. They'd be disappointed not to.'

As she was about to leave he leaned over so close to her that nobody else could hear and spoke rapidly in English. 'Don't worry, Charlotte. I shan't split on you, even though I know. We're all family, don't forget.'

She seemed to feel his hot, treacherous breath on her face as, her expression still fixed in a glazed smile, she turned to go.

PART 3

The Writing on the Wall

August 1943–July 1945

CHAPTER 15

'Oh, this is heaven,' Charlotte exclaimed, throwing back her head so that her face got the full force of the sun. 'No one would ever believe there was a war on.'

No one, Rachel thought, looking tenderly at the pale face of her daughter, except a mother almost sick with worry about her children. At one time, earlier in the year, she hadn't known the whereabouts of all three of them. Ralph somewhere in North Africa; Em probably somewhere in North Africa too, though it could have been Washington or Delhi, or Canberra. For weeks she had received no reports from her and had to rely on Reuters not only for accounts in the paper but for news of her daughter.

When dispatches did arrive they were brilliant descriptions of the final days of the desert campaign, with General Alexander triumphantly reporting to Churchill on 13 May 1943: 'All enemy resistance has ceased. We are masters of the North African shores.' There had been no word of Charlotte, literally for months. Wherever she was Rachel had felt pretty sure it was not on active service with the WAAF.

And then, suddenly, everything had changed – the children all came home at once, and briefly, gloriously, it was like old times again except that the family had transferred itself to Darley Manor which they filled to bursting point. If it really had been old times again they would have been at the Hall or the Grange and there would have been plenty of room for everyone.

But the happiness, the joy, the relief of having them all, however crowded, under one roof, compensated for everything – and not only the children, but grandchildren and friends as well. Ralph had arrived with Jenny, and Charlotte had turned up with a mysterious man called Marc La Fôret who had little to say but seemed perfectly charming. Charlotte and Marc had slept for two days after their arrival; both were still very pale.

'Marc is awfully good with the boys.' Rachel gazed towards the lawn. 'Has he children of his own?'

Charlotte lazily shook her head, opened her eyes and shaded them. 'He's not married, or so he says.'

'Why do you say "or so he says"?'

'You know what men are like, Mummy,' Charlotte glanced at her mother. 'All liars.'

'Oh darling I wouldn't say *that*!' Rachel was shocked. 'Your father ...' And then she stopped. She always liked to hold Bosco up as an example to his family, but over the question of Nimet everyone knew that he'd lied, if not openly, at least by omission.

'All right, Mummy,' Charlotte patted her hand. 'Daddy was perfect. I wish Daddy were here now,' she said suddenly.

'Why do you say that Charlotte?'

'It would make the family complete.' Charlotte kept hold of her mother's hand and once again Rachel was reminded that Charlotte wasn't wearing her wedding ring. Rachel touched the bare finger. 'Except for Freddie,' Charlotte added, then looked sadly at her mother. 'The family will never be complete again, will it Mummy?'

'Not in that way, darling.' Freddie's death was still a wound; a wound so deep she knew she would never recover from it. There had been an inevitability about Bosco's death, but Freddie's was unnecessary. Freddie had died before his time. For Bosco time had clearly been up; the writing on the wall.

'I think Giles is teaching poor Marc cricket,' Charlotte burst out laughing. 'Oh my he *is* good isn't he? Look, he's actually batting.'

'Very good, very nice.' Rachel shaded her eyes too, maybe to hide her expression from her daughter as much as keep out the afternoon sun. 'How did you meet him, Charlotte?'

'At one of the bases.'

'Is he Free French Air Force?'

'Yes.'

'I see.' But Rachel didn't see at all. She didn't believe her and, tired of being understanding and patient, she wanted to know. 'Why aren't you wearing your wedding ring Charlotte? I've never seen you without it.'

'Oh!' Charlotte started and rubbed her finger as though, like Aladdin's lamp, it could be made to reappear. She thought she was not a very good agent to have forgotten something like that in the excitement of being home. For six weeks she and Marc had gone down the line to get back to England through Spain. After meeting Jordan they had decided there was not a moment to lose; no time even to send a wireless message to London. Escorted by Hélène to the first stop on the line they had left that very night ... just in case they were betrayed. For Charlotte was quite certain that Jordan knew and, in his own perverted way, had been trying to warn her to get out.

'Marc is certainly very nice,' Rachel began, 'but...'

'Not having my wedding ring on is nothing to do with Marc! I must have left it in the bathroom or something.'

'You haven't had it on since you came home, Charlotte. It was the first thing I noticed.'

'Trust you to notice a thing like that, Mummy!' Charlotte attempted to laugh it off.

'Of course I notice, especially when you arrive with a charming young man.'

'Marc isn't young. He's nearly forty.'

'He's still very charming.'

Mother and daughter looked at each other and Charlotte knew that there was no point dissembling with someone who knew her so well.

'Yes, he is very charming,' she said slowly looking at Marc playing with the boys on the lawn.

'It's something to do with the secret service isn't it,

Charlotte?' Rachel said, at last, something that had been in her mind for months.

'Oh *Mummy*...'

'I know you can't say.'

'No, I can't.'

'Oh Charlotte ...' Rachel sank back in her chair, hands linked in her lap in an attitude of resignation. 'It makes me very proud of you, and yet frightened. I knew it was the secret service when you were away for so long and no one would tell me where you were. Was it in France?'

'Yes.'

'And you were working with Marc?'

'Yes.' Charlotte closed her eyes remembering the day dislike had turned into love, or had it started earlier? 'I didn't like him much at first. He didn't approve of women in the service and thought I was a security risk. As it happens, he was right.'

Rachel saw the pain in Charlotte's eyes as she opened them again.

'Can't you tell me what happened?' she urged. 'I'm sure it will help. You know that with me a secret is as safe as the Bank of England.'

'I know that, but I think you'll worry, as we shall probably go back.'

'I worried anyway. If I knew I don't think I'd worry so much.'

'All right, I'm breaking official security, but I'll do it. I trust you. I was sent to France with Marc. I only knew him by his code name Plus Fort. I chose,' she looked shyly at her mother and smiled, 'the code name Rachel. I thought it would bring me luck.'

'Well it did. You're here.' Rachel felt very moved that her daughter had chosen her name. For a moment or two Charlotte was silent again. Then briefly, speaking rapidly, very quietly almost in a whisper she told her mother what had happened.

'Jordan Bolingbroke!' Rachel couldn't restrain her indignation. 'That little twerp. Not *him* again. I thought he was incurably ill.'

'Kyril brought him to Paris for some reason no one can fathom. Jordan appears immediately to have begun to chat up the Germans. It was our bad luck to bump into him.'

'And what did he do?'

'Well nothing, immediately, that we know of, but after what happened in Berlin, who could possibly trust him? I had to tell Marc all about it and he made the decision to leave at once.'

'Quite.' Rachel pursed her lips at the memory of helping Jordan to escape from Hitler's Berlin after the night of the long knives. What a terrified young man he had been then. 'I don't suppose he'd have any gratitude.'

'Gratitude?' Charlotte looked at her.

'To me for saving him from Hitler. Thank God you're safe.' Rachel sighed. 'I wonder what happened to poor Hélène and the girls. They're all on my conscience.'

'Hélène is all right, Mummy.' Charlotte pressed her hand. They seemed to communicate by means of signals as much as anything else. 'She is a very brave woman.'

Rachel started. 'She's involved too?'

Charlotte dropped her voice again. 'To the hilt. She has been almost from the beginning and risks her life every day.'

'But surely she can't be living with her parents?'

'She was, but she's not now. She lives in that dingy little apartment that they had near the Gare du Nord. I hope she gets a medal when all this is over.'

Rachel wiped a tear from her eye. 'I'm glad that she's safe and well, being so brave. I knew she had it in her. I always liked Hélène. One couldn't help it.'

The game of cricket was over and the players came straggling up the lawn. With Ralph as wicket keeper, they had practically fielded a full team, the girls joining in.

As she sat back watching them come slowly towards her Charlotte appraised each one, as though committing certain vital details to her memory. There were times when, as far as

277

her children were concerned, she thought she might never see them again. And now here the three of them were, as large as life: Joe, Pascal and Angelica with their cousins Giles and Flora. Ralph's girlfriend Jenny had sportingly been acting as umpire.

The Verdi children were all dark: dark skin and thick, shiny jet black hair. They looked very Italian, taking after their father rather than their mother. The three of them were all slight with fine bones, deeply recessed eyes; the boys rather tall and Angelica, at thirteen, only a little shorter than Charlotte.

Perhaps because they had been bereaved at an early age her children were accustomed to being self-contained and independent. She had few qualms about leaving them, although, of course, there was the unutterable pain of separation, possibly permanent. But they could not share this with her. They had always seemed quite old, quite grown-up. Angelica was given to tantrums as a small child, but she had rapidly grown out of them when she was sent to boarding school.

Her cousin Flora, Adam's younger daughter, was at the same school. There being two years between them, they saw little of each other until they were at home for the holidays when they became inseparable ... to resume the distance when back at school.

Giles was now fifteen – very much a Bolingbroke in looks and temperament; stolid, reliable, good at games. Like his cousins he and his sister had also lost a parent when young and, although the five were very unalike to look at, they all got on very well.

They came up, chatting to Marc, at ease with him but on their best behaviour. By his overarm movements Giles was obviously showing the stranger some of the finer points of bowling.

Ralph had his arm round Jenny's waist. Charlotte, like her mother, gazed at them critically. Next to Ralph in age she had always been close to him, whereas the twins, Em and Freddie, had been inseparable until death separated them forever.

Charlotte knew how her mother felt about Jenny, but she herself liked her. She was completely different from Cheryl but she could see how good she was for Ralph. Besides, she obviously made him happy in a way, and in an important area, that Cheryl never had. They had the contented, slightly bemused air of a couple who enjoyed a satisfactory physical relationship. They were always touching, and although at times it was a bit embarrassing to a family who had always been reticent about open displays of affection, in the context of the war and their separation it was understandable.

And, finally, there was Marc. He was very lean and tall, more cavernous than before the long journey to Spain. His hair was a little grey at the sides and Charlotte couldn't remember whether it had been like that before, because she hadn't loved him before. One only scrutinized people in whom one was interested. It was only on the journey across Nazi-occupied France that she had become that interested in her travelling companion.

As the group approached the terrace Rachel got up to rearrange chairs, and Marc squatted on the ground beside Charlotte. Instinctively Charlotte bent down and touched him lightly on the cheek.

'I didn't see you get that many runs.'

In all the years since Paolo she had never felt about a man like this. Any contact, however brief, with him seemed electric. Briefly he looked at her and in that moment she felt that they were the only two people there.

'I'm out of condition,' Marc laughed. 'I lead too lazy a life.'

'What do you do?' Joseph, called Joe by the family, threw himself on his stomach and gazed frankly at the older man their mother had unexpectedly introduced into their lives.

'I'm in the Air Force.'

'Like Mummy?'

'Yes.'

'Is that how you met her?'

'Yes.'

'Arthur's in the Air Force too.'

'I know.' Marc's face remained impassive.

'Only he's a prisoner. Isn't that tough luck?'

'Very tough.' Marc joined his hands round his knees. The muscles in his jaw were twitching.

'I'm sure everyone wants tea,' Rachel interposed tactfully as her brother Adam staggered on to the terrace with the stumps. 'I'm sure no one wanted to steal the stumps, Adam,' Rachel said. 'This isn't a Test wicket. You could have left them for tomorrow.'

'You know Dad,' Giles said disparagingly, 'he's suspicious of everybody. It's his training as a lawyer.'

'That's not fair.' Adam collapsed into a chair and looked reprovingly at his young son. He was always aware of the great difference in their ages – he was sixty. But his second wife Margaret had wanted children so badly. Despite the difference, however, between him and eleven-year-old Flora there was a deep bond of affection. Flora carefully removed the stumps from his arms. 'You're sweating, Daddy!'

'I'm an old man, my darling.' Adam put his hand out to her and Rachel announced briskly as the maids approached:

'Tea! Tea, everyone.'

The tea was traditional English – cucumber and tomato sandwiches, layer cake, scones with plenty of butter, all things that were possible in the country but not in the city. Sometimes Rachel with her well developed conscience felt rather guilty about it all. The boys, who all also went to the same school, fell almost baying on their food and before very long Giles was dispatched to the kitchen to request more.

Though Adam managed to keep a small complement of elderly servants the children were encouraged to do things for themselves in a way that would have been strange when Rachel and her brother were their age. Even the middle-class relatively poor Bolingbrokes had servants; but the Askhams, when young, would never have dreamt of doing anything for themselves, nor would it have been considered proper. Beds

280

were made, rooms tidied, meals prepared, dishes washed, clothes valeted, shoes polished, ladies' hair brushed by a small well-trained cohort of obedient servants.

Ralph glared at the empty plates. 'I see there's practically nothing left to eat! After all my efforts.' He pretended to shake his fists at the children.

'Aunt Rachel says you eat too much anyway.' Flora made a face at him. 'You're a pig.'

'Flora, don't speak to Ralph like that!' Adam tapped her sharply on her leg.

'Why not?' Flora stared boldly at her father.

'Because it's a very rude way to address a grown-up.'

'*And* an officer and a gentleman,' Ralph said good-humouredly, flopping on the ground beside Jenny just as Giles reappeared, followed by a maid with a laden tray.

'Betty was just bringing it out.'

'It wasn't *all* out, my lady,' Betty protested to Rachel. 'They don't half eat quick.'

'Pigs,' Flora said again, but in a low voice as if she didn't want her father to hear. 'Is Em coming over tonight with that horrible Felipe?'

'Flora.' This time Adam's tap was harder. 'I don't know what's the matter with you today.'

'Well, he *is* horrible. Everyone *hates* him.' Flora seemed instinctively to feel that her youth gave her the advantage of plain speaking. She was a very direct, outspoken young girl who often reminded Adam of her namesake – his lost platonic love.

'No one really knows him.' Rachel seemed annoyed at this washing of family linen in front of strangers. 'And I do wish you *would* not be so outspoken, Flora. We have guests present.' She looked severely at her niece.

'Please don't mind me, Lady Askham,' Marc said reasonably. 'I don't understand a thing anyone's talking about.'

'Oh yes, you do,' Flora went on. 'I think you understand everything perfectly well. You're always watching.'

'I watch because I'm trying to learn,' Marc said kindly, and not for the first time in the short period he'd been here Charlotte marvelled at his tact. He really was the perfect diplomat, never lost for the right word. She was aware that her children regarded him with special interest but, being so polite and well brought up, they would never have commented on him even to her; although Angelica might whisper something when the time for confidences came as she was being tucked up and kissed goodnight.

'I do hope you'll stay a while,' Adam said politely to Marc as he filled his pipe after tea. 'You'll find England at its very best at this time of the year. You speak such good English you must know it quite well. What did you do before the war? The Diplomatic? Or shouldn't one ask?'

Adam sat back, resting his eyes on Marc who had been studying a column of ants walking briskly and in perfect formation along the ground.

'I'm a boat-builder – an engineer by training,' Marc said, looking up. 'I come from Nice. I don't actually physically build them with my hands, you understand, though I can; but I'm the head of a small business building boats, selling them to rich people or chartering them. It was a very thriving little business. Of course I met many English people in the South of France and that's how I came to speak English a little. After I came over to join de Gaulle I was able to improve it.'

Leaning back, her hands behind her head, Charlotte listened to him explaining certain aspects of his life and career to the audience on the terrace. She wondered how much of it was true because she knew that Marc had very early on been one of the pillars of the French Resistance, one of its founders.

She watched everyone on the terrace, their eyes on Marc. They were as charmed by him as she was – well, not quite perhaps. But Adam was right. He did have the accomplished, polished air of the professional diplomat. A boat-builder? Well it might be true. But did it matter? She had promised to marry Arthur.

Shortly afterwards the group broke up. Ralph and Jenny agreed to drive over to fetch Paul who had been spending the day helping Hugo on the farm. Paul was Freddie's young son, now an orphan and entirely in Rachel's care. Paul was only eight but he was a sturdy, vigorous lad. Until Ralph had children he was his heir.

Would Ralph ever have children? Suddenly Rachel – she didn't know why – looked at Jenny and wondered. Was it not, perhaps, the strong desire to breed that had really driven Ralph from his apparently barren wife to this capable, fecund-looking farm girl from the North?

'Ask Hugo if he'd like to bring Amelia over,' Rachel said as she saw the party to the door. 'There's plenty to eat.'

Rachel loved large family dinner parties; they reminded her so much of the past. The precious candles were lit and the table gleamed with polished silver, fine crystal. The excited, chattering faces round it, from the youngest, Paul, to the oldest, Adam, gave it a kind of timeless continuity.

No one dressed for dinner now. The women wore pretty frocks and the men jackets and ties, but formality had gone with the outbreak of war.

Rachel wondered how long it would be until they were all gathered like this again and said very little during the meal which, inevitably, was dominated by talk of the progress of the war.

After dinner the children went to the games room, with the exception of Joe who was rather studious and went to his room to read.

It was a balmy night in late August, quite hot, and the adults wandered on to the terrace and lit cigars and cigarettes while coffee was served.

Em had come by herself. Rachel thought that was why dinner had been so harmonious. When Felipe was there, which was seldom, there was always an argument.

Em and Marc got on well, chatted together in French – Em's

was almost as fluent as Charlotte's. Em always seemed happier without Felipe, in Rachel's opinion. And this was shared by Charlotte as they whispered together while they prepared and dispensed the coffee. Ralph was chatting to Hugo and Cheryl's daughter Amelia whom Hugo had been secretly seeing for over a year. Amelia was now stationed at American HQ in Grosvenor Square and Hugo either went up to see her or, more often when she had forty-eight hours' leave, she came down to see him.

Amelia was a very beautiful girl, there was no doubt of that and, although she wasn't wearing it tonight, looked particularly well in uniform. She was very like Cheryl, but only in looks. She didn't seem to resemble her at all in any other way. She was direct, open and friendly and the family had instinctively liked her. Maybe it helped them to close ranks in favour of Hugo, against Cheryl, who was largely ignorant of the relationship. Hugo was quite mesmerized by Amelia and his eyes followed her around the room when she left his side as if he were frightened of losing her. Hugo, for the first time at the age of thirty-one, had found himself seriously in love.

When Rachel had finished serving coffee she went and sat by Adam who looked more than usually content with his brandy and cigar in the company of his beloved family. Adam was like the grandfather of them all, sharing with Rachel the overall care and responsibility for this extended and complex family. Comforting her when she was worried, sharing the happiness when something nice happened. On the whole Adam was a stolid, reassuring presence – long experience had taught him to maintain an equilibrium, a balance, when possible, in all things. Of the two, brother and sister, Rachel was the more impulsive, the more emotional and, in a way, the more talented. One could also say she had more to worry about, but Adam, with his young family, had worries too – and for many years he had had to cope with the caprices of Melanie. Maybe it was this experience that taught him how to be so patient.

Charlotte perched beside Marc who moved over for her on

the wicker settee. Instinctively his arm stole round her waist, a gesture that, Rachel thought, only she observed. She sighed. It seemed ridiculous even to consider that they might not be lovers though Charlotte, typically reticent, had not confided in her. Maybe she wouldn't because Rachel was so fond of Arthur.

It occurred to Rachel, looking at Marc and Charlotte so close together, aware of the sexual chemistry that emanated from them, even though they were listening to Ralph on the far side of the terrace, that in a way she disapproved of the relationships of all her living children. It was only Marian, lawful wife of dear Freddie, to whom she had instinctively responded and come to love very much before her early death.

What did legality have to do with it, after all, and were these not enlightened times even though she was born well before the end of the last century? It wasn't as though her own emotional life had been so blameless. For years before their marriage she and Bosco had been lovers, a fact that made her future mother-in-law ostracize her and continue to dislike her for many years after their relationship became legal.

No, Rachel didn't think, in all honesty, that her attitude towards her children and their companions had anything to do with legality. What was it then? Well, clearly Felipe was not right for Em – he was too dominating, too selfish and chauvinistic. Everyone agreed about that. Jenny, on the other hand ... For a moment she gazed critically at the woman next to Ralph, thankful for the crepuscular light on the terrace that made such scrutiny possible. Ralph, after all, wasn't an ordinary individual – he was a peer of the realm with privileges, rights but also duties. Divorce was a scandal, even now. It could be a very sordid business. Jenny *did* seem right for Ralph, were she, his mother, not so prejudiced on behalf of Cheryl who had expressed repentance, a desire to reform. She was, after all, Lady Askham, Ralph's lawful wife, and she was prepared to take a fresh look at their marriage. Why wasn't he? Cheryl had redeemed herself in many ways by her care for the homeless evacuees, but Ralph wouldn't even go and see her. Rachel had to admit that, but for the fact that he was married, there would be nothing wrong with Jenny.

Rachel frowned and turned her attention to the pair on the furthest side away from her, as though they wished to conceal themselves.

Marc was clearly attractive in a way that Arthur wasn't. He had the dash and flamboyance, as well as the looks, of Paolo Verdi whom he slightly resembled. Charlotte obviously went for the same type. Paolo had been a racing driver with a limited time in which to be successful. He was successful, but he died on the track and left Charlotte almost penniless. Marc was a boat-builder. Rachel realized that, in her heart of hearts, she liked the professions. Not only was Arthur a professional pilot, he was sure to make good as something in the City once the war was over. The Askhams and the Crewes had known one another for generations. Everything that one could know about Arthur was known, yet what did one know of Marc? What sort of life would Charlotte have as the wife of a mere builder of boats in the South of France? Could Marc match Rachel's expectations for her daughter? The last thing Rachel wanted was that Charlotte should have to work so hard, and in such a way – exploiting her body – for her living again.

Ralph rose and stretched himself, long arms reaching to the now inky sky. 'Anyone fancy a rubber or two of bridge?' he inquired. 'We played a lot of bridge in the desert when we weren't fighting. It helped to calm the nerves. I think I was regimental champion. Darling?' He looked towards Jenny, who said deprecatingly:

'You know I'm not very good.'

'I know you're not very good, but we do need another player. If you study my play you'll soon be *very* good.'

'He's so hideously vain,' Charlotte grimaced. 'I don't know how you put up with him, Jenny.'

But from the look that Jenny gave him everyone could see

286

that she was quite willing to put up with Ralph, in any way at all.

What no one else knew was that Ralph and Jenny had only recently come together again after their estrangement in Cairo the previous autumn. Jenny had wanted time to think, to establish her independence – and she had been successful. Now they were closer than ever, with a better, deeper understanding of each other. But Jenny would be very careful not to criticize his mother again.

'Come on.' Marc reached for Charlotte's hand and tugged her. 'We can beat them tonight.'

'Isn't that rather unfair on those who aren't playing?' Rachel looked up. 'You know Adam loves a game.'

'Oh I'm sorry, Uncle Adam,' Ralph was immediately contrite. 'Play instead of me. I'll score.'

'No, no, no,' Adam shook his head. 'I really don't want to play at all. I'm afraid the sun got to me today. I'm ready for bed.'

'Are you all right?' Rachel inquired anxiously, noticing that Hugo was helping him get out of his chair.

'Perfectly all right, my dear.' Adam patted his chest. 'Just a touch of breathlessness. But that's due to my age.'

'And *all* those cigarettes.' Ralph wagged a finger at him.

'The doctor said it had *nothing* to do with cigarettes.' Adam stared at him indignantly. 'Nothing at all.'

Hugo linked his arm through Adam's and went with him into the house.

'Hugo's awfully fond of Adam,' Charlotte said, watching them go. 'I hadn't realized quite how much.'

'Yes he *is* very fond of him, and vice versa,' Rachel said. 'Hugo is very good and understanding with Adam. But then, he is with everyone ...'

'Except Mummy,' Amelia intervened. 'They can't stand each other.'

'I'm afraid they never did get on, my dear.' Rachel tried to

287

sound solicitous. 'It was instinctive. Does your mother know you're seeing so much of him?'

'I think she guesses. Obviously she doesn't know we see as much of each other as we do, or that I come down to see Hugo and don't tell her. Let's put it like this, Lady Askham: she knows I do see him, but not how much. Still,' Amelia flung her head back and gazed defiantly at Rachel, 'I am of age, aren't I? It *is* my business.'

'Our business.' Hugo coming back on the terrace had stood listening, watching the reactions of the people he loved: Charlotte and Em, Rachel and Ralph.

'*Our* business?' Charlotte, in the act of going into the drawing room to join Marc, who was setting out the cards with Jenny, turned and stared at him.

'Amelia and I want to get married. The trouble is we don't know whether to tell Cheryl before or after.'

During the pause laughter could be heard from inside the drawing room and Jenny called out, 'Do hurry.'

'Coming,' Ralph called. 'Just a minute, darling.' Then to Hugo he said, 'This is serious, then?'

'Very serious.'

'From the beginning,' Amelia took his arm. 'It was love at first sight.'

'I'm afraid Cheryl *will* be very bitter.' Rachel wondered why she hadn't seen the warning signals before. 'It might alienate her from you completely.'

'But Mummy can't interfere with my life, Lady Askham.'

At times Rachel felt Amelia *was* like her mother, although she had no doubt she was genuinely in love with Hugo. There was a certain icy insolence that occasionally showed – which Amelia clearly shared with her mother. It was not a very attractive quality – that hauteur – and although she liked Amelia Rachel wondered if she could really make Hugo happy.

'We wondered, Rachel, we were going to ask you later, but we might as well now ...' Hugo paused and then continued rapidly. 'We wondered if *you* would talk to Cheryl as you get on so well with her?'

'*I* tell her you want to get married?' Rachel was flabbergasted. 'I couldn't possibly do that.'

'Why not, Mother? You're so diplomatic,' Ralph chipped in. 'Besides, now you get on so well,' was there irony in his voice? Rachel couldn't be sure. But Ralph was smiling, 'you might also try telling her again that I'd like a divorce ... and I'll cut her allowance if I don't get one.'

'The atmosphere was *so* charged tonight,' Em said when, at last, she and her mother were alone on the terrace. The four inside were not taking their bridge very seriously and there was plenty of laughter.

'Charged with what, darling?' Rachel, sipping her coffee, looked at her. Although Em was only thirty-five she had some grey hairs and Rachel thought, with a pang, how much her beloved daughter had aged since the war began ... or was it because of Felipe who had insisted on keeping Luis, on bringing him up, who scarcely tolerated her?

'Sex.' Em took a gulp of the brandy from the glass in her hand. 'It's almost palpable. Didn't you feel it?'

'Yes, I did,' Rachel nodded. 'I know what you mean. Everyone is in love. Isn't that nice?'

'It's nice, but difficult,' Em lit a cigarette, blowing a thin cloud of smoke in front of her.

'How do you mean?'

'In every relationship there is a complication. Ralph is not free to marry Jenny. Amelia will be bitterly opposed by her mother if she tries to marry Hugo and, well,' she glanced at Rachel, 'as for Charlotte and Marc ... what about poor Arthur?'

'Poor Arthur,' Rachel murmured. 'I was thinking about that a few minutes ago.'

'She gave him her word.'

'Knowing Charlotte, she'll keep it.'

'Yes, but she's in *love* with Marc, Mummy, and you must have seen that she never has been with Arthur.'

'Did she tell you as much?'

Em shook her head. 'She didn't need to. I must say Marc *is* frightfully attractive. You know, of course, that they met in France?'

It was Rachel's turn to look surprised. 'I thought *that* was a secret?'

'Well, it is, but I know. I've known for some time, but I'm not supposed to know.'

'How did you know, then?' Rachel was curious.

'Because I was in Madrid and met someone who was waiting for them. He knew I was Charlotte's sister and he told me what she'd been up to. I'm afraid the espionage world is like that. It's full of indiscretions, betrayals and danger.'

'Oh my God, please don't tell me. She's going back, you know.'

'Charlotte knows the risks, Mother.'

'I hoped she might not go back. I *pray* she doesn't.' After a pause Rachel turned to Em. 'And you, my darling? What about you?'

'Things don't change with me, Mother. Felipe, of course, wouldn't come tonight, said he was "busy".'

'I only wish he'd let me see Luis.'

'You have every right to see Luis. He's your grandson.'

'Felipe is his father and he won't have me or any of us in the house.'

'It's not *his* house,' Em said savagely.

'Oh darling, if we take the house away we will never see Luis again. I'm quite sure of that. Felipe will go back to Spain or disappear or something ...'

'He can't,' Em said, the same grim, stern note in her voice. 'He depends entirely on me for a living. It's unlikely anyone will be interested in publishing his account of the Spanish Civil War.'

'You've read it?'

'Bits. It's far from finished.'

'Is your Spanish *that* good?'

'It's good enough.' Suddenly Em bent down and put her head in her hands. 'Oh Mummy, what am I to do?'

Rachel got up and took Em's head between her hands. 'It *is* bad, isn't it, Em?'

'It's awful. It's like death. I *hate* going back to be with him. I'm not with him in body or spirit any more. I feel I simply hate him, Mum; but I do so love Luis.'

'We all do.'

Rachel went on staring at her daughter. For one of the few times in her life she felt completely helpless.

'Does your mother know about us?' Marc said in the dark. It had been a warm night but now, in the dawn, a little breeze was wafting through the window making the curtain restless.

'I think she guesses. She's very perceptive.'

'I like her very much.'

'She likes you.'

'Did she say?'

'Yes.' Charlotte smiled at him, though he couldn't see her face.

'She actually said she liked me?' Marc sounded pleased.

'She said you were very charming. That's the same kind of thing.'

'Did you talk much about me then?'

'No.' Charlotte was always truthful. 'But she did ask about France. She'd guessed about that too. I told her I worked with you and, at first, I hadn't liked you much, and then I did...'

'Did you tell her when you did?' Marc's voice sounded a little complacent.

'Don't be silly. Mummy wouldn't ask me about the details. She would be horrified, anyway, if I told her half the things that happened during that journey. Little does she know I was in more danger then than I ever was in Paris.'

'True.' Marc nodded and was silent. He slipped his hand

into hers as he had that night when they thought they were both trapped in a loft on a farm near Amboise and it was a matter of time before the Germans arrived. They had been following them down the lane but, instead of stopping at the farm and searching the outbuildings, they drove straight past. In the relief that followed, the relaxation of tension then, that night, for the first time, they had made love.

After that, though still full of dangers, the escape journey had seemed like a honeymoon. Alone, together, they had faced the world, and willingly; not wanting to die but to have a future together.

And now? There was Arthur. There always had been Arthur and Marc knew about Charlotte's promise. How could she betray a man to whom she had made a promise? Who was very probably now being helped to survive through his memories of her. Who knew what kept Arthur alive in a Japanese prisoner-of-war camp?

And how could she ever betray her promise to Arthur when he came home? *If* he came home.

In the dawn her eyes suddenly filled with tears. Sensing it, Marc bent towards her and kissed her cheek, gently blotting her tears with his fingers.

'What is it, my darling?' he murmured.

But Charlotte couldn't speak. How could she possibly tell one man that she loved him so much that she wished another dead?

CHAPTER 16

Each time Rachel came up the drive towards the Hall, past the ilex trees and rhododendrons, the lilac and azalea that still lined that gracious curve before its two arms broadened into the huge paved forecourt in front of the great Doric porch, Rachel felt what she could only call a twinge of nostalgia, a sense of homecoming.

Not that she had ever actually lived there as the châtelaine. Because of Bosco's death that position had passed her by, going straight from Dulcie to Cheryl. But Askham Hall was linked with so many generations of her husband's family, and she was so much more an Askham than a Bolingbroke now, that it was like coming home.

And yet these days once up the drive she was always assailed by a sense of shock. Instead of the vast, planned gardens beyond were rows and rows of vegetables: cabbages, peas, beans, potatoes, tomatoes according to season. All the rose trees, so beloved of Dulcie, had gone to make way instead for the necessities of feeding a large number of people – no longer the family, their friends or servants, but up to fifty East End evacuees and their teachers.

Askham Hall was now a residential school and, by some strange osmosis, it had begun to look like one. Rachel, who had walked up the drive after being put off by the local bus at the gates (a sight in itself, in the opinion of some locals, who could never remember seeing a member of the family travel by public transport before), stopped in front of the house and gazed at it. Yes, it looked like an institution, though difficult to say why. In outward appearance it hadn't changed at all. But in a mysterious way, it had.

'Good morning, Lady Askham.' The head gardener who

had been at the Hall since Dulcie's time stopped and touched his forelock. He would probably be one of the last of that kind of servant, the last of many generations of family retainers. Some observers of the social scene said this was a good thing. It was the passing of a kind of feudalism that many found abhorrent. Yet what would happen to the Hall after the war? It would always require a vast staff to look after it.

'Good morning, Roberts,' Rachel said cheerily. 'How nice to see you again. How are Richard and Sissie?'

Roberts smiled with pleasure. 'Richard has been commissioned in the Army, your ladyship. Imagine, he's an officer!'

'You must feel very proud of him.'

'I am ma'am, I am. It also shows that in the war there is a chance for everyone, no matter who their fathers were.'

'Exactly.' Rachel showed by her warm smile that she approved of such egalitarian principles.

'Sissie had her third last week.' Roberts scratched his head. 'She ain't so good.'

'I'm sorry about that. I must go and see her. Is she in the Cottage Hospital?'

'She's in London, Lady Askham. Mrs Roberts and I were dead against her going, but she wanted to be near her husband. Then, just before the baby was born, he was sent abroad. I think that's why she's not so good. She don't know where he's gone. Not good enough is it? She's taken it hard.'

'I'll send her a note.' Rachel adjusted the brim of her soft felt hat. 'Do you happen to know if Lady Askham is at home?'

'I did see Lady Askham talking to one of the school teachers ma'am. It is a *very* funny set up we have here now, my lady.'

'It's all part of the war effort, Roberts.' She gestured towards the rows and rows of healthy looking vegetables. 'Your allotment is magnificent!'

'Allotment!' Roberts sniffed. 'My lady, do you remember them roses which were the pride of old Lady Askham's heart?

My goodness she would turn in her grave if she were to see them cabbages and potatoes. Ruined the place they have.'

'You should feel proud of yourself,' Rachel said encouragingly.

'*Proud*, my lady? I've got another word for it but I wouldn't say it in front of you.'

'Well, I think it's wonderful.' Looking towards the house Rachel saw that Cheryl was standing on the steps and wondered how long she'd been there. She waved.

'Bye, Roberts. See you again.'

Roberts touched his forehead again, gathered up the wheelbarrow he'd been trundling and went on. Cheryl came slowly down the steps towards Rachel, her arms held out.

'What a nice surprise.'

'Thank you.' Rachel kissed her on the cheek and gave her a small packet. 'There's some butter for you. Just you.'

'I'll be arrested,' Cheryl smiled. 'Anyway, I believe margarine is good for the figure.'

'You don't need margarine.' Rachel looked at her daughter-in-law who was dressed with her usual care even for a day in the country in the middle of wartime. Her blue cotton dress, though simple in style and gathered at the waist, had that unmistakable air of *haute couture* of all Cheryl's clothes. Rachel wondered if she ever bought anything off the peg or if every single garment were made for her.

'What brings you here?' Cheryl looked round. 'And where's the car?'

'I came by bus.'

'Bus?' Cheryl sounded incredulous.

'You know, a bus, a long thing with several pairs of wheels.' Rachel, smiling, described a bus with her hands. 'I got a local train, and then the bus brought me right to the gate.'

'Well I suppose one *has* to be careful of petrol.' Cheryl looked doubtful. 'Though I think I'd rather stay at home than take a bus.'

'You should try it.' Rachel linked her arm through her

daughter-in-law's. 'It's an interesting experience. Besides, I have a lot of people staying with me. Charlotte, who has a young man with her, a colleague, rather wanted to run down to the sea.'

What she didn't add was that Hugo and Amelia, Ralph and Jenny and some of the children were going with them and that two cars were needed.

'Charlotte has a young man?' Cheryl looked curious. 'Not unfaithful to poor Arthur I hope?'

'He really is a colleague, a Frenchman who got some leave that was due to him and had nowhere to go. Now tell me, how are things here? No school of course.'

'More's the pity,' Cheryl looked harassed. 'It's *far* easier when they are all in classes and I know where they are. I'm a nervous wreck. What sort of school, I ask you, keeps all its pupils in the holiday?'

'Don't they *ever* go home for a visit?'

'Some do.' Cheryl waved to a passing group. 'Some don't want to and some can't ... Incidentally, there's something I want to talk to you about. Shall we go in and have coffee?'

'That would be lovely,' Rachel said. 'I left right after breakfast, or I'd have missed the bus.'

Inside the house Rachel realized why one noticed the difference, even from the outside. The atmosphere had changed so remarkably that it was impossible any more to envisage it as a gracious home. The new spirit had even pervaded the white Chilmark stone of the outside.

In the hall there was a smell of dust mingled with chalk, of feet and not very well washed childish bodies. It wasn't unpleasant so much as vital and vigorous; but it was of an institution not a home. People could be heard calling from all over the huge house; there was the sound of running and they hastily stepped back as a body slid past them down the broad banister, collapsing into a heap on the floor.

'Edna!' Cheryl boomed in a voice that, too, had altered. No

longer the *grande dame* but the schoolmistress, a mixture of Matron and Head, used to maintaining authority.

'Sorry, Miss.' Edna, with a smirk, picked herself up, dusted her grubby knickers and ran away stifling her giggles with a hand clenched to her mouth. To her amazement Rachel noticed a fond smile on the face of that former doyenne of London society, who loved nothing better than her portrait in the social pages of the glossy magazines: 'The Countess of Askham photographed at home, Askham Hall, Askham, Wiltshire. The Countess is wearing ...' By her elbow would be a large bowl of flowers, maybe a dog or two at her feet, borrowed from one of the staff because Cheryl was no animal lover and had none of her own.

'I think you rather enjoy this life,' Rachel remarked when they were seated in Cheryl's comfortable sitting room, littered now with books, papers and endless forms stamped with the logo of some government ministry or the other.

'Do you know, I *do*.' Cheryl had ordered coffee on the way up and as they were talking it was brought in by one of the girls who, giggling, put it rather clumsily on the table nearly upsetting the coffee pot.

'Clare, you must be more careful,' Cheryl chided her, but kindly. 'Is it your day in the kitchen?'

'Yes, Miss.' Clare bit her lower lip and giggled again.

'You're doing very well. This is my mother-in-law, Lady Askham.'

'D' je do.' Clare studied her feet.

'Hello, Clare. Are you enjoying it here?'

'Yes, Miss.'

'You don't mind the country after London?'

'No, Miss.'

'Thank you, Clare,' Cheryl said, 'close the door after you. Please don't bang it.' She smiled graciously at Clare who blushed deeply, slipped on the floor and shot out of the room shutting the door with a tremendous bang.

'Oh!' Cheryl put her hands to her ears, but she was still

smiling. 'Can't have everything can you? Boys and girls all take turns during the holidays in the kitchen, the garden and helping in the house. I've allowed the parents of some of them to stay and that has worked well too. The Ministry is frightfully pleased with me and wants me to serve on some board or the other. They say I'm innovative. Isn't that nice?'

'Oh, well done. I *am* pleased.' Rachel noticed the flush of pleasure on Cheryl's face. Like anyone she liked praise.

If only Ralph could see her now. But would it make any difference if he did? Rachel thought of the way he looked at Jenny, the way he was with Jenny, as he had never been with Cheryl.

There had been something wrong with the marriage from the very beginning, an inequality, an awkwardness – with Ralph being the one too obviously in love. With Jenny it was mutual, a partnership. Despite that, however, Rachel was still unhappy about it. As she hadn't at first liked Cheryl, now, she had to admit, she didn't much like Jenny either. Why? She wished she knew because Ralph was very happy; but then, at the beginning he'd been ecstatic about Cheryl.

'There!' Cheryl finished pouring the coffee and offered Rachel a plate of biscuits saying proudly: 'The children baked these as well.'

Rachel took a biscuit, out of duty, because she didn't really want one and bit it. 'Delicious!' she said, dutifully taking another. Cheryl beamed. 'Did you say there was something you wanted to talk to me about?'

'Well,' Cheryl coloured slightly, something Rachel had seldom seen her do. Maybe she was about to tell her she'd found another man. That would solve a lot of problems. 'Well,' Cheryl began again inspecting the biscuit in her fingers as though trying to detect some culinary flaw. 'I want to adopt two children.'

'I *beg* your pardon?'

'I've given it a lot of thought,' Cheryl hurried on, 'and it's not primarily to do with Ralph, but I *did* think that if Ralph saw the children, and me with them, came here, you know, saw the place and what I'm doing here, things might improve between us.' Seeing the expression on Rachel's face she faltered. 'You don't think they would improve, I can see that.'

'It's not that.' Rachel felt terribly confused. '*Adopt* children did you say. Are they babies or what?'

'Good Lord, no! One of them was Clare who just came in. I wanted you to see her first.'

'That Clare ...' Rachel pointed to the door. 'But she's about eight.'

Cheryl nodded brightly. 'And she has a brother who's ten, Edward, we call him Ned. I'm frightfully fond of them both. That's why I introduced you. Pretty little thing, isn't she?'

'Pretty, but ... eight,' Rachel said again as though the number had some mystical quality.

'They're war orphans,' Cheryl explained. 'Their family were all killed in one of the terrible raids on the East End last April: mother and father, grandparents, and another brother and baby sister! There was a direct hit on their house which was near the docks. The whole family was wiped out.'

'How dreadful.' Rachel shuddered and momentarily closed her eyes.

'Ned and Clare were not the only ones – not the only children who have lost one or both parents while they've been here. You hear the most frightful things you know, Rachel.' She paused and smiled nervously – quite unlike herself. It was only recently she had dropped the formalities and used Rachel's Christian name. 'Rachel' yes, but 'mother' never. Maybe they both knew she had left it too late. 'Sometimes the parents just leave them and are never seen or heard of again, or the mother runs away, or the father does. Or the father is killed or goes missing. You've no idea the things we have to deal with. You have to be a nurse, social worker and administrator all in one. You also have to develop compassion,' Cheryl paused again, 'and understanding, and I don't think I had much of either before.'

'But *adopt* ...' Rachel was still dumbstruck. 'I hope it's not just to try and get Ralph back, because...'

'Oh no, no, no! *Nothing* like that!' Cheryl had coloured again. 'Though I *did* think if he saw ... I hoped that he might ... You know, I *am* different.' The expression on her face was replaced by one of anxiety. 'Is he going back to the war?'

'He's going back to something,' Rachel said. 'He's not quite sure what. His lungs are not strong, you know, and after the dust of the desert ... I think they'd like him to take a desk job. In fact,' Rachel didn't know whether or not to pass on this confidence or not, 'he's been asked to be ADC to the King.'

Cheryl clapped her hands together with what looked like genuine pleasure. 'Oh, that's marvellous...'

'But he's refused.' Rachel smiled and took another biscuit. Was there unconscious cruelty in her revelation?

'Refused?' Cheryl looked shocked. 'How could he refuse?'

'Ralph says there are plenty of people who can dance about the monarch and he doesn't want to be one. He had enough as a staff officer.'

'Ralph always has to prove himself, hasn't he?'

'Yes.' Rachel gazed at the daughter-in-law she had for so long disliked. All that had gone. The bond with Cheryl tightened every time she saw her now, grew stronger. She wished it had come a long, long time ago. Was she blind or had Cheryl changed so much? Or, had they *both* changed? *Or*, and this she didn't really like to think about, was it because of what Jenny might do to Ralph and the family name: 'Earl of Askham in a divorce scandal...'

Bosco had been involved in the libel trial when their names were in the paper every day. Melanie and Adam's divorce had got far more space than it deserved. Her own brief appearance in court in 1913 had seemed to occupy newspaper space for days. Was it the unwanted publicity of all those years ago that still haunted her?

Cheryl had gone to the window and stood looking out. 'I

hoped that Ralph *would* come and see me. I've written, you know, congratulated him about Africa and the MC. He didn't even reply. It makes me very sad.'

'I am sorry,' Rachel said. 'That seems very rude. He didn't tell me that.'

'He's cut himself off from me completely, hasn't he? Can't he give me another chance?'

Rachel shook her head. 'I think he *is* in love with Jenny.'

'But he *was* in love with me.'

'Well, he's in love with Jenny now. I'm sorry.'

'Is that why you're here?' Cheryl's voice became shrill. 'To ask me again to free him?'

'No, no, not at all.' Rachel, reminded of her mission, suddenly regretted undertaking it. She bit her lip. 'It's about Hugo and ... Amelia. I've been sent as a sort of emissary.'

'What *about* Hugo and Amelia?' Cheryl now had the very busy, rather cross expression on her face of a peevish child. Oh no, Cheryl hadn't changed. Some parts of Cheryl had changed, but not all. Cheryl would always keep those swift changes of mood, that mercurial temperament, her inherent selfishness.

'They want to get married.'

In the ensuing silence both women were aware of the shrieks coming up from the playground that had been constructed between the main house and the out-houses. What had formerly been stables were now practice rooms and store houses. Most of the horses, so much a feature of pre-war Askham Hall, had gone. Instead of equine noises now came the grind of an ungifted cellist, the faltering notes of a beginner at the piano or the cat-like screech of a badly tuned violin. Cheryl loved it all – life, if not harmony, all created by her.

'You mean *Amelia* and ... well there *is* only one Hugo, isn't there?'

'I'm afraid so,' Rachel nodded. 'He *does* love her very much.'

'I thought he hardly knew her. You mean they've been seeing each other all this time?'

'Yes.'

'But they didn't tell *me*. How ...' Cheryl groped for the word, 'how *despicable*.'

'I think they knew you wouldn't approve.'

'Well, I don't approve and I'm forbidding it. Hugo ... I have always detested that boy.'

'I know.'

'And he me.' Cheryl stared at her. 'Don't pretend.'

'Oh, I shan't. No, you don't like each other. Never have.'

'It all goes back to that cat.' Cheryl sounded aggrieved. 'Right at the very beginning.'

'I don't think you'd have liked each other anyway, but certainly the cat didn't help.'

'Lenin was such a silly name for a cat.'

Cheryl stared fixedly out of the window, but Rachel knew she was just searching for excuses. Maybe she was making a deliberate effort not to cry. It must be heartbreaking. As a mother too Rachel knew quite well how she felt. In her heart she felt sorry for her. Cheryl would always be a woman for whom life had more pain than pleasure, no matter how hard she tried. Is that why she wanted to do good now and adopt two children orphaned by the London blitz?

'I don't know why they couldn't have told me themselves.' Cheryl's tone had changed to one of petulance.

'I think they were afraid.'

'Why tell me at *all* then?'

'Because you have to know. You're Amelia's mother and she ... would love you to be at the wedding. It's quite soon, actually.'

'You can bet your life I shan't be,' Cheryl said.

Cheryl's reaction put a large wedding out of the question. Not only didn't she go, she didn't send a present. For quite a long time afterwards she blamed Hugo for, among other things, alienating her daughter from her.

But Cheryl was far from the minds of the guests – though

302

not perhaps from that of her daughter – who gathered on the lawn of the Manor for the reception following the wedding at Darley Parish Church. It was a very low keyed affair, which would never have suited Cheryl. At the ceremony itself only family had been present; the bride wore a shantung costume in pale green and Hugo a grey lounge suit.

Hugo and Amelia had selected a late September day for their nuptials – the first day that could be arranged after the banns had been called. There had been a little rain in the morning but that had merely made the earth fresh and now in the late afternoon it was fine. The grand old oaks on the edge of the lawn sheltered the less resilient members of the party who sat under them sipping pre-war champagne.

Ralph was best man. Jenny had returned to North Africa from which the troops had been launched into Sicily and no one knew whether she would follow them or not. Charlotte and Marc managed to get forty-eight hours' leave and Marc was in uniform.

But for the proliferation of uniforms it would have been hard to believe the country was at war. The ladies had managed to do amazing things with austerity clothes, bought with precious coupons but embellished with all kinds of pre-war trimmings taken, perhaps, from *haute couture* models which were by now either too old or had been outgrown by the owner.

Charlotte had a wardrobe of such outfits and as there was a timelessness about *couture* clothes, and she had kept her figure, they would be wearable and would look good on her for years. She wore a midnight-blue Vionnet afternoon dress with a round neck and full bishop-style sleeves. Tiny white pearl buttons descended from throat to her waist and from wrist to the fullness of the sleeves. With this she wore a Florentine hat of blue velvet with a large jewel at the side.

Everyone realized that Charlotte Verdi had the advantage when it came to fashion, but only Marc had seen her recently in more austere and functional garb, a plain blue raincoat and headscarf, and he was lost in admiration at the transformation, the undoubted skill Charlotte possessed in the art of disguise.

From the display of food set out enticingly, buffet style, in the dining room it would also have been hard to guess there was a war on. With the help of Hugo's farm and the American PX stores there were sides of boiled ham, barons of cold roast beef, plump chickens, plates of thick smoked salmon from Teesside, salads of every description, some plain and some dressed with an assortment of mayonnaises; fresh rolls and intricate loaves newly baked with white flour imported from America, and bowls of rich, golden farm butter. There were cheeses from Gloucester, Worcester, Cheddar and Wensleydale and spirits and wines of every description, mostly brought down by car from London.

Maybe they should have been ashamed of such a display of plenty when in Europe many were starving; but it was only for this special occasion that some of the rules had been broken, regulations flouted. After all, the Americans had almost unlimited access to anything and half of the wedding was American, with a number of American Air Force and Military personnel from Amelia's Headquarters in Grosvenor Square. Every American who had come brought a bottle or two, one brought a case, and for the rest of the year the English would be stuck with their ration books and quotas, their coarse brown regulation loaves and margarine.

But if it was a day for grown-ups to be seen in their best, ladies in elegant afternoon frocks and men in lounge suits or uniform, their badges of rank and decorations gleaming with polish, it was also a day for children. Angelica and Young Flora had been bridesmaids, prettily dressed as shepherdesses, and Paul and his slightly younger cousin Luis were pages despite the lack of a train for them to carry. It was felt that the children should have a place in this first wedding in the family since the younger ones had been born although Angelica was now thirteen and Young Flora just eleven.

People who hadn't known her father sometimes wondered

where Angelica Verdi got her looks from, her colouring in particular. She was tall, but neat and very dark; she was also very beautiful with straight black silky hair, an olive skin and black fathomless eyes. So strong had the Italian influence been that those who saw them together, and didn't know them, found it difficult to believe that Charlotte and Angelica were mother and daughter. Yet if their genetic make-up was different the bond between them was especially strong.

Like Charlotte, Angelica was vivacious; she sparkled, she was seldom still. Today she ran in and out among the guests like a much smaller child because she was so happy, dancing attendance upon the bridal pair and greeting, like familiars, guests whom she had never met before. She was captivating, an enchantress; few people meeting Angelica for the first time escaped enslavement.

By contrast Adam's daughter, although as enslaved by Angelica as anyone else, was much quieter, shyer, more withdrawn if not exactly timid. She had always been called 'Young Flora' by the family to distinguish her from the Flora after whom she was named. In a strange way (because there was no blood relationship) she rather resembled the older woman who had drowned in Egypt years before Flora was born.

The older Flora had had strong Askham looks, the auburn hair, the blue-green eyes, but her features had been too bold and strong for beauty. Those who remembered her from childhood – and there were few of them left now – often commented not only on the slight physical resemblance between Young Flora and the old one but, more than that, on their similarity of character. Even at eleven Young Flora was a grave, thoughtful young girl who had always effortlessly been top of the class. The elder Flora had got a degree from Cambridge when clever women were automatically labelled blue-stockings. The pretty shepherdess dress sat rather oddly on one who was rather small for her age and too thin. Her mother Margaret, who had died soon after she was born, had been a pretty, vital woman and Flora had inherited her black wavy hair and blue eyes, but not the neat arrangement of facial features that had so attracted her father, Adam. Flora had a broad nose and a wide mouth and had worn spectacles, like the elder Flora, from an early age. These she kept on pushing up her nose, again in a gesture reminiscent of the earlier Flora, so that Em observing her commented on it to her mother.

'Don't you think Young Flora gets more and more like Aunt Flora?'

Rachel had felt relaxed and happy at the wedding, the first of her children's she had attended since Charlotte's society wedding in 1927. Both Freddie and Ralph had been married abroad. Rachel liked nothing better than to be surrounded by family, to see old friends and familiars again to help one celebrate a happy event or share a sad one. But many of those particular families who had graced all Askham family occasions from time immemorial were missing. Where were representatives of the Lawfords, the Pardoes, the Bulstrodes and the Plomley-Pembertons? Many of them, truth to tell, had gone abroad for the duration. Others didn't consider Hugo a proper Askham even though he was Bosco's son. And others simply hadn't been invited because the Manor wasn't even half the size of the Hall – not even a quarter, and there was very limited space to entertain.

Rachel now turned her gaze from the newly-weds happily circulating, hands clasped, among their guests to the young girl who stood drinking orange juice on the edge of the lawn gazing myopically at the concourse.

'It *is* rather uncanny, isn't it?' she said. 'She even has that mannerism of pushing her spectacles unnecessarily up her nose. I think it's Adam's influence. He seems to want to make Young Flora more like *our* Flora. I think he encourages her to be studious so that she can imitate the woman she never knew. In a way, for Adam, she's Flora's daughter.'

Em shuddered and rubbed her arms with her hands.

306

'You've given me goose-flesh, Mummy. You make it sound as though you believe in spirits.'

'Sometimes I think I do,' Rachel murmured. 'Adam only realized how much Flora loved him or he her, when she was dead. He never got over it. I often think it killed Margaret.'

'Oh Mummy, not today of *all* days with Hugo happy and Amelia looking absolutely stunning. You mustn't be gloomy *today*!'

'I *am* happy,' Rachel assured her, putting up her cheek for Bobby to kiss as he strolled over with Aileen beside him.

'Your Rolls is clogging up the drive, Bobby,' Em chided him.

'Nice, isn't it?' Bobby smirked.

'I didn't think they were allowed in wartime.'

'Whyever not?'

'Don't they consume a lot of petrol?'

Bobby winked. 'Official business,' he said. 'I'm going on from here to Portsmouth.'

'I still think you'll get nailed one day,' Rachel said, smiling at Aileen.

Aileen was a curious woman. It was difficult not to think that she rather resented her husband's family who had all known her for a long time as the daughter of an employee. Thus the family went out of its way to praise Aileen whenever they saw her, as though in a determined attempt to put her at her ease.

'What a perfectly *lovely* dress,' Rachel said with perhaps more enthusiasm than it justified. 'I bet that took a few coupons, Aileen.'

'I had it made up,' Aileen said immediately and defensively, 'from some material Bobby bought me in Paris before we were married.' She always considered Rachel patronizing.

'I should have known. It looks *beautiful*.' Rachel was aware that, once again where Aileen was concerned, she had said the wrong thing.

'Who is that man with Charlotte?' Bobby inquired waving his cigar in her direction. 'He never leaves her side.'

'He's a colleague.' Rachel thought it was best left vague.

'What kind of colleague?'

'Something to do with the French Air Force.'

'Is she attached to the French Air Force?'

'Something like that,' Rachel struggled to change the subject. 'I'm not quite sure.'

'I thought she was engaged to Arthur Crewe?'

'Oh, she still is. Marc, I assure you, is just a friend.'

'Bobby, shouldn't we go?' Aileen asked plaintively, consulting the exquisite little Cartier watch with a diamante bracelet she had persuaded Bobby to give her as a wedding present. 'You *did* tell the Mayor...'

'Yes, yes,' Bobby said. 'But first we must find David. I can never find that boy when I want him. He reminds me a bit of Hugo when young.' Bobby looked sympathetically at Rachel. 'You were always looking for him, remember? Now I know how you felt.'

'David is in the lounge talking to Pascal and Joe.' Sasha, glass in hand, spoke from over his uncle's shoulder. He too had managed to get leave and wore his uniform with the three sergeant's stripes on his sleeve, his gunner's half wing on his breast. Bobby looked at him with suspicion.

'Doesn't David realize we have to leave soon?'

'I think he was hoping he could stay.'

'Well, he can't. It's a civic ceremony at Portsmouth and he's supposed to be there with me and his mother. Please go and get him for me Sasha, there's a good fellow.'

Sasha walked off, Bobby glowering after him.

'I don't know *how* he can be content to remain an NCO. You'd think he'd feel he owed it to the family to apply for a commission.'

'Sasha's very happy,' Em said. 'Why do you want to mould everyone to be like you, Bobby?'

'I'm not moulding him, but he's my sister's boy. I feel

308

responsibility for him. He's the first non-commissioned officer in the history of our family. He doesn't realize how this reflects on us.'

'I certainly don't think it reflects on *me*.' Em laughed scornfully. 'I admire Sasha for being true to his principles.'

'What principles are they? Communistic ones?'

Em was about to make a heated reply when Sasha reappeared with David Lighterman who was on the verge of his sixteenth birthday. David was like his father to look at, if a little taller, but the impact of his height was lessened by an adolescent slouch so that they appeared to be about the same height. Whereas Bobby habitually contrived to have a pleasant, if determined, expression on his face David's good looks were marred by a more or less permanent sneer on his lips. Accompanying the slouch it didn't make for an attractive impression though David was notably different in the company of his peers.

Sasha and David were talking animatedly until David saw his father; he resumed his disagreeable expression and snapped at him:

'Well, what do you want?'

'You know we have to leave,' Bobby said testily looking at his watch. 'I *told* you not to disappear. Go and get your coat.'

'I want to stay here,' David said.

'Well, you can't.'

'Why can't I?'

'Because I say so.'

'Please, David,' Aileen anxiously plucked at his sleeve, '*don't* argue with your father.'

'But it's nothing to do with me what's happening in Portsmouth.'

'I just want you there, that's all.' Bobby's expression was calculated to discourage further argument.

David tried another tack: '*May* I not stay, Aunt Rachel?'

'Well of course …' Rachel shrugged, feeling uncomfortable. 'I mean as far as we're concerned, but your father …'

'My father always wants to show me off when I don't want to be shown off. I don't want to go and sit on some platform and listen to innumerable people drone on and on about nothing, or praising the boring things father does.'

'We all have duties …' Bobby began but David flushed.

'*I* don't have a duty, Father, to encourage the war effort. If you want to know what I think I don't think we should be fighting this war at all. You know perfectly well I'm a pacifist.'

'That's what comes of sending him to one of the best schools in the country.' Bobby sounded close to self-strangulation. 'Can you wonder that I'm ashamed of him? How *can* you speak like that, David, when you're surrounded by brave men in uniform?'

'I respect David's views,' Sasha intervened. 'In fact I admire them. It takes courage to speak out, Uncle.'

'No courage at all when you're too young to fight. I'm ashamed of him. Go and get your coat, David.'

'No,' David said.

'Come on.' Sasha took him by the arm. 'I'll come with you if Uncle wishes. I love sitting on platforms.'

'Like that?' Bobby looked at him in disgust. 'No thank you. The last thing I want people to see is my nephew in a sergeant's uniform.'

For a moment Rachel thought Sasha was going to hit Bobby. She seized his arm.

'Please, Sasha, don't. This is Hugo and Amelia's day and people are beginning to stare.'

'Let them stare,' David cried, enjoying himself.

'No!' Rachel's tone caused a few more people to look up. Sensing trouble, Adam and Charlotte converged from different parts of the garden while Hugo was looking inquiringly over his shoulder.

'What appears to be the matter, Mother?' Charlotte had left Marc talking to Willy Hamble who was regaling him with stories about Dunkirk.

'There's a silly argument going on here and I want it

stopped, at once! This is Hugo's wedding day and I don't want it ruined with a family row.' Rachel put her hand on Charlotte's arm. 'It's quite all right Charlotte.' Then she turned to David, her voice firm and clear. 'David, dear, I want you to go and get your coat as your father requests and then wait for him and your mother in the car. *If* they permit you can come to us for half term. We don't see nearly enough of you and we can arrange something with Charlotte's boys. Sasha, would you go with David to get his coat? And then please come back here. There's something I want you to do for me.'

For a moment the formerly noisy and argumentative corner of the lawn became oddly silent. David, quelled by his aunt, was obviously debating whether to oppose her when Sasha took his arm and murmured in his ear:

'Let's do what Aunt Rachel says, old man. I'll come with you to the car.'

As they went towards the house Bobby, quivering, turned to Rachel.

'Thank you for that, Rachel. For a moment I thought Sasha was going to attack me.'

'There's something I'd like to say to you, Bobby,' Rachel said quietly. 'Could we just pop inside? Charlotte, please circulate. Quite a lot of people here don't know anybody. Adam, could you also come with me?'

Adam, who had looked bewildered by the whole thing, ambled after Rachel and Bobby. Aileen said she had to powder her nose and disappeared up the stairs.

Rachel took Bobby and Adam into the small sitting room next to the drawing room which she and her brother used more frequently in wartime when they were alone to save fuel. Adam drew out his pipe and Bobby leaned an arm impatiently against the mantelpiece.

'What is it you want, Aunt Rachel? We don't have a lot of time.'

As Rachel faced Bobby Adam thought he had never seen her look so angry. Her whole frame seemed to quiver, her light blue eyes unnaturally bright. Adam also noticed that her clenched fists were held tightly to her sides.

'I just want to say this to you, Bobby,' she spoke rapidly. 'Please *never* insult anyone in my presence again the way you insulted Sasha.'

'I insult ..?' Bobby gazed at Adam as if perplexed.

'You were *so* rude to him I couldn't believe my ears. Sasha is the dearest boy and, in order to reconcile David to leaving the company of his cousins, with whom he was having a good time, offered to come with you.'

'But he was going to *hit* me.' Bobby sounded seriously aggrieved. 'Surely nothing I said deserved such an extreme reaction. What I said wasn't *that* important. He over-reacted.'

'It *was* important, Bobby.' Rachel shook a finger at him. 'It was terribly important and wounding. Sasha is a very brave, fine young man. He has chosen not to apply for a commission because he is happy as he is. He likes the company of his fellow flyers in the sergeants' mess. He likes those kind of people...'

'If his father hadn't been a Bolshevik...'

'No matter *what* his father was, or is now, Sasha is his own man. Never ever dare offend him like that in my presence again or frankly, Bobby, you and I will fall out very seriously.'

She then pointed towards the door and Bobby, to his astonishment, found himself walking meekly towards it as though he were a schoolboy being gated after a reprimand. Just before he got to the door he turned, the muscles of his jaw working busily.

'Sorry, Aunt Rachel,' he said. 'You're perfectly right. It's David, you know. David does this to me. He's such a disappointment, after all I've done for him. Sometimes I feel I could weep. I'll apologize to Sasha. I'll make it up to him.'

Impulsively he ran back to Rachel and kissed her on the cheek.

Like many family gatherings hardly any Askham occasion went by without some kind of row or disturbance, and Hugo's

312

wedding was no exception. Usually someone refused to speak to someone else, or somebody snubbed somebody else or various people went away aggrieved and dissatisfied. There were usually some members of the family who weren't speaking to others. But even Rachel with her long memory couldn't recall a row potentially so explosive as the fracas that she narrowly avoided that day by separating David and Sasha in the nick of time from Bobby.

The full story only got around after the incident was over and Bobby and Aileen were driven away in the large Rolls, with David ostentatiously sitting in the front beside the chauffeur as though he needed the glass partition to separate him from his parents.

Sasha had quite a lot to say about Bobby and made the remark that his uncle's attitude made him all the more determined never to apply for a commission. There was some sort of irony in this which Rachel reflected on later as she sat in front of the large drawing room fire warming her hands. The bridal pair had gone to a secret destination in Scotland – Amelia only had a week's leave – and all the guests departed soon after. The family stayed and this was the best part, the part Rachel always looked forward to – the gossip, the letting down of hair, the review of the day.

This gathering was particularly precious to her because it included her three surviving children, Ralph, Charlotte and Em, all gathered for once round the family hearth. When soon after his second marriage Adam had bought this small Tudor manor house in Hampshire, not far from Askham Hall on the Hampshire/Wiltshire borders, Rachel would never have envisaged that one day it would be her home.

In many ways it was the perfect family home, large but not too large, nicely proportioned and set in ten acres of beautifully landscaped ground including woodland, with a cottage at the gates where Vance the butler lived with his wife who also helped in the house.

Rachel was proud of her children, but she was afraid for

313

them too. Looking at each for a moment as they sat in the circle round the fire she realized that they were all in dangerous occupations; any one of them could be taken from her at any moment as they travelled about Europe on their various missions. Sometimes in nightmares she could envisage a life when circumstances might deprive her of all of them, and the only one left would be beloved Hugo who wasn't her natural child at all.

Fear seemed then to strike at her heart and, as if sensing it, Ralph, sitting on the floor by her chair, reached for her hand and quietly gripped it. Grateful for his love, his understanding, she let her hand rest on his head and tried to imagine just for those few seconds that the years had slipped away and they were all round the family fire at the Grange once more as children, Bosco in their midst.

But tonight it was particularly good to have Sasha with them because his exploits in the war had already nearly cost him his life. At one time he had been given up for dead and his reappearance six months after being reported missing seemed miraculous.

Rachel had never been told the truth about his escape and rescue, because he had been forbidden to talk about it and it would be years before the family heard the full story and the heroic part played by Hélène. But as soon as he got home Sasha demanded to be put in the air again and was daily taking part in hazardous operations over Germany. Surely if anyone was a hero in this group – and she knew that, in a way, they all were – it was the youngest, shy Sasha Ferov, who had at last come into his own.

Sasha's brown curly hair gave him the air of a cherub but by nature he was far from angelic. Rachel knew he could be wilful, stubborn and strong. Maybe this is what equipped him with the temperament to sit night after night in the most exposed part of the great Lancaster bombers, his eyes searching the sky for enemies. Then it was up to Sasha, and other bold spirits like him, to put his finger first on the trigger before others did it to him. So far, thank God, he had been successful.

Naturally Bobby and David figured prominently in the after-dinner chat. It was difficult to feel sorry for Bobby because he had grown into a hard man, even to those who had known him as a baby and loved him as Rachel still did. Sasha had few good words to say about him and kept on pointedly referring to his small cousins in wartime Paris. There was seldom any news of them, though Charlotte had told Rachel unofficially that they were well. She had had to be very careful not to be seen by the Lighterman girls in case they unconsciously gave her away.

No one defended Bobby except the oldest members of the family present, Adam and Rachel, who knew how difficult Bobby's own childhood had been – a little boy growing up in surroundings of great luxury, mainly in the care of ageing grandparents while his mother showed very little interest in him.

'You must remember how it was for Bobby,' Rachel said, 'and how much he has idolized David. I must say I'm sorry to see that David is so hostile to his father because Bobby married Aileen just to legitimize David.'

'She seems to have fallen on her feet.' Ralph was lighting his pipe. 'I never saw such a self-possessed matron. I believe she's on at least fifteen committees to do with the war effort.'

'She's highly thought of,' Adam agreed. 'However you judge Bobby I've a lot of time for Aileen. She's made her own niche, regardless of him. She's had a hard life and now she's got what she wanted.'

'Which is more than most of us do,' Em sighed. For once she was happy, on her own with Luis who was tucked up in bed beside Paul upstairs. She didn't for a moment think that the two cousins were asleep. Every time she had peeped in on them there were furtive giggles from the darkened room.

'Have *you* had a hard life, Em?' Charlotte turned an amused gaze on her. 'I wouldn't have thought so.'

315

'Not compared to you, maybe,' Em said. They were always conscious with Charlotte of what had happened to Paolo. 'But recently it hasn't been too happy for me personally.' She looked at Marc feeling slightly embarrassed that this one stranger should be present in the family gathering. 'Mind you, I hate the war but love my work. I suppose I can say that. But ...' she raised her eyes to the ceiling as though to indicate that Luis was the one who was paramount on her mind, and Felipe the main cause of her dissatisfaction with her life.

'I think I should go.' Marc looked at Charlotte. 'Leave the family together.'

'Not at all.' Charlotte carelessly threw an arm round his shoulder.

'We regard you as family,' Rachel said kindly, 'for tonight.'

'Only just for tonight?' Marc smiled and Rachel immediately repented of her generous remark, thinking of poor Arthur somewhere in a Japanese prisoner-of-war camp.

What complicated lives her daughters were leading.

'To change the subject,' she said, 'do you think Amelia minded very much Cheryl not being there?'

'Not even a telegram,' Ralph said. 'Typical. I didn't think even Cheryl could be so small-minded.'

'Cheryl *was* hurt,' Rachel murmured. 'I think Amelia should have told her mother and not left it to me. I should have foreseen her reaction.'

'Mother, you did what you could.' Ralph leaned forward to touch her. 'You always take on the nasty tasks. What I'm not sure is how right Amelia is for Hugo.' For a moment there was an imperceptible collective intake of breath, as though Ralph were voicing the unconscious thoughts of many of those present. 'He didn't know her very well.'

'I think he knows her very well,' Rachel protested. 'Don't forget they met *before* Dunkirk.'

'Only briefly,' Charlotte said. 'I agree with Ralph. Amelia is very beautiful but so was Cheryl. I think she has a lot of her mother in her. She has Hugo round her little finger.'

'As Cheryl had me. Go on.' Ralph gave a rueful smile.

'Well, you said it,' Charlotte agreed. 'I don't know why you men must fall for that type of woman.'

'Jenny isn't that type of woman ...' Ralph began.

'Cheryl has changed,' Rachel went on quickly. 'I *wish* you'd give her another chance, Ralph. At least go and see her.'

'Mother, *please* don't bring this up again.'

'You've no idea how much she has changed. She's awfully sweet about those orphan children.'

'That doesn't sound a *bit* like Cheryl, I agree – unless it's to spite me because I wanted children of our own. Basically you know she hasn't changed. Her attitude to Amelia's wedding is typical. How can you say she's changed?'

'She and Hugo always instinctively disliked each other.'

'Then she hasn't changed.'

'Well, Hugo hasn't changed either.'

'You'd do far better, Mother, to make Jenny feel welcome,' Ralph said quietly, 'when she next comes home on leave.'

'I wasn't aware of not making Jenny welcome'

'I think you were. She thinks you don't like her.'

'Does she like me?'

'That's not the point.'

'It is the point. *Does* she like me?'

'How can she like you when you don't like her?'

'Oh, for heaven's sake.' Charlotte stood up and yawned. 'Who's for bed?'

'It's terribly late.' Adam looked at his watch. 'I didn't realize how late. Well, the day went well, I think, Rachel. The day went well, despite everything?'

'The day went fine.' Rachel smiled as he got up. Then she clasped Ralph's hand. 'I'm not arguing *any* more.'

'I'll come with you, Grandpa.' Sasha sprang to his feet and helped Adam to his. For a moment Adam leaned gratefully on him.

'Thank you, my boy. I'm delighted you're here, you know

317

that, Sasha? And you are right to stand up to Bobby. Be true to yourself, that's the main thing.'

'I'll come too ...' Charlotte began but Ralph said:

'I just want a word with you, dear.'

'Me?' Charlotte looked surprised.

'Yes, you and ...' He watched Sasha and Adam walk slowly to the door unaware, apparently, of Ralph's remarks. Then as they paused on the threshold there was a chorus of 'good-nights'.

Ralph saw them to the door and shut it carefully after them. Going to the sideboard he poured himself a fresh drink after offering to refill glasses. Everyone refused except Marc.

'You're a boozer,' Charlotte said to him and her tone made Rachel realize how intimate they had become in such a short space of time. Marc wrinkled his nose as he flopped down beside her. Ralph stood in front of the fire stirring the ice in his glass with a finger.

'I wanted to have a little family conference, but not with Sasha here.' He looked towards the door. 'If he comes back I'll have to stop.'

'He won't come back,' Rachel said. 'He and Adam like a chat on the landing. Adam so loves having him here.'

'It's good to see them together,' Ralph agreed. 'Well, then. What I have to say isn't very nice. It will be very painful for everyone, especially Mum.' Ralph looked over at her. 'Forgive me, but it concerns the death of Freddie.'

'*What* concerns the death of Freddie?' Rachel said, startled.

'What I am going to say. It concerns a curious conversation that Em and I had in Cairo. This is the first time I have had the chance to speak about it, but, believe me, I've thought about it a lot. Well, do you remember Randy Tucker...'

Ralph sat down and began the story, with Em intervening and from time to time correcting him. After all it was a year since that meeting in the western desert, before the Allied breakthrough at El Alamein. When Ralph finally finished no one spoke for some time and then Rachel leaned back in her

318

chair, face impassive, eyes gazing into the fire, her hand clutching the arm of her chair as though it supported her.

'I can't believe it was Kyril,' she said at last. 'Kyril is Sasha's father.'

'Kyril and Sasha are not a bit alike,' Charlotte said. 'None of this reflects on Sasha.'

'*If* it's true.'

'It's true, Mother.' During the course of the story Charlotte had felt Marc's hand steal round her waist as though to give her support, and now she felt his warm breath on her cheek as he leaned closer.

'What do you mean it's true? How do you *know* it's true?' Rachel sat straight, as though jerked upright by the shock.

'I had a feeling instinctively that it's true. We have never known what Kyril's allegiances really were. Why did he suddenly become right-wing from being so left-wing even after years on a Soviet prison farm? Why, to spy. It's obvious now. All the European capitals are *crawling* with spies – Paris, Berlin, Vienna, London for all we know. I see quite clearly now that Kyril, all along, has never changed his allegiance.

'And meeting Freddie like that unexpectedly in Brunete must have come as a terrible shock – a threat of exposure. Poor, dearest Freddie, who could never be trusted to keep his mouth shut, had to die. The one thing a spy dare not risk is exposure.'

Charlotte caught her breath and Marc's hand tightened around her waist. He knew that she spoke from the heart. Would that he could always be there to reassure and protect her.

'Suddenly, tonight, something that Hélène once told me has fallen into place. She said that before she shot Jamie he told her that her *brother* was responsible for all the mischief that had been created with Bobby. She replied: "You mean my father". Then she forgot about it but she said she never understood it.

319

I can tell you that no one in Paris now trusts Kyril. And now I know for sure that he's a spy.'

'It's a terrible tale,' Rachel said slowly, thinking of Sasha as well as Freddie. 'A terrible thought. Shall we ever know? Shall we want to. Truthfully?'

'I want to,' Ralph got up and began restlessly to pace the room. 'I want to know and one day I'll find out the truth. And if Kyril did kill my brother, God help me but I'll kill him.'

CHAPTER 17

Crouching over the wireless Hélène and Charles began to giggle together in the dark. Hélène felt like a naughty schoolgirl and pressed her hand to her mouth. Charles tapped her playfully on the arm and then kissed her cheek. Their situation wasn't really so funny, constantly moving from one safe house to another since Hélène had decided to heed Charlotte's warning and go underground. Charles was worried that the years of strain were taking their toll of Hélène; she was too easily prey to both laughter and tears.

The wireless in the little attic room was hidden under a blanket which also covered them both in order to keep them warm. They had very few belongings or provisions in the small bare room which belonged to some friends of Charles. They never knew from one day to the next where they would be. It was a very, very hard life.

Since Charlotte and Plus Fort had fled the previous summer, after the encounter with Jordan, Charles had managed the network almost single-handed except for the help of Hélène and a few trusted comrades. But the Germans had been very efficient and there were few networks left that had not been penetrated by German agents, or betrayed by Frenchmen in the pay of the Vichy government.

Yet Charles had grown ever bolder, more fierce in his fight against the enemy. Single-handed he had carried out many acts of sabotage which had at least made a little dent in the self-assurance of the hated foe. Hélène still succoured rescued Allied airmen and ferried them down the line. Every time it was more dangerous for her. Though she didn't know it there was a price on her head and an even bigger one on Charles's, who had ceased to have any connection with his law practice and lived entirely underground.

At least he and Hélène were able to live together, moving around as a pair to give each other comfort and support. At least they kept each other's bodies warm in a winter when there was hardly any fuel in the whole of Paris except for Nazis and collaborators.

But now there was a ray of hope: they were expecting a special message and, maybe, that's why Hélène was as excited as a schoolgirl pressing her hand over her mouth, eyes shining. And then it came:

> *The Lion is stronger than the Lamb – repeat*
> *The Lion is stronger than the Lamb*
> *Little Jumbo sends ...*

But neither of them waited to hear what Little Jumbo was sending. They fell into each other's arms like exhausted travellers in sight of the promised land.

The message was telling them that, by the light of the full moon the following night, Charlotte and Plus Fort would be back – back with provisions, with arms, with new hope: The Lion was stronger than the Lamb.

After they'd received the message they had been awaiting for so many weeks they switched off the wireless and hid it under the rug again. Suddenly they felt revivified, stronger. Together they leapt out from under the blanket and Hélène began to prepare the evening meal by the light of the candle, on a primus stove for which they hoarded precious fuel. Softly she sang to herself not daring to raise her voice because they always spoke in whispers.

It had been a life of almost unbelievable hardship. Since Hélène had gone underground she had not seen her children. What friends she had were abandoned. She had had the option to escape to England, but she wanted to stay with Charles. Charles was life: Charles was hope. With their increasing isolation, their inability to trust anyone, she and Charles grew unimaginably closer, bolder, carrying out more daring enterprises and taking huge risks.

She had had to go underground without a word to anyone – her mother, her daughters and especially Kyril who had given the traitor Jordan a home. But in the peculiar mood of that war, especially the sort of personal war they were engaged in against an enemy who tortured and killed in the cruellest way many of their former colleagues and friends, Hélène found that these personal inconveniences meant nothing to her: the cold, the fear, the constant moving about, the shortages of food and heat, the minimum of creature comforts. Because by the end of 1943 Paris was experiencing the darkest days of the war, when no owner dared let an animal go on the street for fear of its being captured and eaten before its flesh was cold. No cat, however loved, dared slink from one familiar lair to the next for it was unlikely that it would ever be seen again.

Although she had never been religious, and was less so now than ever, Hélène, former Princess Ferova, knew that in one respect at least the Bible was right. One could live without family, without children, without friends, maybe even without love – one could forsake them all for a greater cause.

'I think you should have a rest,' Charles said, grinding the acorns before pouring hot water on them. It was a very long time since they'd drunk real coffee, or eaten fresh meat or freshly baked white bread. It was strange how one got used to anything. Even offal tasted good.

'Rest?' Hélène vigorously shook her head but her face was so pale, her hair so stringy that she did, indeed, look like a woman in the throes of serious malnutrition. Only her eyes remained bright and vibrant.

'When Charlotte comes she can take over,' Charles said.

'Charlotte will need me. You know, anyway, that soon the Allies will invade and all our efforts will be worthwhile.' She threw her hands in the air and then her skeletal arms fell like twigs to her sides. She had so little energy left. Looking at her

Charles suddenly felt afraid. He stopped what he was doing and took her in his arms.

'What is it?' she said laughing. 'You're crushing me.'

'You're skin and bones.' Charles wrapped his arms tightly round her. 'I'm so afraid of what I have done to you.'

'What *you* have done to me?' Hélène playfully pushed him away. 'My dear, you have kept me alive. But for you I would be dead. As soon as Charlotte had left and Jordan had told his friends about her they would have been on to me. It would be Avenue Foch and then Mont Valerian.' Mont Valerian was the place where resisters were shot, if they were lucky. Some never made it out of the Avenue Foch, but were tortured to death in the cellars.

'We only *surmise* that it was Jordan.'

'We know *positively* that Jordan told the *boche*, betrayed his cousin. Don't pretend. Don't save *my* feelings. He is no longer a relation of mine, thank goodness. Why else did Kyril suddenly leave without saying goodbye to anyone?'

'Yes, that's true.' Charles lit one of the cigarettes he managed to roll and roll again from discarded bits of tobacco. A few days after Charlotte left Kyril simply disappeared. He left his flat, no messages; but his car had also gone from the garage. It was unlikely he had been arrested because several suitcases and most of his clothes were missing too. Kyril, of course, had disappeared before. The Nazis might have taken him for interrogation or he may have escaped, or gone somewhere for his own good. No one knew. He hadn't said goodbye.

Occasionally Hélène had managed to telephone her mother, but soon she stopped this. It was too dangerous, her father too untrustworthy, the girls too suspicious. For many weeks she had lived a life of isolation except for Charles. But now all this would change. Charlotte and Marc would soon be back. The war would soon be over.

That night Hélène felt a peculiar kind of gratitude and relief as she nestled down in the straw-filled mattress in the single bed against Charles.

'You're very thin too,' she said pressing his body. 'Your ribs are sticking into me. You know what?'

'What?' He put his mouth to her ear.

'I love you.'

'I love you too and you know what?'

'What?' she whispered.

'The war will soon be over and then we can be together for ever. It can't be very long now before the Allies invade.'

'Charlotte and Plus Fort will tell us everything.' Hélène's eyes shone in the dark. 'Oh how wonderful it will be to see them. I feel it's a new beginning don't you?'

Charles nodded but said nothing. He was glad she couldn't see his face, the expression in his eyes. His arm tightened round her, so full of caring, of love.

But that night, as so many nights before, they were too tired to do otherwise than caress each other, too tired to make love. They were two exhausted spirits, at the end of their tether, who needed a rest and deserved one. But not until the war was over; not until victory was won.

The Lysander had crossed the Channel flying low to avoid detection by the enemy. Occasionally the moon appeared from the clouds, but in the body of the aeroplane surrounded by the bales and parcels that would be dropped with them Charlotte and Marc could see nothing. They sat together on the bare fuselage holding hands, Marc quietly smoking. There was very little to say. They knew that the Allies were preparing to land in France, although they did not know when or where. It was only weeks, maybe a few months away. Their task was to help prepare the ground, stimulate tired and discouraged and, in some cases, terribly depleted resistance forces.

For weeks they had been trained in new methods of sabotage, new techniques of detection and avoidance, and Charlotte, who hated heights, had been taken again up to Ringway to repeat the parachute course she had failed the first time. This time she had passed. Hopefully it would be her first drop and her last one.

The roar of the engines made it difficult to talk. Besides, they had said everything they had to say to each other in the past few weeks. They were in love and they knew their love was lasting. It would be wrong to deceive Arthur when he came back after the war; but nothing would happen until Charlotte had seen and spoken to Arthur, even though Marc wanted to marry her now. Maybe he wanted to spare her being dropped again into France. But nothing would have stopped Charlotte doing that, not even marriage to Marc. And marriage to Marc would not have been possible until she had done the honourable thing with Arthur, and *that* would not be possible until he was home – safe and well. Besides, now, she felt that she had too many scores to pay, debts to settle.

She wanted to see Hélène again, to give her the love and support she knew she must need because both she and Marc were aware, from reports sent to England, what Hélène and Charles had had to endure.

Marc groped for her hand and kissed it. Hers tightened over his.

'Are you all right?' he shouted.

'What?' she shouted above the roar.

'All right?'

'I'm fine. Scared, but fine. I wish we didn't have to jump.'

'The jump will be the easiest thing,' Marc called back, and then the air crew, who were to help them jump and unload the goods being dropped, got to their feet and signalled that they were about to start the descent to the field outside Chartres. Soon the hatches would be open.

Marc squeezed her hand and bawled into her ear. 'I love you. I will love you all my life.'

But Charlotte, about to reply, was stopped by a friendly hand on her arm and a gentle shove towards the doors.

Crouched in the trees they saw the Lysander begin its descent.

They wondered if it would have to return as the low clouds had threatened rain; but every now and then the moon appeared again and Hélène and Charles knew it was vital that the Lysander made the effort, not so much for the sake of Charlotte and Plus Fort but the supplies they were bringing with them.

It was a bitterly cold night and Hélène had her well worn rather moth-eaten fur coat, that had been her mother's pride and joy in happier times, up to her ears. Her hair was covered by a large woollen hat which also covered her ears. She had warm mittens on her hands that had once belonged to Charles. Linking arms they watched the plane come in as the men who were there to guide it fanned out on the field. Hélène, who knew what a fear Charlotte had of jumping, closed her eyes and squeezed her fists together inside the big warm mitts.

'They're down,' Charles called, his voice breaking with excitement and, looking up, Hélène saw the parachutes open as, with almost unbelievable slowness, first one parachute then two, then several began to open and float gently down to earth. Attached to two of the parachutes, only some distance apart, were a pair of legs, impossible from this distance to tell which was which.

First one fell to the ground, then the next. The helpers waiting in the wood began to come forward as the supplies landed, boxes and crates one after another. The Lysander signalled that the plane was unloaded and, after a circle of the field, roared off into the sky. Those waiting looked upwards but did not cheer. It was nerve-racking enough without daring to risk any sound. Everyone knew how vigilant the *boche* had become due to the number of defections there had been in the ranks of the Resistance. Too many people had told too many dangerous tales.

Charles and Hélène ran across the field towards the first of the figures who was struggling with its parachute. A woman's face smiled at them and a woman's voice said in perfect French:

327

'How nice to bump into you like this.'

Oh how she adored her. Charlotte who would never lose her sense of humour, however tense the situation.

'Charlotte,' Hélène whispered. 'Oh it *is* good to see you.'

The two women clung together in the middle of the field as those around them started quietly cutting the parachutes from the bales at the end of each. Charles set off across to where the second figure was crawling out of a hedge, trailing his parachute after him.

When the first shot came they all thought it was thunder – it was like a sharp retort that breaks over the sky on a humid night. But it was too cold for thunder. As the guns opened all round the field, and some of the people started to fall, Charlotte pushed Hélène away, her face tense with rage and shock. 'Run,' she cried, 'run as fast as you can.'

But she was too late. Arms like vices closed round them and guttural German voices left no doubt as to their meaning or intentions.

Now everywhere was chaos. Those who could were trying to flee in any direction. But this was a round-up; the ground had been well prepared. Anyone who moved was shot at.

In the hedge where he'd landed Plus Fort, having finally cut his parachute free, lay inert on the ground. Charles, crouching, continued running towards him and Marc shouted:

'Drop, fall, lie down.'

In the moonlight he could see Charles's face and he seemed to look up at the sky as though he had heard Marc and was about to obey. Then he stumbled, fell to the ground, and lay inert on his face.

They were well away from the main body of troops and Marc thought they had half a chance to get clear altogether. Crawling over to him he grasped Charles's arm and pulled.

'Good man,' he said, 'come on, there's a hole here wide enough for both of us.'

But Charles didn't move. Marc rose to his knees and it was

328

only as he bent over his friend that he saw the hole in the back of his coat, the gushing blood from just above the heart.

Marc knelt and, roughly undoing his friend's coat, put his head to his chest. Then, rising, he quickly crossed himself and, diving low, crept through the escape route he had hoped would be used by them both.

He turned once more to look at the scene on the field: at those struggling with the enemy and some bodies lying inert upon the ground. He couldn't be sure, but he thought Charlotte and Hélène, whom he had seen embrace, were taken alive; but his friend Charles, their friend Charles, would never rise again.

He had got the long, long rest that he so badly needed, but in this finality certainly did not deserve.

The broadcasts began in January 1944, shortly after one of the heaviest of the Allied bombing raids on Berlin when 2,300 tons of bombs were dropped and German morale was at a low ebb. In Russia the German Army was being slowly repulsed by the Communists and in Italy, after conquering Sicily, the Allies had established a beachhead at Anzio.

'My name is Jordan Bolingbroke,' the voice, undoubtedly authentic began. 'I was born into a comfortable, upper-class home in England and you may wonder why I am speaking to you now. I want to tell you that I have chosen to come and live in Germany, no one has coerced me, no one has helped or hindered me. I have come as a fervent supporter of the Führer, whom I have admired since I was a boy, and among many other admirers is my mother Lady Melanie, daughter of the 10th Earl of Askham, a British peer.

You may have heard of the Askham family. It is one of the great families of England. For centuries its members have served the monarch, the last of whom was my grandmother Dulcie, Lady Askham, who was Lady-in-Waiting to Queen Alexandra.

Why I am talking to you today is to explain that there are many people in England who are devoted to Germany and hate what is happening between our two countries. We don't forget that our Royal Family came from Hanover and my family, like many others, admired Hitler and did all they could to prevent war between the countries...'

When she had finished reading a translation of the broadcast Rachel sat with her head in her hands, quite unconscious of the passage of time. Then, as she always did in moments of stress, she got up and went to the window gazing out onto the bombed buildings on either side of Ludgate Hill. The ruins, beneath the bleak wintry London sky, had a skeletal quality like a city of the dead. It was very cold and she shivered. The war had taken its toll of everyone and Rachel could not feel she had been especially singled out by fate. But sometimes she did. She perched on a chair leaning her arms on the windowsill and, as the door opened and Em came in, she wordlessly handed her the transcript:

'Read this...'

Em read right to the end without her expression changing. Then when she had finished she put it on her mother's desk and, going over to her, knelt and took her hand.

'Does Uncle Adam know?'

'Not yet. I only just got it over the wire. I'm afraid it will kill Adam. He's not well.'

'He isn't even Uncle Adam's son!'

'Yes, but very few people know that. I'm afraid it will upset Melanie very much...'

'But she *does* like the Nazis. The thing I heard was that her house in Cannes was a popular resort for the top German and Italian brass on the Riviera! I'm not a bit sorry for Aunt Melanie but I am, very, for Uncle Adam. You can't even rebut it.'

'We can rebut parts of it – this family has *not* supported the Nazis. For once they can quote me, gladly. Oh Em, coming after everything else it *is* a bit much isn't it.'

'A *bit* much.' Em gave a savage smile. 'When you think what Jordan did to Charlotte and Hélène...'

'We're not sure…'

'In a world of uncertainties we're as sure as we ever will be,' Em glared at her mother. 'If he didn't betray them, who did?'

Rachel shook her head and sighed once again, covering her eyes with her hand.

All they knew they had painstakingly put together, piece by piece, with the help of the SOE headquarters and with such messages as Marc could get out to them. But there was such an embargo on secret operations that it had taken weeks to learn as little as they did. For a long time they hadn't even known that they were missing. Then one day Marc had managed to smuggle a letter over to them in which, without giving too much away, he told them what they needed to know.

The landing had been betrayed. The Germans were waiting for them. Charles had been killed, Hélène and Charlotte captured; he had escaped. Most of the others had been rounded up and taken to Avenue Foch. One or two had been shot and several had not returned from their examination. After interrogation Charlotte and Hélène had been transferred to Fresnes prison. From there he had tried without success to rescue them. He had also tried bribing the Germans, but to no avail. He had, however, introduced a ray of hope: Charlotte was insisting that she was an Italian national, and Hélène was the daughter of a well-known sympathizer of the regime. Apart from knowing they were in prison and, as far as he knew, being treated well Marc could tell them nothing more. He was continuing his activities and unless he heard anything would not be contacting them again.

'Someone should go over and shoot Jordan,' Em said, looking at the transcript again.

'Doubtless someone will, at the end of the war.' Rachel slowly lifted her head and Em saw with pain how much her mother had recently aged. The disappearance of Charlotte had almost been too much for her. But Rachel, being Rachel, had gone on; keeping her mind on her family, her work. It was noticeable, however, that she, who was not religious, started

331

going regularly to Sunday church and to popping into St Paul's, symbol of the nation's endurance and pride. Charlotte's sons and daughter also maintained the stiff upper lip the family expected. Being young they seemed protected from any urgent premonition of disaster.

'Sometimes I wonder if we, as a family, have offended God,' Rachel said suddenly, getting up and hugging her coat around her. 'What have we done?'

'Oh, Mother.' Em threw down the transcript. 'It's the same with *all* large families.'

'Yes, but they don't all breed traitors. I suppose I do feel personally about Jordan because, as you say, despite his name he is *not* a Bolingbroke. I wish to God now we had made that clear years and years ago.'

'I can't understand why anyone didn't. When Aunt Melanie married Denton, Jordan was only eleven. Why couldn't he be told then who his real father was?'

'We all get wise, with hindsight.' Rachel apathetically picked up from her desk the article she'd been working on before the transcript arrived from Reuters by special messenger. 'Denton didn't particularly want him to know and it all seemed very awkward. I think everyone thought it was too late.'

'Yes, but *he* thought Uncle Adam was his *father*. Bolingbroke is a revered name in England. Now it will be mud.'

Em was partly right. It took some time for the fact to get through that the son of a high court judge, who was a respected member of the English judiciary, a relation of the esteemed Askham family, was broadcasting to the German people to cheer them on in the dark days of the war. At first it was a tiny paragraph. Then, as Jordan's broadcasts continued while the Allies pressed on attacking the Gustav line in Italy, and the Russians continued their annihilation of the German army in the East, they became more prominent.

Why should an *Englishman* boost German morale?

He was compared to William Joyce, Lord Haw-Haw. Only

in a way Jordan was worse. Joyce broadcast in English to the English, but Jordan was broadcasting in faultless German to Britain's enemy, slandering the British people, its fighting forces, its Royal Family and, above all, his own family. His broadcasts had a horribly personal, intimate quality.

'Let me tell you about an uncle, Lord Askham, who fought at Omdurman. He was a splendid fellow, a very good-looking man whose fatal flaw was women. He was seduced by a prostitute in Cairo and he had a son by her. The English aristocracy had become so degenerate by the beginning of the First World War that half its members were illegitimate...'

'If only he knew he was illegitimate himself...'

Rachel threw the paper disgustedly on the ground, but Adam, who had read it first, continued to stare out of the window. It was February and snow was falling. It was not difficult to think of the dreadful things that were happening in Russia, the corpses that had been found piled up in the streets of Leningrad after the siege was lifted. Adam shivered and drew the rug closer round his lap. He wore half mittens on his cold, chapped hands though a good log fire roared in the grate. Adam coughed and weakly waved his hand.

'Don't upset yourself too much, Rachel. It's not important.'

'But it *is* important. Look what it's doing to you ... resigning from the bench.'

'I was tired anyway, and ill.' Adam managed a bleak smile. 'I'm not the man I was. I'll soon be dead.'

'Adam, don't talk like that.' Rachel rapidly crossed the room and sat in a chair beside him. But it was true that Adam did look wraith-like. He had done all winter, since the bad attack of bronchitis he'd had just before Christmas. It was so severe that Bobby had to take all the children to the country house he'd rented outside Chichester as Robertswood was still being used as a convalescent home.

Now Adam seemed less and less to want the children around him. In term time this was no problem as they were all at school; but holidays were awkward and sometimes Rachel longed for the space of former times when any one of a number of houses could be chosen. She felt specially responsible for Charlotte's three – once again she had to be mother as well as grandmother. Often she didn't know where to turn. Aileen was on so many committees she hardly had time for her own husband and son, and Sylvia Bolingbroke was also up to her eyes in good works. When he first heard about the broadcasts, with their very personal overtones, Christopher Bolingbroke was tempted to change his name. It was, indeed, a great humiliation to a proud family that had served its country well. The whole family felt tainted by Jordan.

But Ralph felt tainted most of all. His father had personally been abused by his cousin and one dreaded which member of the family would be pilloried next, their habits and temperaments dissected by someone who knew none of them very well, by a distant member of the family: a traitor.

Ralph had been transferred to the Intelligence Corps at his own request and was training at a secret destination which actually taped Jordan's broadcasts, so that he had been one of the first to know about them. It was also through his intelligence work that he'd learned of the fate of his sister and the part Hélène had played almost since the war began.

As a soldier Ralph knew that his first duty lay to his country; but his second was to his family. In a way country and family were, to him, indivisible. They were one.

In January 1944 General Eisenhower had had a very important secret meeting in London with his commanders and Ralph, though privy to what was going on, didn't know everything except that it was to do with the Second Front.

When the broadcasts by Jordan started Ralph felt that his very career was in jeopardy. His superiors, however, were at pains to reassure him. No one could possibly blame a fellow for what a cousin did. His family still had a proud, distinguished tradition.

Although Askham House had been closed for most of the

war, and there were no servants, one or two rooms had always been available for those of the family who wished to use it. Instead of going in by the massive front door one went in through the kitchen entrance, through the green baize door and up the servants' stairs to the main hall.

Askham House was also used for fire-watching, its mansard roof, high above the others in the Square, affording a panoramic view of the heart of London.

But Ralph had never taken Jenny there until that cold winter of 1944, when she returned on leave from Italy.

After one of Madame Prunier's special wartime dinners served in the basement of her famous restaurant in St James's Ralph said casually: 'I'd like to take you to see the old home. It's just round the corner.'

'I'd like that,' Jenny said. She'd never seen either of his homes and she knew why. Both, in his mind, were associated with Cheryl. Cheryl never used the London home since all the servants had moved out. Maybe Ralph thought that by now her spirit had left the place.

But when they got there, in by the back door, through the extensive servants' quarters, up to the first-floor drawing room, she knew that Cheryl hadn't left: she was everywhere.

The beautiful room had an air of decay, the furniture covered with dustsheets. There was something indecent about the naked statues that, unprotected, hovered over ghostly outlines of the furniture whose cost had helped so to deplete the family fortunes a decade ago.

'She liked naked ladies,' Jenny said dispassionately, looking at the strangely asexual winged goddesses bearing aloft an unlikely cornucopia of still-life fruits.

'Not really.' Ralph was beginning to regret bringing Jenny here. 'It was just the fashion of the thirties. They seem as old as the Dodo now, but the furniture she chucked out would still be in period. It fitted the house.'

'Why did it go, then?'

'She hated it.' Ralph gestured round. 'Anything to do with

335

my family. My grandmother and great-grandmother were collectors, connoisseurs of art.'

'And your mother?'

'My mother never really felt she belonged in this place. She was never happy here. Part of it coincided with the dark time with my father.' Ralph pointed towards the tall blacked-out windows. 'She once chucked a stone through those in her suffragette days but really she was getting back at him. She'd just found out about Nimet.'

'I can understand that.' Jenny was nervous. She also felt cold in this chilly, unlived-in house. 'Do we have to stay here?'

'Not if you don't want to.'

'It's kind of creepy,' Jenny said. 'I feel there are ghosts.'

'Kindly ghosts.' Ralph took her arm. 'We'll go if you like. I wanted to show you my bedroom when I was a kid.'

'Not the bedroom with her ...' Jenny said guardedly.

'No, not that,' Ralph whispered. 'But never fear, her influence over me has quite gone.'

Sometimes Jenny wondered if it really had.

Ralph took her past rooms on the first floor associated with Cheryl – their bedroom and her sitting room and, still with her hand in his, climbed to the second. Then he went along a corridor to a room at the far end, and slowly crept in like a prowler.

Immediately Ralph was transported to his den as a small boy; the first place he'd raced to whenever he came home from school. The place where he kept his treasures, his trophies and, once, a pet gerbil for weeks until his mother found out about it, led to the room by the smell.

Now it had a narrow bed in one corner over which flew the pennants he had collected from his various sporting activities at school and in the Army. The use of the room could be dated as having stopped in 1926 ... just before Ralph went to Kenya where he met Cheryl. Nothing in the room was dated later than that because he had never used it again. When he brought his bride home he had gone straight to the huge master bedroom on the first floor: it had been his parents' room and his grandparents' before them.

In this small room Ralph Askham had passed some of the best moments of his boyhood and he wanted to share it, now, at a crucial time in his life, with the woman with whom he intended to spend the rest of it.

'See, that's when I was captain of the first eleven.' Like a proud schoolboy he pointed to the pictures on the wall. Jenny, smiling, examined first one and then the other, pressing her face close up to them, searching the ranks of assembled boys in the teams, in the giant school photographs, and in the Army.

She realized then how little she knew about the life of the man she loved; what a lot of secrets he had kept to himself. What further mysteries were there?

'I didn't realize you were in the Army before.' She keenly studied the picture of Ralph on horseback with his cavalry regiment, Blues and Royals. 'Why did you leave?'

'I hated it. There wasn't a war on then.'

'Then why did you join up?'

'My mother wanted it.'

'Funny reason,' Jenny sniffed and, once again, Ralph was conscious of the gulf between his adored Jenny and his adored mother. But since the row in Cairo Jenny was careful not to comment further. She knew how far she could go – any further than Cairo and she'd lose him altogether.

Cairo had been a testing ground for them both. The unsuccessful leave was followed by weeks of separation. They hadn't realized El Alamein was so close, and during the crucial battle which went on for days Jenny had spent many anxious moments bitterly regretting her outburst in the Ezbekiah Gardens. Ralph emerged from that particular part of the desert war more sure than ever of his love for Jenny, his need for her. She, for her part, had no doubt how she felt about him. Ralph was careful what he said now.

'It seemed a good enough reason at the time. My father had been a soldier too and I think she wanted me to be like him.'

Jenny gazed at him in his khaki uniform, the medal ribbons above the pocket of his left breast, on his shoulders the new cloth pip and crown of a lieutenant-colonel. 'Well, she got what she wanted, now, at least.'

'I wanted to farm.' Ralph perched on the bed, suddenly wanting to tell this beloved person all about himself – all the things he'd left out, until now. Explaining the past with Jenny was like a fresh adventure each time. 'I want to farm again after the war. Shall you like that, Jen?' He patted the place beside him and slowly Jenny came over and sat there too.

'It's awfully cold,' she said, rubbing her arms. She too was still in uniform and wore a greatcoat over her military jacket and skirt.

'I'll warm you.' Ralph tenderly put his arm round her and kissed her. 'That's why I wanted to bring you here.'

'I thought there was a devious reason,' Jenny said allowing herself to be taken in his arms.

Maybe it was because they had been parted for so long, because of the danger and uncertainty of war, but that time, in Ralph's old room, seemed the best; better than the first, better than the many, many times since. Ralph felt that, finally, at last and together, they'd come home. It was quite dark when he whispered:

'I never ever want you to leave me, Jenny, whatever happens. If you leave me you must always come back to me.'

Jenny lying in the dark savoured the moment, precious moments: his body, his voice, his presence. They were wedged together rather comically on the narrow bed which was old and sagged in the middle. They were both well-built people and it was a tight fit. Even when Ralph was a boy Rachel had always meant to replace it, but somehow they had never got round to it and then Ralph was a man and sharing the large marital bed with the stranger from Kenya.

'You might leave *me*,' Jenny said, aware of a tremulous note in her voice, a catch in her throat. She always felt Cheryl was a threat that she would never entirely get out of her mind. She knew that she feared Cheryl and her power over Ralph. For one thing Ralph talked about her a lot, as though in a vain attempt to exorcize his memory of her.

Now he'd brought her to Cheryl's home.

But this place was Ralph's, this bed his. He had never slept here with her.

'Did you ever bring her to this room?' she asked after a while.

'When I brought her to the house first of all I showed her the whole place. I was in love with her you know, Jen. I can't pretend I wasn't.'

'Oh, I know that,' Jenny murmured.

'But not now; not in the way you think. I can't help what happened in the past and, believe me, if you knew Cheryl you would know how well and truly I have got over her. I will never leave you, never. I will never be parted from you, even in death.'

They hadn't put the light on in the room, preferring to look out onto the starry sky occasionally lit by searchlights. This side of the house faced across the Square to Whitehall and beyond. Because it was high up the view during the day was marvellous and at night one seemed nearer to heaven. She could imagine Ralph as a small boy lying on this bed looking out of the window as she was doing now. What dreams and hopes then had the little Earl of Askham?

But when he mentioned the word 'death' she was filled with a foreboding, the like of which she had never known – a horror that seemed to seep into her making her tremble.

'I didn't mean death *now*,' he whispered, trying to comfort her, aware of her anguish. 'I mean death when we're very old.'

'Don't even speak of it,' she begged him, and she clung to him tightly for a long, long time like a shipwrecked sailor to prevent herself drowning in a sea of inexplicable grief.

CHAPTER 18

All day long there had been the sporadic sound of gunfire. Only Stefanie was brave, or foolhardy, enough to stand by the window while her grandmother and sisters cowered inside. Grandfather was asleep in his room. For days he had been trying to leave Paris, but without success. All the Germans were packing up and fleeing as the Allied troops – the British, the Americans, the Canadians and the Free French – continued their march on Paris. It was rumoured that General von Choltitz, the commander of the German forces in Paris, was trying to arrange an armistice. In the meantime the members of the Resistance, for so long underground, took to the streets to flush out the enemy. There were snipers on every rooftop, behind every door. A state of near-anarchy prevailed, chaos everywhere. Bands of lawless armed men roamed the streets firing guns. No one dare go out. For days there had been no bread, no fresh food. The Ferovs existed on bowls of thin soup that Irina had somehow managed to make from a few potatoes and turnips together with the bones of a very thin chicken, for which they had paid a high price on the Black Market some days before. They still had plenty of money but no influence, no protection. Their friends were abandoning them; once again they faced disaster.

Yet for someone who had seen this all before, the first time when the Bolshevik armies had been advancing on Batum, it had an air of familiarity. What was not familiar was the total collapse of Alexei, his palpable terror that his friends were taking flight and his enemies were about to reappear. There had always been escape before, but now there was not. Hope had gone.

'But the British are not your enemies,' Irina tried to console him, sitting by his bed, urging the thin soup between his lips. 'They are your friends. The girls are *English*. When the British Army arrives we shall go out and welcome them!'

'Oh no!' Alexei gasped, lying back in his bed, the unpalatable liquid trickling down his chin. 'The Communists will get us before that...'

'But there are no Communists, Alexei.' Practical Irina, concerned that her husband might make himself seriously ill, tried to prop him up on his pillows. 'The Allies are not Communists.'

'The Communists are *here*,' Alexei wailed pointing to the sky. 'Here in Paris. There are more red banners flying from the windows than tricolors.'

For once in a disastrous situation Irina felt quite cheerful. Things, she reasoned, could never be as bad again. They may have been friendly with the Germans – but they would be with the Allies too. Everyone *must* know they were neutral. Irina sighed and, reaching again for the spoon, gently tried to ease it past her husband's lips.

It was true that old scores were now being settled among the different elements of the Resistance before the Allies and the Free French arrived. Many of them were being settled privately, not only with those suspected of collaboration but among those who had spent the past five years underground squabbling with one another. Hatred flared up in the streets of Paris that was not only directed against the enemy.

They came for Alexei, as he had feared they would, late one night. He had spent all day in his bed reviewing the past – the old days in St Petersburg at the court of the doomed Czar, happy family holidays at Essenelli. When he looked into the future he could see nothing at all. It was like staring at a blank wall. The tirade of blows on the front door came at about midnight. Stefanie ran to let them in, rather than leave them to break the door down.

There were four armed men who stared at her. One pointed

341

his gun at the self-possessed young girl, her dressing gown drawn tightly round her breast, who looked at them indignantly: 'What is it you want?' she demanded.

Two of the men looked at each other and a third shook his head. 'This is the wrong house. Come on. Let's go. Pardon, Mademoiselle.'

But the one with the gun still pointing at Stefanie motioned her to get out of the way. Roughly he pushed past her, calling to his comrades to follow him:

'This is the one of the granddaughters. It's the old man we're after.'

Stefanie gave a cry and fled after them but before she could get to her grandfather's room she heard her grandmother scream and the terrifying sounds of blows.

'Stop it! Stop!' she cried running into the room just in time to see her grandmother crouching on the floor while her grandfather was dragged out of bed.

'He's very sick,' Stefanie implored them, tears running down her face, 'he's an old man.'

'Do you know how many people he betrayed?' The leader spat on the floor. 'How many innocent Frenchmen he gave away to the Germans?'

'None, I swear, I swear. He didn't betray anyone. He is not French, but a Russian. He...'

'We know quite well who he is,' the chief spokesman said, pointing his gun into Alexei's thin chest and telling him to get dressed. 'We have had his name on our list for many months, I can tell you.'

'Then take me,' Stefanie said, but the spokesman only smiled.

'As far as we know *you* have betrayed no one. We seek only one person.'

'On whose orders, whose orders?' Stefanie demanded but the men had turned on Alexei who was fumbling in a corner of the room with his shirt and trousers, trying to stretch his braces over his thin, trembling frame.

342

When he was dressed Alexei Ferov, whose family, after all, was older than the Romanovs, seemed to have gathered together some shreds of his former dignity. He asked permission to comb his hair and moustache, and then as he put on his overcoat he shook himself and stuck his monocle firmly into his eye.

'I am ready,' he said in clear French. 'May I say goodbye to my wife and granddaughters?'

'Oh *please* ...' Irina screamed, crawling along the floor and pathetically tugging at the rough jersey of the leader. 'You have no idea how much we have suffered. We were forced to leave Russia ... we ... please, please do not take my husband. A weak man he may be, but he has harmed no one.'

'Did you never wonder what became of your daughter?' the leader snarled and, roughly seizing Alexei by the arm, forced him to the door.

Now that there was nothing else to fear Stefanie stood at the open door of the apartment watching them lead him away. For days they had been aware of his terror, forced to share it. As soon as it was certain the Germans were evacuating Paris Alexei had behaved like a marked man, skulking in his room, behind a locked door. Now there was a curious dignity about him as he was roughly pushed away. In the background Stefanie could hear her grandmother's wild sobs, but she was dry-eyed, watching them until they were out of sight. For a girl who had seen many tragedies in her short life this was just another one.

She closed the door quietly and went back to her grandmother – conscious of her sisters crouching by her side trying helplessly to calm her because they were as fearful as she.

'It is like the Terror all over again,' Stefanie said quite calmly recalling her lessons from school. 'I wonder who will play Robespierre?'

Then she went into the kitchen to make tea for her stricken grandmother. She felt too tired, too numb, too emotionally cold even to mourn. For it *was* a mourning. They knew what happened to collaborators now that their friends had gone.

On the first floor of a house not very far away from the Ferov apartment a man sat at a bare deal table with a light in front of him, a packet of cigarettes by his side. To the other side was a glass and an ashtray overflowing with butts. The man seemed to be waiting impatiently, listening, and when at last he heard what he was expecting he went to the door and threw it open.

Alexei, blinded by the sudden light, stumbled into the room and all he saw at first was the table, the chair, the naked light bulb. Then a man came out of the shadows and, after staring at him for a moment, curtly ordered him to stand in front of the table behind which he sat. He lit a cigarette and, through the smoke, stared at Alexei again.

'Prince Alexei?'

'Yes.' The man had a cultured voice and Alexei stared hopefully at him for a moment, pressing his monocle more firmly into his eye. 'Do I have the pleasure of knowing you, Monsieur?'

'You do not, but I know you,' the man said. 'I know everything about you but, above all, I knew your daughter Hélène. I knew her very well...'

'Oh ...' Alexei swallowed. 'My daughter left home a long time ago. What became of her, do you know? Why do you talk about her in the past?'

For a moment the man seemed nonplussed by the bewilderment in Alexei's voice. Then he bent to consult some papers on the table in front of him.

'It is our information that you betrayed your daughter to the Germans.'

'I? Why should I betray my daughter to the Germans?' Alexei cleared his throat, clearly nervous, but appearing to gather more confidence as he went on. 'I had no knowledge of what my daughter was doing until I heard that she had been detained by the Gestapo. I tell you, it was a shock for her

344

mother and me.' Alexei mopped his brow. 'I can't tell you how much of a shock, for her daughters too. Treasonable activities when she was not even a citizen of this country...'

'Treasonable!' The man thumped the table and rose, glowering at the prince. 'Did you never consider such actions to be heroic?'

'We are not French Nationals,' Alexei mumbled. 'You must try and understand our position. Our main fear was of the Bolsheviks not the Germans.'

'Nazis,' the man corrected.

'Nazis,' Alexei agreed, running his fingers round his collar.

'You are a fascist, too, I think, Prince Alexei?'

'It's not a word I would have used. Democrat is better. Believe me, if you went through what I have been through you would certainly not support the Communists.'

The man stared at a paper before him and frowned.

'You don't appear to know very much about what any of your children were up to.'

'Any?' Alexei gazed at him in bewilderment.

'Your son Kyril, your daughter Hélène...'

'Well they are no longer children. Hélène is, was,' Alexei glanced at his interlocutor almost apologetically, 'is over forty. Kyril has a grown-up son who is fighting in the war on the Allied side. How could *I* be expected to know what they get up to. To tell you the truth,' Alexei leaned forward conspiratorially, 'I was quite relieved to know that my daughter was suspected of being in the Resistance. I can tell you in confidence that it was a great weight off our minds. A member of the Ferov family ... She had men in, you know, and of course we didn't know what to think. Then when she moved out...'

'You thought she had set herself up in business as a prostitute? Is that what you told your Nazi friends?'

'I told them nothing,' Alexei said.

'Then who told your Nazi friends?'

Aware of the proximity of the Allied Forces to Paris, Alexei began to stammer.

'They were *not* my friends...'

'My dear Prince,' the man's tone was sarcastic. 'You have been seen all over Paris dining with the *boche* in restaurants, entertaining them, or being entertained by them. I find it very difficult to believe you didn't mention your daughter...'

'I might have mentioned she no longer lived at home. I don't think I ever said...'

'Think, think, think.' The man tapped his head, glancing at his watch. 'Time is running out for you. It is impossible for us, this tribunal,' he glanced at the other men in the room who were lounging against the wall, 'to think that you and your family were other than heavily involved with the Nazis, that you conspired with them to betray Madame Lighterman and Lady Charlotte Verdi, who was captured at the same time. If we could find them, Kyril Ferov and Jordan Bolingbroke would be here in the dock with you. But we will catch up with them, Prince. Don't worry, we will find them. We will find all the traitors to France who have conspired with her enemies. You are sentenced to be shot.'

The man signed a piece of paper, gave it to another on his right who roughly grabbed Alexei and began to lead him from the room.

In his final moments Alexei, that frightened man who had spent the last few days quaking in his bed, acquired a courage he hadn't known he possessed. As a captain in the Preobrazhensky Guard his duties had been mainly ceremonial. Faced now with eternity he remembered his dignity as a Russian prince, heir to all those descendants of that seventeenth-century Ferov who had helped to establish Michael Romanov as the first Czar of a line which would last three hundred years.

He didn't falter, or beg for mercy, but drew himself up, screwing his monocle more firmly into his eye, and imperiously studying his tormentor.

'You make a very grave mistake, monsieur,' he said with

only a catch in his voice. 'May God forgive *you* for it. And, please, tell my poor wife what happened to me.'

With that he turned on his heels and pushed away the hand of the man who tried to lead him away.

'There is no need,' he said. 'I will follow you.'

After the prince had gone Marc La Fôret sat for a long time, staring at the door. Had he condemned an *ingenu* to death, a fool who was genuinely ignorant of the consequences of his actions? Was he guilty of behaving like the enemy with their summary executions in the Avenue Foch? Had he acted only out of bitterness and anger because of what had happened to Charlotte, Hélène and Charles? Was he inspired only by vindictiveness – a feeling that had carried him through the tense months since the fateful landing at Chartres? Was his prime emotion one of hatred for the father of the brave woman whom the Nazis had sent to a concentration camp?

But, if she knew, would Hélène thank him for what he'd done? With a silent exclamation he rose from his chair and walked swiftly to the door, but before he had the chance to open it and halt the execution he heard the muffled sound of a shot. For a moment he stood with his head bent and then slowly he returned to the table.

Pulling a piece of paper towards him he struck another name off the list, writing beside it 'died bravely'.

But he knew that he, himself, would not forget how Alexei Ferov died, or whether he should have died at all.

Jenny sat on the edge of the small bed and suddenly the room seemed to swim for several seconds before it righted itself. She put her head on her knees and Ralph, tying a knot in his tie, saw her sway and rushed over to her.

'Are you all right?' he said, sitting down and supporting her with his arms. Jenny nodded, fighting the violent waves of nausea that threatened to overcome her.

'Just a dizzy turn.'

'Darling, you're overdoing things.' Ralph looked abashed.

347

'I should feel guilty, but I couldn't resist the chance of forty-eight hours' leave and grabbed the first plane that could carry me.' Telegrams to Aldershot, where Jenny was now based, had been arranged for her to get forty-eight hours too. They had spent most of it at Askham House, in the room Ralph loved with the woman he loved.

'I'm pregnant,' Jenny said, straightening up at last. Her voice seemed oddly detached. 'I wasn't going to tell you if you hadn't come home. I'd have just got rid of it. I'm awfully sorry.'

Ralph drew her into his arms. 'You must never say that again,' he said. 'Never even think it.'

'You can't possibly *want* a baby.' Jenny tried to turn round and look at his face but his arms trapped her.

'I do want a baby.'

'Like this?'

'Like this. You can't possibly *want* to get rid of it? I shan't let you.' Ralph sounded angry.

'Of course I shan't, if you don't want me to. If you don't want me to that badly.'

'Very badly,' Ralph said. 'There's no reason for Cheryl not to give me a divorce now.'

'You do believe it all, don't you Ralph?' Jenny's voice sounded strange.

'Believe what?'

'The happy ending...'

'Of course I do.'

'That Cheryl will divorce you, that we'll be married. That everyone will live happily ever after.'

'Not everyone,' Ralph's voice was grim. 'But those who deserve to. There'll be a hell of a mess in Europe after the war. You can't imagine the devastation as our troops advance ... and France! Some people say it is worse than the last war. Thank God Paris escaped because they say Von Choltitz disobeyed Hitler's instructions to destroy the city. But there is a peculiar devastation about Paris and a terrible shortage of food.'

It was October 1944 and the Allied troops were fighting on the German border pushing on for their ultimate goal: Berlin. It was Ralph's job with the Intelligence Corps to round up the Nazis and make sure that none escaped justice.

'You know that I'll have to leave the Service?' Recovered now, Jenny freed herself, and going over to the window looked out onto the Square. 'I'll have to give a reason. I'm a serving officer.'

Ralph went over to her and put an arm round her. 'Well tell them. It's our baby. The father wants to marry you. *I'll* tell them if you like.'

'You'd better not,' Jenny smiled, brushing her hair back from her forehead. 'I don't think you and our commanding officer would get on very well. No, I'll do it, if it's what you want...'

Jenny stopped speaking suddenly and raised her head, listening. Ralph looked at her, then out of the window. From the far distance came the steady chug-chug of a V1, a Flying Bomb. When the engines cut out was the time to worry. That was when everyone held their breaths. Launched shortly after the D-Day landings the flying bombs had struck terror in London but did nothing to diminish the progress of the war. Ralph's arm tightened round Jenny.

'I hate the blighters,' he said. 'Think of all the needless misery they inflict.' Suddenly the engine cut out. Out of sight now, it was probably directly overhead. Ralph pulled Jenny onto the floor. 'If we go we all go together,' he said, 'all three of us.' A moment later an explosion rocked the ground on which the house stood and the sound of tinkling glass could be heard.

'All clear,' Ralph said, kissing Jenny's hand. 'Let's go and tell Mum the good news.'

* * *

'This is David,' Bobby said rather stiffly, 'your half brother. David, Stefanie.'

'How do you do?' Stefanie said politely shaking hands, every inch the Russian princess once removed.

'How do you do?' David said awkwardly.

Aileen, smiling, pushed forward Olga, then Natasha, an arm round the shoulder of each. They still looked tired from the journey. In the background Irina twittered, both excited and alarmed by the sudden turn of events. A summons had come from Bobby and the British authorities in Paris had, with difficulty, managed to arrange the journey through that part of France which was now free.

Sasha, on leave, had met them at Victoria and returned with them to the newly opened Lighterman House. The upper rooms were still closed because of the threat of flying bombs and none of the pictures or valuables had been returned but, gradually, the huge house had the feeling of being a home again even though to the family it was like camping.

If Bobby was emotional about seeing his daughters again after so many years he concealed it well. He was affable and gracious, but unpaternal. He had kissed each girl but without warmth, a peck on the forehead as though he were some kind distant uncle, which was rather what he felt. He had only succumbed to family pressure in sending for the girls at all after they had heard that Alexei had been murdered in some travesty of a court marshal by the vengeful Resistance. In those early days of the liberation there had been many acts of retribution which could only be attributed to the climate of the times. In a way it *was* an act of God. Or was it of the devil?

Some said the devil himself descended on France in those dark days before the Gaullist provisional government began to impose a structure on the shattered country. Some people may have deserved to die, but some did not and, in any case, those kangaroo courts bore no resemblance to any form of known justice or legality.

Lunch had been set in the newly reopened dining room and

when the girls saw the spread before them there was an almost audible gulp. Although he regarded himself as a patriot Bobby had hardly been touched by deprivation during the war. You could get anything if you wanted it, and to him rationing was just a form of self-control to be flaunted at will. Sasha, smiling, sat down next to Stefanie.

'How long is it since you've seen a piece of beef like that?'

Stefanie shook her head. Irina was obligingly about to tell them how good to them the Germans had been when she remembered Alexei. She also saw the look in Stefanie's eyes – a look that told her to be careful.

David Lighterman regarded his half sister across the table. 'Is it true they ate dogs found in the street?'

Stefanie, thinking the remark had been addressed to her grandmother, looked from David to Irina; but Irina was busy patting her mouth with a napkin, still remembering the goodness of the Nazis with their little gifts: a side of ham or a bottle of fine cognac, truffles from the Dordogne.

'We never ate dogs,' Stefanie said disdainfully. 'It is true *some* people were near to starving, but we always managed. My grandmother was such a good cook.'

Irina helped herself to vegetables and, watching her, Aileen thought it was amazing how soon some people recovered from what one would have thought was an overwhelming tragedy. The corpse of Alexei as well as those of other suspected collaborators had been found in the cellar of a house occupied by members of the Resistance before Paris was liberated.

Aileen could dimly recall Irina from her reign, over ten years before, as companion to Bobby's grandmother. There was still some of the glamour left even if the voluminous georgette dress looked a little tattered, the high-heeled calf shoes a little scuffed and the rows of pearls, disguising the withers round her neck, obviously false.

Irina looked like a brave, sad woman more used by time, probably, than she thought she deserved. She was much more gaunt than Aileen remembered, but great care had been taken

351

with her make-up and her false hairpiece was quite skilfully arranged to cover the wrinkles on her brow, a series of crinkly waves rather reminiscent of the style of Queen Mary. The powder on her cheeks was a little too floury, the rouge a trifle too pink, but the fine eyes, ringed by kohl, blazed forth the essential Irina – courageous, philosophical, accepting the worst but looking forward; ever hopeful that the good times once promised by Alexei – now a martyr in her eyes – were just round the corner.

The conversation was desultory. It was hard to know what to say: two sides of the same family who had hardly ever met. An awkward situation. What did the little girls remember of those splendid days before their banishment? How much did they resent? And what was going to happen to them now? Were they here for a visit, or were they going to stay? They were penniless, motherless and, clearly, Irina couldn't cope on her own. Apart from developing a conscience about them, rather late in the day, Bobby didn't appear to have thought the matter out.

After lunch Sasha and David took the girls to see the streets of London, maybe go to Regent's Park or Hyde Park, and Aileen, Irina and Bobby sat in the lounge drinking coffee. Bobby wouldn't be there for long, Aileen knew. He was so important to the war effort, the massive demands for arms as the Allies continued their march on Germany, that there were constant calls on his time.

'Now to the girls,' Bobby said, lighting a cigar, after fiddling a great deal with the band and the cutter, the only way Bobby ever betrayed any agitation. 'I have given the matter a great deal of thought.'

'I knew you would, Bobby,' Irina said flatteringly. 'You are always so thoughtful.'

Aileen nearly choked on her coffee, but Bobby appeared to consider this tribute justified and nodded, stroking his narrow moustache.

'You know we're very short of room, Irina,' Bobby gestured

round the huge house. 'I mean there *are* plenty of rooms here, but not many of them are in use. I don't suppose you would want to return to Paris eventually?'

'Well ...' Irina eyed Bobby balefully. After what had happened to Alexei she doubted whether she, or even the girls, were safe. Many of the collaborators were having their hair shorn and marched through the streets of those towns and villages of France which had produced so many victims of the Nazis. 'It *is* Charlotte's flat.'

'Charlotte is probably dead,' Bobby said in an unemotional voice.

'But that's not the point. I haven't a home and nor have my granddaughters. I realise Hélène may be dead too.'

Bobby examined his cigar. 'It was never my intention to punish my daughters for the sins of their mother,' he continued, earning a look of contempt from Aileen. 'It was, after all, not their fault she was a whore. I felt it was best they should grow up with her, but things didn't work out the way I intended. As you know, Stefanie was meant to go to school the year the war started. Well, it's too late for that now, unless she wants to go to some finishing school to get a little polish. I don't mind, I must say. Olga and Natasha will go to school, boarding school, and you, Irina ...' Bobby stared at her through his cold blue eyes. 'I wondered if you'd like to look after Robertswood? As a sort of housekeeper, you know, as you were with my grandmother.'

'*Companion*, Bobby,' Irina coloured. 'I was never a *house-keeper*. What a *vulgar* word.'

'Times have changed, Irina. I realize how you feel; but Robertswood is going to be restored to me in the new year because it has served its purpose as a convalescent home. We have bigger, better equipped units elsewhere, many of them financed by me. A grateful government,' Bobby smiled modestly, 'is quite prepared to restore my family home to me. That will be the girls' home too, for the time being. Incidentally, Stefanie comes into money when she is eighteen. If she

353

likes she will be able to afford a little place of her own. I tell you, property will be very cheap in London. I'm going to buy a lot myself, war-damaged property, and do it up. I'm even going to make an offer for Askham House which is on its last legs. I should think Ralph would be glad to get rid of it.'

Bobby looked at his watch and said he must go but Irina, who had been plucking at the folds of her dress with an unusual air of agitation, stood up before he did, clutching in her hand a rather pathetic little pocket purse which had seen far better days. She opened the flap with a trembling hand and, drawing something out of it, held it up. It was a tiny photograph which Bobby rose to peer at, drawing his spectacles out of his breast pocket to try and see it better. When he saw it, he started back.

'It's my daughter Hélène,' Irina said, a quiver in her voice. 'She was not a whore but a heroine. I never want you to call her that again, or *dare* to demean her to me or the children, or anyone else for that matter. Hélène saved the lives of many Allied soldiers and airmen, including Sasha...'

'I know that,' Bobby said awkwardly.

'How *can* you call her a whore, then? Or diminish her in front of me? We don't know where she is now, or if we shall ever see her again, but I am proud of my daughter, Bobby, and my husband, for he was a hero too. He was slain by the Communists, as he knew he would be. He betrayed no one to the Germans, certainly not our daughter, or any of your family. He was killed as an act of revenge by madmen.'

Irina paused for a moment and dabbed at her eyes with a lace handkerchief that was both genteel and very old. Its edges were frayed like her and her purse and the clothes; it too looked pathetic – pathetic but brave, like the flag of a defeated army. Suddenly Irina possessed in the eyes of the two astonished people who beheld her a nobility that neither of them had seen before. She had invested herself with dignity.

'I've been through a lot, Bobby, I and my family,' Irina went on, 'and I never wish to hear my daughter, or my husband

354

criticized.' Shaking her head she gave a sniff and tucked her handkerchief back in the band of her sleeve. Her little speech appeared to have given her a resolution she had lacked before, her voice growing stronger minute by minute. 'I shan't deny that we're poverty-stricken, but we're not beggars. We are of the Ferov family who closely served the Romanov dynasty for three hundred years. Both Alexei and I attended, as honoured guests, the celebrations commemorating the coronation of the first Czar Michael, in 1914, when our own dear imperial family was still alive.

'Now my dear Alexei, a martyr too like them, has joined them. Maybe Hélène too, God knows, and maybe, too, poor Charlotte who was always such a devoted friend of ours, never patronized us, as you do.

'As for Robertswood I will do what I can to help you. But I am not a menial, Bobby, and will not be one now. Please don't think you're doing me a favour because, believe me, you owe a lot to me for looking after your daughters.' She moved a step nearer Bobby and quickly he took a few steps back, but there was nothing threatening in her gesture. 'You have neglected them, Bobby, shamefully. You can't buy everyone, you know. You can't buy me and you certainly can't buy *them*. They're fine girls, girls with spirit. Don't think they're going to be grateful to you because they're not, I can assure you of that. They're taking what is due to them. I, as their grandmother, shall see to that.

'Now, on these terms I accept what you want me to do, is that clear?'

Bobby looked at Aileen, and Aileen looked at Bobby with a cruel smile on her mouth. To see her husband for once in his life get his come-uppance was sweet. For once Bobby was speechless.

'Bobby never meant to offend you,' she said to Irina, going over to her and taking her hand. 'Bobby will be more than grateful, and so shall I, for *anything* you can do.'

* * *

'The Askhams have no money you know,' Cheryl said looking sharply at her daughter as if wondering if Amelia had married Hugo for the reason she had married Ralph. 'They used to, but they squandered it all away and now they haven't a bean. I really don't know what I'll do after the war, or how I'll manage. Ralph will have to get work of some kind I expect.'

'There's the farm.' Amelia sat closer to the fire because she felt very cold in the vast house. Despite the flying bombs many people were starting to drift back to London and it was thought that after Christmas would be the last term for the school. Even now many of the children had gone home for good. Amelia thought her mother looked chilled and rather lonely. Yet try as she would she couldn't feel much compassion for her. Cheryl seemed one of those people who had brought everything on themselves and deserved what came to them. Her attitude to Hugo had been unspeakable and continued to be. She never lost the chance of deriding him, when she was with him and when she was not.

In many ways Cheryl had had her heyday in the early years of the war, and was now in a decline. Her usefulness to the nation was passing. There were many who said the war was almost over, could not possibly last more than six months. What would Cheryl do then with this vast house and all the money it would need to restore it to even a semblance of its former grandeur? It would cost thousands and thousands of pounds, perhaps millions, and, as Cheryl said, everyone knew that the Askham family fortune had been whittled down to almost nothing.

'Ralph was always hopeless at money,' Cheryl continued. 'Hopeless at most things.'

'Yet still you want him back I understand?' Amelia's voice was brittle. These visits to her mother were infrequent, regarded as a painful duty. But it was better than having her visit them. Those occasions were awful, dreaded equally by Hugo and Amelia.

'My dear he's my husband,' Cheryl looked surprised at Amelia's remark. 'I believe in marriage, you know.'

'Except when the man's name is George Lee.'

Cheryl paused in the act of pouring fresh tea and examined a rather hard rock cake that Clare had made. As some people rely on the love of their animals Cheryl relied on that of the evacuees she wanted to adopt and who now lived with her permanently. It was true that Ned and Clare did seem to love her very much. In them she was humanized, but when she saw members of that family again who irked her so much, the Askhams – and now Amelia was one of them – all the bad, old traits of the pre-war Cheryl came to the fore again.

'Amelia, that's *very* impertinent.' Cheryl decided not to eat the cake after all. Too much powdered egg. 'You may be a married woman and think yourself very clever, but there is a big difference between Ralph and your father.'

'Money, I believe, in those days.' Amelia got up and walked to the window peering outside. But it was too dark to see the lake. A wind sighed through the trees and the dry branches crackled. '*And* a title,' she added.

'I shall really have to ask you to go I'm afraid.' Cheryl put her cup to her lips and drank from it as though it were the elixir of life, greedily gulping it. 'I don't know what's happened to you,' she said when she'd finished. 'It's the effect of *that* man.'

Cheryl looked pointedly at the door.

Instead of leaving as she was being asked to do Amelia sank into a chair and lit a cigarette. 'I'm sorry, Mummy. I'm very unhappy that you are so nasty about the Askham family. It upsets Hugo a great deal. I didn't marry him for his money...'

'A good thing,' Cheryl cut in but Amelia held up a hand.

'He works hard, he really does, and makes a success of the farm. Hugo will *never* want. I came over here, Mummy, meaning for us to be reconciled, and then...'

'How can we be reconciled when you come out with those nasty remarks?' Cheryl looked indignant. 'What a *way* to speak to your mother!'

357

'Did you know that Ralph's girlfriend is having a baby?'

Cheryl, stooping to light a spill from the fire, straightened slowly and didn't put it to the cigarette in her mouth, but let it go out.

'Who on *earth* is the father?'

'He is.'

'Oh no,' Cheryl gave a sarcastic laugh and lit the spill again, this time completing her task. 'Is that what *she* says?'

'Yes.'

'I very much doubt it. In fact I know it can't be true. I was living with Ralph Askham for nearly ten years and I was never pregnant, or anything near it. That man is sterile.'

'Can you prove it?' Amelia coloured slightly. 'I mean, did you have tests and that kind of thing?'

'Ralph wanted to, but I wasn't keen.' Cheryl sighed. 'I didn't much like children, you know. If that girl says she's pregnant it is *not* by Ralph Askham. I shan't be fooled in that way.'

'Well Ralph thinks it's his baby, isn't that the main thing?'

'Certainly not if he wants to use it as a ploy to get a divorce from me. The baby could not be his. It would have no right to the title. There are enough bastards in his family already ...'

Cheryl hardly saw her daughter as she made for the door. One minute she was there and the next she had gone.

'How touchy some people are,' she murmured, looking into the fire. It was nearly Christmas and she was a very lonely woman indeed.

'I was going to ask your mother here,' Hugo said after Amelia had told him of their meeting. They were eating in the kitchen as they usually did, after the cows had been milked and the animals locked up for the night. It was a time Hugo always loved, always felt grateful for, sitting by the kitchen grate with his wife after a good day well spent.

'You mean for Christmas?'

'Why not? She's lonely, isn't she? I still will if you want.'

'You're too good for this world, Hugo,' Amelia said gazing

358

at him and aware, not for the first time, of a tiny spasm of irritation as she did. He really was so nice, too good, had something to say for everyone. Sometimes it got on her nerves. People said that he and Ralph were alike and maybe that's why Ralph had got on her mother's nerves too.

Hugo got up and went to pour himself more beer. He'd seen the look in her eyes, and he'd seen it before. It was a critical look that rather unnerved him, reminded him a bit of Cheryl. It worried him. But life was good, too good to think that his darling wife could in any way resemble her mother.

'Well, she's very welcome if she wants to come. Rachel and the family are going to be at the manor, and Jenny's coming too.'

'That's good,' Amelia said. 'I really *like* Jenny. Look, let's ask Jenny to come here, seeing that she and Rachel don't get on all that much. Forget about my mother. Why should we ruin our Christmas?'

'That's a fine idea,' Hugo said as, of course, Amelia knew he would. He always agreed with her about everything.

She let her finger stray across the plain deal table on which they ate and looked at him slyly. 'What do you think of the suggestion that the baby...'

'Isn't Ralph's? It's perfectly ridiculous,' Hugo said scornfully.

'But what about him being sterile?'

'I'm quite sure that if Jenny says Ralph is the father then he is. He's the happiest man in the world. Over the moon when I saw him.'

Hugo, having finished his meal, began to fill his pipe. He had a healthy brown face from so much time spent in the open. His work on the farm had strengthened his muscles and he had grown into a powerful man. He gazed at Amelia and thought how much he loved her. She had given up the Army when they married and now ran the farm: doing the accounts, ordering grain and feedstuff. She was the perfect wife, the perfect

359

helpmeet. She was also a wonderful cook and an attractive, much sought after, hostess.

'What about us having kids,' he said. 'Don't you think it's time?'

'Darling, we've only been married a *year*.' Amelia looked at him in mock surprise. The only real surprise to her was that he hadn't asked before. She knew it was his inhibitions about this subject that prevented it. They'd never discussed it. Maybe he thought babies happened like the livestock on the farm.

'Well a year is a year,' Hugo muttered. 'I would love for us to have kids, Amelia.'

He went over to her shyly and let his finger run down her cheek. Amelia seized it and playfully bit it. Then she got up and, putting her arms round his neck, nuzzled her face against his. 'There's *plenty* of time you silly boy,' she said softly. 'Let's have all the fun we can first.'

The look she gave him was tantalizing, frankly sexual, as she tugged him playfully towards the door. Hugo quickly put the light out, allowing her to lead him by the hand upstairs.

Amelia was a tease. She was her mother's daughter after all.

CHAPTER 19

Unless one has seen it, [Em wrote to her mother] it is almost impossible to describe. I think the stench of these camps is something that will remain with me all my life and as for the sights ... the mounds of rotting corpses, and the rows upon rows of people in the last stages of mortal illness. Many will never be cured by the camp doctors rushed in by all the liberating powers. All they can do is try and make the last days of these poor people more comfortable.

The things I have seen in these camps – they are all over Germany, some very large, some quite small – make me despair of ever being able to convey the reality of the horror. Fortunately the news cameras can do that quite silently ... captured for all time so that we never forget. Thousands, perhaps millions of people have been allowed to die from starvation as well as unmentionable brutalities inflicted on them. Can the people who have done these things really belong to the human race? I don't think so.

I think the Allies might have been prepared to deal more leniently with the German people had it not been for the discovery of these concentration camps and the horrors they hold. It is impossible to believe that the general population did not know of them, yet did nothing to help. The Americans who liberated Buchenwald camp which housed, in wretched conditions, over 21,000 people forced many of the inhabitants of the nearby town of Weimar to go round the camp and see conditions for themselves. Some tried to make excuses, but many of them wept.

It was Peter Klein, Mother, who told me that Charlotte might still be alive. His camp, at Dachau, was liberated in April by the Canadians and, incredibly, many of the inmates were still in reasonable shape. Peter Klein heard I was in the area and sent a message to me. I can tell you it was a very emotional moment when I saw him. I told him we had all long ago thought him dead. He said that many of the earliest political prisoners, who had been sent to Dachau, had somehow survived because they began to make themselves indispensable to the running of the camp. Peter was a Kapo, a man in charge, and he said he was able to make life easier for a lot of his fellow inmates than it might otherwise have been. Peter remains for the time being in Dachau as it is impossible to find transport or accommodation for so many thousands, most of whom are now homeless. Peter himself has no idea what happened to his father or whether his mother and sister were still alive. I had to tell him about Marian ... the sadness of this was compensated for by the fact that he has a little nephew, Paul. He wept when he heard about this.

This brings me, Mother, to the main story of my letter which I promised to elaborate after my wire to you.

You will have heard of Belsen Concentration Camp which was liberated by the British. Among the first to go in were the Intelligence Corps and Ralph found a pass for me, as we had heard through the grapevine that Charlotte had at least been here – moved on from Auschwitz in Poland before the Russians came. A man who reached Dachau from Auschwitz remembered her, but he said that many of the women had been force-marched to other concentration camps, and others too ill to be moved remained behind.

When Ralph first went into Belsen he could not believe that anyone could have survived such appalling conditions and his first inquiries brought no news of Charlotte, or Hélène, because, of course, we have constantly asked for her. It was strange, and sinister, that we could pick up a trail to Charlotte but nothing about Hélène.

Ralph spent several hours in Belsen, but it is such a huge place that he drew a complete blank other than hearing that a group of prisoners from Auschwitz had arrived there. He thought they had been shot.

Mother, the day that Ralph came for me to take me to Belsen as a last hope was one that I shall never forget. The camp commandant, who is called Kramer, is a byword for bestiality and brutality. Ralph who interrogated him said that the man seemed to have no interest in the fate of the inmates at all or concern that he may have done anything wrong. Ralph felt like shooting him on the spot, but thought it was too good for him. Incidentally, summary execution by infuriated Allied armed troops has been the lot of many concentration camp personnel. It is impossible to stop.

I will pass over, Mother, the sights we saw that day, as we

walked around peering at the huge piles of lifeless bodies, completely naked, waiting to be buried; we dreaded what we might see ... but would we have recognized her?

The camp is a huge place like a small town with rows of huts divided by streets, by the side of which men and women sat with great vacant eyes staring into space. Many seemed past caring that they had been liberated; some were unaware of it, but stared at us uncomprehending, their minds completely gone. Some apathetically put out their hands as if begging for food. The RAMC have to be very careful to regulate the diet of these people because too rich food too quickly could kill them. So they add a little meat and vegetables to the thin gruel which is all they are capable of digesting, and the meagre ration of bread is increased.

It was towards evening that Ralph and I, sick at heart, were standing by the corner of one of the huts which, like all the others, was in unspeakable condition when a woman in a white coat walked out. We had heard that some of the guards, fearing retribution, had disguised themselves as prisoners and Ralph stopped this woman and, despite her emaciated condition, said to her in German: Are you a guard?

The woman looked up at him and then she looked at me ... and the three of us instinctively put out our arms ... Oh, Mother, I can hardly bear to go on except that it was one of the most beautiful, most memorable moments of my life. It was a long time before Charlotte – because, of course, it was she – Ralph and I could say anything remotely logical. We still have not heard all of the terrible story she has to tell since she and Hélène were transferred to Germany from France. She has been in several concentration camps, among them the awful Auschwitz and Flossenberg. She owes her survival, she thinks, to the fact that she was treated as an Italian national and also because she developed a flair for lying. She told them that she had nursing experience and so she always worked in the prison sick bays, such as they were. The stories she has to tell are too frightful ... mostly, such is her weakened state, they reduce her to tears.

But, Mother, Charlotte is *alive*. She is painfully thin (she said Chanel would love her now! – she still has her sense of humour) but much better than many of her fellow inmates. She is still in the camp because she has charges she doesn't want to leave – typical Charlotte – until they are transferred to a proper hospital. Ralph and I go and see her daily, though he must soon move on to Berlin which the British are at last being allowed to enter. The Russians have kept us out for their own questionable purposes and everyone is livid, as you can imagine, Monty especially. It is said that Stalin wants Berlin for himself. It was Eisenhower who insisted that the Allies stay at the Elbe while the Russians took Berlin. Apparently the casualties were fearful.

Mother, isn't it wonderful ... Charlotte is *alive*? I keep repeating it over and over to myself and, despite the horrors I have witnessed, it is the one thing that irradiates every day for me and will for the rest of my life.

Mother, the sad part is that there is no news of Hélène. She and Charlotte were split up at Auschwitz because Hélène was too ill to go. The camp was "liberated" by the Russians in which case, as a White Russian princess, there would be very little hope for her.

The stories told about some of the Russian "liberators" equal those told about the Nazis. Everyone is terrified of being taken by them and Ralph feels very angry that the Allies weren't the first into Berlin as they could easily have been ...

When the letter came to an end Rachel removed her glasses and gazed at Joe, Pascal and Angelica. Of the three, Joe had tears in his eyes and busily blew his nose when the first mention of his mother was made. But Pascal and Angelica were dry-eyed; they had done all their weeping in the years their mother had been missing, and when the first cable came to say that she had been found alive amidst the horrors of Belsen. Then it was almost impossible for the English people to grasp what had happened inside the camps: the true facts were only available on newsreel and not everyone went to the cinema.

'When will she be home?' Angelica asked thoughtfully, as though she had a lot of adjustments to make which, in fact, she had. As a young girl she had grown up almost without the care of her mother and, good as her grandmother had been, it was not the same. Of the three Angelica seemed to feel more resentment than pride in her mother's achievements in France, because these had led to her capture and disappearance for two years. Angelica was nearly fifteen, and four years was a long time to be without a mother.

Rachel had folded the letter and tucked it back in the official envelope Em had managed to use through Ralph to send the letter quickly.

'I gather from this letter it will not be very soon,' she said. 'It is so like your mother to stay until all those who need her are well looked after. You must be very proud of her. I am.' At that moment Rachel's self-control broke and she hid her head in her hands. It was so unusual for the children to see any untoward display of emotion from that bastion of calm and common-sense that at first they looked at her, and one another, in amazement. Then with one accord they went over to her, Pascal leading her to the sofa beside the open window.

It was going to be a warm, beautiful May – the month that marked the end of the war in Europe. Rachel had received the letter in her battle-scarred office and, summoning the children from their respective schools for the weekend, she had gone to collect them and brought them back to Darley Manor with Flora who, being at the same school as her cousin, had got permission to join them. Flora was out in the garden now, waiting, because Rachel had wanted Charlotte's children to hear the details about their mother alone with her. The children still standing solicitously by her, Rachel blew her nose and looked up, smiling.

'There, I'm a silly old woman aren't I? After all, she's safe.'

'But you're *her* Mummy,' Angelica said understandingly. 'There's nothing to be ashamed of, Gran.'

Thoughtful, sensitive Joe put his arm around Rachel's shoulder. 'You've had an awful lot to put up with you know, Gran. You've worked all during the war, nearly been bombed several times; you've looked after us, looked after Paul and Flora and Giles; looked after Uncle Adam when he has been so ill. And you're worried. I don't think you realize, Gran, just how much of a burden you've carried.'

'Dear Joe.' Rachel groped for his hand. 'You make me feel like crying again. But you make me proud too, all of you. You've been splendid children and your dear mother will be the first to say so when she gets home. As to when that will be,' recovered, she leaned back and put her arm around Angelica's waist, 'I would think in the next few weeks. Won't it be exciting to have her for the summer? Oh, there are so *many* things to look forward to now.'

As she turned towards the door it opened and Jenny put her head round. Rachel waved the letter to her.

'I had to read it to the children first, Jenny.'

'Of course,' Jenny nodded.

'But it *is* the most wonderful news. Read it.'

As Jenny took the letter Rachel looked towards the window. 'Why don't you go and get Flora and tell her about the letter?' she said to Pascal. 'We don't want her to feel left out. Besides it's a lovely day. Oh, a lovely day.' Rachel stretched her legs and her arms before her. It was as if her whole body were unwinding after years of strain. As the children went outside she watched them, then she murmured to Jenny, 'I was the one who did the weeping. They were *very* calm and controlled. Sometimes I feel they hardly know Charlotte, hardly remember her.'

'I think that's natural,' Jenny said, rapidly turning the pages of the letter. 'They're bound to be a bit reserved at first.'

'Oh Jenny, you're so sensible.' Rachel put a hand towards her. 'I've got so used to having you around. I can't think what I'd do without you.'

Jenny hardly appeared to heed her, except for a brief smile, but when Ralph's mother had gone into the garden to join her grandchildren and great niece, Jenny put down the letter and gazed for a long time in their direction.

Her son had been born in March and Ralph had yet to see him. A tentative name had been John, but nothing positive was to be decided until Ralph came home. She knew that Ralph was keen on the name 'Bosco' after his father but somehow Rachel was against this, rather as no one in the Royal family wanted to use the name of beloved Albert because of its sacred meaning to Queen Victoria.

Ralph's mother's thaw towards Jenny had been very

gradual, the ice only finally melting after the birth of John. The months after Jenny left the QARANC had been hard because, as well as being pregnant and alone, there was the worry about Ralph from whom they sometimes didn't hear for weeks.

Jenny had taken a room by herself in the Swiss Cottage part of London and used to lie on her bed listening to the buzz bombs fly over, experiencing, alone, the terror when they cut out knowing she had no strong body to protect her as Ralph had that night in St James's Square. Occasionally Rachel would ring or ask her round to tea, the implication being that Rachel was very busy with all the things she had to do – her newspaper, the family, while Jenny only had to take care of herself.

Jenny carefully put the letter back in its envelope, laid it on a small table and walked to the window. She could see Rachel on the lawn, her face shaded by a large straw hat, surrounded by her grandchildren and great niece.

She was a remarkable woman, Jenny conceded, gazing critically at her, even a great woman. She was sixty-eight and sometimes she seemed to have the strength, vigour and even looks of someone much younger. Her pale ash-blonde hair was only streaked with grey and that smooth, healthy skin relatively unlined. Beside her Jenny felt rather insignificant by comparison, ungainly. Rachel, the matriarch, did inspire her with feelings of awe.

Jenny had never really doubted herself in her life until she met the Askham family. She was a capable farmer's daughter, a north countrywoman, and feelings of inferiority were not part of her nature, until she met Ralph. He would have been horrified to think that he or his family could induce these feelings of inadequacy in her and she would never tell him, or his mother. She realized it never occurred to them either; it was something in herself that she hadn't known was there.

When John was born Rachel asked her to stay in the country. She said she didn't like to think of her all alone in London. But Jenny knew that the real reason was John: a new member of the Askham family had been born; Ralph's first son, a grandson of Rachel and the legendary Bosco. This, and only this, gave her acceptability in Rachel's eyes.

It did occur to her to refuse but in many ways it would be an empty gesture, which would hurt Ralph and which he might misinterpret. She knew that his love for her had no strings attached – son or no son he loved her. But he also loved his mother and Jenny didn't want Rachel to turn into an enemy – so she accepted gratefully and she tried to make herself useful. There was a lot for her to do. Since the affair of Jordan Bolingbroke and his broadcasts to the German people Adam had seemed to be a broken man. He stopped going to London altogether and stayed at home pottering in the garden and listening to endless news broadcasts about the progress of the war. She didn't think he missed one.

During term time all the children were at school, even Paul who was at his father's old prep school, and Jenny had the place almost to herself and her baby. Rachel came down at weekends and, occasionally, one or two of the children came home too. There was the celebration for VE Day when a bonfire had been lit on the village green and she and Rachel had cooked all day to provide a feast for the evening.

Although Adam was younger than the Prime Minister, Winston Churchill, he was like a very old man, waiting for death. Unlike his sister he had been broken by life. Too many mistakes, he told Jenny, especially over Bosco's sister Flora who had been the real love of his life, and not the woman he eventually married, Margaret, the mother of Flora and Giles.

Adam confided a lot in Jenny whom he found congenial, and she'd grown very fond of him. Yet he was like a man riddled by guilt. The presence of Young Flora seemed to remind him constantly of that great love, which had magnified over the years. He lived in the past, in his dreams, even the bad ones, and seldom took much part in what was going on. Rachel in turn valued Jenny's help with Adam. Indeed, she had come to value her very much.

From the garden Rachel looked up and saw Jenny staring at them. She wondered if, in her eyes, she saw a trace of sadness, of envy, or was she simply missing Ralph? She beckoned to her and as Jenny slowly came out of the French windows towards her she said:

'Is there anything wrong? You look quite sad.'

'I thought there might be some news of Ralph in the letter.'

'But there is.'

'Yes …' Jenny ran her hands through her short hair. 'I haven't heard from him for so long, sometimes I worry.'

Rachel grasped her hand and pulled her onto the bench beside her: 'You silly girl,' she said fondly. 'The war is over. What on earth is there to worry about now?'

There is no doubt the Allies could have been first into Berlin, Ralph thought with a savagery mixed with sadness as he viewed the ruins of that once great city. Scarcely a house or a building was left standing and there was a dreadful air of desolation, as though some paranormal event had struck the town.

Everything was deathly quiet – literally deathly because, beneath the mounds of stones and debris that littered either side of the thoroughfares both approaching the city and within it, still lay the bodies of many Russians who had entered Berlin with the Red Army and whose advance had been resisted, street by street, by the Germans. It was said that, had the Allies been the conquerors, those in charge of Berlin might have surrendered at once perhaps even when Hitler was alive. It was the thought of that implacable Bolshevik foe that had kept the Germans fighting.

There were few people about in the streets and the once beautiful broad avenues which Em, who frequently accompanied him, remembered from before the war. Hélène and Bobby used to come here quite a lot and stay at the Kaiserhof. Hélène loved the shops and cafés on the Unter Den Linden. Now, in his chancellery near that famous thoroughfare, the body of Hitler had allegedly been burnt by his faithful staff after he poisoned his wife and then shot himself. The circumstances of the deaths – if deaths there had been, some people were still sceptical – were obscure.

For many weeks, perhaps months, the Berliners had been without water and electricity. There had been scarcely any food in what shops could remain open or what markets managed to survive – pathetic little street markets manned by hapless, hopeless people, with a few scraggy vegetables, maybe some cheese, for sale.

Berlin had finally fallen on 4 May and, in the weeks that the Red Army had been in charge, things had improved. They could scarcely have got worse. The resourceful Germans had started to creep out of the ruins of their homes and businesses and there was a semblance of life beginning again. One or two cafés were open, the chairs and tables hopefully dusted down, fresh cloths laid. It was almost impossible to get a place in one of the few hotels which could take guests, and the war correspondents and those on official business mostly had billets in any remaining houses standing in the city. Ralph was at the British Army barracks in Wilhelmstadt, the southern part of Spandau.

The normal government of Berlin had been suspended and there was strict military rule.

Berlin was to be divided into four military sectors: French, Russian, American and English, while Germany itself would be divided into two, East and West. Some thought this was a good thing as it would prevent the resurgence of power that had in this century caused two major wars. In this one alone the number of deaths was incalculable.

Ever since he had come to Berlin at the beginning of July with the advance party of British troops Ralph had had his hands full. The task of finding the Nazi war criminals, and stopping them fleeing to safety, at times seemed insurmountable. Many were already dead, some had committed suicide, but many more were missing. It was not until he drove past the

Reichstag one day and saw the red flag with the hammer and sickle of the Soviets hanging over it that he remembered that one of his tasks, in this most complex of complicated jobs, an officer in the Intelligence Corps, was to find Kyril.

Yet his search for Susan's husband, possibly Freddie's killer, now seemed that much less important than it had been in the days before El Alamein when he and Em had heard the story from Randy Tucker. That was nearly three years ago. He had never heard from Randy Tucker again and wondered if he had perished in the desert. Somehow he didn't think so. There was something very enduring about that tough old 'digger', that soldier of fortune, who once boasted he had fought for the Bolsheviks in 1919.

On one of his rare breaks Ralph had arranged to meet Em at a bar in the Kurfüstendamm. You could have a drink there and a snack of delicious German sausage with the blackest of bread, all hideously expensive. Ralph was sitting at a table on the pavement of the café writing to Jenny and looked up as a shadow fell over him. Em, in her correspondent's battle dress, her bag slung over her shoulder, stood before him. Ralph got up to greet her and pointed to a chair. The other tables were quickly filling as it was past noon.

'Isn't this a heavenly day?' Em said with a levity in her voice that was almost pre-war. 'Who would ever have thought that two months ago they were having a battle here?'

It was true. Even the famous linden trees had started to bloom, although the trees in the Tiergarten remained blackened stumps. Birds were returning, no one quite knew from where because the countryside for miles around Berlin had been devastated. The streets now were clear of rubble, much of it removed painstakingly bucket by bucket by the German, largely female, population known as *Trümmerfrauen*.

Em had lived in Berlin for two years in the middle of the thirties, her stay coinciding with the rise of Hitler whom she had frequently warned the readers of her mother's paper about.

Yet looking around her now, fascinated, as much as anything, by the devastation in that once beautiful city, it was almost impossible to remember those years. In many ways she felt that Berlin had purged itself for the sins committed by Hitler in the name of its people.

Phoenix-like, reborn, surely it would rise again? She looked thoughtfully at Ralph, who had ordered two beers, and said: 'I've got important news.'

'I thought you looked mysterious.' Ralph signed his letter to Jenny, put the cap on his fountain pen and the letter in his pocket. 'Hélène ...' he said hopefully, but a shadow passed over Em's face.

'No, not Hélène, alas, but something close. Do you remember Cairo and ...'

'Kyril,' Ralph finished for her. 'I was only thinking about him the other day.'

'Kyril *is* in Berlin.'

'I don't believe it.' Ralph put his glass of beer to his lips. 'Have you seen him?'

'No, but he's here. He's been described to me, and there's no doubt. He is here, under his own name. He's a colonel and has something to do with Stalin's security at the Potsdam Conference which starts next week.'

'Who told you all this?'

Em tapped her brow and said in a heavy foreign accent: 'Do not forget I am ze newspaper correspondent. I ask ze questions, a lot of zem. If *you* have forgotten Kyril I certainly haven't ...'

'Nor I.' Ralph's face grew grim. 'I once made a vow ...'

'Would you still kill him?'

Under the steadiness of Em's gaze Ralph lowered his eyes. 'I see you wouldn't.'

'I've seen too much killing.' Ralph gestured around him. 'Besides, we have no proof.'

'True,' Em nodded. 'After the concentration camps I am

ready to forswear killing forever. What do we do? Forget about him?'

'How can we forget about Kyril?' Ralph felt uneasy. 'We know he killed our brother.'

'We *think*; as you say, there's no proof. Unless Randy Tucker could identify him.'

'I've not the slightest idea where Randy is, or what happened to him.' Ralph, still frowning, studied the froth on his beer. Then he looked at Em. 'I'm sure Kyril was there at Brunete, as Randy said. The scar is the most vital evidence. Kyril fitted the picture, no doubt, but ...' Ralph folded his arms and leaned back in his chair. 'It doesn't seem quite so important as it did. Freddie was our brother and, if he was murdered, he should be avenged. But you and I, Em, have seen so many outrages perpetrated in this war, so many acts of revenge, so much unfairness and injustice ... how can we feel as we did about Freddie's death, in battle, eight years ago? The sum of human bestiality sickens me – I'd hate to add to it with as much as one more victim, however richly deserved.'

'I feel you don't care so much about Freddie, but *I* care,' Em said stubbornly. 'He was my twin.'

'Of *course* I care,' Ralph interrupted crossly. 'Of *course* I care. But Kyril, even if he were there, might not have killed Freddie. *How* can we possibly know?'

'I think we ought to try and find Kyril. After all, he is our cousin's husband. The father of lovely Sasha. Brave Sasha.' Sasha had been shot down again, this time in the North Sea, where he managed to survive until picked up by a fishing boat. 'I *do* agree with you about the killing, Ralph, don't think I don't. There has been too much of it but, I think, for our own sakes, we should see Kyril, if we can, and talk to him. Get it over. Get the thing out of our minds.'

Ralph agreed.

It was not as easy to find Kyril as might have been supposed, because Berlin was swarming with Russians. After the arrival

373

of Stalin to join Churchill and Truman at Potsdam, a suburb of Berlin, for the first important post-war conference on the future of Europe there were more than ever.

Ralph had very little time for detective work, other than seeking Nazi criminals and all the paperwork that went with it. Em, who had turned into one of the top correspondents of the war, having seen active service in almost every European theatre, was busy reporting on the conference and immediate post-war Berlin. Her reports sent home to *The Sentinel*, somehow before those of anyone else, were guaranteed a vast readership.

The villas where the three leaders were staying overlooked a large lake. Every night one or other of the statesmen entertained, and there were drinks and cigars on the balcony to admire the view. Occasionally service personnel were invited, and one evening Ralph found himself included as part of Churchill's staff for drinks at Stalin's headquarters at the Cecilienhof Palace.

Ralph nearly didn't get to the reception because at one point it was thought that Martin Bormann, Hitler's deputy, had been apprehended leaving Berlin and a man had been detained for questioning. But Ralph soon satisfied himself that the frightened man before him was not Bormann, though he was undoubtedly a Nazi trying to escape and was arrested.

The reception was in full swing when Ralph, producing all the requisite passes and authorizations, collected his drink in the large gracious salon full of Service personnel and from there he wandered towards the balcony, looking around to see if there was anyone he knew.

At first the man in military uniform standing by the window, a cigar in one hand, a drink in the other, in earnest conversation with a colleague, looked like any other Russian officer but, as Ralph excused himself to pass him, the man recognized him first and called out:

'Ralph!'

Ralph turned. There was no mistaking Kyril even after all

374

these years, though he looked pale, was much thinner, and his hair was almost entirely grey.

'Kyril,' Ralph said as if the sound of the name had a mesmerizing quality. Then he extended his hand. 'How are you?'

Kyril put his cigar into his mouth in order to free one hand and shook Ralph's warmly.

'I heard you were here,' Ralph continued rather awkwardly as Kyril murmured something to his colleague who moved away to the side of the room.

'Oh? How did you hear that?'

'Em is a war correspondent. She hears everything.' Ralph studied the uniform of the shortish man standing in front of him. 'I see you in your true colours at last, Kyril,' he said smiling, but Kyril didn't smile.

'What do you mean, Ralph?'

Ralph indicated his uniform. 'Of a Soviet soldier.'

'Well.' Kyril appeared to hesitate and when he spoke Ralph had the impression that his reply was carefully calculated. 'No one could but admire the heroism of the Red Army.'

'Oh agreed,' Ralph said. 'But how could you bring yourself to change sides so often?'

'The exigencies of war.' There was a hard note in Kyril's voice and he took Ralph's arm. 'Why don't we meet and have a meal? We have an awful lot to talk about. Right now I can see the private secretary of the Generalissimo signalling to me.' He indicated the stocky white-uniformed figure of Stalin standing surrounded by officers near the massive double doors of the salon. 'Have you got an address?'

Ralph gave him the address of the military command and shortly afterwards left. He was quite sure he would never hear from Kyril again but more certain than ever that all thoughts of revenge had gone. Let Freddie's spirit – along with all the millions who had perished in this war to end wars – lie in peace.

Some days later Em, who knew about the encounter, called

375

Ralph at his headquarters and said she was soon leaving Berlin to cover the British elections at home to which Churchill was also returning. She suggested that Ralph should try and get hold of Kyril because she didn't feel she could rest until she had spoken to him.

Ralph spent a fruitless few hours trying to cut through the red tape to contact the Russian delegation at the Cecilienhof Palace but he was unsuccessful. Then he forgot about it until later in the evening when the duty sergeant phoned up and told him a Russian colonel was waiting for him in the hall.

Ralph put away his papers, picked up his cap and flew down to the entrance which still bore the scars of the fighting in Berlin. Many of the windows had been boarded up and there was a large crater by the side of the entrance. Ralph held out his hand. 'I've been trying to contact you all day.'

'And I you,' Kyril said shaking his hand. 'What a coincidence. You see, I am shortly to return to Moscow.'

'And Em to London.'

'Em? She is here?' Kyril looked surprised.

'I told you she was a war correspondent. She would love to see you before she goes home. You know we have elections in England?'

'Ah yes,' Kyril nodded wisely. 'They say Churchill will lose.'

'Oh, I don't think he will,' Ralph protested. 'After all, he won the war.'

'People are never grateful you know.' Kyril walked towards a car parked by the pavement. 'They have short memories.'

'I think you'll find you're wrong.' Ralph was surprised to see the car but prepared to get in, nevertheless. 'Where are we going?'

'I've arranged for us to eat where I'm staying. A meal of sorts is being laid on for you. I hope it's convenient for you, but I may be sent back any day.'

'I wish we could find Em.' Ralph looked anxiously towards the car as though, by some miracle, Em would appear from round one of the battered corners in the by now deserted street.

Suddenly he felt apprehensive. 'If I could leave a message,' he said before getting into the car. 'She might phone the office.'

Kyril tapped the wheel. 'We will see Em another day.'

'But she might not be here.' Ralph looked pointedly at Kyril. 'Nor you.'

'There will be plenty of time later you know,' Kyril said soothingly. 'We have years and years of peace and friendship ahead of us now that we are allies.'

Kyril's billet – which they reached after a short journey – had remained completely unscathed by the war. Not only were its windows intact – or had they been replaced? – but crystal chandeliers blazed from the rooms and salons, many of them decorated in the rococo theme.

'Trust you to fall on your feet, Kyril,' Ralph said as they climbed the stairs. 'You should see my barracks.'

'Ah, I have connections,' Kyril said. 'Remember I frequently visited Germany before the war.'

'I thought you were in Spain?' Ralph looked over his shoulder, but Kyril gave him a little push as they continued up the broad staircase with its beautiful wrought-iron banister.

'That too. Here we are.' Kyril carelessly flung open a door and Ralph found himself inside a pleasant room with antique furniture, a little shabby now, maybe through years of neglect. Ralph had the impression that the house had not been lived in for some time.

'This belonged to the Von Spee family.' Kyril went over to a table and, lifting a bottle of vodka, poured two quite full glasses. 'Do you remember Gunther von Spee?'

'No I don't.' Ralph shook his head, accepting the glass as Kyril gestured towards a chair.

'He was a friend of my father's...'

At the mention of his father's name Ralph started. Was it possible that Kyril didn't know? But Kyril, watching him closely, shook his head. 'I know all about my poor father, Ralph, assassinated by the fascists when Paris was liberated.'

'Some say it was the Communists.' Ralph pointedly studied

his glass then looked at Kyril. 'The trouble is no one knows the truth.'

'I know all about my family,' Kyril said breathing heavily as though, Ralph thought, he had had quite a lot to drink already. It hadn't shown before, but now it did. Ralph wished they had Em with them. He wished it very strongly. 'I know that Hélène was killed by the Nazis in Auschwitz, and that Sasha was a hero in the war. Anna and Susan have remained untouched and are safe in Venice. My mother and nieces are in England.'

'Are you sure Hélène was killed by the Nazis?' Ralph searched the impassive face of the man who now sat a few paces away from him across the room.

'Of course. Who else?'

'Some say that the Russians liberated Auschwitz and that she was among them. As an emigré she had little chance.'

'That is nonsense,' Kyril said brusquely, standing up and leading the way to an adjoining room where a small table with two places had been set. 'The Russians would never kill Russians.'

'That's not what I heard,' Ralph said grimly, sitting down and unfolding a starched white napkin.

'Well unless they were traitors ...'

'Who is to say who a traitor is?' Ralph leaned over the table and pointedly looked at him as Kyril took the cork out of a bottle of white wine and began to pour.

'Georgian,' he said, lifting a glass and peering at the liquid, 'from the same region as Stalin comes from. Taste it. It's excellent.'

He raised his glass, and silently the two men – allies, adversaries – toasted each other.

'Excellent.'

'Yes, the business of loyalty is very interesting.' Kyril gestured for Ralph to serve himself from the simple spread of various kinds of German cold meats – bierwürst, bratwürst, smoked ham and frankfurters – with sauerkraut and a large salad of cold potatoes. 'Who, as you say, is a traitor? You asked me the other day how I could change sides so often. In fact I have not.' Kyril sighed, drained his glass and immediately refilled it. He raised his glass again and looked at Ralph. 'You see, Ralph, I have always been devoted to the Communist Party. I first joined as a boy before the Revolution. I have been faithful to the Party, and the Party has been faithful to me.' Kyril pointed at the medal ribbons on his tunic. 'These are my reward.'

'So in Paris you were a spy?' Ralph now spoke the word that had been hovering at the back of his mind since the meeting with Randy in Cairo.

'Well, "spy" is not a word I like to use.' Kyril sounded aggrieved. 'I considered myself a servant of my country.'

'And in Spain too?'

'Of course in Spain,' Kyril acknowledged. 'I have always been loyal to the motherland.'

'Then you were loyal to the motherland, but *disloyal* to a lot of other people whom you deceived.'

'One has to do that, unfortunately, in peace as well as in war.'

Ralph had begun to feel very warm and, asking Kyril's permission, undid the buttons of his jacket. He thought, perhaps, that he too had had too much to drink. He decided he must be careful. Had he been foolhardy to come at all? But he was in uniform, and so was Kyril. It seemed some sort of protection.

'You were seen with Freddie in Spain.' Ralph almost heard his statement with surprise, a kind of *déjà vu*, as though it had come from someone else.

Kyril inclined his head. 'I met Freddie, Em and that tiresome young man of hers in Madrid. That is no secret.'

'I'm talking about Brunete,' Ralph's voice seemed to come from far away. 'That was some time later.'

'Brunete ...' Kyril pretended to study the ornate rococo ceiling. He wasn't even a very good actor, Ralph decided, realizing how much he now hated the man.

379

'A ruined town, I understand, outside Madrid. You were seen there with Freddie and someone later claimed that it was you, not the enemy, who shot him.

'You see that's why I said no one knew, or knows to this day, which side you were on – or are on. Are you really a Russian colonel for instance?'

'Oh yes.' Kyril pushed his chair back from the table and restlessly got up. 'You can be quite sure about that.' He turned to Ralph and studied his face for a minute or two before resuming his seat. 'Tell me, I find all this very bizarre, almost paranoic, but who told you this tall story?'

'A man whose word I trust. He was with the International Brigades and I think would recognize you.' Ralph instinctively fingered his chin and Kyril imitated him.

'The scar?'

'The scar.' Ralph nodded his head. 'He has absolutely no doubt at all. He also said Freddie appeared apprehensive after meeting this man – you – and was shot in the back while running *towards* the enemy. He pitched forward ...' Ralph made an awkward movement with his hands as though propelling himself towards the ground.

In his mind's eye Kyril could see that hot Castilian plain that day – it seemed so long ago and, indeed, now it was – as the men of Freddie's battalion ran towards the hill. As Freddie fell Kyril remembered feeling as little emotion as if he had shot a rabbit.

'But why should I shoot Freddie?' Kyril avoided Ralph's eyes and leaned over to fill his glass. 'I'm quite curious to know, I must say. This is a very tall story, but it intrigues me all the same.'

'To prevent him telling anyone that you were there. That you were not what you said you were, an anti-communist.'

'But it's no secret.' Kyril looked, or pretended to look, surprised. 'I'm telling you now, here.'

'Yes, but that was before the war – eight years ago. You still had a lot of work to do, Kyril.'

'Well, it was not the case I assure you,' Kyril said, but Ralph detected a note of unease in his voice. 'You have no proof except the word of this mysterious man.'

'I have no proof, and I will never see him again.' Ralph got up and began to walk slowly around the room. 'I confess Kyril that, for three years, since I first heard this testimony, I have wanted to kill you. It was deeply etched in my mind that you were responsible for my brother's death, and I wanted you to pay. Now,' Ralph made a gesture of futility, 'I have seen so much killing, so much war, so much brutality that the urge has gone. I don't know if you did kill Freddie and I don't suppose I ever shall know. But now that I've told you I feel better. I do not think, however, that we will have much to say to each other in future, even should our paths cross again. I imagine you intend to go back to Russia where, in time, you may see your wife and children, who knows? Maybe in this post-war world we shall be able to forget old scores and live in harmony. Somehow I doubt it, but let's hope.' He held out a hand. 'Do you mind if we go now? I have lost my appetite for food.'

'Of course,' Kyril started buttoning his jacket. 'I'll run you back. Wouldn't you like a coffee, a brandy perhaps, before you go?'

'Nothing.' Ralph shook his head. 'I just want to get out of here.'

'I understand.' Leading the way into the next room Kyril gave Ralph his cap and then, taking his own, put it smartly on his head, glancing at himself in the mirror. He looked at Ralph, his expression affable. 'Shall we go?'

Ralph was glad to get out of that large empty house in which he had heard no other sound of life. He began to breathe freely, more calmly as Kyril led the way towards the car parked in the drive.

Ralph felt no fear of Kyril, no bitterness as he stood watching that enigmatic face, illuminated briefly in the dim indoor light. It was not quite dark, but the light seemed like a flare and the scar going from his chin to the cleft below his lower lip was clearly discernible. It was strange that a boyhood accident should leave such a deep impression on a man's face.

Kyril raised his head, saw Ralph looking at him and gave a rueful smile.

'I hope you don't intend to bump me off?'

'I told you the time was past.' Ralph got in beside Kyril who reversed the car then drove back down the drive.

'You're wrong, anyway, if that gives you peace of mind. I was not there and I did not kill Freddie. Yes, I will go back to Moscow and in time I hope Sasha and Anna will come and visit me.' He stopped as he got to the road looking to right and left though the traffic was very sparse, motor fuel still being almost unobtainable by the ordinary citizen who might still have a car left to run.

'And Susan?'

'I will divorce Susan. I want to marry a Russian woman – oh, I have no one in mind – but maybe I can live out my days in peace. I never wanted to leave Russia, you know that? You can blame the Askhams, particularly your cousin Bobby for much that has happened.'

'Bobby doesn't consider himself an Askham. I think he would be quite insulted to hear that.'

Ralph marvelled at the banality of their conversation. Looking about him as they drove along he thought the suburb was like a ghost land with few living beings and, occasionally, a startled cat or a pathetically thin dog scavenging among the ruins for the unlikely chance of a meal.

'Well, Askham or not he is a man with much to answer for.'

'Helping you I presume you mean? He did his best.' Ralph looked sideways at Kyril and was surprised to see a savage expression on his face as he hunched over the wheel, his chin thrust forward, all urbanity was gone. To his surprise Kyril pulled into the side, in the shadow cast by a giant ruin of a building, and stopped. Then slowly he drew off his gloves and began to root for something in the driving compartment in front of him.

Ralph didn't know why he was so astonished when Kyril produced a gun, cocked the barrel towards his face and sniffed it. Then he polished the gun with his sleeve, as though it had not had much use and casually pointed it at Ralph.

'I'm afraid this is where we part,' he said. 'It was foolish to think I could ever let you go with all the evidence you had to connect me with Freddie. I want to start a new life, not be haunted by the past. You really are a very foolish man, Ralph, to talk as you did. Maybe it runs in the family. Bobby was foolish too and Freddie was very foolish.'

'Yes, we were all foolish,' Ralph said, realizing his mouth was suddenly dry. 'How foolish – to trust you.'

'Not quite cricket is it?' Kyril said with a wan smile. 'But it was a game we Russians never learned. You gave me the idea of killing, but if you get out, Ralph, I'll give you the chance to run. You may just miss the bullet.'

He was about to stick the pistol in Ralph's side when Ralph, knowing he had nothing to lose, lunged at him. It was a move Kyril hadn't been expecting and he fired his weapon straight into Ralph's body.

Ralph had a searing sensation of heat, but with it came a feeling of enormous power. He wrenched the gun from Kyril's clasp and put it to his adversary's head, almost immediately firing it as he did.

Kyril, half his face blown away, slumped towards the wheel and Ralph fired again. This time he missed and the bullet went straight into the body of the car. A second later there was a flash, followed by a roar as the petrol tank caught fire.

As Kyril fell across him Ralph, his senses ebbing, knew that his own escape was impossible.

After all, there was no victory in death.

PART 4

The Frontiers of Freedom

Autumn 1946–Summer 1948

CHAPTER 20

In the autumn of 1946, Hugo looked from the windows of Nimet's apartment onto a tree-lined avenue which linked the City of Cairo to the old Shubra Palace, once the magnificent home of Mehemet Ali, founder of the dynasty of which King Farouk was the present head. Though Hugo didn't know it, the luxurious flat had once been a brothel in which his mother had first welcomed his father, many years before he was born. In fact forty-seven years had passed since the beautiful, willowy Nimet el-Said had seduced the younger son of the Earl of Askham, and thus started a whole chain of circumstances that was to haunt the family for years.

Now much had changed, including the City of Cairo which had become a vast, sprawling Metropolis compared to what it had been in 1899 when Bosco had first met Nimet, the year after Omdurman. And Nimet had changed too, being not only older and wiser but much, much richer. She also retained much of her former beauty; her hair was black, her figure was good and only lines of wisdom were etched on her forehead and those very faintly. She was still a beautiful, elegant woman and her son was proud of her, if a little in awe of her as he always had been ever since he first knew she was his mother. For a while he had been so mesmerized by her that he forsook his adopted mother Rachel for the home of his real mother and her husband, a Turkish businessman called Theo Igolopuscu. He had travelled the world with them and enjoyed good living such as he had never imagined it, even though his upbringing in the Askham household had been comfortable.

But, after a while, the good but empty life of luxury palled. The pull of his adopted family was too strong; but it was also a real bond because Ralph, Freddie, Charlotte and Em were his half brothers and sisters, flesh of his flesh. The blood tie was important to Hugo. He went back to farming with Ralph and had many years of contentment until the war and even, partly, during it. Then had come happiness ... and tragedy.

He turned as the door opened and Nimet sidled into the room with that special oriental way of walking she had perhaps acquired in the brothel. It seemed to indicate elegance and sophistication, but also a desire to please.

Hugo went across the soft Persian rugs to embrace his mother savouring, as he always did, that faint exotic perfume that immediately conjured up the infinite mysteriousness of Egypt. Nimet, who was very much smaller than Hugo, always pressed her head into his neck in an endearing expression of familiarity, a suggestion of intimacy that was faintly incestuous.

Nimet was so different from Rachel that it was impossible to imagine the same man being in love with them both, as Bosco was alleged to have been – and at the same time, if the received wisdom of his family was to be believed. It showed him different aspects of the father he had known only for a short time, but always admired and yearned for, in the way only a child yearns for the parent it has lost.

Nimet's tailored, sequinned dress was also a blend of the east and west, a dress designed for her in Paris and made for her at a fraction of the price in Cairo. Her many years of poverty had made Nimet very shrewd about money. Only she could drive such a bargain and get anyone to accept it; but in Paris, after the war, people willing to spend vast sums of money were not easy to find and even the best designers of *haute couture* clothes, trying to re-establish themselves, were not averse to a deal.

Nimet had some papers in her hand and there was about her an air of gravity that made Hugo gaze down at her with a smile.

'Something important, Mother?'

'Very.' As she sat down Nimet patted the place beside her on the brocaded settee that had come from one of the Bey's houses in Istanbul when Nimet decided after his death to sell them all except one. This left her with, besides a house in Istanbul, an apartment in Cairo, a villa in St Tropez and permanent hotel suites in London and Paris. She had not, as yet, established herself again in New York since the war.

Hugo, who wore a white alpaca suit for the Cairo winter– it was never very cold – perched next to her, his hands linked in his lap, a smile on his dark handsome face. In Cairo he was accepted as a Cairene and this was never called into question except that he didn't speak Arabic.

'Why do you look so serious, Mother? I thought this was to be a happy holiday?'

'It is and it will be,' Nimet briefly touched his face, 'once you have recovered from the fatigue of your journey and the last few exhausting months. My poor Hugo, you should have written to your mama about it before.' She searched his face for a moment but, as he volunteered no further information, she went on.

'I sent for you, not only because I wanted to see you and wanted to know first hand about the tragic events that have afflicted the poor family of your father, but because I have something to tell you.' She put a hand on the papers on the cushion beside her. 'While you are here we have a lot of business to attend to, lawyers and bankers to see, and it is important that we get this part out of the way first. Now,' she extracted from a jewelled spectacle case a pair of rather severe gold-framed half-moon glasses and put them carefully on her nose as though she were not quite used to them. Then she pressed them firmly into place with her index finger and began to study the documents, most of which were written in Arabic.

Hugo, who had only arrived the day before, continued to stare at her, bemused still, as his mother had surmised, befuddled by the journey, by the startling contrast between the wintry England he left and the Egypt he had arrived in – winter too, but very different. Hot, warm, the sky eternally blue.

Tourists considered it the best season for exploring Egyptian antiquities, but eighteen months after the end of the war the tourist trade had scarcely got going again.

'Ah!' Nimet, having perused the documents, nodded, pushed them to one side and removed the spectacles, replacing them neatly in their case with as much ceremonial as she had removed them. Hugo was already learning that in Cairo things went at half the pace, and with far more ceremony, than would ever be the case in England, even in rural Wiltshire or Hampshire.

When this was all finished Nimet regarded him with a bright smile, her head on one side.

'I want to tell you my dear,' here she paused to take his hand, 'that you are a very wealthy man. Ah,' she pressed his palm, 'in your *own* right. It was always the wish of your step-father, the Bey, that you would inherit the bulk of his fortune after I was dead, but my dear,' Nimet raised an arm to pat her sleek *coiffure* and also at the same time, her susceptible son suspected, to show the firm outline of her bust, the neat circle of her waist, 'I assure you I am not about to leave this world for quite a while. Having survived the war I intend to make good use of such years of peace as remain.'

'Do you think there'll be another war, Mother?' The indulgent smile on Hugo's face was replaced by an expression of concern.

She looked at him in surprise. 'My dear, I, who remember so clearly the terrible war of 1914/18, never thought I would live to see its like again. Not only did I see its like, but something far, far worse. Even *I* was obliged to leave Cairo to live in Luxor and, at times, before the Allies established their supremacy in North Africa it was not thought we would survive for so very long *there*. My suite in the Paris Ritz was occupied by Germans and in London by Americans! My house in St Trop was the headquarters of one of the German military commanders. You may wonder what *I* did in the war.

I can tell you. I provided accommodation for the armies on *both* sides. So I should be *persona grata* to both.'

'It's hardly *suffering*, Mother...'

'We'll come to that.' Seeing the look on his face she patted his knee again. 'Suffering is relative after all and, compared to some, mine was very light. Now. The Bey, as you know, was the most astute businessman and, moreover, he could see this war coming long before it started. He also knew who would win and he removed all his assets from Germany, and they were considerable, and reinvested them in America. What he had then, and he was a very wealthy man, increased fourfold. You may not know it but he also invested in Askham Armaments when it became a public company. I don't know if even Bobby Lighterman knows *that*, though they did share a string of racehorses. Consequently when the war was over and I was able to take stock, I found myself possessed of more money than I could ever possibly need. For the last few weeks I have been arranging my properties, my shares and my assets so that you, from the moment you sign these papers, are the sole owner of three-quarters of everything I own. Certain things like my houses, my apartments, I keep to myself, but when I die everything is yours. As from now, though, you are a millionaire.' She thrust the papers at him and sat back with a triumphant expression on her face. 'Pleased? Free from the Askhams at last eh?'

'Mother!' Hugo laid the papers aside without even glancing at them and, getting up, began to pace across the room. Just then with that expression of his face, the gesture of his hands he reminded her of his father. It was quite incredible how so much of Bosco survived in his youngest son. When at last he stopped he stood facing her, his arms extended. 'Mother, I have never felt myself *trapped* by the Askham family. They have never been anything but good to me.'

'Oh I know that, dearest.' Nimet looked apprehensive. 'Nothing but good, I do agree; but what I mean to say is that now, since they have no money anyway, from what I hear, from what discreet inquiries I make, you have no need to be dependent on them.'

'For a long time the farm has paid its way.' Hugo sat down beside her again. 'Like Bobby I, too, did well out of the war. Everything I grew, milked or bred I sold. I am quite a prosperous man. If I do have any money, and I'm not turning down your generosity, Mother, I shall be glad to help Rachel a bit.'

'Oh I'm sure Rachel doesn't need any help,' Nimet said airily. She had never quite forgiven her old rival though she really had very little to forgive, if she'd been honest. It was Rachel who had given a home to the young boy who, but for that, might have been lost to her forever.

'Rachel is really quite poor,' Hugo looked serious, 'with a lot of responsibilities. Ralph hardly left anything except debts. It was only then that the full extent of the disaster to the former Askham fortunes were realized. All he had left was property and that was in poor shape, almost valueless except the land that Askham House stands on – valuable real estate in central London.'

'What a lovely place that used to be,' Nimet sighed, recalling the very few times she had, unwelcome as she was, been inside its walls.

'Well it's soon going to be a block of offices, or an institution of some kind. Because there was no money, and very few assets, Bobby was able to break the trust and the house is now to be sold. It was in poor shape, anyway, having been unused since before the war. The Hall, likewise, is almost derelict, having been a boarding school for so many years. Cheryl went off without a backward glance to Kenya taking her two adopted children with her. She was glad, she said, to shake the dust of England from her feet. No, Rachel has very little money. Adam, broken by ill-health and the scandal of Jordan's broadcasts during the war, is almost completely dependent on her emotionally. I think he has a little more money than she has because he was left the bulk of Aunt Flora's fortune.'

'Bobby must be as rich as Croesus,' Nimet raised a neatly shaped eyebrow, 'and, don't forget, half his fortune came from the Askhams in the first place, when Ralph so foolishly sold him most of the family business.'

'Ralph sold *all* the family business. He thought that the sum Bobby paid for it, and the income, would give him more than enough to live on. But he was wrong. He gravely miscalculated, was badly advised. Also he was in love, newly married and ... there is no doubt that most of what fortune remained was squandered by Cheryl. What a *ghastly* woman she was.' Hugo shook his head and his mother laid a sympathetic hand on his arm again.

'Poor Hugo. How unfortunate you were in your marriage too. Amelia was just like Cheryl.'

'Oh, Amelia wasn't like Cheryl at all, except that she was a liar. The first year was all right, but then she started to lie to me about children, the way Cheryl lied to Ralph.'

'How do you mean, darling?' Nimet's mascaraed eyelashes fluttered wildly. 'Or is it too delicate to ask about?'

'It's delicate, but I don't mind telling you. Cheryl used to tell Ralph he was infertile, couldn't have kids, and Amelia started to tell me the same. Both women seemed to have a horror of childbearing...'

'I can't say I blame them,' Nimet said, 'but that's not the point. Women, especially women in certain classes, have duties however much they dislike them. In the poorer classes of course, no one asks them, so the problem doesn't arise.'

'Ralph, poor Ralph, as we know was capable of fathering a child and so, I'm sure, am I.'

'Of course you will be darling, when you get the right girl.'

'Just now I don't feel I want one,' Hugo said angrily, 'either a woman or a child. I'm building up the farm, and acquiring new horses for the stable. The money will be marvellous for that.' He looked at Nimet and bent over to kiss her cheek. 'I should say how grateful I am, don't think I'm not. Thank you, Mother darling.'

'Hugo,' Nimet murmured into his ear, 'you know that the only thing I want is your happiness. If you ask me you're well rid of that girl. I'm glad she's gone. If she's anything like her mother think just how jealous she'll be when she knows what a wealthy young man you've become!'

The sound of a baby's cry always made Charlotte jump, in those first weeks after Jeremy was born. She would look round as if to see where it was coming from and then realize, with a shock, that it was her own new-born son, usually in his nursery across the way or, if she were on the ground floor, upstairs. For a mother of three nearly grown-up children, for someone who had lived through such dangers in the war, including two years in a concentration camp, a new baby was something quite extraordinary not only in her life, but in that of the family.

As soon as she heard Jeremy's cry Charlotte put down the phone and ran upstairs, but Nanny was already bending over him. Charlotte sighed.

'I always seem to forget about you, Nanny. It's such a long time since I had anyone to help me, and I never had a nanny for my other children.'

Nanny, who was Norland trained and rather superior, had only taken the job because Charlotte was a 'lady' and lived in a rather nice house in Holland Park. It was quite a shock to her to see such a mature woman having such a young baby, because Charlotte had been affected by the war. Although she was not yet forty she had the lines on her face of an older woman and her rich, chestnut hair was streaked with grey.

The baby had come before Charlotte was really ready, and the doctors had been against it. But a woman who was nearing her fortieth year, and whose husband was desperate for a child, didn't try and stop a much-wanted pregnancy. There were many who thought that, owing to the deprivations of the war, her general poor health and loss of weight, she would never have one. The strain was a lot on Charlotte, but to please her husband a baby there was, and not for a moment had she regretted it.

There were other things that Nanny, who was an awful snob, thought unusual about the household: the freedom the older children were allowed would never have been tolerated in her last appointment. They came and went as they pleased, and as for their clothes ... Then there were all their friends and relations, an odd assortment of cousins, who seemed to have little regard for the proprieties either. There was something too unconventional about the whole place for Nanny, and she was on the point of giving notice when she heard that her employer was a war hero, and his wife a war heroine who had been decorated by the French government for her undercover duties in France. Both of them were also related to two of the best families in England, so Nanny carefully shredded her written notice into little bits and decided to stay. Whatever the inconvenience the social cachet would certainly be a help in her next post.

Charlotte looked at little Jeremy, only six weeks old, lying in his crib. This life alone was precious because it made up for so many that were no more. Still the family couldn't get over Ralph or Hélène and nor could she ever forget, nor would she want to, the horrible things she had seen in the concentration camps during the war ... babies wrenched from their mothers, tiny children led to the gas chambers ... These and other terrible memories afflicted her a dozen times a day – not so much the fear as the expressions of despair on the faces of the doomed – and gave her nightmares at night. Charlotte once more closed her eyes in horror and held tightly to the side of the wicker crib.

'Are you all right, my lady?' Nanny said solicitously. 'I don't think you've allowed yourself enough time to recover from the birth.'

'I'm perfectly all right, thank you, Nanny,' Charlotte said.

'Sometimes when I look at Jeremy I think about what I saw in the war and I am so grateful for this life, this precious little life.'

She put her finger in Jeremy's hand and he gurgling, clasped it and started to suck. The tears came into Charlotte's eyes as Nanny, raising her head, said:

'I think that's your husband home now, my lady. Shall I tell him you're here?'

'No, I'll go down and see him, thank you.' Charlotte bent and kissed the warm bundle, then, putting both hands to her hair in a futile effort to flatten it, ran along the hall and down the stairs.

Watching her come down Arthur thought that she did, indeed, look ill. She had had the baby too soon and she hadn't recovered. A terrible fear gripped him that he would lose the wife he loved so much, and he held out his arms to her as, running into them, she laid her head on his shoulder.

'What is the matter, my darling?' Putting both arms tightly around her he looked anxiously into her face. 'Has something happened? Are you ill?'

Charlotte shook her head, wiped her cheek on his shoulders and, with an arm round his waist, walked with him to the drawing room overlooking the gardens of once beautiful Holland House that had been bombed in the war.

'I guess I feel just too emotional and sad, for some reason. I was talking to Mummy when I heard Jeremy cry and I felt anxious and ran upstairs forgetting about Nanny... oh Arthur, I am so grateful for him, for you...'

He thought she was going to cry again and he went to the drinks table pouring healthy measures of whisky for them both. Giving her her glass he said: 'You look absolutely awful, darling. I'm terribly worried about you, and I feel guilty.'

'Guilty? About what?'

Arthur looked thoughtfully for a moment into his glass then consumed, in a gulp, half the contents.

'About Jeremy. It was too soon. You didn't really want a baby, and I did.'

'I did too. I couldn't wait five years or anything like that. We couldn't afford the time.'

It had been a difficult birth because the hospital told her, rather disapprovingly, that she was rather too old to be a mother. That hadn't helped, or the fact that she'd been in labour for three days. But Jeremy was a full term baby, a healthy baby and from the moment he was put into her arms she adored him.

It hadn't always been the same about Arthur, but it was now. She held out her hand and he kissed it.

'How's your mother?' Arthur said. 'You were talking to her on the phone?'

'She's certainly much better. The doctor said it wasn't a heart attack, but she must take care. He says really she's quite strong, but she's just had so much on her plate.'

'Why don't you and your mother go away?' Arthur said suddenly.

'Where to?'

'The south of France, Scotland, wherever you like. They say winter on the Riviera is marvellous. You'd be back for Christmas. Paris, though that wouldn't be much of a rest. You and Rachel deserve a break alone. No Jeremy, no kids, home. I'll stay here and I'll take care of everything.'

'Oh *Arthur*,' Charlotte said, throwing her arms round him, 'you are *such* a brick.'

It was hard to get Rachel away but it was done. There was somewhere for them to go to – Melanie's villa, untouched in Cannes since she'd fled from it to Venice after the liberation by Allies. She'd dreaded the vengeance of the Maquis against those who had collaborated with the enemy. That was even before she'd heard about Alexei Ferov and, when she did, she was more than grateful that she'd got out in the nick of time. No one had been to the villa since, though the housekeeper and her husband, who looked after the garden, kept it in perfect order.

'Just so that whenever her ladyship comes back it will be as she remembered it,' the housekeeper, Martine, had said tearfully. 'I hope it will be soon. She has nothing to be afraid of here, you know.'

'I think she just wants to be sure,' Charlotte replied as she and Martine were cutting vegetables outside the kitchen door in the bright sunshine. Arthur was right – though early November it was warm enough to sit out in sheltered places. 'She'd hate to have her hair all shorn off. She was so proud of it.'

Charlotte smiled at the very idea but Martine looked horrified.

'Her ladyship was *English*, you know. His lordship too. They had many German cousins and they all came here to visit them. They couldn't help it. Anyway it was only the French who had their heads shaved, not that they deserved it if you ask me,' Martine grumbled, 'some of the Maquis were far worse than the *boche*, the things they did.'

'War is relative,' Charlotte agreed and looked up to see her mother standing by the doorway smiling at them. Charlotte's heart leapt. Already Rachel looked much, much better.

'Come and have a drink for goodness' sake,' Charlotte said, putting down the knife, 'it's nearly lunch time.' Rachel took her arm and they strolled round the back of the house to the terrace that overlooked the Bay of Cannes.

Rachel who, for over forty years, had never given up over anything, finally surrendered when she heard of Ralph's death. She gave up the paper, retired to the country and took to her bed. For days she wouldn't see anyone except Em, who had rushed home to be with her – not even Jenny.

Death was never pleasant however it came but the circumstances surrounding Ralph were peculiarly harrowing. At first he had just disappeared. He didn't return to his office and then the rumours started: that he was associated with the Nazis through Jordan, that he was a spy, that he had defected to the Russians. Em stayed in Berlin to uncover what she could about

Ralph, but no one knew anything except that he had worked late in his office one night, as he always did. After that it was a stone wall, no trace, nothing.

The duty clerk had remembered someone enquiring for Ralph. He thought he was a Russian officer, but couldn't be sure. He could have been French, or American, or, possibly, even English. So much happened in Berlin in those days for people to have long memories.

Then slowly, painstakingly, with the aid of Ralph's colleagues, who always believed in him, she began to wear down the high command who got onto the Russians. It was in the middle of the transfer of power from the Russians to the various Allied zones and it was not easy. Em had seized on the suggestion that Ralph's visitor was Russian. She worked at it as a dog worked at a long-buried bone ... tugging this way and that to get it out of the ground. If Em lacked anything it was not perseverance.

Then one day, weeks after his disappearance, she was called to a mortuary in the Russian zone and told that a charred, refrigerated corpse lying under a sheet might be that of her brother. It had been found in a street, shot through the stomach and badly burned. The top clothes had been removed and all identifying marks or labels. Nearby there was a burnt-out car. It was as though he had been ambushed and had tried to escape. The Russians, thinking it was Russian because the car was Russian, said they had been investigating ever since. Then they had the enquiry from British HQ.

Em was told that recognition was impossible and she should spare herself the anguish. She didn't and wished she had because it was impossible to recognize Ralph. He was finally identified by his dental records, and the remains of his body were buried, as the family thought he would wish, in the nearest British cemetery for those soldiers who had also died in the war.

For, like them, Ralph was a victim of the war. He had died in battle, even though no one knew why. No one had ever found out what he was doing in that dark street on that dark night on the outskirts of Berlin.

It was Em who suspected Kyril was involved, but no one would listen to her. Here she drew a blank, especially from the Russian authorities who were already showing that attitude of non-cooperation with the Allies, a hostility that was going to result in the next few years in the Berlin airlift and the Cold War. They said: *Niet, niet, niet* and that was that. No one could shift them. It was a wonder they had ever released the information about the body, and both military authorities – Russian and British – did what they could to minimize the incident: passed it off as just one of the many mysterious happenings in a city that had been decimated by war.

At home there was the usual memorial service, the usual obituaries:

MYSTERIOUS DEATH OF THE EARL OF ASKHAM

The twelfth Earl of Askham was found shot in a street in Berlin nearly two months after his disappearance. His body was badly charred and was only identified by dental records flown from England. The mystery of the Earl's death has not been solved, but it was thought to be the work of one of the many snipers or saboteurs that still roam the streets of that ruined City where a state of near anarchy prevails.

Ralph Askham was born in 1906, the son of Bosco, the eleventh Earl of Askham and Rachel, Lady Askham. His father had a distinguished career in the Army and the City and was killed in Flanders in 1915 in an action for which he was awarded the Victoria Cross.

Ralph Askham was intended for the Army and joined the Blues and Royals when he was eighteen, but the life never appealed to him and he went to Kenya to farm. There he met the woman he was to marry, Cheryl Lee. The Askhams returned to England where they settled at Askham House in London and Askham Hall in the country, near to where Ralph Askham ran a very successful stud.

He enlisted in 1939 and served first in the Grenadiers then in the Guards Armoured Division in North Africa, where he was awarded the bar to the MC he had won during the evacuation at

Dunkirk. He later transferred to the Intelligence Corps, a fact that might not be unconnected with his death as he was looking for Nazis trying to escape the net put out for them by the victorious Allies.

Lord Askham, whose family of Down went back to the Conqueror, came of a very distinguished family and added lustre to it. He was a cousin of Mr Robert Lighterman whose work during the war has just been rewarded by a Barony. The lives of Lord Askham and his family were blighted during the War by the behaviour of his first cousin Jordan Bolingbroke, son of Mr Justice Bolingbroke, who broadcast scurrilous messages to the Germans from Berlin. Jordan Bolingbroke, sought by the Allies, managed apparently to escape from Berlin before the end and has disappeared.

Lord and Lady Askham had no children. Lord Askham's younger brother the Honourable Frederick Down was killed in the Spanish Civil War and it is his son Paul, who is 9, who succeeds to the title at, incidentally, almost the same age as his uncle succeeded after the death of his father.

Lord Askham's sister, Lady Charlotte Verdi, widow of the racing driver Paolo Verdi, distinguished herself during the War, surviving two years in various Nazi Concentration Camps after her capture in France. She was recently awarded the *Legion d'honneur avec palme* by the French government.

Charlotte and Rachel ate in the garden under the huge oleander tree whose thick leaves almost, but not quite, obscured the view of the sea. They ate sparingly at lunchtime, always took an afternoon nap and had a good dinner. Apart from Martine and her husband there were no servants, and they shared the cooking and some of the household chores. It was an idyllic life and in the two weeks they'd been there both of them had been transformed to some approximity of the people they had been before.

Rachel had survived, but only just. Ralph, after Bosco and Freddie, was too much and she took to blaming herself for their misfortunes – as though it could possibly be anything to do with her. But her mental state was confused and for several weeks her family, who had never seen anything all their lives but her stiff upper lip, were appalled and confused too. In time

Rachel got better, but very slowly because she had decided it was time that she gave up.

Then in the autumn of 1945, Arthur had come back and, although no one had expected it, somehow Arthur's arrival transformed everything. Everyone was pleased to see Arthur in a way that no one, least of all himself, would ever have anticipated. Incarcerated in a Japanese prison camp, at work on building a railway in the course of which hundreds of his fellow prisoners died, Arthur had been cut off from the rest of the war. He never knew that Charlotte had been captured and imprisoned, that Hélène had disappeared or that Ralph and Alexei had been murdered.

He couldn't understand why everyone was so happy to see him, but he was overjoyed. Thinking of Charlotte was the only thing to which he attributed his survival and when he told her this she cried. Charlotte kept her promise and they were married almost immediately – the first happy thing that had happened in the family, Rachel said, for years and years. There was something so right and normal about Arthur.

After that Rachel really got better though recently she'd had pains in her chest which she feared was her heart. The doctor said it was still the effects of stress and so, gladly, she had agreed to join Charlotte at Melanie's villa still looked after from England by the ever efficient Bobby, now Lord Lighterman of Robertswood. Bobby at least had got his heart's desire.

After lunch Rachel lay back in her long, low chair under the oleander and Charlotte and Martine cleared away. Charlotte finally emerged with the hot, strong black coffee.

'Oh!' Charlotte said leaning back in her chair and closing her eyes. 'This is *so* marvellous. Every time I see coffee I still taste acorns.'

Rachel held out her hand, without opening her eyes. 'Was it too awful, darling? You never talk about it.'

'I hardly ever want to, to be truthful,' Charlotte said after a pause, after she had inhaled that wonderful smell of pine and lavender that seemed to be the essence of Provence. 'Even now, even to you. Sometimes I have memories, nightmares, mostly about Hélène ... I often feel I could have saved her, you know, Mummy.'

'How?' Rachel opened her eyes and gazed with love at her daughter. When one had lost two children those who survived were especially precious. 'What could you *possibly* have done to help her?'

'She wanted me to take her when we left and I couldn't. I always kept the side going, you know, in the camp, stiff upper lip, like you, Mum, but Hélène did too. Then at Auschwitz she started to get ill and everyone was terrified when they got ill because the Germans always took the sick away to be gassed...'

Rachel closed her eyes with an involuntary gasp.

'It is too awful to think about, even now. I kept Hélène in the hospital, hiding her whenever the camp guards came around; but when we heard that the Russians were coming and the order came to go I knew Hélène would never make it. We were being force-marched away from the advancing Russians though, of course, we didn't know it then.

'I had to leave Hélène behind. I can still see her eyes, her hand held out to me: "Don't leave me, Charlotte, please help me ..." Oh Mummy,' Charlotte bent over, rocking her head in her hands, the tears, finally, gushing down her face. Rachel, with an agility she didn't know she still had, leapt out of her chair and went over to Charlotte, kneeling beside her.

'Charlotte,' she said quite sharply, 'you did *everything* you could. You couldn't have done more.'

'But I could. I see those eyes, Mummy. I shall never forget them. I should have helped her, found some way. But, you see, we were by then so weak. We were hungry and it was affecting our brains. We were slow. I'm sure I could have thought of something now; but then I couldn't. *That's* why I can't forgive myself. It will haunt me all my life, "help me Charlotte, don't leave me, please".'

Then, Rachel wept too.

It was fitting, she thought a few minutes after, that they should weep for Hélène. There was nothing to be ashamed of for that, or for weeping for all the millions who had died in the war. She wept almost every night for Ralph. It was like a fresh wound that had been opened after first Bosco's death, then Freddie's. One never really got over a death. A husband and two sons: was it worth being a wife, a mother, to go through such suffering?

Yet always there was something, someone to take their places. After Freddie there had been Paul and now there was Jonathan – Jonathan Down, Ralph's son. Jenny had taken the surname by deedpoll after Ralph's death. To all the world she was Ralph's widow, but never Lady Askham and Jonathan could never be his heir.

Hélène had left three daughters – and a heroic memory: *Legion d'honneur avec palme*, like Charlotte. Hélène left a memory of bravery and self-sacrifice to make up for the spoilt, selfish but rather sad and frightened woman of pre-war years.

After a while Rachel and Charlotte, worn out by emotion, comforting each other, stretched out their legs and slept, close together on their comfortable wicker chairs, their hands touching.

It wasn't clear which one of them was first woken by the footfall because the stranger had already spoken.

'Charlotte?' he said, bending over, his eyes half fearful, half hopeful. 'Do you remember me? Marc?'

CHAPTER 21

Rachel, on the phone to Arthur, said: 'No she's not in. Oh I don't know. With friends, I expect. She knows a lot of people in Cannes. Shall I ask her to phone...'

Rachel had a chat with her son-in-law about when he would be in, how the baby was, what the weather was like, state of the Stock Exchange and so on and when she replaced the receiver she looked thoughtful. This was the third time Arthur had rung and Charlotte hadn't been there. Rachel felt as though she were conniving at Charlotte's deceit and, suddenly, she hated the whole thing.

One couldn't help being pleased to see Marc, Charlotte's boss during those Resistance days, the legendary Plus Fort; to know that he'd survived the war to resume his business as a prosperous boat-builder on the Riviera.

However, in a very short space of time, within a couple of days in fact, Rachel felt less happy about Marc's reappearance because of his effect on her daughter. Charlotte, who had begun to look very well, to lose her haggard appearance and put on weight, suddenly lost ten years. She bloomed, became incredibly youthful. Clearly she was hopelessly and radiantly once again in love with Marc. They started to go everywhere together; she to the boat yard with Marc, out to sea, visiting friends of his all along the coast. Rachel said nothing. Charlotte was a mature woman, her own mistress; but was she also Marc's? Clearly it seemed that she was.

Rachel went slowly into the garden to read *The Sentinel* Marc had brought up from Cannes when he called for Charlotte. Although it was still warm on the Riviera there was a distinct chill in the air. They could no longer stay out as much or for so long, and soon they must think about going home.

Sitting down on the porch, rather than under the tree, Rachel shook out the paper. It was a day late, but she never liked to miss an issue, now capably, but temporarily, edited by Em. Em had a lot of sorting out of her own life to do, one of the reasons for which was staring at Rachel from the leader page of the paper:

HOW KIND SHOULD WE BE TO THE GERMANS?
An examination of Allied post-war policy by Peter Klein.

Em had brought Peter Klein back with her after one of her frequent visits to Germany to try and unravel the mystery of Ralph's death.

Peter and Em had worked together in the thirties and the Kleins had been good friends to Em and Freddie until Hitler's savage laws against the Jews turned them into fugitives. Freddie had married Peter's consumptive sister, Marian, to help her out of the country. Only later he fell in love with her and had a son by her before she succumbed to her mortal illness.

Peter and Em had never been lovers, only friends and colleagues, but even so Felipe refused to have Peter in the house, so Em had had to billet him on Bobby and Aileen who were gradually reopening Lighterman House, though without much enthusiasm.

In the end Em found a home for Peter with Irina at Robertswood. Peter, who had survived eleven years in Dachau, was nevertheless an invalid; he needed mental and physical care and Irina, with her own well-developed instinct for survival, found that looking after him took her mind off brooding about Alexei and Hélène.

Peter now had a flat in London, and was trying to rebuild his life. Technically he was a displaced person, a new breed of stateless citizens created by the war; but he would never lack for a home or security in England as a friend of the Askhams and, particularly, Em. For something had happened between

406

the two that had not been there when they had been colleagues in the thirties: love had burgeoned and, with it, the problem of Luis and Felipe, with whom Em had long since fallen out of love. Like Peter, however, he was a dependant. Em seemed to have a talent for collecting people with a multiplicity of needs. Yes, Em was another problem.

Rachel sighed and turned over the pages rapidly scanning the columns. She heard the car crunching in the drive round the side of the house and sat there holding the paper, feeling rather tense, looking over the rims of her spectacles. It was Charlotte by herself, looking very happy, swinging a bag. She waved before she was within earshot and broke into a little run. At that moment Rachel thought she would burst with love for her daughter, love and thanksgiving but, also, apprehension.

'You look *very* thoughtful Mummy!' Charlotte, all her old ebullience having returned, flopped down in the chair beside her mother. 'Anything nasty in the paper?'

'It's all nasty,' Rachel said, shutting it and folding it by her side, her spectacles placed as usual neatly on the top. 'Sometimes I wonder what we fought the war for. Things certainly aren't much better except that no one's actually fighting.'

Charlotte folded her arms around the back of her head. 'I wonder too. I mean to say we did it to rid the world of the Nazis but what have we got in their place? Apparently Stalin's concentration camps are just as huge. Did we really want to replace Hitler by Stalin occupying half of the free world with his eyes on the other half?'

'There's no short answer to that,' Rachel said. 'Oh – Arthur rang – *again.*'

'Why do you say *again* in that way?' Charlotte looked suspiciously at her mother.

'You know, I think, why I say it.'

'Haven't a clue.' Charlotte shut her eyes to the rays of the sun, quite low on the horizon in the late afternoon. 'Do I detect a chill in the air?'

'It's definitely getting colder. Shall we be going home soon, Charlotte?'

'I suppose so.' Charlotte kept her eyes firmly shut, as though closing them, too, on the future.

'Darling, don't you want to see Jeremy, and Arthur? Don't you *miss* them?'

'Very much.' Charlotte's tone was prosaic. 'But, you know Mum, I haven't had a real holiday like this since before the war.'

'What about your honeymoon?'

'Well,' Charlotte appeared to be groping for the right choice of words. 'Yes, that was fun too. I'd forgotten about it.'

'Because it wasn't with Marc?'

'Ah, *now* I see what this is all about,' Charlotte opened her eyes and sat forward on her chair, gripping her knees. 'It's about Marc, isn't it, Mum? Can't I have a bit of fun?'

'Is that *all* it is, darling?'

'Of course that's *all* it is. I'm a married woman.'

'Yes, but should married women have fun ... in *that* way?'

'You mean, are we having an affair?'

'Well, you are, aren't you?'

'Yes.' Charlotte paused and then said in a very low voice, 'I didn't realize it would upset you all that much. I'm sorry. I should have been more discreet.'

'Of course it upsets me.' Rachel looked miserable. 'You've only been married just over a year. You know I'm enormously fond of Arthur...'

'So am I. Truly.' Charlotte waited for her mother to say something and, when she didn't, went on: 'But I don't love him. Is that my fault?'

'I don't know.' Rachel bit the side of her nail. 'Why did you marry him?'

'I promised him, didn't I, all those years ago? Arthur said

408

the memory of me kept him alive. I hadn't even *met* Marc then. Besides, Mum, there was you...'

'Oh, you married him for my sake did you?' Rachel said bitterly.

'In a way. At the time we both needed Arthur; solid, dependable Arthur. You were cracked up by Ralph's death and so was I. I hadn't been home long. We were all at sixes and sevens and dear old Arthur seemed just the ticket to restore us all to normality. After all, I hadn't seen Marc for over two years. How did I know I'd ever see him again?'

'Did you think of him?'

'Oh I thought of him, but not crazily. I didn't really think an awful lot about love in the concentration camps. There wasn't a lot of point. For one thing, I never thought I'd survive. You live in a completely different world; the past is irrelevant, the future uncertain. I *was* pleased when I saw Arthur. I may have thought I loved him. I could see a nice home with Arthur, solid and settled, for me and the children. Ralph was dead. Uncle Adam was ill. Bobby was busy – he'd changed anyway. Where was a dependable man in our family to lean on any more?'

'I know what you mean.' Rachel reluctantly nodded her head. 'Sorry.'

'That's all right Mum.' Charlotte gazed at her mother. 'Believe me, I'm worried too. You see, to be honest, now that I've found him again, I don't really know how I can live without Marc now.'

'My mother knows,' Charlotte said later that night.

'Oh good, so you needn't go home. I always wondered why you didn't tell her. You're a grown-up woman, after all.'

'I knew it would make her unhappy, and it has.'

'That's only to be expected, darling. Your mother is a very moral lady.'

'It will make Arthur very unhappy too, *and* all my family. I tried to tell Mummy how you and I felt about each other; but I don't think she understood. She thinks my duty is to Arthur.'

'In a way it is. No one likes divorce.'

At the word 'divorce' Charlotte involuntarily shivered, nestling closer to Marc. Hugo was getting divorced from Amelia and, although it was mutually agreed between them, no one liked it. Years ago when her Aunt Melanie and Uncle Adam were divorced the family felt it was never the same again.

Besides, Arthur was so good.

'I can't *possibly* divorce Arthur, just yet.' Charlotte gazed at the strong profile of her lover outlined in the moonlight which reflected off the sea to his cottage in the old port of Cannes. The situation reminded her strongly of the time they were escaping across France. They'd been rather furtive then ... brought together by secrecy and danger.

How different Arthur and Marc were. Arthur was like a dear old ox, Marc like a hare. How could she ever have *married* Arthur? This she didn't understand.

'I can't live without you,' Marc said, his arm tightening around her bare waist.

'I told Mummy the same thing this afternoon about you.'

'And what did she say?'

'Well, she said it would have a most frightful effect on poor Arthur.'

'Arthur's had a whole year of you. You're mine. I've been longing for you ever since we parted. I thought you were dead. How do you think I lived with that torment? Oh Charlotte, why didn't you try and find me before committing yourself?'

'You don't understand.' Charlotte shook a cigarette from the pack of Gauloises by the side of the bed and lit it. 'You've no idea what the end of the war was like for us. I know it was bad for everyone ... but Ralph, my brother, was our life, our anchor, the mainstay of the family. First I'd been missing and then Ralph was. The way they found him was horrible. An unidentified corpse, almost completely naked. Mother, who had always been so strong, cracked up completely. She had a

410

sort of mental breakdown because she thought it was all her fault.'

'How could Ralph's death be her fault?' Marc took the cigarette from between Charlotte's lips and drew upon it. Little intimacies like that, which were characteristic of their relationship, would never have been considered by Arthur. Life with him conformed much more to a stereotype of reasonable, not too sensuous, behaviour between a sensible, not too young, married couple.

'Well Mother thinks, thought, that Ralph went off because she didn't approve of Jenny, his girlfriend. *That* reminded her of Father who enlisted because he and Mother didn't get on at the time. With Freddie she felt he shouldn't have been there at all; she should have done more to dissuade him. But for Ralph she did feel the most enormous guilt, and has been trying to make up for it ever since in her attitude to Jenny. You see, darling, don't you, how I couldn't possibly set off to look for you? Then dear old Arthur came back and here was a capable male again, someone who knew his mind, and ours. He drew us all together, and Mother began to get better. I thought, if I thought at all, that ours – you and me – was an affair of the war. Too much had happened, Marc. I'd been through Auschwitz and Belsen. I'd seen thousands of dead and dying people. I'd left my best friend behind – maybe to die horribly too. Physically, and emotionally, I was like a dried-up apple.'

Marc squeezed her again. 'I understand. I think I do. For me, too, there was so much as we settled old scores. The fighting and recriminations went on for a long time after the war. France had committed a terrible self-wound when she surrendered to Hitler. She will never forgive herself.'

Marc sat up abruptly and put on the light at the side of the bed to look at his watch. Then he put it off again and lay down beside Charlotte, his eyes on the ceiling.

'There is something I have to tell you, of which I am not proud. I have to make it straight between us, if we are to have a future.'

'You had an affair with another woman.'

'No, that would not make me ashamed.' Marc smiled at her. 'After all, you married another man. That is a far worse crime than a mere affair. What I did I have on my conscience. If we are to live together and be straight with each other, as I hope we shall, I must tell you this first. It concerns someone we both know.'

'Hélène, but how..?'

'Not *Hélène*. Her father.' Marc looked at her as if trying to determine in the dark the expression on Charlotte's face and then continued. 'I was on the tribunal that sentenced him to death. I *was* the tribunal in fact.'

'I thought it was a sort of kangaroo court...'

'It was a kangaroo court and I was judge and jury. I wanted Ferov dead. I sought him out.'

'But why?' Charlotte sat up and leant on one elbow. 'Why that poor, silly, old man?'

'Because I thought he had betrayed you. He was well known as a collaborator.'

'If anyone betrayed us it was Jordan. I doubt if Alexei knew a thing about it.'

'I realize that now; but at the time I didn't think about it.'

'But Jordan was *there* the night you and I...'

'I know, I know, I know,' Marc shook his head too vigorously, as though he were vainly trying to convince himself. 'I had it fixed in my mind that Ferov was in it too. He may have been, for all we know. He was such a crawler. I knew where he lived and I didn't know what had happened to Jordan. He'd disappeared and so had Kyril. I decided they were all in it together. I wanted Ferov killed and I ordered it because I thought you were dead. It was an act of revenge.'

Charlotte said nothing and when he turned Marc could see, in the moonlight, the tears on her cheek. He brushed them with a finger but they continued to come.

'That poor old man,' she said. 'He was just a fool, a vain

fool. He was not bad – a kind of joke. He was always so insecure. His granddaughters loved him...'

'I know.' Marc hit his hand with his fist. 'For God's sake I *said* I know, and I'm sorry. I tried to stop it, but it was too late ... he'd gone. It was very quick. He was very brave, very dignified – I'm glad I can at least tell you that.'

Charlotte could see Hélène lying on the bunk, her large, cavernous, haunted eyes turned pleadingly towards the door: *'Help me,' she said, 'please don't go. Don't leave me, Charlotte. Take me with you.'*

Charlotte knelt and kissed her looking at her emaciated form, feeling her hot, fevered forehead bathed in sweat.

'Darling you can't possibly come with us,' she said. 'You will die on the way. Here you have a chance. I can't stay. They'll shoot me.'

'I'd rather come with you and die than stay and meet the Russians.'

From the door the Kapo called, roughly ordering Charlotte to be quick or they'd all be shot. She kissed Hélène and then without another word, even of comfort, a last goodbye, she fled.

Charlotte got out of bed and sat on the side, her head in her hands. In the light Marc could see the arc of her body; a beautiful, almost celestial arc, like the moon. He touched her and she quivered.

'You don't know how that family have affected me,' she said. 'How I shall always suffer and I'm suffering now.' She turned and looked at Marc. 'Don't you see – I'd be betraying Hélène? Hélène may not have been very close to Alexei in the end, but he was her father and she'd be appalled if she knew how he died ... and your part in it.

'How could we ever live happily together with that guilt between us?'

The next day Charlotte phoned Arthur and then she told her mother she wanted to go home. Rachel, without asking questions, said it was about time anyway and began making

413

arrangements for them to take the train from Cannes to London. She noticed immediately the change in her daughter but asked no questions. It was not until they had left Dover for London and were sitting alone in the first-class compartment that Charlotte told her about how Alexei Ferov had died, and the difference it had made to her relationship with Marc.

For a long time after Rachel too was silent, her hands folded in her lap, watching the beautiful welcoming countryside of England, so quickly recovering from the war, as the train slipped past. Life renewed itself again and again.

'Poor old man,' she said at last.

'That's what I said. Not a way he deserved to die. Marc did it because of me, you see, so I'm responsible too.'

'Oh Charlotte.' Rachel leaned forward in her seat, studying the agonized expression on her daughter's face. 'You can't possibly say that.'

'Well then *you* can't say you were responsible for Daddy or Ralph. We are not responsible, Mother, on the whole for what happens to other people. If we felt we were the whole time, we couldn't go on living. I know I'm haunted by Hélène. I wonder if I *should* have stayed with her, insisted on staying...'

'You wouldn't be here now if you had.'

'Did I know that, Mother? Or did I know that, by leaving, it was my only chance of survival? Maybe I could have succoured Hélène, helped her. Maybe we could have got away together.'

'Maybe, maybe ...' Rachel reached out for her hand. 'Maybe you can't live the rest of your life properly unless you exorcize this guilt. I'm sure Hélène, wherever she is, would forgive you, and understand.'

The train was drawing into Victoria Station and Rachel searched the faces of the people waiting on the platform to greet it. 'Look,' she said, pointing eagerly, 'there's Arthur! Oh how happy he looks.'

And there was dear Arthur, anxiously scanning the windows as each carriage slipped by. Charlotte stood up and, pressing her nose against the window pane, waved.

Arthur thought the tears when she greeted him were from happiness. He clasped her to him, pressing his cheek against hers, his hand round her waist.

'Oh darling, it's perfectly ripping to see you again,' Charlotte said, looking at him at last with rain-soaked eyes. 'You've no idea how marvellous it is to be back.'

In the background Rachel quietly got a porter and told him where the bags were.

Rachel took a cab from Victoria to Paddington because she wanted Charlotte and Arthur to be on their own. Somehow she hoped that a new beginning would be made, that Charlotte would never wish to see Marc again. So she resisted a peep at her latest grandson and phoned Adam from Paddington, asking him to send the car to meet her.

Instead Adam came himself, standing on the platform as the local train steamed in, leaning on his stick. Rachel was delighted to see Adam and as they embraced he said, 'You look jolly well, old girl.'

'Not so much of the "old girl".' Rachel turned to him with a smile as they got into Adam's large pre-war Bentley which still had a double de-clutch. 'I feel rejuvenated. How are all the children?'

'They're fine. And Charlotte? Is she well too?'

'She looks like a million dollars, as the Americans say. Absolutely marvellous.'

'You should have stayed longer.'

'Oh I think five weeks is *quite* long enough. Charlotte missed the baby.'

'And Arthur too, I suppose.'

Rachel had decided not to confide to her brother, who had extremely old-fashioned and conventional ideas about morality forgetting that, in his time, he had broken many of them.

'Oh of course she missed Arthur. He was at the station waiting for us.'

'Very good man, Arthur.' Adam turned the car out of the station drive and set off at his usual ten miles an hour along the narrow lanes.

'But it *is* good to be home. Isn't that the nicest thing about a holiday? Coming back?'

'I think so,' Adam grunted. 'Prefer not to go away myself.'

'Well you should. Melanie's house is really lovely. You've never seen it and it would do your lungs good.'

'My lungs are very well actually.' Adam coughed as if to show in what fine condition they were. 'The doctor says I have only to smoke a pipe and I'll live another fifty years. By the way, Hugo has got some very exciting news.'

'Oh? Is he back from Cairo already?'

'He is, and with a fortune. Nimet has made most of her money over to him.'

'Well I don't know.' Rachel clicked her teeth.

'What don't you know?'

'I can't help remembering when she hardly owned the clothes she stood up in.'

'And you seemed to own the world. Well, the boot's on the other foot now.'

'I'm not jealous, Adam,' Rachel said with dignity. 'You know money has never meant anything to me and we have always had sufficient.'

'Well those days might be coming to an end, my dear.' Adam looked grave. 'Hugo might just be in the nick of time.'

'I wouldn't dream of touching a penny of Hugo's money.'

'But he's going to offer it and you must think seriously about it, Rachel, because we are really very skint indeed.'

'Are we? Why is that?'

'The war, my dear. The rise in the cost of living. Ralph left under £15,000, imagine that for the Earl of Askham! His grandfather left three million in 1910 – and that was worth much more then than the same sum now. We aren't the only family to be ruined by the war.'

'Are *you* ruined by the war?'

'I never had much,' Adam said. 'I've got even less. The manor largely took care of Flora's legacy – it's expensive to run. Bobby pays me a nominal fee for my few directorships. I lost some of my pension because I left the bench early. I do own the house and we can keep the car ... but not much more.'

'How depressing to hear all this the moment I get home,' Rachel sighed as they turned into the gate.

'Well, I don't want you to be too shirty with Hugo. He *does* regard himself as family and, if he can help, let him. Incidentally he's been seeing a lot of Jenny since he returned. He comes over a great deal.'

'He did before.'

'Did you know it was to see her?'

Rachel recognized that familiar pang of jealousy. Yes, she had realized Hugo came to see Jenny, and she didn't like it. But why? Didn't the woman deserve something for all she'd lost? Or was it, now, that Rachel felt she was being disloyal to the memory of Ralph?

'Yes, I suppose I knew he came to see her. I thought he was lonely. Amelia going off with that Air Force colonel hurt him a good deal.'

'She was always a strumpet ... like her mother. Good riddance to both of them.'

'I must say I incline to feel that way myself though, at first, I did like Amelia. She seemed so unlike Cheryl, but then she got more like her. Mind you at the end I liked Cheryl a lot better than I had; poor woman. I shan't miss her though.' Rachel sighed and smiled at her brother as he stopped the car in front of the main door. 'It *is* good to be home! Thank you for coming to meet me, dear.'

Adam looked better too. She had noticed that his breathing was not so stertorious and his face looked healthily pink instead of having the unhealthy flush of the bronchitic. His grey moustache, which seemed like a barometer of Adam's health, had a spruceness about it, and his silver white hair was still thick at the back of his head, though balding on the top.

One could be quite proud of Sir Adam Bolingbroke at the age of sixty-nine. Like her, so far he'd weathered many storms.

For the first few days after she came back Rachel had several occasions to regret that she had gone. There were all kinds of tiny problems about the house, but the main thing was the family. Em wanted Felipe to leave the Grange so that she could live there with Peter, and Felipe refused. He also declined to acknowledge that his relationship with Em was over and he was adamant about refusing to let her have their son whom, he claimed, with some justification, he had brought up.

In a sense Luis was another casualty of the war, a child growing up without a mother. Because of the attitude of his father he missed, for the most part, the company of his grandmother and other relations who would all have rallied round as the Askhams and their kin always did. Luis had grown up in virtual isolation, as though he'd lived many miles away – maybe in Spain. At the age of eight he was a withdrawn young boy, unnaturally attached to his father who refused to send him to boarding school. At home he and Felipe spoke Spanish all the time, which was another factor isolating the family.

However, apart from all this, Rachel wasn't sure that Peter and Em should set up home together. Professionally they got on well, but personally they quarrelled a good deal. Em said it was because Peter had spent eleven years in a concentration camp, each day a struggle for survival and one could hardly expect him to be entirely normal. He was a proud man without a country, 'displaced' and dependent on the Askhams.

'Then why do you have to live with him?'

'Because I love him.'

Rachel, who was arranging holly that Jenny had brought in during her afternoon's walk with Jonathan in preparation for

Christmas, stood back and gazed at her arrangement with dissatisfaction.

'I was never any good at flower-arranging,' she said beginning again. 'The damn thing won't go right.' She paused and looked at Em over her spectacles. 'Em, you *do* have a penchant for lame dogs...'

'What a perfectly *foul* thing to say,' Em threw the cushion from her chair onto the floor in a fit of temper. 'There is nothing the least bit "lame" about Peter. Nor was there about Felipe. Don't be so patronizing, for God's sake.'

'I didn't mean to be. It was a silly thing to say,' Rachel felt cross with herself. 'I mean people...'

'You mean people who cannot live in their own countries. Exiles. You call them "lame ducks". I'm surprised at you, Mother. Anyway, did you never think that Peter would make a marvellous editor of *The Sentinel*, that is if you don't want to go back?'

'I don't want to go back,' Rachel stuck a sprig at an awkward angle in the vase. 'I'm nearly seventy.'

'I don't suppose you'd believe me if I said you didn't look it.'

'Well I feel it, sometimes. And I *certainly* don't want to go bustling up to London every day, or every week as I used to. Besides, Adam says we haven't any money.'

'None?' Em looked rather amazed.

'Well not much. No capital. Two white elephants, or rather one – the Hall which no one wants – and nothing much else that anyone can see.'

'You could sell the Grange and fling Felipe out that way.'

'Do you *really* want him to be homeless?'

Em flushed. 'You know I don't. Not at all. But until I can get my son I shan't leave him. He will have to put up with me as a snail does the case on its back, that is when I'm here. Mum, I'd like to go abroad again. There's a lot going on in Europe. I thought if you made Peter editor...'

'What would people say to a German editor ... so soon?'

'Mum, he's no more German than you or I. He hates the Germans and never wants to go back.'

'He hates the Nazis. It's not the same thing.'

'I don't think you like Peter. You never seem to like *anyone* any of your children are involved with...'

'Now *that's* a beastly thing to say.' Rachel stamped her foot and the vase fell over.

'Except Arthur, of course,' Em caught it before water spilled, 'and that's because *you* chose him.'

'I did *not* choose him!'

'You did. You thought he was very "suitable" for Charlotte and you practically forced her into marrying him.'

'That is *absolutely* untrue.'

Rachel felt so enraged that the pain in her chest returned again. She sat down in the chair near her abruptly and Em felt a twinge of alarm.

'Mum, are you all right?'

'I'm perfectly all right, but I'm absolutely furious with you and I think you should go until we've calmed down. I'm sorry, but I do.'

Em left without a word, passing Jenny on the drive without a wave.

'Are you all right?' Jenny asked as she came into the room.

'I've got my pain again but we know it's stress.'

'I wonder if you should see a specialist?' Jenny gave her a professional look.

'Well, if the doctor says I should I will, but my pain is caused by my children who, at times, can be a pain in the' Rachel looked about to explode, then laughed, 'the chest!'

'I saw Em flying by. She looked very angry.'

'She *was* very angry. So was I.'

'Can you say what about?'

Jenny always felt diffident in front of this woman who was her son's grandmother without being her mother-in-law. Ralph's death had not even left her a widow. There was some kind of respectability in that.

Rachel turned once again to her arrangement of holly, berries and twigs – tugged the whole lot out of the vase and began again. For a few moments there was silence as Rachel worked, watched by Jenny. It was an odd, unenviable situation and she always felt like a poor relation, though she did what she could to make up for it. She ran the house like an experienced housekeeper and looked after Adam with the expertise of the first-rate nursing sister she was. She thought that much of Adam's good health was due to her. She watched his diet and made him cut down smoking. His chest had improved and his blood pressure was almost normal for a man of his age. The year that Jordan Bolingbroke had started broadcasting it was so high the doctor feared a stroke and sent him immediately to bed for several days.

Rachel was aware of Jenny's diffidence and knew it was because they never felt completely at ease with each other. They were alike, but they were also dissimilar. They were both strong personalities and they both thought that what they wanted was right. Finally she paused and looked at Jenny as though wondering whether to tell her – tell her what?

'Em would like me to make Peter the editor of *The Sentinel*.'

'Wouldn't that be a good thing?'

'He's German.'

'Yes, but a refugee.'

'Still German, and *The Sentinel* is a very British paper. I think there might be an awful lot of resistance to him by the public.'

'But that's prejudice, surely?'

'No, in a way it's logical. We have just fought a war with Germany, and why should we have to print in the paper every day that the editor was as much a victim as any of us? Because that's what we'd have to do. Oh dear.' Rachel looked at her watch. 'Nearly time for tea. Thank heaven. I need it.'

'Let me get it.' Jenny who had sprawled on the settee, jumped up. She felt awkward and she wanted to be out of the way when Hugo arrived.

'Oh, would you? Are we just three for dinner?'

'I think Hugo's coming.' Jenny looked deliberately vague, but her heart was behaving oddly and she was glad to leave the room to make tea.

Rachel said: 'I can see you're excited about something.'

She embraced Hugo as soon as he walked into the room and, for a moment, they clung together like mother and son, though Rachel felt the restraint she always did when he had seen Nimet. 'How was your mother?'

'Very well. Wonderfully well really. I think she had quite a good war.'

'Well go on, tell me all. Get it off your chest.'

Rachel smiled at him. She could see he was bursting with news.

'Do you know?'

As Rachel shook her head in mystification he continued.

'Can't you *guess*?'

'Well, to be honest I *have* got a little idea. Adam told me in the car coming home.'

'And you don't mind?'

She looked at him in bewilderment before it dawned on her just what he'd said. 'I'm absolutely delighted for you. Why should I *mind*?'

'Jenny thought you might mind.'

'*Jenny*. You're talking about Jenny?'

'We're going to get married. I thought you might guess.' Rachel always had difficulty in disguising her emotions and as he studied her face he said, 'I can see you're not pleased.' His voice was flat. 'She thought you wouldn't be.'

'Why should she think that?'

Hugo gestured with his arms like a man who suddenly had had the wind taken out of his sails.

'I think she feels you think she should be loyal to Ralph...'

'Well it *is* a bit soon.'

'Rachel, it's eighteen months since Ralph died. How can you say it's a "bit soon"?'

'Yes, but you've been feeling this way for some time haven't you? I guess you weren't all that sorry when Amelia left you.'

'Amelia and I found after a year we were incompatible. I assure you I didn't fall into bed with Jenny because of that.'

'I didn't know you'd "fallen into bed" with her at all. I can see there's a lot I don't know,' Rachel said frostily.

'Rachel I'm sorry.' Hugo's handsome face had a wry smile on it. As he tried to touch her she moved away. 'People *do* sleep together you know, now. It's all very different...'

'I don't know that I like it in my house.'

'Well, we never did it in your house.'

'Really I find this conversation very distasteful. I don't know, Hugo.' Rachel put a hand to her hair. 'I feel somehow as though I've been deceived. I *should* feel happy for you and Jenny...'

'It *is* Ralph.' Hugo sat beside her. 'You don't like me marrying the woman he was in love with.'

'It sounds rather indecent somehow, I'll admit. It's not only that, but I'm rather surprised that Jenny could get over Ralph so soon. I'd always thought, been led to believe, she was so much in love with him.'

'She was.'

'Oh I see. If he had married Jenny I don't think you could have, in law. Didn't Henry VIII have trouble over that sort of thing?'

'Well Henry VIII was an awful long time ago and we shan't have any trouble because I've already talked to the vicar. He won't marry us, of course, because of my divorce, but he does approve and will bless us after the service in the registry office. Oh Rachel, I wanted this to be *great* news. A great day. You've heard about the money, I suppose that's what you meant?'

'I certainly heard about that.'

'Well what you don't know, what nobody knows, is that I plan to use some of it to try and buy Askham Hall. I want to live there and farm and raise a family with Jenny.' Hugo looked happier than Rachel thought she had ever seen him look in his life – certainly since he'd been grown up. 'I want it to be a home again, Mum, for all the family.'

CHAPTER 22

Lord Lighterman of Robertswood stood in front of the imposing fireplace in the large drawing room of his new Hampstead home practising a suitable stance with which to receive his eldest daughter.

First he clasped his hands behind his back and stood with his feet apart, chin thrust in the air. But he thought somehow that wasn't right. Stefanie was a shade taller than he was and he would find himself looking up at her. So he crossed to the far side of the room by a window that gave a beautiful view across the heath to Kenwood and sat down, sticking his cigar firmly between his teeth. That way Stefanie would be at a disadvantage because she would look round for him, wonder why he was so far away and didn't rise to greet her, and might momentarily feel the icy blast of parental displeasure.

Stefanie was almost as much of a problem as David, but in a different way. She was very polite whereas David was invariably rude, and she worked whereas David did nothing, nor did he show any indication of wanting to be anything other than a rich man's son. Bobby would have been quite happy were it the other way round: if Stefanie didn't work but applied herself to finding a suitable husband and settling down, preferably in the country where she would be out of harm's way, remote from the bright city lights which seemed to have such an attraction for her.

He would have liked David, his treasured heir, to have gone to university to meet the right people, the contacts he would later need in the City, and then come into the business, to the place that had always been there for him. But David showed no inclination even for the mild kind of scholarship, leading perhaps, at best, to a pass degree that his father had in mind for him. He also made it quite clear that he absolutely detested the idea of business.

People said that it was all part of growing up, David would change; but David, who would be twenty this year, didn't show the least sign of changing. He had no interests, nor was there anything he seemed to enjoy doing or did particularly well, except one thing: he was particularly skilled at annoying his father. He was very good at that indeed and Stefanie came a close second.

Stefanie, however, did not set out purposely to annoy her father. She had no strong feelings about him at all, either of love or hate, and it was this total indifference on her part that irked Bobby: she was too like her mother – cold, detached, impossible to fathom or understand.

The drawing room with its glorious view of the Heath was at the back of the house so Bobby didn't hear his daughter's sports car roar up the drive or hear her being admitted by the butler. He was locked in his reverie by the window, brow furrowed, chewing at his cold cigar, wondering whether they'd been right to leave Lighterman House, now his generous gift to the nation, when Stefanie came in without being announced and went right over to him as though she had known where he was all the time.

Stefanie too peered out of the window into the February fog. 'Is there something especially interesting to see? I can't see a thing.'

Bobby removed the cigar from his mouth, silently cursing. Stefanie was always like this. However carefully laid his plans, they always misfired where she was concerned. She utterly refused to be cowed or intimidated by him.

'You're very late,' he said petulantly.

'The fog is all over London, Father. I nearly didn't come at all, but was told you wanted to see me urgently.'

'Will you have tea?' Bobby kept his tone chilly and Stefanie sat on one of the Louis XV chairs that had been brought from Lighterman House and, crossing her legs, lit a cigarette.

'Please.'

She was a very confident young woman, Bobby thought, going to the bell push by the side of the fire. Irritatingly like her mother, though of his three daughters – or rather Hélène's three daughters – she was the only one who strongly resembled him. In a way he was proud of her – her spirit as well as her looks. Bobby was now rather an over-weight, middle-aged man, but when he was younger he had been considered handsome. She had his colouring – Lighterman rather than Ferov – his clear blue eyes, long lashes and firm well-moulded mouth. She was very tall for a woman and had a good figure which is why she'd taken up modelling. However, she was the casual type so the clothes she modelled were usually the chunky sweaters, tweed skirts and trousers favoured by the post-war young. In contrast their elders were corseted in the curved New Look line with which the daring and brilliant designer Christian Dior was trying to entice women away from the uniformed drudgery, the economy and utility of the war years.

'What is this "very urgent" thing?' Stefanie said, tapping her foot impatiently, as her father made his way across the Aubusson carpet to resume his seat.

'In time,' Bobby said joining his hands and crossing his legs, 'all in good time. How's your grandmother?'

'Grandmother is fine. Very happy. That was a brilliant idea of yours to put her in Robertswood. She has a fantasy that she is in St Petersburg at the time of the last Czar.'

'Well she's doing a good job,' Bobby said grudgingly. 'She has extremely good taste and flair. When I imagined her there it was more as a housekeeper. I simply wanted a home for her, and you girls. I imagined that Aileen would see to the refurbishment and redecoration of the house.' Bobby sniffed and stroked his silky moustache with the back of his hand. 'However, Aileen's not a bit interested. You would think there was still a war on with the number of committees she sits on and good causes she supports. Resettlement this, rehabilitation that. I never see her.'

Bobby looked aggrieved and Stefanie suddenly smiled. 'You sound like a housebound wife.'

'Well I'm certainly not that.' Bobby sounded affronted. 'I'm an extremely busy man; but I have to *do* everything. When I decided to give Lighterman House to the nation and move up here there was so much to *do*, so many decisions to make. What furniture to take, what furniture to leave, that sort of thing – pictures, carpets, *objets d'art*. I didn't want the nation to have *everything*.'

'Naturally not.' Stefanie looked up as a servant brought in the tea. The house on the edge of the Heath, though large, was nothing like as vast as Lighterman House and a much smaller staff was required, which was as well. People who had found independence in the army and factories didn't care much to return to domestic service, and there was a shortage of good staff. Bobby ran the house with a reduced staff of five indoor staff, two gardeners and a chauffeur.

'Shall I be mother?' Stefanie inquired. Moving to the edge of the chair she leaned over the silver tray and began to pour from the tall silver pot into the porcelain cups. 'Are you really going to keep Robertswood? It's so *huge*.'

'I feel I have to keep it for the time being. I did think of turning it into a hotel. It's a marvellous position, but it does have important links with my grandfather, with my roots. After all, this fortune came from him.'

'And the Askhams,' Stefanie gave him a cheeky look.

'From *Sir Robert*,' Bobby said firmly. 'All the Askhams could do was lose money, or throw it away. For Sir Robert's sake I want to live there, at least for the foreseeable future, especially now that Lighterman House has gone. But it was always his intention to turn it into a museum. That, alone, perpetuates his name: The Lighterman Collection. No,' Bobby accepted a cup from his daughter and put two lumps into it before thoughtfully beginning to stir, 'I have other plans. I like the idea of the hotel business. I think it's going to be boom time for holidays, and it will be years until Europe is fit or fun for anyone to visit. I thought of turning Askham Hall into a hotel and installing young David there to give him something to do and get him off that bottom of his. He's bone idle...'

'I thought that Hugo was going to take over the Hall?' Stefanie looked surprised, then sat back and, tucking her legs under her, sipped her tea.

'That's what *he* thinks, but not what *I* think.'

'But isn't there a Trust?'

'There is, and a devil of a job it's been to break it. It was made in the days when the Askhams, the Down family, had a huge fortune. In those days – and I'm talking of the 1880s when it was made – one would never have envisaged it going the way it has. A depression and two world wars have seen to that.'

'And *you* I understand.' Stefanie said, looking at him from under those thick brows which were a legacy from her mother.

'How do you mean me? I kept them alive for years, still do.'

'Well I understood that you bought the Askham part of the family business for much less than it was worth.'

'Well.' Bobby's shifty expression did not escape his daughter. 'When people want to sell they have to take what price they can get. Ralph, newly married, wanted to go back to Kenya with that wife of his. He took what I offered.'

'People say you diddled him.'

'Well people are wrong.' Bobby thumped the cup and saucer onto the silver tray. 'People, whoever they are, don't know what they're talking about. You shouldn't listen to gossip. I gave a good price and it wasn't my fault that Ralph's wife had the habits of Croesus but not his gifts. Do you know she spent two hundred thousand pounds on those two houses alone? And now we can hardly get the market price for one, it's in such bad repair and the other – the Hall – is a white elephant. For five years it's been used as a school and the grounds are in ruins. I don't think Hugo who, like the Askhams, has no head for business, knows how much it will cost him to do it up and make it liveable in again. The fine old bedrooms have been used as dormitories! You should see the graffiti of those East End kids! The priceless woodwork on some of the walls and the hall are full of carved initials and crossed hearts. It will have to be all taken down; all rebuilt. Government compensation will be a pittance.'

'Then why do you want it?'

'Because I *do* have the money,' Bobby said smugly. 'I have a lot already and I'm still making it. I can see it as a fine hotel with a golf course and a boating lake.'

'But the Trust doesn't want that?' Stefanie helped herself to fresh tea.

'Rachel Askham doesn't want it,' Bobby corrected. 'With her usual blindness she has convinced her fellow trustees, a banker and a lawyer, that it should stay in the family. She says it is the traditional family seat of young Paul who should properly inherit it when he is twenty-one. What purpose there is in inheriting a shell when you haven't a penny to pay for the upkeep I don't know. Do you know that Ralph Askham left *under* fifteen thousand pounds?'

'So I heard.'

'Compare that to what *I* give you a year.'

'I know, Father, and I'm grateful.'

'Which brings me to what I wanted to see you about.' Bobby looked at her gravely, shifted in his chair and rekindled his cigar. 'I don't like that man you're going around with. I don't like him at all.'

'I didn't think you knew him?' Stefanie carefully arched one of her brows.

'I don't, but I don't *like* what I hear.'

'Do you check on me all the time, Father,' Stefanie's temper was mounting, 'like the KGB?'

'No I don't, and don't be rude to me young woman. Everything you have you owe to me. You have a title, you're an "honourable", thanks to me, and you have a name to keep up. "Lighterman" is a very important name in London these

430

days not only in the City, but in society, in cultural activities. The King and Queen are going to attend the official opening of the Lighterman Collection. I don't want you going around with some half-baked ex-army officer who came from nowhere. You're a Lighterman, an honourable, and don't you forget it.'

'My mother was a Ferov *and* a princess,' Stefanie said heatedly, 'and you seemed to forget that pretty quickly.'

'Don't you mention your mother to me,' Bobby said furiously. 'I don't want her name thrown up at me all the time.'

'I bet you don't, "Lord Lighterman",' Stefanie jumped up, 'because she was a much, much better person than you! She was a war heroine, not someone who made a fortune out of guns, out of the miseries of others...'

'Your mother was a *whore*.' Bobby stabbed a finger at her and only just managed to duck as Stefanie's hand came out to hit him. He caught it and held onto her wrist so strongly she thought it would break. She also thought her father was about to have a stroke because his eyes bulged and the veins throbbed on his forehead. Only very slowly did he collect himself and calm down.

'I'm sorry, that was a very provocative thing to say.' Bobby released her hand and extracting a large white handkerchief from his breast pocket began to mop his brow. 'I shouldn't have said it. I realize how you and your sisters feel about your mother and I wouldn't have had what happened to her happen.'

'It only happened because you threw her out. If you hadn't she would have spent the war in England and be alive today instead of in some unmarked grave, or dust from the crematorium.' Stefanie's voice suddenly broke and she collapsed onto the sofa. Bobby stared at her with an expression which was, for him, curiously like despair.

'We can't go back to what happened all those years ago Stefanie,' he said pleadingly. 'Your mother had a lover, a man

431

she'd known before we were married, and continued to see. I had to divorce her. What else could a man of pride do?'

Bobby got up and, still mopping his brow, his hand trembling, anxiously inspected his face in the mirror over the mantelpiece. 'I'm sorry about what happened, now, in retrospect, but I was a very hurt and angry man. I sent you there to be with your mother. It seemed the proper thing to do. I never knew that the war and all that would intervene. I know they were terrible years for you and I regret them, believe me I do. You were meant to come to school in England. I've tried to make up for it by letting your grandmother have a free hand at Robertswood – as you say, it's beginning to resemble Tsarkoe Selo, but never mind. She enjoys it and there are many bargains to be had from the great houses of Europe, from the Balkan countries and Russia. I'm glad to do that for your grandmother. I know how much she did for you. You, yourself, have an income that many a family man would envy. Five thousand a year is a lot of money for a young woman. You're not yet nineteen.'

'I know it is and I said I'm grateful.'

'The thing is, Stefanie,' Bobby walked towards her theatrically, wringing his hands, 'I want you to live up to what you *are*. There is no need for you to work. You could be part of London Society. Your mother always used to love it and I hoped you would too. You can go anywhere you want and do anything you like. This man I hear you're consorting with is absolutely nobody. Who is he? Someone you met in the rag trade? Is that the sort of man I want my daughter to associate with?'

'He had a very good war.' Stefanie looked mildly amused. 'Maybe you should meet him and talk about it.'

'I hope you're not sleeping with him or anything like that ...' Bobby began, but Stefanie stopped him.

'It's more serious than that, Father. I want to marry him. We only have to ask you because I'm under age. He's really very nice.'

Bobby's eyes began to bulge again but he remembered the trembling, the tight feeling across his chest and controlled himself. Instead he slumped in the chair.

'If you marry him I'll cut off your allowance. I'll cut it off for good and never restore it. I promise you that.'

Stefanie began to look very angry again. 'But, Father, you don't know him. You've never met him. Who told you about him, anyway?'

'Everyone knows about him, as far as I can tell – all the members of the family. None of them like him. Even Rachel doesn't like him and you know how she always tries to see the good side.'

'You really have been spying on me haven't you?'

'I have to know these things. You're not yet nineteen. Marriage is quite ridiculous. My mother first married when she was twenty and regretted it immediately. You know nothing about life. I should never have let you have your own flat, but insisted on you living with me. As we were moving from one house and looking for another it was very difficult, but I see now that I should.' He regarded her sombrely for a moment, then pointed a warning finger at her. 'You've got your mother's wild streak in you, Stefanie, and I warn you: this man is no good for you. Give him up, or you'll regret the consequences. She did. Remember, please, what happened to your mother – and I don't mean her tragic fate in the war.'

Stefanie drove very fast all the way down Highgate Hill through Camden Town and across Euston Road to her flat off Marylebone High Street. She felt so livid with her father, with her family, that she didn't care if she crashed on the way. She drove through two sets of lights as they were turning red and nearly collided with a lorry on the Marylebone Road.

Jack looked at her with great concern as she flung open the front door, and paused in the act of pouring himself a large gin and tonic.

'You've been to see your father, I can tell that,' Jack said and put even more gin in another glass, splashed tonic into it, bundled in some ice and handed it to her. 'Was it about us?'

'Yes.'

'I thought it might be.' Jack settled down on the sofa beside her, beckoned her over to his side, and put a large hand round her waist. 'I knew none of your snobby family would like me.'

'But you were a major in the war. Doesn't that sort of thing count?'

'No, not with people like them.' Jack laughed and removed his hand to extract a cigarette from his silver cigarette case and light it. Then he gave the cigarette to Stefanie and she puffed it too while Jack lit another. They always did this. It was one of the sensuous things she liked about him, like Humphrey Bogart saying to Ingrid Bergman: 'Here's looking at you kid' in *Casablanca*, which was probably where Jack got it from, as he had an entirely unimaginative mind. 'I knew your father would check up on me as soon as your family knew. And you never wanted me to meet him did you?'

'Not yet. I told him we wanted to get married.'

Jack chuckled. 'What did he say to that?'

'He said I was under age and he would cut off all my money. I think he must meet you, Jack. He likes self-made men and I'm sure he'd like you.'

But Jack Blackstock-Thomas wasn't so certain. He went into the kitchen to get fresh ice for their drinks, thinking over what Stefanie had told him.

He was forty-one and had had a good war. He had served in Africa, all through Sicily and had been wounded at Cassino. But before the war he had been a salesman in ladies' fashions and it was to this that he returned after his demob, going round the stores selling ladies' lingerie in his shiny new demob suit.

Jack Blackstock was very good at what he did and he soon got promoted. He liked to be known as 'the Major'. He was a tall, well-built man with black Brylcreemed hair and a very charming smile which showed a good set of teeth. He was very successful with the ladies and Stefanie Lighterman was bowled over by him. He had sold ladies' knitwear and she modelled it.

When he met Stefanie he had no idea of her background, or that her father was the newly ennobled Lord Lighterman because she used her mother's maiden name, and her slightly Slav looks made some people think she was an impecunious refugee. There was no 'side' to Stefanie, no gracious airs to recall a bygone age. But the impression of freedom and independence she gave was deceptive: she was vulnerable and she needed a man, a protector.

Jack Blackstock was perfect because he had learned a lot of things in the Army and had acquired a veneer and a taste for good living. He'd added the 'Thomas' to his name as an afterthought when he was demobbed and it was as Major Jack Blackstock-Thomas that he had been introduced to Stefanie.

They had been together for a year but they didn't live together although they slept together. Stefanie had detected that slightly common touch about Jack, that trace of cockney accent he had tried so hard to get rid of in the Army. She knew quite well what her family would think of him. She had never met her mother's lover, Jamie Kitto, and although there was nothing at all common about him – he was related to her grandmother and his family were impeccable – he was very like Jack Blackstock-Thomas to look at. Those who had met him and knew them both thought it was remarkable that the tastes of mother and daughter, so different in many ways, should instinctively be for the same kind of *louche roué* of a man.

Jamie had been a charmer, a womanizer and Jack was one too. He had his eye on the main chance with Stefanie, but he had quite a few other girlfriends as well. He liked women and he liked danger. The war had cemented a taste for both in a lingerie salesman who had very little to show for the first thirty-three years of his life, until the war began.

Jack came back into the sitting room and sank onto the sofa next to Stefanie.

'I've been thinking,' he said. 'There may be something that

will change your father's mind about me.' He put ice in their glasses and drank from his.

'What's that?'

'I've been offered a very good job in the cinema business. I think it's the fact I'm associated with ladies' garments that your father doesn't like. If I'm in films it's something different isn't it?'

'I suppose so.' But Stefanie was still doubtful. She knew that Jack was common and nothing he did would dispel that.

'Let's go to bed,' she said, tugging at his coat.

She always felt terribly sexy when she saw him. Also it made her forget, suspend criticism about the other things that weren't right because he was so good in bed. As Jamie Kitto had been.

How odd the large FOR SALE notice attached to the railings of Askham House looked, Rachel thought standing on the pavement outside, rather as she had that day in 1912 when she had lobbed three large stones through the first-floor window.

The thought of it now didn't even make her smile because it brought back memories of Bosco and how sad it had made him. She tucked her arm through Hugo's who, somehow, seemed to share her thoughts and said:

'Let's go in.'

They had a key from the estate agent because, although the house had been acquired, the new owners had not yet exchanged contracts and completed the final formalities. Rachel had begged for a last look round.

'It feels so funny,' she said, climbing the five steps to the door and inserting the key in the dusty lock. 'I haven't been back for years, you know, though Ralph sometimes stayed here during the War.' She was about to say: 'I think it was where he and Jenny used to meet' and then thought she shouldn't. She thought, too, it was why Jenny had decided not to accompany them, but to do some shopping for her

436

trousseau in Bond Street and meet them at Fortnum's round the corner for lunch.

When she had lived here she'd hardly ever opened the door herself, but Bromwich, the watchful butler, or a footman invariably stayed just inside the door, peeping through the stained-glass panes on either side in case any member of the family should return. One person did that all day. It was incredible to think of now.

It was quite dark inside the hall and when she tried the electricity nothing happened.

'It's been cut off,' she said, a catch in her voice, 'of course.'

'Do you think you should have come?' Hugo whispered. 'I mean was it necessary?'

'It was something I wanted to do.' Rachel, with a quick look round the hall, started to climb the stairs. 'It was very much part of your father's family, and had been for two hundred years. I think he never expected that by the middle of this century it would no longer be ours.'

They were now on the landing and Hugo slowly opened the large double doors of the main drawing room and peeped in. Rachel tiptoed after him and then burst out laughing.

'I don't know why we're whispering and tiptoeing about. There's no one here to hear us.'

'Except ghosts.' Hugo put his arm round her and led her through the room, by now completely empty of furniture and carpets, to the window overlooking the Square. It was April and the buds were just beginning to burgeon on the trees, the birds hopping from branch to branch. In the herbaceous borders surrounding the grass there were daffodils. Rachel and Hugo stood for a long time looking out, saying nothing.

'This was the first real home I had,' Hugo said, a lump in his throat. 'I think I shall miss it. I didn't, but I do now.'

'Then maybe *you* shouldn't have come,' Rachel pressed his waist, 'though I clearly do remember the day I brought you here and how excited and happy the children were to see you, their new brother. You were a very quiet, controlled little boy then.'

'No wonder,' Hugo said, knowing quite well what his life had been like before. He looked at her for a few moments, then: 'I do love you, Rachel.'

'Oh Hugo ...' Rachel turned to him and pressed her head against his shoulder. 'And I love you, very much. I always did, but recently you've been so good to me. Since all this awful money business, coming on top of Ralph ...' Distressed, she put a hand to her eyes. 'I don't know what I would have done without you.'

'And I don't know what I'd have done without you because it's through you I'm going to get the Hall. I won't let happen to the Hall what's happening here.'

'Oh yes, you'll get the Hall all right, if it's what you want.' Rachel pursed her lips. 'Poor Dulcie, if she saw what was happening to this house she would be sad enough, but the Hall, that she loved so much, passing out of the family...'

'Not *out* of the family, if David is going to own it...'

'And turn it into a hotel?' Rachel expostulated. 'The very idea! David, anyway, is not an Askham and never has been. Poor boy, he has no sense of family, or anything else very much. It's not his fault.' She turned away from the window and ran a finger down the wall. 'Well I shan't miss Cheryl's "refurbishment" I must say. Come on, let's go upstairs.'

She turned towards the door and Hugo followed her. 'I'd be surprised, anyway, if David wanted the Hall or to run it as a hotel. He apparently doesn't want to do anything, which is hardly surprising since Bobby has spoilt him all his life. I don't think David ever wanted for a single thing.'

'Except, perhaps, the love of a father.' Hugo carefully closed the door after them. 'I don't think Bobby could give him, or anyone, that.'

'Poor Bobby certainly lacks a fatherly image.' Rachel clasped the banister as she began to climb the stairs. 'But I know he loved David. He adored him and he feels very unhappy and let down by him. The irony is that if he'd done the right thing by those little girls they'd have loved him so much. They are all simply bursting with affection, which is why Stefanie has gone off with this most unsuitable man ...' Rachel shook her head in disapproval, 'this adventurer.'

The whole family had been shocked and upset by Stefanie's relationship with this man twenty-three years her senior. Stefanie, with everything to offer, surely deserved something better than that? The attraction was hardly credible so that one was forced to delve into Stefanie's past for the reasons: her desertion by Bobby, neglected by Hélène, hence the search for a father figure coupled with the desire to shock.

'She hasn't "gone off" with him.' Hugo caught her hand as they came to the top of the stairs.

'Well, you know what I mean. She wants to marry him! I think it's only the thought of losing Bobby's money that's stopping her. She loves that more than him which is perhaps, for once, rather a good thing!'

She fell silent as they walked along the corridor, pushing open first one door and then another. There was the room she'd shared with Bosco. She looked round it trying to summon up the ghosts, but it didn't have any special memory for her now. They hadn't lived here very long and they hadn't been particularly happy here. It was soon after they moved here that he'd met Nimet again. She shivered but she didn't want to tell Hugo why and rapidly closed the door behind her. They climbed more stairs.

The Grange had the happiest memories of her marriage to Bosco – all the love they had enjoyed there, and it was where her four children had been born. She stepped back to let Hugo push open a door, a smile on his face.

'Your den,' she murmured. 'I can see you've happy memories of it.'

'Yes my den.' Hugo wandered round. There was nothing there now, no furniture, but the marks on the walls where his trophies and shields had been, his favourite pictures. He stood by the window and, flinging it open, looked out to the ledge of the one next to it. 'Do you remember when Lenin got stuck and couldn't go forward and couldn't go back?'

'Oh yes,' Rachel laughed, 'and one of the footmen risked his life to rescue him. Dear old cat. My goodness, that was years ago because we only got Lenin when you were small.' She touched his head affectionately and he took her hand and held it. 'You were a lovely little boy then and you're a lovely man.'

'I was a bit naughty.' Hugo hung his head in mock sorrow.

'Well there *were* moments when I was worried,' Rachel admitted. 'How quickly one forgets those things. You ran away from school, if I recall...'

'Rachel.' Hugo let her hand fall and moved over to the wall leaning against it, his hands in his pockets. He really was vastly handsome, Rachel thought, looking at him with pride. He seemed to improve all the time, to grow even better with maturity. He was a big man, heavy framed, powerful and, yes, he grew more and more like his father.

'What is it?' Rachel said encouragingly.

'I would like you to like Jenny.'

'But I do like Jenny!' Rachel looked surprised. 'I like her very much.'

'I'd like you to love her.'

'Ah!' Rachel paused. 'Love is something else. Love comes.'

'But you've lived with Jenny for long enough for it to come.'

'Then I can't force it.' Rachel half closed her eyes, thinking back to a similar conversation with Ralph. 'Does she love me?'

Hugo started. 'I – er – I think so.'

'Well, why don't you ask her? Love must be a mutual thing. I think Jenny feels the same about me as I feel about her ... a little cautious, a little restrained. I don't know why. Maybe it *is* to do with Ralph. People say it is. But I do like her and I think you'll be very happy married to her. But love ...' Rachel again trailed a finger along the wall, this time examining it for dust. 'Love will come.'

The last room they visited was Ralph's, and this Rachel

entered as though it were a sacred shrine. Perhaps this was really why she had wanted to come to the house. She looked at the place where his bed had been, his trophies, marks of all the family portraits on the wall that Hugo hadn't bothered with because they didn't mean so much to him.

Hugo noticed that Rachel had gone quite quickly through the girls' rooms as though they were impersonal, not meaning all that much to her. Perhaps the memories were not so important because they were still alive.

In Freddie's room she had stayed a little longer, but in Ralph's room she lingered, her eyes roving restlessly round as though she would summon him back.

'Shall I go?' he asked quietly, after a while, wondering if she wanted to be alone.

'No!' She held on to him fiercely. 'You're my son now. Ralph's gone.'

It was a long time before, slowly, with all the tenderness of which he was capable, he could draw her out of the room again, gently shutting the door after them forever.

CHAPTER 23

Hugo and Jenny were married in the summer of 1947, the month of August being one convenient for most of the family to attend. Weddings and baptisms and, of course, funerals were always occasions for a gathering of the large circle of relations who were associated with the Askhams: the Boling-brokes, the Lightermans, the Kittos and the Crewes. Then there were the various friends who had attended these occasions since records began: the Bulstrodes, the Dugdales, the Mackenzies, Frobishers, Smith-Forresters and so on, whose descendants had continued to be friends of the family into modern times. If rarely seen otherwise, they were always there for big occasions.

And the wedding of Hugo was the biggest family occasion since the end of the war. Ralph's memorial service and the wedding of Charlotte and Arthur had been much quieter affairs. And here Hugo broke, or was forced to break, with tradition. Again, for the first time since anyone could remember, the gathering was not held at Askham Hall but at the Oak House Manor Hotel near the village of Darley. That neat little manor house where Rachel and Adam lived was far too small for the kind of reception planned by Hugo and Jenny after their registrar's office wedding.

Now with the ceremonial part behind them Hugo and Jenny stood at the doorway of the hotel ballroom to receive the guests who were announced in a suitably sonorous voice by the hired master of ceremonies.

Those who filed past congratulating the bride and groom thought it all a far cry from the days when Askham Hall was seen at its best, as though it had been built just for that kind of thing: splendid parties, huge glittering occasions that attracted the very best of society and the nobility from all over England. A reception taking place at a *hotel*? To what had the family come? Those who knew, and most of them knew everything, blamed Bobby for the feud which had divided the family into two quite clearly defined camps: those who thought that Askham Hall should be leased to Hugo, and those who thought that it should be turned into a hotel by one of Bobby's many investment groups.

For, whatever one said, Hugo was not *quite* family. Despite being Bosco's son Hugo was not quite family because of the other half of his parentage who stood now in the line of those receiving the guests. Everyone said that Rachel showed surprising magnanimity in standing next to her, even though she was in her seventies and Nimet not far behind.

In between receiving guests Rachel and Nimet chatted together for all the world like old friends, instead of one-time rivals for the love of the same man. One-time? Was it really over thirty-five years ago?

Hugo looked resplendent in morning dress, every inch the earl he might have been, if his father and mother had married, because he was Bosco's last surviving son. But it was Paul, Bosco's twelve-year-old grandson, politely greeting guests, most of whom he didn't know, who had inherited the title.

Title, but no money. The very few present who remembered the Askham splendour before the First World War found it hard to realize there was not a penny left; only liabilities and a huge empty house going to ruin while the family disputed over it. It was for this reason that Bobby had forbidden his family to attend the wedding of his adversary which, needless to say, made his two eldest children only more determined to be there. The younger ones still at school had to obey their father, and Princess Irina, who adored Hugo and loved any excuse for a party, had reluctantly to stay at Robertswood with them for fear of offending that mighty lord to whom she literally owed her comfortable existence.

As the guests passed the line there were handshakes, kisses, more handshakes, more kisses, congratulations, greetings. To the casual observer, maybe the photographers and reporters scattered around the grounds of a hotel that, prophetically, had once also been a gracious country house, it seemed not so much a celebration for Hugo and his wife as a chance for pre-war finery to be shaken out of mothballs. For those who could afford it to show off the latest *haute couture* fashions, frocks maybe in printed crêpe with side drapery, or with ruched hiplines and flared skirts, and all eleven inches from the ground in accordance with the dictates of Dior.

As the names were called heads were raised as this or that interesting name was announced, or this or that person, or couple who, maybe, had not been seen since before the War, passed in the relative safety of the United States or South Africa.

The Honourable George and Mrs Petwith Forsyth, the Honourable Henrietta Mackintosh, Sir Meredith and Lady Hallet, Mr and Mrs Anthony Devine, the Honourable Stefanie Lighterman and Major John Blackstock-Thomas...

Stefanie, known for her casual approach to clothes, had decided to startle everyone who expected her to wear something unsuitable for the occasion. Her afternoon frock of sheer crêpe had a gored skirt with a tight bodice and a wide, deep décolletage which let those, who hadn't suspected the fact, see that she had a bosom. Long white gloves reached three-quarter length sleeves but, and no one could ever remember seeing this, she wore a hat, a modified straw cloche set forward on her head with a little half veil tantalizingly over her eyes.

Major Blackstock-Thomas too was impeccably attired in morning suit carrying a grey top hat. His thick dark hair was brushed back from his forehead and his attractive smile, under a black moustache, much in evidence.

Hugo kissed Stefanie warmly and shook hands with the major, whom he had heard of but not met, and, as they went down the line, there was a similar response from the rest of that well-brought-up family – whatever they thought of Stefanie's fiancé – including Charlotte who was standing not far from her mother talking to an aunt of Arthur's.

The Crewes had been at the ceremony, along with close family. Charlotte, a much beloved half-sister of Hugo, had been matron of honour to Jenny together with the bride's sister Mary who felt very out of place in this exalted company, despite the attempts of the Askham family to make her feel at ease. Jenny's mother had died during the war and her father didn't want to leave his small farm, so Hugo and Jenny had promised to go there on their way to their honeymoon destination and Mary was the sole representative of the family at the ceremony. Mary had never been further south than Keswick so it was all a bit strange and frightening, proud though they all were in Cumberland of Jenny, and relieved too, even if her son was the son of an earl, that she had finally got herself a lawful husband.

Charlotte kept Mary near her so that she wouldn't feel left out and as soon as Stefanie and Jack came over she introduced them, exclaiming at the same time at Stefanie's striking appearance and greeting the major with more than her usual warmth so that he, too, wouldn't feel out of place.

However, there was little chance of that with Major Blackstock-Thomas. He hadn't been five years in the Army as an officer for nothing. He was also used to mixing with people of all kinds in his long and peripatetic career. Just in case, he had also well fortified himself with several whiskies at the hotel where he and Stefanie had stayed the night on the way down from London, and his gait was slightly unsteady, although this was scarcely perceptible in a gathering where the consumption of champagne was well under way.

Charlotte was one of the few members of the family who had already met Jack because to Stefanie she was like a second mother, preferable, indeed, to the one who had disappeared during the war. Stefanie's attitude to her mother now was one of pride and a love that had come too late. Because Charlotte had so loved Hélène, she had instinctively reached out to her

445

daughters who had arrived in England confused and bewildered, bereaved by the death of their grandfather. They had still not recovered when Charlotte came home from Belsen.

In the months that followed Charlotte had often talked to the girls of their mother, had recreated an image they had never had, building up a picture in their minds of a noble, self-sacrificing woman who had given everything, maybe even her life, for liberty.

Gradually their mental picture of Hélène changed from that of a selfish woman who neglected them, to a loving mother whose patriotism, and that alone, had taken her from them. It also reinforced – though Charlotte did not necessarily mean to do this – an image of Bobby as the cruel, remote father who had abandoned them and their mother, who had only sent for them when family pressure on him became too much. They knew how important Father was in their lives, because they didn't want to be sent back to a flat like the one behind the Gare du Nord, with the paper peeling on the walls and not enough to eat. But their affection for him was insincere, and hypocritical, when he was around. When he was away it was openly hostile. Bobby had, thus, whatever his worldly success, failed dismally as a father.

Lord and Lady Harris, Miss Amanda Nightingale, Mr and Mrs Bertie Hope-Barlow, the Honourable David Lighterman...

Heads turned again, all of them this time, though few had missed the importance of the entrance of Stefanie and her gentleman friend of whom everyone knew instinctively, if they did not know for a fact, the family disapproved. Even regardless of his age there was something not quite right about the major, and those with an ear tuned for these things immediately detected those nuances in his intonation that showed he had not been to public school.

Mr Lighterman, however, was quite a different matter, indubitably top drawer even if his appearance did its best to disclaim all aristocratic connections. However much he wished to dispel the past, young Mr Lighterman, like his father, had been to Harrow; and Harrow, together with Eton, Winchester and, possibly, Haileybury and Rugby, was one of those things that one could never quite get out of one's system, no matter how much one tried or wished to. As the flamboyant young man strolled confidently along the receiving line, quite sure of his welcome, his place in the gathering, with his long hair, sidewhiskers and colourful, spiv-like clothes, it was difficult to remember the shy young boy, studying for Common Entrance, whose mother had married his father when he was eleven years old.

Some could recall his presence at Freddie's memorial service at about that time, but no one would have recognised him. David, dark like his father, appeared to have *dyed* his hair which was now curly, not straight as most remembered it; and his morning suit would have looked more in place in the window of a theatrical costumiers from which, perhaps, it had come. There was a blue tailcoat over white trousers and a jabot-type white shirt with a profusion of lace at the neck. David wore white shoes and a collection of rings and bangles and, from his left ear, a solitary emblem that looked like a miniature bird cage hung at the end of a gold chain. David had dark skin and blue eyes and in this outfit he looked like a prosperous gypsy. There was even a little gasp in some quarters, though it was discreet: it would never have done for the family to hear it because, like all the best families, they protected their own and David was their own.

'I must say, David, you look *splendid*,' Stefanie said with genuine admiration and leaned forward to kiss him. 'Have you been down the King's Road? Do you know my fiancé, Jack?'

'*Fiancé* is it?' David shook the major's hand vigorously. 'How do you do, Jack?'

'This is my half-brother, David.' Stefanie tucked her arm into Jack's. 'We are *both* absolutely beyond the pale as far as our father is concerned.'

447

'I hear you're in films,' David said chattily, stopping a passing waiter to commandeer a glass of champagne.

'You hear right,' Jack said, further lightening the load of the same waiter.

'Do you know Arthur Rank?'

'Pretty well,' the major lied.

'I'd like to get into films,' David said. 'It's the only thing I really want to do, act, or play in a band.'

'I can see why.' The major looked at his clothes and Stefanie couldn't tell whether he was laughing at David or with him, anyway she joined in. All three of them were a little tipsy by now.

Stefanie and David had joined forces, soon after they met, united in a common loathing of Bobby. It was odd they had this in common because Bobby had rescued one but jettisoned the other; however, they both agreed he was foul. They recognized rebellion and non-conformity in each other, and David would have met the major long ago had he not just spent a year in America, sent by his father in the hope it would improve him.

David occasionally saw his father, when he wanted money. Although he was only nineteen he had been allowed his own flat, though Aileen would have preferred him to live at home. The anxious parents had consulted advisers of all kinds about their son, and professional opinion, medical and psychiatric, was that David would change: this rebellion was a passing phase, something he would grow out of. But they had been saying that for years; pocketing large fees and saying the same thing, again and again. David didn't grow out of it. He had grown more into a Bohemian way of life after those stifling years in a semi-detached house with lace curtains at the windows in Harrow, waiting day after day for his father to come: the father he so idolized until he came to live with him. It was all very ironical that Bobby, who had sacrificed so much for David, who had married a woman with whom he wasn't in the least in love in order to legitimize him and make him the heir to his business, should find that he had a misfit on his hands, a social pariah who didn't get his School Certificate and neither wanted to work, nor give any reasonable account of himself.

Almost to the day Bobby and Aileen were married David changed – and no one really knew why.

All Bobby could do was pray and pay up, hoping that one day the experts would be proved right and David would change back.

In the middle of the spacious green lawn behind the hotel was a marquee where a very passable buffet was being served, despite the fact that wartime rationing regulations were still in force and many items were still unobtainable. Hugo had provided a lot of the food produce from the farm and, of course, even in the war there never had been a shortage of wine: wine went on being made in the vineyards of France, no one knew quite how, and, as soon as the French ships could freely cross the Channel, wine went with them.

Just outside the striped marquee Peter Klein asked Em who was the man in the colourful dress and Em was explaining about David when Paul ran over to his uncle and asked him to come and meet some friends of his from school. Peter had been an immediate favourite with the orphaned Paul who had inherited the kind of insecurity that Hugo had, inevitable with people who are never quite sure of their parentage.

Em told Luis to go along with Paul, but Luis didn't want to go. He was an introverted boy who felt foreign and awkward in large gatherings because he only spoke Spanish at home. Every day he went home from the local school to his father, and he had few friends. Felipe was very possessive and Luis didn't see his mother very often though he knew what she did and was proud of what she wrote.

Luis felt cut off from the Askham family, his cousins and their friends. He knew that his parents had quarrelled bitterly and wouldn't ever live together again. Thus, when his mother's lover appeared, a thin, emaciated man yet with tremendous spirit who had been for so long in a concentration camp, who had seen the worst of the war, he took to him with the passionate sensibility of the insecure. He loved his Uncle Peter, but he loved even more that rarely seen creature, his mother. Whenever he had the chance to be with her he never left her side; he clung to her and now, as Paul went off with Peter, he preferred to be with Em.

Em felt happy about Hugo and Jenny. She'd been introducing Peter to her cousin, Douglas Kitto, who lived on the family estate in Scotland, whose father had been her grandmother's brother, when Paul ran up and now they continued the conversation.

'Don't you think Jenny looks rather like Mother?' she asked him. 'People who remember him say how like Father Hugo has become, and I thought it rather a gentle irony that he marries someone who resembles our mother rather than his.'

'Rachel and Hugo have always been very close,' Douglas said, reaching for a sandwich. 'And, yes, I do think there's something about Rachel in Jenny. They are the same build and colouring and, don't you think, they are both very English types, and you are an English type, whereas Charlotte is a polyglot and her family look so extraordinarily foreign.'

'Except Arthur!' Em said reproachfully. 'Arthur would be *extremely* upset to think that people thought of him as anything other than the perfect English gentleman.'

'Which he is,' Douglas hastened to correct himself. 'There's nothing the least bit foreign about Arthur, nor little Jeremy whom I saw for the first time when I was in London last week. Now do tell me exactly who that fellow is with Stefanie...'

Even though Lord Kitto had never met him, and knew nothing about him, being out of the mainstream of gossip in his country seat on the Scottish borders, he instinctively knew that Jack wasn't quite right. He bent his ear attentively as Em began to explain.

Hugo, an arm lightly round Jenny, took her once again

among the family friends, though many people there had met her. She wore a pretty outfit in cream shantung, the dress with a pleated skirt and a bolero-type jacket over it. Her hair, which she wore coiled, was tucked into a little straw hat. Jonathan was not at the ceremony, or the party, but remained at Darley Manor with his cousin, Jeremy.

But there were many there that day who remembered Jonathan's father Ralph and the reason for Jenny being there at all, and they talked about him: fond memories of a good man who had not had the happiness in life he deserved and had died a horrible death. Many glasses were raised to Ralph, though not when Hugo or Jenny were present.

Arthur had acquired a small country house not far from Salisbury, within easy reach of the family. Arthur would quite like to have been much further out, say in Somerset, but Charlotte, so family minded, wouldn't hear of it. When she was in the country, which was quite often as the house was being done up and prepared for occupation, she saw her mother every day. The two women naturally gravitated together from time to time at the party, exchanging trivial items of gossip, small bits of news.

'Someone said Jack Blackstock is getting rather drunk,' Rachel murmured with a worried frown midway in the afternoon when the party was in full swing. 'He's talking very loudly.'

'He does that anyway.' Charlotte picked up a mint from a silver dish. 'He has a naturally loud voice. I think he got it in the Army.'

Rachel couldn't tell whether her daughter was being sarcastic or serious. Because she loved Stefanie so much she only wanted her to be happy, and if she was happy with Jack then Charlotte was happy too. But *was* Stefanie happy with Jack?

Rachel said: '*Are* they engaged? She's introducing him as her fiancé.'

'So I hear,' Charlotte frowned. 'I don't know how serious it is. She hasn't a ring. I think it's just a bold move to defy Bobby. Maybe she doesn't care, if she's so in love.' She screwed up her eyes, looking for Angelica who had a habit of roving off, on occasions like this, with eligible males. 'I mean I hope she really *doesn't* care. The fact is that Jack has got some sort of job with a film company and he and Stefanie seem to think this means he'll be rich. I know she'd love to be independent of Bobby, do without his money.'

'But do you think the business of marriage is serious?' Rachel began to feel thoroughly alarmed. 'I so hoped it was just some kind of bravado. Do you think he is in any way attractive?' Rachel looked once again at the tall figure of the major, his arm round Stefanie's waist – as if in defiance of her family – in profile to her further up the lawn.

'Not to me he isn't attractive – but I don't need someone like Stefanie does. She has never had a strong man or men around her. She only had her grandfather. At least Em and I had brothers, uncles and cousins – all Stefanie ... Oh *look* who's come!' Charlotte put a hand on her mother's, pointing towards the open French windows of the hotel from which a trickle of late guests still issued. 'Mother, is that Sasha? Isn't that wonderful? I thought he was still in Singapore.'

Sasha Ferov stood with his hands in his pockets looking at the crowd of people assembled on the lawn. There were much more than he had expected and he felt rather bewildered until he saw the familiar head of Hugo towering above the rest.

Sasha took his hands out of his pockets and walked over to them pressing through the throng. He saw nobody he knew, until he reached Hugo, and no one seemed to recognize him. Even Hugo looked at him for a minute or two as if in disbelief and, as Sasha held out his hand, Hugo released Jenny and flung his arms around him.

'Sasha, so you came!'

'I'm very sorry I'm so late. My plane only landed at Northolt this morning. I changed, borrowed a car and came straight down.'

'That's very good of you Sasha.' Beaming, Hugo wrung his hand as Jenny looked on rather shyly, thankful, at last, for a genuine friendly face. Jenny hadn't known Sasha well, but she liked him best of all the family. He had gone abroad soon after the end of the war and hadn't been back since.

Jenny hadn't looked forward to her wedding and she wasn't enjoying it. All she'd wanted was a quiet ceremony, preferably near her home town, with just a few of the family present. Instead Hugo and Rachel between them had organized this enormous gathering at which, from the beginning, she'd felt out of place rather than the focus of attention.

For Jenny was, and remained, self-conscious. She loved Hugo too much to forgo marrying him even though she knew that it also involved marriage to his family: his real mother, Ralph's mother, his sisters and cousins all of whom were represented in full force at the reception. If eyes were on anyone they were not on her, dressed prettily but very simply in cream, but on the flamboyant Stefanie, the ultra-chic Charlotte, in pale blue and white with the customary large eye-catching cartwheel hat that so suited her, and the interesting and intellectual Em who was rumoured to have the ears of statesmen since she had been editing *The Sentinel*. Jenny felt that everyone in the family was of more interest than she was: the only interesting thing about her was her past. Briefly she had enjoyed, though that was not the word, some notoriety; but now that was over. She was not beautiful and she was not stylish; maybe they thought she was rather pathetic, a single woman with a child whose lover was dead and whose brother had taken pity on her.

Everyone had wanted Jonathan to be present at the wedding, even though he was so small, but Jenny had absolutely forbidden it, impressing everyone by the strength of her feeling. This was her day, she seemed to be saying and, as much as she could, she wanted to hang onto it; but even then

453

it hadn't worked and as the crowds swarmed into the ballroom towards the line in which she stood with Hugo and his family she had all but panicked.

Jenny said little; people seemed to ignore her, or patronize her with a few carefully chosen words. In time she felt like a guest at her own wedding and she longed to be gone, wondering if her very mediocrity would change the way her bridegroom felt about her. Amelia had been beautiful, a personality as her mother, Cheryl, had been and she, Jenny, had come in the wake of these two controversial women like calm after the storm. Only the calm was rarely exciting.

Now she stood looking on as Hugo and Sasha talked excitedly together and the family began to gather round. It was only then that anyone seemed to think of her and, as Sasha stopped and looked at her, she said: 'It is *very* nice of you to come, Sasha,' and, as he stooped to kiss her – he was very tall – she blushed.

Then he greeted Charlotte and Em and when he saw Rachel further off with Arthur's mother he said: 'Where's Uncle Bobby?'

There was a little silence in the family group until Hugo spoke: 'Bobby and I are feuding over the Hall. He has forbidden any of his family to come, including your grandmother.'

'That's too bad.' Sasha looked annoyed. 'I so wanted to see her. I didn't realize the feud was as bad as that.'

'Actually it's very bad. Bobby is threatening to go to court on the grounds that I'm not a legitimate member of the family. Lawyers are trying to work that one out now.'

Sasha's face clouded with rage.

Jenny said boldly: 'Lord Lighterman is so unused to being thwarted, not having what he wants, that he behaves like a spoilt child.'

'A dangerous, spoilt child,' Hugo said grimly. 'Rachel has a horror of court cases.'

'Who hasn't?' Sasha looked around at the crowd. 'That's an astonishing looking girl. Who is she?'

Charlotte, following his gaze, smiled. 'Don't you recognise her?'

'No I don't.'

'Let's introduce you then.' She led Sasha through the throng smiling and shaking hands as they went, rather like a procession of royalty. 'You remember my cousin, don't you? Sasha Ferov ... just back from Singapore ...' A path was finally cleared for them and, as they arrived, the woman Sasha had admired looked straight into his face:

'I don't believe ...' she said.

Sasha had last seen Stefanie as the rather gauche, bewildered and rebellious girl who had arrived in 1944 with her sisters to join her father after so many years of separation.

'My goodness ...' he began as she flung her arms round his neck.

'Sasha it's you!'

'With the hat ... I didn't recognize ...' he tried to explain, aware of the warm, pliant body so close to his. His arms tightened round her and, for a long moment, they pressed each other. Slowly they drew apart, still holding on to each other.

'No one said you were coming.' Stefanie looked reproachfully at Hugo, who with Jenny had followed Charlotte.

'No one knew,' Hugo said. 'We thought he was in Singapore.'

'Sasha...'

'Sasha...'

'Sasha...'

All the family started to arrive. Rachel came up with Lady Crewe, Em with Douglas Kitto, Peter and Paul, Arthur with the boys and Angelica; Adam with Flora and Giles. Christopher and Sylvia Bolingbroke joined the queue of wellwishers and, last of all, there was Nimet who, gazing gravely at the stranger, held out her hand:

'How do you do? I don't think we have met.'

'This is my mother.' Hugo ushered Nimet forward while Rachel faded into the background.

'I'm very pleased to meet you, at last.' Sasha gallantly kissed her hand. 'I hear you were stranded in Egypt all during the war.'

'Hardly *stranded*.' Nimet gave her still fascinating silvery laugh. 'I had a very good time at Luxor in the little house I own on the banks of the Nile. You would hardly have known there was a war on.'

Stefanie was hovering by Sasha's elbow, trying to get his attention. He looked from Nimet to her and, then, across to the man next to her.

'This is my fiancé, Jack,' she said.

'How do you do?' Sasha shook Jack's hand realizing as he did that the major was very unsteady on his feet.

'Whoops,' Jack said pulling himself up straight. 'The ground's got a bit wobbly.'

'*You've* got a bit wobbly,' Stefanie chided him. 'You've had too much to drink.'

'I think *everyone's* had a bit too much to drink,' Rachel said tactfully. 'It really *is* a lovely party, Hugo. Don't you think so, Jenny?' Always, as usual, even at her own wedding, she was trying not to exclude Jenny from the proceedings.

'I have *not* had too much to drink,' Jack said pompously, and rather loudly, trying to shake Stefanie's hand off his arm.

'There, there old man.' Arthur, hovering in the background, stepped forward; solid, capable old Arthur who never had too much to drink or scarcely did anything to excess.

Arthur was about to grasp Jack's arm when Jack pushed him right in the chest and, as the ground at this point sloped slightly, Arthur fell headlong on the ground.

'Oh!'

There was a chorus of concern as everyone, except Jack, moved towards Arthur, and many willing, helpful pairs of hands tried to pull him up.

456

Dusting himself Arthur, red-faced and polite as ever, said he was perfectly all right. Stefanie, also flushed, said:

'I'm *awfully* sorry, Arthur.'

'No need for you to apologize, my dear.' Arthur rubbed some grass from his elbow while Charlotte straightened his tie as she looked anxiously into his eyes.

'Are you *sure* you're all right? That was a heavy fall.'

'I really am fine.' Arthur brushed back his hair.

'I do think you should apologize to Arthur.' Stefanie looked angrily at Jack.

'I *do* object to being told I'm drunk when I'm not,' Jack said, swaying forward. 'I don't think I've *anything* to apologize for.'

'Arthur never said you were drunk. All he said was "there, there".'

'He tried to take me by the arm.' Jack glowered at Arthur. 'I didn't like the esp ...' Jack screwed up his eyes in the effort of pronouncing the difficult word, 'esp ... expression in his eyes.'

'You should still say you're sorry.'

'Nothing to be sorry about.'

Rachel, aware of all the family looking accusingly at Jack, felt unexpectedly sorry for him.

'I'm sure that Jack didn't mean...'

'No need at all,' Charlotte echoed her mother...

'Oh forget about it.' Arthur took Charlotte's arm and turned away, but Jack called after him in a loud voice that was heard above the buzz of conversation:

'I say old man, don't go away.'

Arthur stopped, despite the tug of Charlotte's arm and, half turning, looked at him.

'Yes?'

'I wanted to tell you I'd knock you down again if you dared ever to lay a finger on me.' Jack raised his fist threateningly and shook it at Arthur. Stefanie appeared about to burst into tears and Sasha quickly whispered in Hugo's ear. Hugo, anxiously looking at his bride, nodded.

457

'Jack,' Sasha said smoothly, hands in his pockets, careful not to touch him, 'can you show me where there's any good whisky to be had at this party?'

Jack, leaning perilously forward again, leered at him and winked. Rachel signalled to the others to start drifting away, and Sasha whispered in Jack's ear.

'Up at the house, I think.'

'You're a frightfully good sort you know,' Jack mumbled clasping Sasha's arm for support as they turned towards the house. Stefanie, watching helplessly, humiliated, felt a friendly hand in hers.

'Sasha will know what to do. He always did.'

'Oh Aunt Rachel!' Stefanie buried her face in Rachel's shoulder, looking as though she were about to weep. Rachel said quietly, 'Keep going darling, just for a little while longer.'

'It's so *awful* ...' Slowly Stefanie disengaged herself.

'People soon forget. Quite a lot here have had a bit too much to drink.'

'Jack had *much* too much. I've never seen him like that. And with Arthur of all people. Oh Arthur...'

Arthur, coming up behind Rachel, caught her as she ran to him.

'It's absolutely all right, Stefanie. It's the sort of thing I've done myself.'

'I bet you haven't.'

Stefanie stared at him and then at all the sympathetic faces of the family gravely watching her. People in odd groups were still peering at them or casting surreptitious glances but they were too polite, too well brought up to stare. It was quite clear to all that the man was a cad and one wondered what he was doing in a gathering such as this.

'Shame,' several of them said, but it was true: they would soon forget.

Inside the house Jack still had his arm through Sasha's; to his surprise, he found he needed it for support.

'I think I've had a bit too much, old boy,' he said, wobbling.

'Do you think so?' Sasha looked at him in surprise.

'I don't think we should have that whisky.' Jack's eyes roamed round the large hall of the well-run establishment. 'What I'd quite like is a nap.'

'I'm sure that can be arranged.'

Sasha, who had arranged it already and had the key in his pocket, led him to the stairs and, as they walked up, Jack's step got heavier and heavier until by the time they were at the top he was nearly flat on his face.

'There we are, steady.' Sasha caught him just in time and half led, half dragged him to the first-floor room overlooking the grounds where the party was continuing as though nothing had happened, the members of the family dispersing again among the guests. Hugo had taken the room for him and Jenny to change, and Sasha only hoped that when they were ready to depart Jack would feel better. Maybe they should have transported him back to Darley Manor by car.

'This is a terrific room,' Jack said looking round him in surprise. 'Whose ... whose is it?' He blinked his eyes again, another difficult word.

'It's where Hugo and Jenny are going to go away from, but you can have a little nap until they do.'

'Delighted,' Jack said getting on the bed and, almost immediately, he began to snore.

Sasha skilfully removed his tight patent leather shoes, untied the natty cravat at his neck and undid the top button of his shirt, covered him with a blanket and left.

Stefanie, who had removed her hat, so that her dark, silky hair fell onto her shoulders, was waiting for him in the hall downstairs, distressed and anxious.

'Is he all right?' she asked.

'He's fine.' Sasha looked at her. 'A bit drunk but he'll sleep it off.'

'I don't know what came over him.'

'Don't you?' Sasha smiled.

'No, do you?'

'Don't you think meeting all the family is rather an awesome experience? I think Jenny feels it too. Luckily she's on orange juice.'

'But Jack's a man of the world. He's over forty.'

'Tell me, how long have you been engaged?' Sasha took her arm casually and steered her out onto the terrace. There were several chairs there and very few of them occupied. Drawing two aside he indicated to Stefanie that she should occupy one of them.

'Would you like a drink?'

'I don't think I'd better.' Stefanie smiled ruefully as Sasha sat opposite her.

'How did you meet him?'

'I was modelling for some time doing casual clothes and he was a rep selling them. He'd had a very good war,' Stefanie said defensively. 'He was a major.'

'I don't think that matters, do you, what he did, just who he is. He seems a very nice bloke.'

'Oh do you *really* think so, Sasha?' Stefanie looked grateful and clutched at the straw.

'Well from what I've seen of him.'

'No one else thinks so. They think he's common.'

'Oh!' Sasha sat back and joined his hands. He was trying to calculate how old Stefanie was.

'I hate these class distinctions, don't you?'

'I do rather,' Sasha agreed. 'Besides, they're extinct, but no one realizes it. The war has destroyed them all, as the last war destroyed titles and the worst of the social system.'

'Are you a Communist?' Stefanie looked at him with interest.

'No, but I am very much against social barriers. If you love Jack and want to marry him go ahead and do it.'

'My father is going to disinherit me.'

'Let him. Does it matter to you?'

Stefanie studied her knees. 'A bit. We lived in such poverty for so long. I hated it. There was a horrible flat near the Gare du Nord.'

'I know,' Sasha said. 'I was there.'

'I was so angry you didn't come and see me that time.'

'I'd love to have seen you, but it was too risky. I had to see my father, Gran and Grandpa ...' Sasha stared at his cousin feeling suddenly with her a bond of tremendous tenderness. They had in common Russian grandparents, a common family background. Here, among the Askhams and their friends, they were as much aliens as poor Jack. He and she were aliens too – part Russian, part English, part nomad. They were doubly related – brother and sister marrying brother and sister – as had happened before in the family. He knew he had always loved his cousins – lost little girls. Did he now love one more than the others? One who had developed surprisingly quickly into a beautiful woman – yet only eighteen. She couldn't be much more.

She didn't know where her mother was, he had lost a father. They had so much in common. He bent over and took her hand.

'I heard about Grandpa. It was a mistake.'

'It doesn't help though now does it, because it's done?' Stefanie looked fiercely at him. 'You can't bring him back any more than you can bring my mother back.'

'Your mother may come back. I hear all sorts of people keep on turning up who were in the concentration camps.'

'My mother will never turn up,' Stefanie said with a profound air of fatalism. 'She's dead. I know that as much as I know anything, and I will never forgive myself for as long as I live because of what I said to her and thought about her. She will never know, now, how sorry I am.'

It had been a bad day. Stefanie bent her head and, as the tears rolled slowly down her cheeks, Sasha saw the little girl that she had been, the resentful, rebellious, high-spirited little girl who had now become a disturbed and unhappy woman. He kissed the hand he held between his.

461

'Let's go and join the others. You know, I haven't seen them for over three years?'

When she had had her little weep and blown her nose they went down onto the lawn again. The crowd was already beginning to break, drifting in twos and threes towards the car park. The shadows were lengthening on the lawn and the hotel, positioned on a slight hill against a beautiful background of hills and a wood, looked like the gracious country home it had once been – who knows when? Before the First World War perhaps. Who had lived there? What tales could that house have told? That gracious country house, a little smaller than Askham Hall, but not unlike it to look at.

Relaxed in each other's company Sasha and Stefanie strolled about arm in arm. Her beautiful springy black hair glowed in the soft rays of the sun, setting below the level of the trees. Her face seemed to reflect its radiance.

'Don't they look well together?' Charlotte whispered to Arthur as they tried to gather together their brood to leave.

'Well, they're first cousins. They're rather alike.'

'Not really. Stefanie takes after Bobby and Sasha takes after his mother. I agree there is a slight family likeness, but what I mean is that they just seem to go together.'

Charlotte sighed. After two years of marriage to Arthur she could say she was a contented, happy woman; but she always felt she was missing something. Now she was a housewife, a mother, wife of a respectable and rising businessman. Arthur was doing well in the City, where his connections with the aristocracy and his war record certainly had helped. They had two homes – in Holland Park and, now, a country house not far away where they were spending the weekend for the first time. He belonged to all the right clubs; they mixed with the right people.

Most nights Charlotte entertained Arthur's friends, or was entertained by them. Most of them were men who, like Arthur, had gone to the right schools, acquitted themselves well in the war and had now settled into City life. Some of their wives, but

462

not many, had been in the Services or had busied themselves with voluntary work.

But none of them had had a war quite like Charlotte, and the concentration camps had left their mark on her. There was the guilt that one had survived where so many had perished; the luck that one had been able to see normality again. To marry, to have children, to live in a comfortable house. But with the guilt, the relief, there was the nostalgia for days that had gone before; those secret activities in France that she was never allowed to talk about, the very existence of the SOE still being a well-kept secret of the war. People knew she had been in the concentration camps, but not why. If they suspected she had been a spy most people, who she knew anyway, were much too well bred to ask.

So Charlotte lived for her husband, her children and her home as a good wife should; but she still remembered the days of danger, of excitement, of love – of Plus Fort.

'You look awfully thoughtful darling.' Arthur tenderly stroked her cheek. 'Are you thinking of that awful man Jack?'

'No I wasn't as a matter of fact.' Charlotte shook her head.

'We must stop Stefanie from marrying him at all costs. She says she doesn't care about the money.'

'I don't think *we* can do anything to stop her,' Charlotte said with a mysterious smile. 'She's as stubborn as a mule. But there *is*, maybe, someone who can. We talked about him a while ago. Did you by any chance notice the way Sasha looked at her?'

CHAPTER 24

At the age of twenty-five Sasha Ferov was a quiet, controlled young man who seemed much older than his years. He had had rather a lonely childhood, first spent exclusively in the company of his mother and then, uncomfortably, at an English public school as a boarder which he hated. Both experiences had seemed to isolate him from the world even more. Though popular at school, because he was athletic, he was withdrawn and liked to spend a lot of time on his own, reading or walking alone as much as possible in the English countryside.

Accordingly when the war came Sasha was more prepared for its ordeals than many young men of his age, scarcely more than schoolboys. He was resourceful, he could fend for himself and he was unafraid, even in the gunner's cockpit of a Lancaster bomber, the most vulnerable part of the plane, with fires raging below from Berlin, Hamburg or Dresden.

Sasha knew that a lot of people were critical about saturation bombing, but he felt about this, as he did about most things concerning the war, a detachment that helped him to face many of the horrors that, as a sensitive man, he would otherwise have found overwhelming. Many of the air crew who survived became psychiatric cases or alcoholics. Some made bad marriages, and one or two went to gaol for petty crimes. Most found it hard to settle down to civilian life.

Sasha, who had been shot down twice, survived not only physically but mentally. He was in good shape, better, he thought, than when the war had begun, because despite his horrifying experiences he had learned so much.

Though he was not aware of it, what had happened to him, and its part in determining his attitude to life, was very similar to what had occurred to his father Kyril in the eight years he had spent in a Russian prison farm in Siberia.

Both became very detached, emotionally controlled men who avoided exhibitionism of any kind.

Yet, unlike Kyril, Sasha wasn't a cold person. His experiences had not chilled him to the soul as they had a father who could deceive, cheat and kill with impunity, no matter whom. Sasha was a warm man who looked for love in his life, but had not yet found it, not in the deep satisfying way that he craved.

Sometimes he wondered if he ever would, or if he would remain a solitary upon the face of the earth, the cat who walked by itself.

Sasha had liked Air Force life and he stayed on after the war. Finally he accepted a commission and was sent to Singapore as a Flight Lieutenant with a bomber squadron. At the time of Hugo's wedding he had come home on leave; but there was a question mark in his mind about the future, about what he should do with the rest of his life.

Immediately Sasha saw that there was a lot wrong in the family. Bobby obviously had not enjoyed having his daughters at home and had once again banished them, this time with their grandmother, to the country. Here Sasha stayed for part of the time because he loved Irina and more so now that, in her widowhood, she was still so ready and happy to forgive, to make the best of life, to help others, even though the war had so cruelly deprived her of a daughter and a husband.

In the house in which she had worked so many miracles since she had lived there she liked nothing better than sitting after dinner on the terrace in the evening sun with her grandchildren around her. Then she would talk to them of Russia in the days before the Revolution, of the Ferov homes in Petersburg and Moscow and Batum, of those lovely Caucasian summers at Essenelli with the apples lying ripening in the attic rooms infusing the whole house with the smell of cider; of the fat bunches of grapes hanging on the vines along

465

the walls; of the big, fat pink trout in the lake in which, as children, they used to swim and fish.

She would talk to them in Russian and they would listen and answer in the same language, drawn together by that bond of hope that now seemed forever unattainable.

'Your father and mother were married from that house,' Irina said to Sasha with a knowing smile that meant 'and there you were conceived.' Sasha knew what she meant and returned her smile aware that his parents had never lived together again until Bobby had had his father released some eight years later on the direct command of Stalin. Sasha knew that he was conceived in Russia but born in England. In his heart he was an Englishman, but in his poetic soul he was a Slav. It was perhaps this dichotomy of spirit, as well as the war, that had left him with a sense of restlessness.

Listening to Irina, he now leaned forward, his hand on his chin.

'Did you hear from Stefanie,' he asked, 'after the wedding?'

'No, but I heard what happened *at* the wedding.' Irina shook her head. 'He is no good, that man.'

'Baba, you're being prejudiced, like all the family.'

'Why, are they prejudiced?' Irina's wide, kohl-ringed eyes looked at him in surprise. '*I'm* not prejudiced, certainly not. I just don't like him. She wants a father, not a husband and that is what she sees in him. He's *much* too old for her.'

Irina dusted her hands as though in a gesture that would banish him forever if only she could.

'I agree he's too old for her; but to oppose her is to make her more determined to marry him.'

'And the money!' Irina stared at him open-mouthed. 'Did you ever hear of such foolishness? Her father settles a fortune on her and she is prepared to give it all up. They *will* live in poverty, I can tell you, and soon she'll have babies and nothing to feed them on. I know what it's like. Don't tell me please.' Irina shook her head and pulled her shawl over her shoulders as if she were a Russian peasant woman rather than a princess.

At the thought of babies Sasha started. He didn't like to think of Stefanie having babies by that man. He thought of her as she had looked that day, proud and beautiful, very different from the small, rebellious girl growing up in Paris before the war with a mother in prison and never quite enough to eat. He realized then that he felt very possessive towards Stefanie, but he thought that his attitude was that of a brother, who didn't want to see her hurt, married to the wrong man.

A few days after the talk on the terrace Bobby arrived on one of his infrequent inspections of the house which was still not finished. Half of it remained closed, as the country was still in the grip of austerity, and Bobby did not want to appear too obvious in vaunting the wealth he had made from a war that had ruined the lives of so many millions of people, including his relatives. He was surprised to find Sasha still staying with his grandmother, and one day he invited him for a walk in the garden and asked him about his intentions for the future. Bobby didn't like Sasha or, rather, he didn't like his nephew's independence of mind. He had seen a lot of Sasha when he had been at school in England, often spending weekends or short holidays with him and Aileen, and they could never be said to have got on.

For one thing Sasha had always disapproved of the way Bobby had treated his daughters, and not infrequently said so.

Those, however, seemed very far-off days now and Bobby could not help a sneaking admiration for a young man who had performed bravely, and anonymously, in the war and, instead of hanging around as many men did afterwards, had stayed on for a further term in the RAF in order to sort himself out.

Bobby had dined quite amicably with the family, approving of the respectful silence that his daughters maintained in his presence without speculating about the reason for it. He questioned them about their prospects for the future – Olga now being seventeen and preparing for Oxford entrance. She had missed so much because of the war and took her School

467

Certificate a year after everyone else, but quickly caught up and superseded them. Olga had a brain.

Natasha, at fifteen, was at the same school as her sister and had no intention of following her academic aspirations. Natasha wanted to marry and have babies as soon as she could; she yearned for security and domesticity, an end to living off other people. Sometimes she felt that she and her sisters were like hens scratching around in the earth for nourishment. She wanted nothing better than a prosperous husband, a nice home and a life that went on in a smooth, relentless course from one year to the other and didn't change from day to day.

'They've turned out well those girls,' Bobby said as he and Sasha began a turn round the garden puffing at large Havanas, naturally a gift of Bobby which were, in turn, a gift from one of his many grateful clients. Bobby practically lived on graft: bribing others and being bribed in return. Almost everything he used, even some of his cars, were the result of favours done or received. Like many very rich people he was an expert in the art of not spending money.

'Did you expect them *not* to?' Sasha smiled to himself in the growing dusk.

'Well, after what they've been through ... not that I can say the same of Stefanie. Well, she knows how I feel.'

'You mean about Jack?'

'Is that that person's name? She always calls him Major something or other to me.'

'Blackstock-Thomas.'

'Blackstock-Thomas!' Bobby stopped and roared with laughter. ' "Thomas" he added himself after the war. Just the kind of jumped-up cove I detest. They had a good war and think they own the world. They're nothing, yet they can't go back to what they were.'

'All the same, why won't you let her marry him if she loves him, Uncle? It's a very different world to what it was when you were young.'

'You can say that again!' Bobby said. 'My goodness, don't I regret the old days when women knew their place, and kept it. Not that I could say that for many of the women of my family,' he added, after a moment or two of reflection, 'but I'm not talking about the gentry.'

Sasha wondered if he were talking about Aileen who had kept her place for years and had now quite firmly left it, but he said nothing.

'No, I don't like that Major fellow,' Bobby went on, frowning. 'But there's nothing to stop her marrying him. When she's of age I shan't stand in her way. I'm not saying she can't marry who she likes when she's twenty-one,' a note of caution crept into Bobby's voice. 'But not with my money. I'm not supporting someone I don't like and disapprove of to live on my money for the rest of his life. There have been enough people like that in this family. I've told Stefanie she can marry whosoever she likes when she's of age but not on my money. If she is to be an heiress, and that was my intention, she must marry someone I approve of, someone of her own class.

'I most emphatically do not approve of Blackstock, and that's that.'

Sasha didn't want to persuade his uncle to change his mind; he didn't even try. In his heart he knew that he didn't like Blackstock either, not only because he felt he was unsuitable for Stefanie, too old for her and in all probability a gold digger, but his own feelings about his cousin had caused him some emotional turbulence ever since Hugo's wedding. He could hardly get her out of his mind.

'What are your own plans now, Sasha?' Bobby said expansively as if reading his thoughts. 'I know we haven't always got on, seen eye to eye. But now that you're a man perhaps you can see what makes someone like me behave like I do. I feel I'm responsible for an extended family, and it's no mean burden, I can tell you. I can do with a capable chap like you – and I admire what you've done – to help me. Tell me, do you want to stay on in the RAF? I hear you have three months' leave.'

'Six weeks is almost up,' Sasha said, glad of his uncle's confidence even if he didn't agree with most of it. Bobby was an artist in self-deception. He kicked the stones of the path at his feet as they walked towards the river. One half of the house was completely covered with scaffolding, for restoration and repair. Then, according to Bobby, it would be one of the finest properties south of the Wash if not in the whole of England.

'Are you going back to Singapore?'

'I don't think so. I did think I might not renew my commission, Uncle. See a bit of the world maybe. After all, I helped to free it.'

'Capital idea my boy,' Bobby said approvingly, 'and, of course, you have the money to do it, thanks to your mother. No problems there I suppose?'

'Financially you mean, Uncle? Oh no, none at all. Even without mother's allowance I have achieved independence on my own. I have no family and my pay has been quite adequate for my means.'

'That's what I like.' Bobby felt more and more satisfaction as the conversation progressed. 'A man who knows the value of money.'

'I thought I might go and see Gran, Mother and Anna in Venice. They seem to have decided to live there.'

Bobby frowned. 'Well your grandmother is very nervous about returning back to France until memories of the war have quite cleared. I say she is in no trouble, she's English; but she was perhaps unwisely too friendly with the Germans. I daresay I might have done the same thing myself if I'd been there. We always had many good German friends – a very civilized people, but for Hitler. Your grandmother's attitude was, – what can one person do against so many?'

Thinking of Hélène and Charlotte, Sasha felt his anger beginning to rise but Bobby went on.

'Well, maybe you don't approve, but your grandmother is

470

an old lady now. She seems to like Venice anyway and there is a casino for dotty old Denton there as in Monte Carlo. He spends his time on the Lido, playing roulette. Yes, do go and see them, they'd love it. As for your father ...' Bobby paused to puff smoke in the air, 'God knows what's happened to him.'

'I *am* worried about my father,' Sasha said quietly. 'You know we have completely lost touch with him? I did think I might set out and see what's happened to him too. I hoped that by this time we'd have heard from him, or something about him.'

'Well you'll be dabbling in murky waters there,' Bobby frowned again. 'Never could make out that man. Never liked him, to tell you the truth.' He slapped an arm round Sasha's shoulder. 'But you knew that didn't you? He was never at all grateful for what one did for him. Was he a Fascist or was he a Communist? No one knows. Did he side with Germany or did he continue to be a Bolshevik? Who can say?'

'Em said he was in Berlin as a Russian Colonel.'

'Yes, but she never saw him. No one did. She said Ralph did, but we can't know for sure ...' Bobby sighed. 'I feel a real burden of responsibility with Ralph gone. I feel that I'm virtually the head of the family.' His hand tightened round Sasha's neck. 'You know, Sasha, I'm getting quite fond of you. I'll be honest with you, I never liked you much as a boy. You had a touch of impudence which I found offensive. You were quite rude to me at times. But that's all over now. Why don't you think about coming into my business when you've been round the world? Don't say anything now, but think about it. In time, of course, I'm hoping to persuade that young scamp David to join me and I'm sure he will; but another member of the family ... think about it eh?'

After his talk with his uncle, Sasha resigned his commission in the RAF, not because he wanted to go into Bobby's business but because he did want to have time to think and reflect. He took a short lease on a flat in Mayfair and decided to have the good time he'd missed as a young man by going on dangerous bombing raids nightly over enemy territory. He decided to enjoy himself.

Much later Sasha wondered why he did leave the RAF when he hadn't meant to, and why he stayed in London instead of immediately going abroad. He wondered how much of it was fate and how much a deliberate, if largely subconscious, decision on his part.

He knew even then that Stefanie had something to do with it. He was drawn to his cousin by a force, the source of which remained obscure. He didn't think it was because of love, though he loved her; he thought that it was because he felt unhappy about Stefanie and, because of her mother, who had helped to save his life, felt a responsibility for her. She was always somewhere in his thoughts, somewhere at the back of his mind.

Stefanie was the person the whole family loved and worried about. She had a quality that attracted love and admiration – a spirit of independence, yet a vulnerability. She was constantly on people's minds, because of the way her lifestyle resembled that of her mother.

The other two – Olga and Natasha – although with the same background and parentage, somehow didn't occupy the attention so much of those who cared for them. Their destinies seemed much more straightforward – over that of their sister there hung a question mark.

In those months at the end of 1947, while Stefanie hesitated about marrying Jack, Sasha saw a lot of her. He became a dear familiar, not only a friend but a cousin with whom she shared so much of the past, and he used to pop in at all hours for a drink or to take her out to lunch. Although there was still strict rationing, many of the better restaurants were slowly regaining their former glamour, and there was good food and wine to be had by those who knew where to look.

Stefanie kept up her modelling in a desultory kind of way, but Sasha could tell she wasn't happy.

'If it's Jack,' he said one day, 'why don't you get rid of him?'

'Oh, I couldn't get rid of Jack!' Stefanie looked quite shocked. 'Besides I wouldn't want to.'

They were lunching at a small restaurant in St Christopher's Lane near Stefanie's flat. Sasha seldom saw her at night, because nights were reserved for Jack and Jack was jealous, not only of Sasha but also of all Stefanie's 'toffee-nosed relations', he called them, who tried to come between him and her. Jack had very little recollection of the stir he'd caused at Hugo's wedding, so that didn't disturb him much or strike him as a reason for Stefanie's relations disliking him even more than they had before.

'Are you really in love with Jack?'

Stefanie didn't notice how tense Sasha's face had gone as she looked at him in surprise.

'Of course I'm "really in love" with him. I want to marry him.'

'Is it your father, or rather the money, that's stopping you?'

'Not at all.' Stefanie gave a derisive laugh. 'You forget how many years I lived in poverty, Sasha. I'm *quite* used to being without money. The real problem is my age and the fact that I can't marry without Father's permission. I've told Jack I'll go away with him to some place where we can marry, but he's reluctant to do this. He thinks it would be a bad start to the marriage. Money is certainly no problem. Jack now has very good prospects in the film business, you know. He's doing really well.'

Somehow the look on Stefanie's face made Sasha doubt that she believed much of what she'd said and, after he'd seen her home, he went back to his flat feeling sick at heart.

It was probably then that he realized his love for her was not only that of a cousin.

Jack was in a very bad mood when he came in one night a few weeks later. As usual Stefanie was lying down and he stormed into her room and dragged the bedclothes off her.

'For God's sake get up,' he shouted. 'Are you ill or something?'

'I feel tired.'

'You *always* feel tired,' Jack said. 'You're a young girl and you shouldn't always feel so bloody tired. Oh my God, I've had a terrible day.'

Jack suddenly collapsed onto the end of the bed and held his head in his hand, swaying backwards and forwards.

'Jack, what is it?' Alarmed, Stefanie sat up in bed and put out her arms.

'Everything has just gone so bloody wrong,' he said. 'Things never seem to come out as I expect them to. There are so many dishonest buggers around, you mark my words.'

'Darling, let's get married,' Stefanie said urgently. 'Tomorrow, the day after.'

'You have to have your father's permission and you know you won't get that. It's not his money I'm after, you know that.'

'Let's go to Gretna! Oh Jack, it would be the most wonderful present in the world for me.'

Jack gazed at her and putting his arms round her kissed her harshly on the lips. Then he drew her shift over her head and stared at her, his eyes almost starting from their sockets. She could smell drink on his breath and after he'd pushed her roughly back on the bed his lovemaking was functional and crude, leaving her dissatisfied. Not for the first time Stefanie lay beside him afterwards wide awake, for a long time wondering what his power over her was. For he had power, even though he was no gentleman, even though he had no money, and even though she saw through his bluff. He had a power over her that induced in her at all times this slave-like servility and submission.

Was it his age, the fact that he was twenty-three years her senior, only a few years younger than her father, that gave her this compulsion to do his bidding? As he snored beside her she gazed at the ceiling and remembered the story about her

474

mother and the man she'd killed. Had her mother felt like that about him – loving him yet hating him too. In a way, a bit as she felt about Jack?

Stefanie looked at him lying beside her, his face on the pillow puffed with sleep. Like that he was quite repulsive ... but she knew that very soon he'd be transformed, freshly shaved, in a clean shirt, the shiny surface of his thick black hair gleaming, the perfect Brylcreem Boy. He had power and he had fascination.

Yet she knew she could never leave Jack if only because she would be acknowledging her mistake in the eyes of her family. She remembered Hugo's wedding – the way she had flaunted Jack, introducing him as her fiancé, and defended him when he made a fool of her, and himself, in public.

The family would remember her mother and then they would say about her ... like mother, like daughter.

No, this affair had gone too far.

She sighed and, for a moment or two, she closed her eyes and slept.

Later that night, Jack's good humour restored, they dined by candlelight at the window overlooking Marylebone Lane. Stefanie was a good cook, having learned the domestic skills by the side of her grandmother and old Masha during the hard days in Paris. Jack always said it was a miracle how she could turn out the good things she did. She even made potato soup delicious.

'Never thought I'd eat potato soup again after those days in the Army. God.' Jack shook his head and reached over for her hand. 'We'll live as happy as two bugs in a blanket. But, darling, no Gretna Green for us, we do need your old man's cash...'

Stefanie looked at him in amazement. 'You just said we didn't.'

'When did I say that?' Jack looked up from greedily spooning his soup.

'An hour ago, when we were in bed.'

'Oh, people say all kinds of things then.' He smiled and winked. 'Can't say I remember it.'

'There's a lot you don't remember,' Stefanie said in a steely tone that many people were familiar with but which Jack seldom heard. With Jack, Stefanie was quite different.

'If you want a row I can't be bothered, Stefanie,' Jack said in a weary voice. 'I've got a lot of worries and I don't want any more. I'm telling you though ...' and here he looked up at her, 'I'm not marrying you at Gretna or anywhere else without your father's cash. I can't.'

Stefanie drew back her chair from the table and reached over for her cigarettes, food forgotten.

'I thought you said you loved me?'

'I do love you, but I can't marry you if that old man cuts you off. I couldn't have the responsibility of a wife...'

'And kids ...'

'Well, yes, and kids. I couldn't have the responsibility.'

'I'm pregnant,' Stefanie said, and for a moment Jack, who had returned his spoon to his plate, went on eating as though he hadn't heard. Stefanie said it again.

'I heard you the first time,' Jack said, raising his head; 'you'll have to get rid of the bloody thing. You should have taken more care.'

'*You* should have taken more care,' Stefanie shouted. 'You knew about these things and I didn't. You were the one with all the experience.'

'Well what's done is done.' Jack also lit a cigarette. 'If you're sure.'

'I am sure. I went to the doctor because I've been so tired. I thought I was run down, anaemic. He said I was three months pregnant.'

'My God,' Jack said shaking his head, 'and you didn't know. You really are a child.'

'Don't you *want* to be a father, Jack?' Stefanie adopted a wheedling tone and, rising, went over to him attempting to lay her head on his shoulder.

'Not at the moment, I certainly don't. A bride, a baby and no job ... no thank you.'

'No job?' Stefanie said, raising her head. 'I thought things were going well?'

'Well they're not and that's honest.' Jack roughly pushed her away and got up from the table. He went to the sideboard and poured himself a large whisky, about the fifth he'd had that night. 'I thought I had a good position with this new company cashing in on the nostalgia film market, but they've gone bust. Not enough capital. I heard today.'

'That's why you were in a bad mood? It's not the end of the world, Jack.'

'Well it is at the moment.' Jack drank from his glass. He smiled ruefully and held out his hand. 'Sorry, darling, but it was one hell of a day to talk about babies and weddings. You'll just have to get rid of it.'

'How?'

Jack wrinkled his nose as though he hated talking about something unpleasant. 'I don't know. Don't you have a girlfriend you can ask? There are these places, these women...'

'But it's horrible *and* dangerous ...'

'Well I'm sorry,' Jack shook his head, 'that's the way it will have to be.'

'And if I won't have an abortion?' Stefanie stepped back thrusting her head in the air.

'You're bloody well going to *have* to have an abortion, my girl. Either that or ask your bloody father for some money to make the whole thing respectable and set me up in business.'

'You know he won't do that.'

'I haven't even met the bastard.' Jack tipped more whisky recklessly into his glass. 'He doesn't even want to see me. Doesn't like me sleeping with his daughter, the High and Mighty "Honourable" Stefanie. Wait until he knows I've put the Honourable in the pudding club.' Jack chuckled and leered at Stefanie swaying slightly on his feet.

'What a horrible thing to say.'

'Well it's true isn't it Miss High and Mighty Princess? I'm nothing, you know, and your family know it too. I'm nothing and I never will be anything.'

'What about the war?'

'What *about* the war? Commissioned in the paymaster corps? All I ever did was sit at a table and hand out cash.'

'I thought you fought at El Alamein?'

'That was just a story, wasn't it?'

'I said my cousin Ralph was there and you said you were too.'

'Bloody Earl of Askham.' Jack raised his eyes to heaven. 'I'd have shot him in the bum if I'd have seen him.'

'Jack – you're drunk again. Don't be so *foul* ...'

'*Foul?*' Jack turned slowly and looked at her. 'You call *me* foul you little tart? Threw yourself at me, couldn't wait to get your drawers down, you horrible little slut you...'

'You ...' Stefanie rushed over to him and began to tear at his face. As Jack gripped both her hands she could see the hatred in his eyes.

'Now look, Princess, don't you start doing that to me. You're a little tart and your mother was a tart. You told me her room was full of airmen...'

'That was because she was *helping* them ...' Stefanie tried frantically to free herself from his iron clasp.

'Helping them? Yes, I bet she was. Helping them – I know how. You've got bad blood in you, my girl, and it shows. My God it shows. How your family can look down on me I don't know. At least my mother was respectable. She may not have been rich or very high and mighty, nor an "honourable", but she wasn't a tart and she wasn't a murderess...'

Jack gave a scream as Stefanie bit hard into his wrist, so hard that a gash appeared from which blood started first to ooze and then pour.

Jack released her hand and, one hand over his wrist, hopped about on one leg shouting: 'My God the bitch!'

Stefanie rushed into the bedroom to get something to wrap

478

round his wound but seizing a knife from the table Jack followed her. As she turned he kneed her in the crotch and she fell back onto the bed. Crouching on top of her Jack began hacking at her clothes with the blunt knife, stopping every second or two to brandish it at her, like a spear.

'I'm going to bloody well give you an abortion myself you little whore. Just you wait. Pregnant are you? You won't be when I've finished…'

The blood from his hand was now all over the bed and the weight of his body stifled Stefanie so that she couldn't even scream. She tried to open her mouth but no sound came, and as the waves of nausea started to overwhelm her she slid slowly from under Jack onto the floor.

Jack recovering himself, shaken into sobriety, looked at her and thought she was dead. Hastily he rearranged her clothes, pulled the cover over the bed and went into the bathroom to put a towel round his hand. Then, steeling himself, he went into the sitting room, poured himself another whisky and sat down breathing hard. After a while he went into the bedroom and saw that she was breathing. He lifted her onto the bed and covered her with the bedclothes. Then he put the lights out in all the rooms and quietly left the flat.

'Sasha.' Stefanie's voice sounded very weak and faint. 'Sasha, can you come? Come quickly, Sasha.'

Sasha looked at the clock and saw it was nearly dawn.

'Where are you?' he said.

'At home. Come quickly. I'm dying, Sasha. Hurry.'

Sasha dressed in three minutes and was out of his flat in five, hailing a cab which happened to be cruising up Park Street on its way out of Park Lane.

Only twenty minutes or so had passed since she'd rung him when he pressed the street bell of Stefanie's flat, his heart painful in his chest. For a minute nothing happened and he rang again, and then he was about to ring all the other bells in the block when the street door swung open and he rushed up to the second floor two steps at a time.

The door to Stefanie's flat was half open, but the only light was from the bedroom. When he saw the blood on the bed he cried 'My God' and then he turned to find Stefanie limping out of the room towards him, her gown clasped round her naked body. There was an ugly gash by her mouth, and blood everywhere.

As she rushed to him he folded her in his arms.

'What happened Stefanie? Who did all this? What happened? Are you all right?'

She started to nod her head and then he felt her body go slack and she would have fallen in a heap onto the floor but for his arm holding her up.

He gently laid her on the sofa, covered her up and then he dialled 999 and asked for an ambulance.

'Miss Ferov is much better now,' the doctor said several hours later. He was an impersonal, competent young man doing his first house job after qualifying. 'Are you a relation?'

'Her first cousin.'

'I see. Did you know that she was pregnant?'

Sasha shook his head. 'Has she lost the baby?'

'Oh no.'

'But there was blood all over the place.'

'Apparently someone with her, her boyfriend I gather, got bitten in a fight. Wounds like that bleed a great deal. They can also be dangerous so he should have it seen to. I expect they were both drunk. She can go home when you're ready. Has she anywhere to go to?'

'Of course.' Sasha resented the fact that this supercilious young man seemed to think she was someone from the street.

'Well, she can go when you like. She should rest for today and then have a check-up with her own doctor in a week's time. There's nothing wrong, no bones fractured, no lacerations. It was just some awful drunken row. People should take more care.'

'I'll get a cab at once,' Sasha said, and went out onto the street in Paddington to look for one.

The first snow of the winter had fallen and the grounds of Robertswood were covered by what looked like a very faint layer of white dust. The trees were for the most part completely bare, though Stefanie's great-grandfather, Sir Robert, had planted a number of conifers and firs to hide the house from the curious gazes of those passing by on the river in the summer. These now waved back and forwards against the skyline, swaying in the wind, causing Stefanie to imagine that they made a fanciful pattern of shifting turbulence. Like her life: back and forwards, back and forth, no stability, ever.

The family were told that Stefanie had had a nervous breakdown and that Jack had gone. Everyone was thankful for that, though they thought it was a pity that she had to have a nervous breakdown before she saw how unsuitable he was. The flat in Marylebone, cleaned up by Sasha, was handed back to the landlord with the keys. Sasha had always thought it a horrible place anyway, functional and impersonal, like a den of sin.

He brought her to the family home where she was received with love by her sisters and grandmother, even by her father who said it was a pity she had to learn the hard way. Rachel sent flowers and Em and Charlotte came over to visit. Charlotte, who suspected more than everyone else, stayed a few days; but she could get nothing out of Stefanie and very little more out of Sasha, who protectively hovered around the invalid lying languidly in her bed like the lady with the camelias.

'It's a very good thing that she sent for you,' Charlotte said to him, looking at the same swaying trees that Stefanie could see from the bedroom window. It was a cold day and Charlotte stood hunched in a warm coat and a woolly hat.

'I'm glad I was there,' Sasha said. 'I was on the verge of going away. I thought I'd spend Christmas in Venice with Mother.'

'Why don't you go, and take Stefanie with you?' Charlotte said. 'It would be an excellent thing for you both.'

'Do you think she'd go?' Sasha looked at her and then again at the trees.

'I think she'd probably love to get away from the memories of that awful man. I suspect he beat her, but neither of you are saying anything. She's very special to us both isn't she?' Charlotte said gently, taking his arm. 'We both love her, because we loved her mother. Take her away with you, look after her, Sasha, for the sake of Hélène ... wherever she is.'

'If you think I should, and she'll come, I will,' he said looking at her with gratitude. 'Thank you Charlotte.'

In the event there was no problem at all. Stefanie was only too glad to go, her secret still safe from the family.

They were married in Paris, on the way to Venice, in an abbreviated service in the Russian Orthodox Church. There were no family present and only the priest and his house-keeper, a sacristan and some pious members of the congregation.

It was a most un-Askham-like wedding because the family had always liked a fuss. When eventually they heard about it they would be furious; but, had they known the truth, perhaps Sasha and Stefanie would be forgiven for the haste.

CHAPTER 25

Peter Klein never spoke much at breakfast time. He had toast and black coffee while he read *The Times*, then he usually went into his study to read the foreign papers and work. Emily had moved into a large flat in Earl's Court for the sake of Peter, so that he could have plenty of space and privacy.

In the time they had lived together, nearly three years, Em had done everything she could to make Peter happy. But she'd never felt she'd succeeded. He was a quiet, withdrawn man of few words, haunted by the past, and he never shared confidences with her. In a way he was very like Felipe, and Em wondered what it was in herself that attracted men who didn't appreciate her. Her mother thought it was a need for self-sacrifice because not only had she acquired two very difficult lovers at various times in her life, both exiled from their homes, but she had lost her son into the bargain, the only person that she really adored. Felipe had kept Em's house and Em's son, and Em's income was divided between two rather selfish men who felt they had a right to what they could get.

It wasn't that Peter Klein was intentionally selfish. But he felt he was living on borrowed time, time to which he had no right. More than Charlotte he was obsessed by guilt, by the memory of the thousands of those who died while he had survived, by the atrocities and horrible things that went on in the camp.

Peter was grateful to Em and the Askham family. He didn't like to think he had taken advantage of her or them, as Felipe had. But he couldn't live on gratitude any more than he could live on memories and, one morning, as he watched Em buttering her toast, reading *The Sentinel* propped up on the coffee pot while he flicked through *The Times*, he said:

'I think I should go back to Germany.'

'Oh?' Emily didn't look up. 'How long for?'

'For good.'

Em then raised her head, removed her glasses, shook back her hair.

'For ever?'

'It is my country.'

'I thought you said you never wanted to see it again?'

'That was in 1945. This is 1948. A lot of Jews are going back. There is compensation, reparation. In my own country I could get a job on a newspaper. Here I can't because I can't get a work permit for anything else than domestic work.'

'Mummy *has* tried,' Em said apologetically. 'It's just there are so many people after jobs.'

'Exactly,' Peter said. 'I'm not complaining. Why should they make a German Jew an editor of an English newspaper when there are so many Englishmen more suitable for the job? I quite see your mother's point of view.'

'I think you're being deliberately nasty now.' Em swung her glasses in front of her.

Peter mopped his lips and neatly folded his napkin in the ring with the Askham crest. 'I assure you, my dear Em, I'm not being nasty. I'm grateful.'

'What about me?' Em said.

'Do you want to come back with me?' Peter looked surprised.

'Do you want me to come back with you?'

'I never thought about it,' Peter confessed.

In fact he'd never thought about her at all. Suddenly he felt even more guilty – guilt added to guilt. He put his head in his hands. 'Sorry.'

'That's quite all right. Why should you think about me when it's your future?'

'But you're part of my future too,' Peter said, not very convincingly.

Em got up and walked to the fire, tapping the log with her

foot. It was very cold, and nearly three years after the end of the war fuel was still short. In fact there were still many shortages in England as well as the rest of Europe. These logs came from Robertswood.

'Am I?' Em said turning to him. 'I don't think I am, Peter. You *have* tried to love me, but you can't.'

'That's not true,' Peter said. 'I do love you, but in my own way. I am not a demonstrative man.'

He was certainly not that, Em thought bitterly. They had made love six times in the last six months. She always felt that Dachau was responsible for Peter's lack of passion, but was it really very important, anyway, when people loved each other?

But did they? It was love of a kind, as Peter said, love based on necessity and gratitude. Peter seemed to be always saying 'thank you'. The Askhams didn't give because they wanted thanks; Bobby didn't send the logs because he wanted gratitude; but Peter couldn't seem to understand this. He went round and round saying 'thank you' until people got sick of it and told him to stop.

'Well, when shall you go?' Em said.

'I thought quite soon, if you don't mind. Then you can come and join me if you want to.'

'I'm not sure about that,' Em said. 'I'd have to think about it. Frankly, I'd like to have been consulted.'

Peter got up and, coming over to her, kissed her chastely on the cheek. 'You're very understanding Em,' he said shyly. 'Thank you. I'll start making arrangements today.'

Peter walked out of the room with more of a spring in his step than Em remembered ever having seen for some time. He really was glad to be going; glad to be independent. Maybe he'd thought of her, of the family, as gaolers.

Em looked at the mirror over the mantelpiece and then put her forehead on the cold marble top. She was nearly forty and, once again, she was going to be on her own.

Rachel thought the business about Askham Hall had dragged

on for long enough and she had agreed to go to court on Hugo's behalf. Hugo had been married six months and he knew how long it would take to get the Hall into any kind of order. The place, empty now for nearly three years, was falling apart. Sometimes Rachel thought that was what Bobby wanted, so that it would have to be pulled down and he could build something else in its place, maybe a fine new hotel with all modern conveniences. If they didn't act soon that's what would happen.

So she and Adam and the other family trustees decided to issue a writ to get Bobby to take some action. This was done with great reluctance, because it would widen the rift in the family – a rift people would like to see closed since the surprising and sudden secret marriage of Sasha and Stefanie who were still honeymooning abroad. Rachel also had memories of the awful scandal in 1912 when the Askhams last went to court but this move was not intended to end up in court, but to try and get Bobby to see some sense.

Christopher Bolingbroke, now a prosperous solicitor with his own large practice, acted for the trust and applied for a writ on behalf of the trustees which was served on Bobby.

When he received it Bobby was so enraged he nearly tore it into pieces and instructed his own solicitors to issue a counter writ. Bobby had the money, and the time, to get into a very long legal wrangle indeed. He didn't mind what happened to Askham Hall so long as Hugo didn't get it. That property was reserved for his son, David. It was that which would bring David back to him again.

Bobby was only a year away from his fiftieth birthday. He had been born in 1899 when Queen Victoria still ruled over an empire that had been created in her lifetime. That empire had twice come to the aid of the mother country in time of war in the present century, and on both occasions Bobby had remained at home while others of his family fought in the field. The first time Bobby had been too young, a boy of fifteen when war started; and in the war that had recently finished he had considered himself too old. He had thought he could serve his country in other ways.

For Bobby service of one's country and self-interest happily coincided. As the nation fought for freedom and survival Bobby's business expertise helped considerably in the process. Not only did he become a very wealthy man, as a result – wealthier than he had been before – but he achieved a lifetime's ambition and became a baron of the United Kingdom, thus fulfilling the dream of his grandfather.

Bobby had known that business interests alone wouldn't bring him a barony, so he had used his money for charitable purposes where people noticed it most; where members of the Royal Family were patrons or where the cause was dear to their hearts, or those of other prominent people. Bobby had taken with one hand and given away with the other, keeping just a little more in the right hand than he gave away with the left. Thus his charity was as self-interested as his entrepreneurial activities.

But at the age of forty-nine, although he could consider that he had everything he had ever wanted in life, great wealth, a peerage, large houses, a string of racehorses, he lacked one thing: love. He had always found it hard to give love and people always found it hard to love him. Their love, like his, was self-interested too.

There was one person however for whom Bobby would sacrifice everything he had in exchange for his love: his son David. He would beg, borrow and steal for David; sell his soul for him. He loved David with all his heart and wanted to be loved by him.

Yet David's progress or lack of it had worried him. David had no ambition. David seemed to lack direction and Bobby felt that he must do all in his power to give it to him.

This was really what the fight over Askham Hall was all about. If David had no ambition Bobby would be ambitious for him. He would tie his son down, give him a career and, at the same time, a stake in the ancestral home of his grandmother's family:

Askham Hall. Once David had Askham Hall the Askhams were virtually finished; written off the map. Paul would be a minor for several more years; the family had no money; Askham House was sold and Askham Hall would be renamed after the Lightermans.

Subconsciously, all his life, Bobby had worked to obliterate the Askhams, and at last he was on the verge of success.

Bobby prepared the ground very carefully before he spoke seriously to David. He made sure that he was in as relaxed and happy a frame of mind as he could before he invited him to lunch at the Hampstead house. Aileen was away in connection with some charity she was interested in to do with the displaced persons who were still housed in camps all over Europe.

David seemed naturally suspicious at receiving this summons from his father and delayed it as much as he could, putting him off several times at the last minute, something that made Bobby fume.

Eventually David arrived in the MG Sports Bobby had given him for his twentieth birthday. For once David looked neat and conventionally attired in a tweed suit with a tie. His hair was quite short. Expecting a roasting for something or the other David had decided to placate his father for once if he could. He knew he usually gave him a bad time but now he wanted a favour.

'Cheers, Father,' he said, raising his glass before lunch. 'Very good news about Sasha and Stefanie.'

'Isn't it good?' Bobby looked pleased that David was in such a harmonious frame of mind. 'I don't normally approve of marriages between close relations, but in this case I do. Stefanie needs to settle down and Sasha is the man to help her settle. I don't quite understand what happened with "the Major" but she was lucky Sasha was on hand. He wrote me that he'd always loved her. Does she love him, though?' Bobby looked at David as though wishing to draw his son into his confidence. David though wouldn't be drawn. He wasn't close to the sisters he hardly knew and scarcely ever saw. So he remained standing, drinking his pre-lunch sherry and nodding affably with his father.

'I hope he'll come into the business.' Bobby looked at David from under his furrowed brow. 'As I know you're not keen.'

'Not a bit, Father.' Relieved, David helped himself to another sherry, pleased to find the old man in a good mood, for once. 'I *did* want to ask you...'

'Ask away, but over lunch,' Bobby said expansively as the butler appeared to announce it was on the table. 'And I've one or two interesting ideas to put to *you*.'

David liked his food and Bobby had ensured that the meal was excellent. At first the conversation was desultory, about the state of the nation and the awful things the Labour government were doing. Bobby prophesied that Churchill would soon be asked once again to run the country.

'Nationalization is the sure way to ruin,' Bobby said. 'My goodness, if they try and get their hands on any of my businesses, I tell you, I'd go abroad.'

'Anywhere special, Father?'

'I've always liked America,' Bobby said, pouring wine into David's glass. '*That* is the land of opportunities.'

David brightened.

'About what I was going to ask you, Father.'

'Ask away,' Bobby said again, helping himself to sole.

'I rather wanted to get into the music business.'

'The what?'

'Music: you know – da-de-dum-dum,' David hummed a popular tune.

'Oh *that* sort of music? You don't want to be a conductor and have me buy you a symphony orchestra do you?' Bobby laughed, evidently enjoying his own good humour.

'No, but I'd quite like a band, Father.' David strummed an imaginary guitar.

'Like Geraldo?'

'No, no, jazz, you know, *that* kind of thing.'

'You want a *jazz* band?' Bobby's attitude changed dramatically. 'But it's out of the question.'

'But why, Father?'

'Because I don't like that kind of thing. I'm prepared to be indulgent to my only son but I don't want him to be a *jazz* musician...'

'Why not?'

'I just don't.'

'Well, whatever I do, America's the place to be. I'd like to live there.'

'Well, you're not having a penny of my money to do it,' Bobby said shortly, 'and that's that. I've asked you to join my business and you won't. All right, you're not attracted to business. But I have asked you here, David, to put another plan to you. I'd at least like you to consider it. I think you'll like it.'

'I'm sure I shan't,' David said truculently, drinking his wine.

'Well listen,' Bobby's tone was placating. 'I think you may. You know Askham Hall...'

Bobby outlined, with painstaking detail, the problems of Askham Hall, its past and his plans for it. David scarcely appeared to be listening until Bobby said:

'And you could run it any way you liked, a fine country house hotel with, say, the best golf links and stables in England. The lake could be used for fishing and boating and...'

'Did you say *me* run it?' David said incredulously.

'Yes, you. I'm prepared to go to court to get that place. It is part of our family. It was my grandmother's home, my mother's home. Generations of the Earls of Askham have lived there. I don't want that bastard to have it.'

'What bastard, Father?' David gave him a rather cheeky smile. 'Are you talking about me?'

'I am certainly *not* talking about you,' Bobby said crossly. 'As you know quite well you were legitimized when I married your mother. I have always done the right thing by you, young

490

man, so don't give me any of your lip. Hugo wants it to run as a farm and I...'

'Let Hugo have it...'

'I don't want Hugo to have it! You don't seem to understand what I'm driving at.'

'I *do* understand, Father.' David stabbed his finger at him, waving it rudely up and down in front of his father's face. 'You're up to your tricks again. Always interfering. Hugo wants the Hall, you don't like him and you don't want him to have it.'

'Hugo has been opposing me and getting all the family to oppose me too.'

'Good for Hugo, and good for them. I oppose you as well, Father...'

'You always have,' Bobby snapped at him. 'That's nothing unusual. At last I find something that I think might appeal to you. I can't see why it doesn't appeal to you. Your own country hotel. You can go to the Ritz or the Savoy, any hotel you like in London or the Continent to train. While I'm doing up the place you'll have the time. I'm sure that once the family realizes that I'm adamant and you're interested they'll back down.'

David neatly put his knife and fork together and rose from the table. He stuck his hands in his pockets and strolled rather insolently round to where his father was sitting. Then he leaned over him:

'Lord Lighterman of Robertswood, *Baron* Lighterman, I do not want to run a hotel. I have no interest in the catering business whatever. I don't know how you got the idea I would be. I don't like catering, I don't like business, I don't like you. How long is it going to take you to realize that, Father? You are the most disliked man I know. I can't think of one friend you have in the world. Even Mother can't stand you and keeps as far away from you as she can. She's never here – or haven't you noticed? None of the family have more to do with you than they can help. You've practically ruined the Askham family by your greed and now you want to snatch the Hall. Don't think

I don't know about the deal with Ralph Askham when he was too besotted by love to know what he was doing...'

Bobby jumped up and flung his napkin down on the table, pointing at his son.

'Don't you *dare* talk to me like that. I did Ralph Askham a favour. He was such a fool...'

'All the family are fools, Father, except you, grasping Bobby who turns every shilling he makes into a fiver, a tenner, a hundred pounds.' David dramatically flung his arms into the air. 'Who cares? Who wants it? I don't. You stopped Stefanie marrying a man she loved. You kicked your first wife out of the house, plus your three daughters, yet when Stefanie wanted to marry the man she loved you wouldn't let her. Mind you he *was* a bum and maybe you were right, for once, I won't argue there. But you didn't know; you didn't care. You didn't even meet him. Money, money, money, Lord Lighterman, that's all you're interested in. Money and getting your own way. Someone opposes you? Bankrupt him, threaten him, take him to court.

'You may think I don't know all this business about Askham Hall, but I do. I may not see much of the family but I do know what is going on. I like Hugo and I want him to have the Hall if he wants it. It belonged to *his* father. You're not an Askham, by the way, but a Lighterman, grandson of a grocer. Hugo *is* an Askham and I'm sure he'll make a wonderful thing of running the Hall. He deserves it.'

David paused to recover his breath and Bobby slumped into a chair, pouring himself more wine, with hands that shook. He started to mumble in a low voice but David raised his hands, like a man summoning the avenging angel.

'Let me finish, please. I don't want Askham Hall, Father, to run as a hotel or a brothel. I don't want any part of it. I don't want Robertswood or this huge, airless, graceless mansion or any of your money. If you think I can't manage by myself I can. If you think I'm lazy I am, I have been, but I'm going to change. I'm going to America and I'm going to stay there. I came here to ask for your support, but after today I'll make my way without you. Frankly, Father, I hope I never see you again.'

David finished his wine, banged the glass on the table and left the room.

Hugo was in the stables when Rachel arrived, driving herself in her small car. Since she had given up the paper and the worry of running it with the shortage of newsprint she felt she had a new lease of life. She'd wanted to sell it but Em asked her not to for a few years. 'It's almost the only thing that Daddy had that we still own,' Em had pleaded. 'Don't sell it, Mummy.'

Rachel hadn't sold it, but put another editor in. If she lived that long she would give it another five years and then see.

Jenny met Rachel at the entrance to the farm, drying her hands on a towel.

'I do look a sight,' she apologized. 'I didn't expect you.'

'Don't dress up for *me*.' Rachel kissed her warmly on the cheek. 'How's Jonathan?'

'He's with Hugo in the stables. He calls him "Daddy".' Jenny suddenly looked apologetic. 'I hope you don't mind.'

It was a bit of a shock and, for a moment, Rachel didn't reply, then she said: 'Of *course* I don't! I'm glad, and Ralph would be glad too. Ralph loved Hugo – and he loved you.'

This was the first emotional thing that Rachel had ever said to Jenny and the two women looked shyly at each other for a moment or two until Rachel took Jenny's arm, and together they strolled up the drive to the stables. There Hugo was talking to one of the grooms while Jonathan energetically rubbed down a steaming mare just in from a canter. When he saw his grandmother he gave a squeal of delight and came running across to her, dropping his brushes. Rachel felt a surge of gratitude for the goodness that was Hugo and Jenny in giving this beloved little boy such a good, loving home. She squeezed him to her until he was breathless.

'Great news!' she cried, holding on to Jonathan but passing a letter from her pocket.

Hugo, after kissing her, wiped his hands on a cloth, apologized for his appearance, took the letter from her, and hastily scanned the pages.

'It's ours!' he cried raising his head. 'Bobby's given in. Oh Rachel, that is *great* news.'

'It came this morning. I wanted to tell you myself.' Rachel clasped him as he came over to her and kissed him again.

Jenny took the letter and read it.

'But why?' she said. 'I thought we were going to have *years* in court.'

'Adam phoned Christopher this morning and he *thinks* that it's something to do with David. There's been a terrible row and Bobby had some kind of turn. Aileen had to come all the way back from Poland to look after him. Christopher thinks Aileen has made him do this, so that he can get the whole thing off his mind. It's yours, darling, yours and Jenny's.'

'*And* Jonathan's.' Hugo ruffled his hair. 'He's going to be a wonderful horseman, just like his daddy.'

'You're his daddy,' Rachel said, the tears in her eyes scarcely perceptible. 'You're going to love him and bring him up and be his father.'

'And be another father too,' Hugo said, gazing at Jenny.

'You mean Jenny's expecting?'

'We were going to tell you at Sunday lunch.'

'Oh I'm so happy.' Rachel got between Jenny and Hugo, putting an arm round the waist of each. 'Who would ever have thought that, in the twilight of my life, God should be so good to me?'

'God?' Hugo looked at her sceptically. 'I thought you didn't believe in Him, except at special times.'

'Well, this is one of those times,' Rachel smiled.

'Do you think God would mind if we had a drink to celebrate?'

At lunch they talked about the house and the plans, the

finance that would be needed. Rachel told them that Peter was going back to Germany, and Em was not sure whether she was going with him.

'It's too far from Luis,' she said.

'Isn't there anything she can do about getting Luis? It sounds most unfair.' Jenny looked up from serving the pot roast with fresh vegetables.

'It *is* unfair,' Rachel agreed, 'and sometimes, with hindsight, I think we did the wrong thing. Felipe was an alien in this country and we could have made things difficult for him. But no one wanted to. It would have looked very bad, very cruel. We did what we did and who knows whether or not we were right? I grieve for my daughter who is unhappy, and for the little grandson whom I hardly know. Felipe took advantage of us.'

'Perhaps Em may go back to Felipe?' Hugo was still too excited to concentrate on anything other than Rachel's news about the Hall.

'She may; but they've been apart so long I doubt it. I think Em will stay on awhile in London. She'll help the new editor who is a very nice young man, ex-Army, get into the swing of things. It's very sad, you know, that Em can't find happiness. It seems to elude her.' She looked at Hugo and Jenny. 'I'm glad you two found each other. I really am. It's been just right.'

Hugo looked at her with gratitude for her words. Now he knew that, at last, two of the women he loved best in the world loved each other.

The busy chatter of pigeons reminded Stefanie of home. But which home? She wriggled deeper in the huge four-poster bed trapping in the warmth, though outside the warm Italian spring had begun early. Home, Stefanie thought, was Robertswood, because that was the place she had instinctively thought of when listening to the sound of the pigeons.

Robertswood was really the only happy memory she had of a home until she had come here and, in a very short time, this had become home too. Or maybe home was her mother's home, so often described by her grandmother, that long, low white building overlooking the lake and hung with vines: Essenelli. Grandma's description of it was so vivid that Stefanie often felt she had lived there herself and now, when she thought of it, she remembered her mother and wondered if, perhaps, after all her wanderings she had returned home: to rest in peace?

Stefanie was haunted by the memory of a woman she felt she had maligned, spurned – a mother whose warmth and courage had gone unrecognized by her. It was difficult to look back on the days of her extreme youth and account for her thoughts and actions, as she must do now.

When was it that her mother went away and when had she last seen her? What were their last words to each other? Try as she did she couldn't remember, except for that vision of a solitary figure going out into the dark with a battered old suitcase. The vision faded. She was gone, never to be seen again.

'Oh Mother ...' Stefanie would begin, then stop, not knowing how to go on, how to apologize, or how to atone to that solitary woman who had died – no one knew how, or where.

Stefanie opened her eyes and the reflection of the water of the canal, dappled by sunlight, swirled about the ceiling making the room seem upside down. She always had tears in her eyes when she thought of her mother, even in sleep, and now she brushed them from the corners and looked at the big old-fashioned clock by the side of the bed.

Eleven o'clock! Sasha and her grandmother always let her sleep. There were strict orders that she was not to be disturbed but should stay in bed for as long as she wished. Then when she awoke she would ring the bell and, after a maid brought chocolate, Sasha would come and lounge on the bed asking her what she wanted to do that day.

But sometimes Sasha had gone off early with his sister

Anna, and today was one of those days, the maid when summoned informed Stefanie in her halting English. Her husband had gone to the Lido with his lordship and the signorina to see if it was warm enough to swim.

Stefanie thanked the maid who pulled back the shutters letting the full glory of a Venetian spring day flood the room. She wriggled her toes with pleasure and as the maid silently departed lay back against her pillows to sip the hot chocolate revelling in the luxury of being warm, alone and safe.

The Palazzo Quinducale was very safe. It had withstood so many centuries, including attacks from the enemies of the Venetian Republic, that one felt as long as Venice survived so would the palazzo. When they had arrived by boat from the station they had entered the building directly from the water onto a wide stone courtyard where the pigeons that she could hear now strutted about. The pigeons rose as they had entered, fluttering onto the eaves and craning their short necks, peering curiously down at the new arrivals.

Approaching it from the canal the thirteenth-century palazzo was a yellow stone building with tiny latticed windows criss-crossed by iron bars; it looked solid and formidable, impenetrable. The quadrangular courtyard with its covered cloisters and tiny windows barred by grilles gave it, initially, the appearance of a convent.

But inside, the palace, with its waxed floors and stone walls, became a medieval fortress, a refuge and also a place of shadows, of mystery. Stefanie wondered if one would ever know all the rooms, however long one lived there, and her grandmother had replied quite happily that no, one probably wouldn't; she certainly didn't.

Susan and Melanie, Denton and Anna lived in the old palace with its memories as though they had been there all their lives. It had been Susan's home since the war, and Melanie had joined her in 1944 as the Allies swept through southern France from North Africa. Melanie had been a very frightened woman then, but the peace and timelessness of

Venice had worked its magic on her guilt-ridden, tormented, bewildered soul. Lady Melanie, daughter of the tenth Earl of Askham, had certainly never expected to live the sort of life that she had after a tranquil Victorian childhood in one of the great houses of England. Now she had seen three wars, had lost a husband, a brother and two nephews in battle and numerous other vicissitudes had overtaken her family, not the least of which was the defection of her son Jordan to the enemy. It was one thing to fraternize with them discreetly, as she had. It was quite another to broadcast on the wireless and publicly betray one's family.

Yet, at the age of seventy, Lady Melanie remained a fascinating woman who mesmerized her granddaughter. Susan, Sasha's mother, at forty-five had the same air of timeless preservation as Lady Melanie, though she had never had her looks. Plain as a child, she had grown into a handsome, rather formidable woman whose appearance had changed little since she was in her twenties.

Stefanie had known her since she was a small child when Aunt Susan dispensed presents, largesse and comfort from her grand apartment on the Quai d'Orsay to the unfortunate Ferov family who lived next to the railway station. Aunt Susan had inspired awe then and she did now; Stefanie was only marginally less frightened of her than she had been as a little girl.

Stefanie finished her chocolate and got with difficulty out of bed. Her baby was due in the next month and she was big. Every time Stefanie thought about the baby, Jack's baby, she felt overwhelmed by such a dejection of spirits that, for a moment, it seemed impossible it would ever lift. But it did and Sasha had helped, as Sasha had helped her every minute since he had found her on that night that Jack left.

Sasha's approach to the baby as to everything else was positive: it was her baby, it was their baby and they would love it. There would never be again between them, and never was, any mention of Jack.

Stefanie shuddered at the thought of Jack. There was no need to mention him, but sometimes he couldn't but intrude on one's thoughts. And then, deliberately, she would focus her mind on darling Sasha and Jack disappeared as an evil memory.

Sasha was like a dream; that miraculous cousin who had come out of the past with his compassion, understanding and good sense, to rescue her. He had guided her through Europe, smoothed all paths, awkwardnesses, irregularities. A phone call to Bobby from Paris had ensured that permission to marry was forwarded at once to the British Embassy with the necessary documentation. Everywhere they stopped she consulted the best gynaecologist available to ensure that all was well. They had gone to Paris, Lyons, Cannes, Menton, then up through the Italian Alps to Geneva where he thought they might stay until she had the baby.

But somehow Venice, and an urgent letter from Susan who had just heard about the baby, proved irresistible, and to Venice they went, and safety.

Stefanie opened the creaky old door of the large bedroom she shared with Sasha and made her way towards the bathroom at the end of the corridor. The old palazzo was built round the quadrangle so that the end of each corridor was a sharp right angle. Stefanie thought there must be about a hundred rooms but Susan said she never counted; there were so many tiny ones that nobody used, so what was the use?

The plumbing was relatively new in the palazzo having been installed by Susan shortly before the war. For a time she had shut up the old ducal palace and thought of selling it when she bought her house on the Lido overlooking the Adriatic. But when the war came she and Anna felt safer in the heart of Venice and the house on the Lido was boarded up and, ultimately, it would be sold.

The bathroom was large, with a huge solid tub with gilt taps in the middle so that it could be approached from either side. Sasha had asked her not to bathe unless he were there, but she never felt any fear. She stepped carefully into the bath and lay there luxuriating in the warm water, watching the reflections play on the ceiling as she had when she was in bed.

After her bath Stefanie rubbed herself well, put on her robe and went out into the corridor shutting the bathroom door carefully behind her. Suddenly, like the swish of a curtain, a door opened just round the corner and, thinking it was one of the servants, she pulled her gown more tightly round her. She was about to proceed to her own room when a face peered at her, startled, and then suddenly vanished.

For a moment Stefanie stared at the face, searching in the recesses of her memory, brushing back the cobwebs, and suddenly she turned again and called in a clear, penetrating voice: 'Jordan! Uncle Jordan. It's me, Stefanie.'

But there was no footfall, no sound of closing doors, no reply. It was very eerie. Stefanie tiptoed along the corridor in the direction she supposed the apparition would have gone, but it was empty – the morning light playing on the old stonework, the wide black beams in the ceiling. After a while she returned, reflectively, to her room.

Stefanie felt too excited by her discovery to keep it to herself. She told Sasha when he got back from the Lido but Sasha said she must be imagining it. They had been here for two weeks and no one had mentioned Jordan.

'No one will either,' Sasha added. 'It's a name that is absolutely forbidden to be mentioned in the family.'

'But just supposing he is here?' Stefanie whispered. 'He has never been found.'

'Many people were killed in the fighting in the last days in Berlin,' Sasha said, lying on the bed beside her. 'Some think he was among them. We must say absolutely nothing about this to Grandma. We don't want to spoil the atmosphere.'

'But it *was* him,' Stefanie insisted. 'It was not an illusion. Why should I suddenly see Uncle Jordan?' Wide-eyed she looked at Sasha whose expression had grown thoughtful. 'I tell you, he is here.'

Lunch was always a family occasion eaten at about one o'clock. It was always Melanie, Susan, Anna and any guests they happened to have, but never Denton who spent his days on the Lido, adapting to the Venetian coast a way of life he had found so congenial in Cannes.

It was rather formal eaten at a long, oval table and waited on by Susan's Italian butler Luchonti and a full complement of staff. The food was invariably Italian: pasta, a meat or fish dish with vegetables and fruit eaten with a glass or two of white wine. After lunch Susan and Melanie always went to their rooms to rest. Usually Stefanie went too and, since his arrival, Anna spent the afternoons with Sasha, showing him the sights and treasures of Venice which she knew well.

Anna had been born in 1930, the child of Kyril and Susan's second honeymoon, after he had returned from Russia. There were eight years between brother and sister and they didn't know each other very well. Anna had gone to school in Paris but, since the war, had attended an Italian convent and at eighteen was an accomplished young woman, very like Sasha to look at: reddish-brown hair, blue-green eyes and an oval, rather interesting face. She was not a beauty, but she was decidedly good looking and proud of her aristocratic inheritance.

Anna had grown up cut off from the rest of her family who were like strangers to her. Her friends were the wealthy daughters of the Italian nobility or bourgeoisie. She was a rather imperious self-contained young woman whose life had almost been a steady progression, except for the interruption of the war, but even that hadn't affected her very much.

She looked, and was, unmarked by suffering.

But as soon as Stefanie arrived as the bride of Sasha, Anna underwent a change of mood. She wanted her idolized and idealized brother for herself, not to be shared with someone else. Anna regarded Stefanie as an interloper and she went out of her way to be unpleasant to her, insinuatingly insulting and suggestive: it was quite obvious to the whole family that

Stefanie had been pregnant when she married Sasha. Anna's insinuation was that the marriage had been a necessary, one-sided affair forced on her susceptible brother, fresh home from the war, by a scheming woman who had bad blood in the family.

For a young lady of eighteen Anna was very knowing. She had a developed chic; a distinct style unusual in one educated in a convent though not, perhaps, in Italy where religion and learning took second place to the cultivation of elegance and the art of attracting men. Many of Anna's contemporaries were married within a year of leaving school. Their husbands were the wealthy sons of wealthy men who had old titles and large estates, or business interests in Rome and Milan.

In a way Anna had regarded the advent of Sasha and Stefanie as an inconvenience, to be got over as soon as possible. Susan and Anna disagreed a lot. Anna was very unlike her mother, who thought she had no depth, and her childhood bore no resemblance to Susan's. Anna had always been very attached to Kyril, and blamed her mother for the fact that they saw so little of her father. Now they didn't even know where he was. Susan frequently had a headache when Anna was around and her earnest prayer was that some young nobleman, or the wealthy son of a wealthy father, would take her tiresome, egocentric, irascible daughter off her hands for good.

The even tenor of life at the Palazzo Quinducale was interrupted by the advent of Sasha and Stefanie, the news of the impending arrival of a baby. It transformed Susan, whose tiresome headaches disappeared. She was able to forget about Anna and concentrate on her son and daughter-in-law. She spoiled them both and made an immediate pet of the vulnerable, motherless Stefanie, ensuring that she got the maximum of rest and the minimum of irritation and vexation, as she waited for the birth of her child.

That day, watching her family round the table eating with the equanimity of those who had never gone hungry, making desultory conversation, Stefanie felt a need to throw a little pebble in the pond of tranquillity, complacency and self-satisfaction.

'I saw Jordan this morning,' she said, aware immediately of Sasha's horrified expression, Anna's look of shock, Melanie and Susan glancing at each other in disbelief. 'Upstairs.'

'You're quite mistaken,' Melanie said at once, carefully laying her fish knife and fork together on her *majolica* plate. 'You couldn't have seen Jordan *here*. It is a name we never mention.' Even though her voice sounded curiously strangulated she continued firmly: 'It is a name we have forgotten. That was a perfectly *awful* thing poor Jordan did, betraying the family. They had been so good to him, especially Rachel who got him out from Germany in 1934 at some risk to her life.' Melanie tapped her brow. 'I'm afraid there was something not quite right in the head about Jordan, poor darling ...' Melanie sighed and immediately tried to change the conversation to something else.

Stefanie, however, wasn't satisfied.

'I thought I saw his face today, here in this house. I was coming out of the bathroom and this face looked at me from round the corner.'

'You must have imagined it,' Melanie said kindly. 'When is your next appointment with Dr Felicci, Stefanie dear?'

'I'm quite all right Grandma.' Stefanie too tapped her head. 'I'm not mental, or deluded. I did see Uncle Jordan. Then he ran away from me.'

Stefanie noticed that Anna was looking fixedly at her plate.

'Do you know anything about Jordan?' she said to her, but Anna vigorously shook her head, her eyes not meeting Stefanie's.

'Nobody here knows anything about Jordan, you can be sure of that.' But Susan's tone too failed to convince as she raised her head to look at the clock that ticked away over the ducal stone fireplace, that was supposed to be as old as the

Palace. 'I think it is time for your nap, Stefanie dear. Didn't you sleep well?'

'I do object to people thinking I'm mad,' Stefanie said angrily, attempting to rise from the table while they all sat back and stared at her. 'I *saw* Uncle Jordan and you're all hiding the fact that he's here. Even you ...' she glanced at Sasha who quickly rose to help her and, leaning heavily on his arm, she left the room.

Outside in the corridor he said: 'Why on earth did you do that?'

'You know he's here, don't you? Everyone is in the secret but me.'

'Do you think they'd tell *me*?' Stefanie thought she had never seen Sasha so angry in all the time she had known him. 'I fought in the war. If I knew he were here I'd kill him. I'm the last person they'd tell. Frankly I don't want to know, Stefanie.' Sasha turned away and perched on the wide sill of one of the latticed windows that overlooked the narrow canal. 'If they're hiding Jordan, let them; but for God's sake don't ask. If you do that again you might stir up a hornets' nest.'

But despite all the implications Stefanie felt restless and dissatisfied, hating the constraint that her revelation had imposed on them, the suggestion that, maybe, she was not all there. Besides, if Jordan were in the house she had to know; she had to speak to him.

Accordingly the following day, after her bath, as usual she made sure that the coast was clear and then she tapped at the door next to the bathroom and, when there was no reply, she opened it.

It was a small boxroom full of dust, perfectly empty. It looked as though no one had been in it for years. She walked along the corridor on a thorough inspection, opening all the doors, but there was no one there. No sign of the missing black sheep of the family.

Stefanie realized she couldn't go along the whole of the

504

Palace looking into every room; it would take days. She felt too fatigued and, now, too despondent and also strangely full of self-doubt.

Gradually her suspicions receded – nothing more was said and everyone behaved as though she had never raised the subject in the first place. But several days later the family went out to tea with an acquaintance of Melanie, a contessa who had an apartment in a palazzo near the Accademia. They seldom used the gondola belonging to the Palace, preferring the convenience of speed, but Sasha fancied his hand as a gondolier and volunteered to take them via the network of canals, avoiding the Grand canal, that eventually led to the bridge.

Melanie and Susan thought it a charming idea but Anna declined and Stefanie had been ordered to rest, as the birth was imminent.

She was accordingly lying once again on her bed trying to read, her eyes feeling heavy-lidded and tired, when there was a tap on the door and she sat up, her heart beating.

'Who is it?' she called in Italian.

'It's me, Anna,' the voice whispered. 'May I come in?'

'Anna, do come in.' Stefanie put down her book and sat up, pleased with the diversion. 'I thought you had a headache?'

'That was just an excuse,' Anna said sitting on a *chaise-longue* by the window. 'I wanted to talk to you.'

Anna lay languidly against the high back of the old sofa staring interestedly at the hump in the middle of Stefanie's stomach.

'It must be awful to have a baby,' she said. 'Don't you hate it?'

'I rather like it,' Stefanie said defensively, wondering about the reason for this strange visit. 'I didn't think I would, but now I do.'

'Don't you feel terribly *young* to be a mother?' Anna let her finger run through her fine hair which fell in locks on her shoulders keeping one curl twined round her forefinger. She

505

wore a cashmere jumper and a plain grey skirt which made her look half like a young girl and half like a woman. 'You're not much older than me.'

'These things happen,' Stefanie said guardedly, reluctant to confide. 'Both your mother and grandmother were very young when they married. I think both were under twenty when their first children were born.'

'I suppose you must have slept with him before you were married?' Anna had one of her rather unpleasant, suggestive little smiles on her face. 'I suppose you *had* to get married, really. I would hate to *have* to get married.'

'You'd better be careful then ...' Stefanie began heatedly, but Anna held up a hand to forestall her.

'Oh don't get angry. I didn't come about that anyway. I just wondered ... I came because I know something you want to know.' Stefanie, alert, sat up and leaned on her elbow. 'He *is* here you know.'

'Jordan?' Stefanie realized her breath was coming in rapid gasps.

'Yes. You did see him. No one is supposed to talk about it and not even the servants are supposed to know, except Luchonti who takes him his food; but of course everyone does and, one day, I'm sure the police will come for Uncle Jordan and take him away. He's a war criminal you know and if he were found he'd be hanged like William Joyce.'

'How long has he been here?'

Anna studied the ceiling, her hands behind her back. 'Oh, he came quite soon after the war. He'd had a terrible time escaping from Berlin and that kind of thing. Naturally Mother didn't want him, but she couldn't throw him out. Gran wept for days after he arrived, whether with relief or anger we didn't know.

'They decided to put him upstairs and never to talk about him or refer to him. After all, he was family. We all had to pretend he wasn't there.'

'Does he never come downstairs?'

'Never. He's a bit like Mrs Rochester,' Anna touched her temple, 'a little mad, you know, but harmless. We all go up from time to time to visit him and I read to him. I quite like him, really. He did what he did because he loved Hitler. He really hero-worshipped him, he told me. He thinks he's not dead, but hiding somewhere like him.'

'I *wish* I could see Uncle Jordan,' Stefanie said lying back on the bed. 'I used to quite like him.'

Anna looked at her solemnly and slowly got up. 'You can if you want. He likes you too. He wanted to talk to you the other day, but he was frightened too. Only you must promise *not* to tell.'

'I promise,' Stefanie said, realizing she had never felt more excited, or frightened, in her life. Not even on the day the Communists came to take Grandpa away.

The late afternoon sun lit the corridor at the top of the house which, like an attic, was cut off from the rest of the house by a short flight of stairs and a door. From the low hanging eaves the pigeons cooed quite loudly. Stefanie had never been so high up and when she looked out of the tiny windows she could see over the multi-coloured roofs of Venice; the reds, the browns and the terracottas towards the Campanile and the great gilded domes of St Mark's Basilica.

Anna, who had been leading the way, stopped beside a door, looked both ways, as if caution were instinctive to her, and tapped three times. Then after a pause she tapped again. To a sound from inside she answered: 'It's me, Anna.'

Stefanie could hear a bar being pulled back and, slowly, the door opened creaking on its hinges. She was quite afraid and wished she hadn't come but Anna, looking excitedly at her, drew her in.

'This is Stefanie, Uncle Jordan. You do remember her don't you?'

'Oh my dear.' Jordan held out his hands to clasp hers which, she found to her surprise, had somehow instinctively reached out to him.

'Jordan,' she said. 'I'm so happy to see you.'

Jordan's appearance surprised her. He looked much older. His thick, luxurious black hair had gone prematurely white, even though he was not yet forty. As he turned back into the room he walked with the faltering step of quite an old man. She was surprised that he could have vanished that day along the corridor so quickly; she guessed now that he must have hidden inside one of the rooms. Yet Jordan's pale face, when he turned to her again and bade her sit down, was unlined and his bright, handsome, dark eyes glinted as boldly as they used to do. She thought he probably had something like the appearance and personality of Dorian Grey. He was ageless, though aged, and still beautiful with his white hair and unlined skin. His clothes too were old-fashioned – a black corduroy suit that had something of the 1920s about the cut – padded shoulders and flared trousers – as though it had come from a theatrical costumiers. With it he wore a green silk shirt and a large black floppy bow tie at the neck, as though he were in mourning.

The room was part of a suite of rooms which ran one into the other to make, Stefanie guessed, a self-contained flat. It was well stocked with books and comfortably furnished. There was a large wireless in the corner with a wind-up gramophone by the side, and stacks of records, as though Jordan spent a lot of time listening to music.

'I see you like my apartment,' Jordan said approvingly as Stefanie looked round. 'Above all, it is so light. You see,' he pointed towards the blue Italian sky, 'I am so high up, above the rooftops. It's much better than prison, Stefanie, although it is like a prison because I am never allowed to go out.' He paused for a moment and gazed solemnly at her. 'Oh Stefanie, it *is* good to see you. I thought you mightn't want to come. Sasha must never know, you know, because his father was a Communist. It was the Communists who killed your grandfather and they would quite cheerfully kill me.'

'But Uncle Kyril didn't kill grandfather!' Stefanie looked shocked.

'Oh no, he'd gone by that time. But he was never a true Fascist you know. He was a Communist and he betrayed many people. I found out a lot about him before he left Paris because the Nazis knew his book. Kyril left just one step ahead of them. Those were very dark days, Stefanie, and we mustn't upset ourselves about them now.' He gazed at her again only this time smiling with pleasure.

'A baby.' He nodded towards her stomach. 'I feel quite thrilled about the baby, and Sasha. Sasha is a nice boy though I haven't seen him for years. I follow all the family affairs, you know, from my little eyrie. I am *so* pleased about you and Sasha but, please, never tell him about me.'

Stefanie, remembering what Sasha had said about killing Jordan, wondered if he would still feel the same if he saw this strange, fragile man whose pathetic life seemed suspended in time.

'I will never tell Sasha,' she said. 'I promise, and after today I will never talk about old times; but I wanted to ask you, now, about my mother…'

'Your mother?' Jordan looked surprised. 'I seldom met your mother after Bobby divorced her. I spent many years in Cannes, you know. When I came to Paris your mother was no longer with you. You remember you used to tell me that she was a prostitute…'

'Oh don't say that,' Stefanie said attempting to rise. 'Please don't remind me about the awful things I said about her.'

'Well I was just trying to remind you that I never even *saw* your mother during that time,' Jordan said gently.

'I thought it was you who betrayed her,' Stefanie said in a small voice. 'Everyone said you did. Mother and Charlotte … caught in a trap by the Germans.'

For a while Jordan didn't reply but turned in his chair so that he could look out of the window. From somewhere a clock started to chime the hour of four and then this was taken up by all the other clocks, large and small, in Venice: time to get up, they seemed to say, the end of the siesta: time to get up and go to work. Anna had remained just inside the door sitting on an upright chair like some sentinel guarding Jordan, not participating but listening to the conversation with the expression of one being faintly entertained.

'Charlotte should have been more careful.' Jordan finally turned round to stare at Stefanie. 'I have often thought about it, and I blame her. She should *never* have appeared in a public place in occupied Paris. I was there with a member of the Gestapo. I didn't know I was going to bump into her. He asked me who she was. I couldn't say I didn't know, we'd already greeted each other, but I *can* say and I do that I didn't betray her or your mother. Charlotte betrayed herself, and Hélène ... I'm very sorry, I really am. When I do think about it – and I often go back on the past – I wonder what else I could have done that night.'

'Mother never came back ...' Stefanie felt the familiar tears that pricked her eyes whenever she thought about that sad, noble creature she had so misunderstood.

'A lot of people never came back,' Jordan echoed sadly. 'A lot of my friends too. Berlin was utterly fragmented by the Communists. They were, you know, the biggest menace the world has ever seen, and remain so. The Allies were extremely misguided in not seeing what a bulwark against Communism Hitler was. He too may be dead, poor man, shot to death in his bunker. Yet I still hope and pray he is somewhere where he can prepare to lead the world again to sanity and freedom.'

Jordan leaned back in his chair, his hands on the sturdy, carved wooden arms, and closed his eyes, as his voice sank to a whisper. 'You see, my dear Stefanie, we are all of us victims of war.'

It was then that Stefanie realized that Jordan, in all probability, was quite insane. It was his air of calm, of certainty that seemed, more than anything else, an indication of his state of mind. He was insane, and he was also sad. The precariousness of his situation could not help but enlist one's sympathy, and also for the family who protected him ... daily fearing discovery and with it the threat of scandal.

Jordan had spent a very large proportion of his life either suffering from his delusions or incarcerated in a self-made prison. And so he would remain for the rest of his life.

In a way it was his punishment, but more comfortable, surely, than death in a concentration camp far away from loved ones?

'Come and see me again,' Jordan pleaded before she left, a little while later, realizing how pointless it was to talk to a man who had lost his reason. She promised she would. But, somehow, she knew she would never make that journey up the many flights of stairs again. Poor, mad Jordan and his isolated existence reminded her too much of a lost, fragmented world that nothing could ever put together again, or bring her mother back.

CHAPTER 26

Hugo worked hard to bring Askham Hall to even an approximation of what it used to be in the great days of his grandparents, Dulcie his grandmother and Frederick the tenth earl. His toil on the ancestral home coincided with Britain's gradual transformation from austerity to some semblance of prosperity, though there was still a long way to go before all ration books could be consigned to the fire and shortages were things of the past.

Naturally Hugo's labour wasn't single-handed. He was a wealthy man, but he couldn't have afforded the army of workmen that his ancestors would have had to do a similar task in times past. Also he liked to work with his hands. He restored most of the stables himself with the intention of breeding horses again. The stables were his particular pride because they were somehow a link with Ralph. He and Ralph had used to love to groom the horses, chatting as they worked, and Hugo enjoyed a similar kind of relationship with Ralph's son.

Dulcie's beloved rose garden was not restored. Instead Hugo wanted to develop the market-garden side of his farming activities and acres of the arable, fertile land were converted to crops; potatoes, beans, peas, lettuces, onions and cabbages. Large greenhouses were constructed for the cultivation of tomatoes and in time Askham produce became known for its quality. It was given the brand name 'Askham' and was extensively imported into the Covent Garden Market and Les Halles in Paris, recalling the days twenty years before when the Askham motor-car made its first journey across the Channel to conquer Europe.

Jenny largely supervised the restoration of the house which

had been a school and had then lain empty for nearly four years. She went about this with the help of Rachel who remembered the old place as it used to be. What was left of Cheryl's expensive refurbishment of the thirties, which had played a large part in bankrupting her husband, was removed: the mirrors, the lacquered furniture, the silks and screens, such as remained after the depredations of wartime evacuees; precious little. It hadn't seemed meant to last.

The old woodwork and panelling was restored and, where possible, the plasterwork, but the precious works of art of eighteenth-century masters were gone for ever, committed to the auction-room nearly twenty years before. All the old paintings had gone and much of the antique furniture which, had they still possessed it, would have restored the Askham fortunes several times over. Instead Rachel, Charlotte and Jenny went round local salerooms, old houses that were being cleared in places as far away as Yorkshire and bought, where they could, pieces that would fit into the old house at a fraction of the price they were worth.

Thus by late August 1948 the work was well on its way, the outside shone with fresh paint and new glass and Hugo gave a party to celebrate the birth of his daughter who was christened at Askham Parish Church the day before the party and given the name of Jenny's mother, Elizabeth.

The wide gates leading to the Hall had been flung open to welcome all the villagers. So had the great double doors of the house itself, and the wide French windows which led onto the terrace on which were newly-painted wrought-iron tables, chairs and large gaily striped umbrellas.

Strolling round the grounds greeting all and sundry, Rachel tried hard to visualize those days long ago when the guests at parties like this were always attired in their best; the men in white suits or blazers and flannels, the women in long afternoon dresses, hats and twirling parasols. She could recall a day like this when Ralph had given Hugo a beating after a quarrel in the boats and Bobby had been the one to save the situation. That was the day, it was rumoured, that Bobby first thought of marrying Hélène, and Melanie and Denton had come home from abroad for the first time since their marriage. It was also the first in what was to be a long line of visits by the Ferov family.

Now Melanie's grandchildren, Sasha and Stefanie, were here for the first time since their marriage with their baby son Nicky. Stefanie was sitting on the terrace now next to her grandmother, who was nursing the baby, and both smiled up at Rachel as she joined them, flopping thankfully into a chair after the steep climb up the hill.

'Do you remember that day, Irina, when all the children, yours and mine, were playing on the lake...'

'Oh I remember,' Irina began to laugh, 'and Hugo did something naughty...'

'Ralph gave him a beating ... your mother was here too.' Rachel looked at Stefanie, at once regretting what she'd said as she saw again that sadness come into her eyes, as though Stefanie never gave up hope that one day Hélène would walk through the door.

'Well that was a long time ago, and so much has happened since.' Irina kissed Nicky's plump little cheek. 'Good things and bad.'

'Where's Sasha?' Rachel inquired. It had been lovely to see them home again after staying at Melanie's villa in Cannes on their way home from Venice. They were looking for a house in London.

'He's playing tennis with Pascal and Joe and Angelica. He's quite mad about tennis.'

'I wish Melanie and Susan had decided to come. We hardly know Anna.'

'The journey is too far for Granny.' Stefanie's eyes were on the far distance as if her mind were on something else. 'But Aunt Susan said she would try and come for Christmas and bring Anna.'

Rachel watched Stefanie as she chatted to her grandmother. It was difficult to see in this self-possessed, calm young matron the rather reckless girl who had startled her family with a man so much older than she was at Hugo's wedding only the year before. Rachel had no doubt that Stefanie's baby was by Jack. She had had four children of her own and, without complicated calculations, she knew that almost until she left for France with Sasha Stefanie had been Jack's mistress. Thus this time last year she must have been just pregnant, as Nicholas was three months old. Luckily, as yet, he was not a bit like Jack to look at, although he was dark, unlike Sasha, but like Stefanie. Whatever his faults – many, by all accounts – Jack had been a good-looking man and as long as his son only inherited his looks and not his personality he should come to no harm.

Rachel suspected that all the family must have made the same guess as she; yet none of them would ever mention it and Nicky would be brought up as a Ferov, Sasha's son. Hopefully the young couple, loving but perhaps not quite in love, would have more. Rachel sensed it was a dutiful marriage but one that, for the moment, gave each of them happiness and a solid base for Stefanie's son.

'What's Anna like?' she said, leaning towards Stefanie. 'Excuse me butting in, but I can hardly remember her.'

'Anna was a dear little thing,' Irina volunteered. 'Like a waif. How I long to see my granddaughter.'

'Waif's not the word I'd use now,' Stefanie laughed. 'These Italian girls are very sophisticated, and Anna is Italian. She speaks the language fluently and all her friends are Italian. I don't think you'd recognize her, Baba.'

Baba was such a dear term, 'grandmother' in Russian. Rachel liked to hear the language spoken, didn't resent it in her presence because she knew that to be reminded from time to time of the old country was the thing that bound them all together, the genuine exiles and the first generation who had been born out of the mother country. In a way Sasha and

Stefanie successfully combined aspects of both Russia and England.

'Anna misses family,' Stefanie said thoughtfully. 'She would like to know you all. She misses Baba, and her father.'

'Ah Kyril ...' At the mention of his name Irina's mouth always drooped. Somehow they all suspected that Hélène had died in Auschwitz, but it was impossible to know what had happened to Kyril. The uncertainty about the fate of two children was very hard on their mother.

Stefanie said she'd go and look for the others, and after she left Rachel and Irina sat in a companionable silence side by side on the terrace as the baby slept in Irina's arms.

Yes it was a time for nostalgia. Below them Em and Charlotte were standing by the side of the lake keeping an eye on the children playing on it in boats – reminiscent of that incident so many years ago when Ralph had thrashed Hugo. Ralph had been about eighteen, on the brink of manhood; who, then, could have foretold the life he would have led or that Hugo would now be the owner of the Hall, already twice married and the stepfather of Ralph's child? Paul was on the lake too with Giles who was in his second year at Edinburgh University training to be a doctor; being a Bolingbroke, he was rather on the large side for the fragile waterborne craft.

Young Flora, a careful, cautious girl, not at all adventurous, was nevertheless standing on the prow of a boat clutching a pole and making the boat wobble for all she was worth. There were gales of laughter from the people in the over-crowded boat and sharp warning gestures from the adults on the shore.

Of all her nieces and nephews Rachel thought Flora one of the most interesting, the least predictable, the most insecure. What would Flora make of her life?

As for Em, she had stayed on in London and Joe Verdi had joined *The Sentinel* as a reporter. Pascal had gone to Durham University to study engineering. It was interesting how the younger generation had gravitated away from automatic entrance to Oxford or Cambridge. There had never been an

engineer in the family though Bobby had been very knowledgeable and Pascal's father, Paolo, had been trained as one.
Charlotte feared that Pascal too wanted to follow his father's
footsteps onto the racetrack, a prospect she hated.

Em never complained about her life in a large solitary flat
without a companion. She loved coming over to Rachel or the
Hall because it gave her one of the few chances she ever got to
see Luis, now playing in the boats with his cousins. Paul kept
on diving in and out of the water, soaked to the skin, and little
Jonathan had to be restrained at the water's edge by Em who
had a strong arm round him. Em went to Europe a lot to write
about post-war reconstruction but, as far as Rachel knew, she
never saw Peter Klein. That curiously unsatisfactory chapter
was closed.

Charlotte, the devoted wife, mother, and now a magistrate,
was the perfect companion for Arthur who, as well as his
important contacts in the City, was standing for Parliament at
the next election as a Conservative. The Labour Government,
of which the people had expected so much, had been a
disappointment, never quite achieving what it set out to
achieve. Everyone predicted that Churchill would be back.

Willowy Angelica, dressed in tennis white and carrying a
racket, appeared on the terrace:

'Sasha says we should get more players,' she said flopping
down by her grandmother. 'Anyone for tennis?'

'Not us geriatrics,' Rachel said. 'Where's Sasha? Stefanie
went to look for you all.'

'He's there. She's not. I must say *he's* rather super.' Angelica
pulled a face. 'What a pity I didn't get to him before Stefanie.'

'Darling!' Rachel looked shocked.

'Only joking, Gran.'

Rachel wasn't sure. Angelica had a flirtatious nature and
there was a certain instability about this beloved granddaughter that worried her. It certainly hadn't been present in
Charlotte or Em and, in temperament, Angelica reminded her

very much of fun-loving Freddie, who had chased all the pretty girls before he settled for Marian.

'Anyway they're disgustingly married,' Angelica said sweeping back a lock of hair and looking at Nicky. 'Fancy producing *that*. I thought she had some other man?'

'Must you gossip?' Adam, who had been fast asleep in a shady corner of the terrace, had been awoken by the arrival of his great-niece. 'Your chatter disturbed my slumbers.'

'Sorry Uncle,' Angelica said without any obvious contrition. 'And I *am* a gossip. This family has a lot to gossip about.'

'What do you mean by that?'

Angelica touched her nose and winked at Rachel, who wondered if the whole world speculated on the truth about Nicky's father.

'If you go down to the lake tell Paul he'll catch pneumonia,' Rachel said, 'and I don't know what else from that dirty water.'

'And ask Flora to come up. She's worrying me with that pole,' her father added, peering anxiously down the hill.

'You're awful old fuddy duddies. I'll do no such thing.' Angelica jumped up abandoning her racket. 'I do see Mummy though and I want to talk to her. If Sasha comes tell him I won't be long ... to play tennis,' she said with a cheeky laugh, glancing at them over her shoulder.

Irina looked disapprovingly after Angelica, clicking her tongue.

'She is too beautiful that one. Too wilful I think.'

'She's not at all serious,' Rachel murmured. 'Stefanie has no need to worry.'

'Hasn't she?' Irina inquired darkly and shifted Nicky from one arm to the other sighing deeply. 'We shall see.'

'I'd like tea,' Adam announced and Rachel rose to go and look for Jenny and organize it. Guiltily she felt that, as usual, they were talking too much to the family whom they saw often anyway and not enough to the guests. That's where Dulcie had been so good in the old days. She made every single person

518

from the highest to the most lowly feel welcome. Rachel sighed and went into the house.

Bobby was not at the party. He and Aileen would probably never attend any family gatherings again. That era was past. The two sides had never come together after the row about the Hall and only met at official functions which these days were few. David had gone to America where he played in a jazz band and Bobby was reported to be suffering from depression. Aileen had had to abandon her charitable activities to look after him.

Rachel sometimes saw Bobby alone on family business, visiting him at his gloomy home in Hampstead, but he was a sad and embittered man, who had discovered, too late, that the things of the world did not bring happiness. It was rumoured that Robertswood was up for sale but Irina denied it. Bobby meant it to be a home for his children and would never sell.

Bobby claimed he had put all his emotional life into his children, none of whom appreciated him. He hadn't even been told about the birth of his grandson Nicky, but had to read it in the paper. Bobby grumbled all the time, but there was no one to hear him.

Rachel thought that you got from people what you had invested in them, but perhaps that was too trite, a truism. Some people returned love where none had been given in the first place, and others were never grateful for anything they got. It was quite true, though, that no one loved Bobby; not his children, not the wife he had kept for years as a mistress because he thought she wasn't good enough to bear his name. He had no close personal friends. Maybe his mother loved him, even though she hadn't seen him for years. But then Melanie had always only loved one person best: herself.

Rachel wandered through the large rooms of the Hall, some of them barely furnished. Much of the house had not been touched at all. It had just about been made habitable for those who lived there. It looked, now, like a functional, comfortable, family house, not a museum of art as in the past or a temple to

519

modernity as in Cheryl's day. Privately Rachel wondered how long even Hugo would be able to keep it up, despite the Bey's vast wealth, because of the general austerity and shortage of servants. In winter it would be a very cold house, hard to warm.

But to Hugo it was home; the family home. She found him and Jenny in the huge kitchen, like any young couple organizing the small troop of helpers who had been bullied or bribed for the day.

Rachel paused, unnoticed, at the door of the huge kitchen which once employed a staff of about fifteen – a chef, a sous chef, a pastrycook, a still-room maid and numerous minions whose sole function was to attend the Earl of Askham and his family, whether there were guests or not. Once the staff complement at Askham Hall had numbered in excess of fifty including kitchen staff but excluding gardeners, grooms, stable lads, gamekeepers and foresters who accounted for another twenty-five.

The village of Askham had, over the centuries, grown up round the Hall and most of the cottages in it had been tied to work in the house or on the estate. Thus it had at one time been a perpetual source of supply, a kind of breeding ground to the nobility, son succeeding father, mother daughter. At one time the Rectorship of Askham Church seemed to be the provenance of one family and it had even been fashionable for medical care to follow the same pattern, as one Doctor Fraser succeeded another.

The first erosion into this cosy and convenient scheme of things had come with the First World War when many men went away and some did not return, including the then Earl. There were thus left a number of widows or marriageable young women with no possibility of finding a mate in the locality, and gradually there was a drift to the neighbouring towns – Salisbury, Southampton and Winchester.

In the twenties many of the cottages had been occupied by workers at the Askham Motor works ten miles from the Hall, but after the death of Paolo Verdi Bobby lost interest in his motor car and sold the goodwill to Ford with the consequence that the factory was shut down and the workers dispersed. Some cottages fell vacant and remained so, slowly falling into disrepair as Dulcie grew older and her granddaughter-in-law, Cheryl, showed little interest in the servants, the estate workers or their welfare. Gradually their numbers depleted too as the Askham fortune declined. When a servant retired he or she was not replaced, and the children who had been groomed for the succession had to find work elsewhere.

When the Second War came the progress of gradual disintegration of that once harmonious disposition of people and places was complete. Half the men from the house went to the war – either to the Forces or into the factories, and the latter attracted many of the women and girls. The Hall as a school was run on such a small staff that the children had been encouraged to do a lot of the work themselves. When Cheryl left for Kenya, almost as soon as she heard of the death of Ralph, the Hall was closed and all the staff, except for one or two who were retained for maintenance, given notice.

The village of Askham now had hardly enough people to make morning service on a Sunday worthwhile whereas in the old days there was a full congregation led by the Earl, his family and guests. Half the cottages were empty and either for sale or to let. More and more city people were beginning to find it attractive, and also financially possible, to have a weekend cottage out of town, and the countryside round Askham was of considerable beauty.

Now the few workers who lived in the village were supplemented by people from further afield – friends of current or former servants, women who worked in the towns during the week, and liked to make a little extra money.

So instead of maids neatly dressed in black and white, or footmen in the Askham livery, there were cheerful, motherly ladies in overalls with rolled sleeves, and men and boys in trousers and shirts with hot perspiring faces. Between them they kept up a continually moving line between the kitchen and the lawn with trays laden with oven-hot cakes, scones and freshly made sandwiches.

Looking at the busy scene surrounding Hugo and Jenny, both hard at work at the table in the middle, Rachel realized that it was not until she was a widow that she herself had ever seen inside the kitchens properly and she was quite sure Bosco's father, the tenth Earl, who lived in the Hall from the time of his birth to his death, never had. To visualize him and his wife, sleeves rolled up, took a great feat of imagination and nothing seemed to emphasize the contrast more between Hugo and his wife now and his grandparents who had owned the Hall thirty years before. Jenny was a working girl, a country girl, and would be as incapable of emulating Dulcie, even had she wanted to, as Rachel had ever been.

In that period of time more had passed than a mere generation: an entire world had gone and been replaced by a completely different way of life.

Natasha Lighterman, who was helping Jenny, looked up and saw Rachel. She told Jenny who smiled and called over to her to join them. 'Adam would like tea,' Rachel said, going over to them. 'Could I take him a tray?'

'I'll take him a tray.' Natasha gave her aunt her sweet, customary compliant smile. She was a happy girl who wanted to please everybody and invariably did. Some said that she even tried to please her father, and was the only member of the family regularly to go and see him.

Being a modern mother Jenny took Elizabeth with her everywhere she went, dumping her down on a blanket or in a carry-cot where she happened to be. In the old days there had been a plethora of nannies at family parties, but now they were a rare breed. Needless to say, Jenny didn't approve of them at all. Elizabeth now gurgled up from her carry-cot gurgling attractively at Rachel who bent to smile at her.

'Anything I can do?' Rachel said.

'You wouldn't like to take Elizabeth for a little walk would you?' Jenny, pink-faced and harassed, was taking a tray of newly-baked scones from the hot oven while Hugo, sleeves rolled to the elbows, was cutting and buttering them.

'I'd love to.' Rachel reached for the delicate baby clad only in a romper suit.

'It's so hot in here,' Jenny said.

'I'm off down to the lake anyway.'

'Her pushchair's by the door. Thanks.' Hugo spoke without looking up and Rachel realized that now, at last, she was part of the family too – not a person they deferred to but one they accepted, part of the furniture: grandmother.

Skilfully carrying Elizabeth in one arm she managed to get her into the pushchair without help.

'Thanks again,' Jenny called and Rachel waved without looking back, wheeling the chair round the side of the house to the tennis courts which bordered the flat piece of lawn at the top of the meadow.

Quite a party was in progress – on one side were Pascal and Joe with two girls she didn't know. On the other Sasha was partnering Angelica, who must have returned pretty quickly, against Christopher Bolingbroke with Olga. Sylvia Bolingbroke, her children Mark and Alice busy on the lake, sat out gossiping with Stefanie, and behind them stood Young Flora and Paul, still soaking wet, both eating ice cream. As soon as he saw his grandmother he pretended to duck and Rachel called.

'I only said you'd get your death of cold.'

Paul grinned and pretended to shiver. He was only thirteen but he had the sensitivity and responsibility of someone much older. He was the darkest Askham she could recall in this century. His hair was jet black, like Marian's, and he had black eyes and thin, clever lips. He was lean and athletic and looked very Jewish though he had been baptised into the Church of England with Marian's agreement. Paul was a scholar, a serious young man on whose shoulders it was good to feel the House of Askham lay.

'Fifteen all ... fifteen thirty ... thirty all ...' Little Elizabeth leaned forward with excitement, as though studying the game, and Rachel steered the chair along the narrow path that led towards the lake where the boats were being vacated and pulled towards the shore.

On the left a cricket match was in progress, mostly composed of local lads though in the old days Ralph and Freddie would have been among them. Now the young in the family, perhaps due to the foreign influence, seemed to prefer tennis. In the meadow to her right the marquee was filling with people seeking tea and there were groups on the lawn balancing paper cups and plates. In the old days white-coated servants would have been circulating among the guests, but now it was self-service and not a waiter to be seen – tea, sandwiches, buns and cakes still a peculiar colour because the flour wasn't fully refined.

The clothes were different too – summer frocks and open-necked shirts, most of the men jacketless, something that would have been unheard of in Dulcie's day. Many of them waved to her and she waved back and even Elizabeth, tiny baby that she was, pretended to wave too though she could hardly sit upright without help. She had the instinct to be gracious – Dulcie's great-granddaughter, every inch an Askham.

How she would have loved her, Rachel thought, and this party on the sort of day it was: a perfect English summer's day. How she would have loved the house sparkling with new paint, the sun at its height catching the windows as it had that day, the last year of the old century when Flora and Rachel stood looking at it, nearly fifty years before.

Suddenly the years slipped by and Rachel was a young woman again, standing there with Flora looking at the Hall, not yet married, not even yet in love or engaged to the man who, briefly, had owned all this. All too briefly.

Not surrounded by the family she and Bosco had engendered between them or her family's family, or all those young people, relatives and friends, whose lives over the years had interwoven with theirs.

'Mummy,' she could hear Charlotte call, though it seemed to come from very far away.

'I'm coming,' she heard herself answer, reluctant to turn round, to leave the past with its priceless recall of time, and join the present.

Her eyes misted over. Briefly it had been possible to imagine it was the year 1899 and the heyday of Askham Hall all over again – and a life, not nearing its end, but yet to be lived.

SELECT BIBLIOGRAPHY

Berben, Paul. *Dachau 1933–1945. The official history, 1975*. London, 1975.

Blake, Ehrlich. *The French Resistance 1940–1945*. London, 1966.

Brett-Smith, Richard. *Berlin '45. The Grey City*. London, 1966.

Charles-Roux, Edmonde. *Chanel: her life, her world and the woman behind the legend she herself created*. London, 1976.

Cottrell, Leonard. *Egypt*. London, 1966.

Darling, Donald. *Secret Sunday*. London, 1975.

Deacon, Richard. *The British Connection: Russia's manipulation of British individuals and institutions*. London, 1979.

Des Pres, Terence. *The Survivor: An anatomy of life in the death camps*. London, 1976.

Dodds Parker, Sir Arthur Douglas. *Setting Europe Ablaze: Some account of ungentlemanly warfare*. London, 1983.

Foot, M.R.D. *SOE in France*. London, 1966.

Foot, M.R.D. *SOE: The Special Operations Executive 1940/1946*. London, 1985.

Fuller, Jean Overton. *The German Penetration of SOE*. London, 1975.

Garlinski, Josef. *The Swiss Corridor: Espionage networks in Switzerland during World War II*. London, 1981.

Hawes, Stephen and White, Ralph (eds.). *Resistance in Europe 1930/1945*. London, 1975.

Hawkins, Desmond (ed.). *War Report: D-Day to VE-Day. Despatches by the BBC's war correspondents with the Allied Expeditionary Force 6 June 1944–5 May 1945*. London, 1985.

Jackson, Carlton. *Who Will Take Our Children? The story of the evacuation in Britain 1939–1945*. London, 1985.

Kee, Robert. *The World We Left Behind: A chronicle of the year 1939*. London, 1984.

Kee, Robert. *1945: The World We Fought For*. London, 1985.

Lord, Walter. *The Miracle of Dunkirk*. London, 1983.

Marshall, Bruce. *The White Rabbit*. London, 1952.

Masson, Madeleine. *Christine: A search for Christine Granville GM, OBE, Croix de Guerre*. London, 1975.

Mee, Charles L., Jnr. *Meeting at Potsdam*. London, 1975.

Minney, R.J. *Carve Her Name With Pride*. London, 1956.

Moorehead, Alan. *The Desert War*. London, 1965.

Noel-Baker, Francis. *The Spy Web: A study of Communist espionage*. London, 1954.

Novik, Peter. *The Resistance versus Vichy: The purge of collaborators in liberated France*. London, 1968.

Rositzke, Harry. *The KGB: The Eyes of Russia*. London, 1982.

Ryan, Cornelius. *The Last Battle*. London, 1966.

Salmaggi, C. and Pallavasini, Alfredo, (compilers). *2194 Days of the War: an illustrated chronology of the Second World War*. London, 1979.

Strawson, John. *Desert Victory: The battle that changed the course of World War II*. London, 1981.

Trepper, Leopold. *The Great Game: The story of the Red Orchestra*. London, 1977.